FATAL VOW

Marnie Reilly Mysteries Book 3

SHARI T. MITCHELL

Also by Shari T. Mitchell

Marnie Reilly Mysteries Series

Divine Guidance, Book 1

Torn Veil, Book 2

Fatal Vow, Book 3

Marnie Reilly Mysteries Novellas and Short Stories

The Island

Christmas Eve in Creekwood

Praise for Fatal Vow

Creekwood is one deadly town, but Marnie Reilly isn't letting a maniacal killer get away with it. A great cast of characters, a solid plot, creepy scenes, and dogs! What more can a mystery/thriller reader ask for? Why, a great ending, of course - checkmate! You won't forget it!

—Chronicles of Crime, Victoria, BC, Canada

Author Shari T. Mitchell has me hooked! If you love thrillers, this series belongs on your bookshelf. Fatal Vow delivers a stunning conclusion to a complex storyline spanning three books while expertly setting the stage for book four. I'm eagerly awaiting the next release.

—TL Brown, Door to Door Paranormal Mysteries

Dedication

For Harper, Dougal, Callee, Midget, and Mags;
without them, I would have finished this book two years ago.

Table of Contents

Introduction

Hey there! My name is Marnie Reilly, and right off the bat, I'll tell you, the last year has been an absolute shitstorm here in Creekwood!

That's where I live. You won't find it on a map, but it's in the Adirondack region of New York State where I'm a psychologist. I'm also a clairvoyant, which comes in handy when spirits make themselves available for consultation. I've used "divine guidance" to help solve a murder or two. I think we're up to seven with a few pending. But I'm getting ahead of myself.

I've lived here on the Hudson River most of my life. After college, I lived in DC, but when a maniac murdered my mother, I moved home to be with Dad. My friend and colleague Carl Parkins thinks I did that because I'm a rescuer. He could be right.

Let me give you some family history. My mother and father have both passed and my brother was a federal agent until a few years ago when he entered a building during a drug raid and the whole place exploded.

My best friend Tom Keller is a detective with Creekwood PD, and Danny Gregg is his partner and also my boyfriend. I have two beautiful Border Collies named Tater and Dickens. They are incredibly loyal and smart, and if they had thumbs, they would be dangerous.

Anyway, I'm here to fill you in on the unsavory things happening here. Now, Creekwood is typically a peaceful, sleepy place—like those towns you read about in a cozy mystery. I should warn you; *cozy* is not a word I would use to describe the recent shenanigans.

Just before Thanksgiving last year, a crazed killer murdered my abusive ex, Ken Wilder, and dumped his corpse in my shed, setting me up to take the fall. Fortunately for me, the murderer didn't succeed, even though I was a suspect for a while. Danny Gregg was the lead detective, and let me tell you, he and I argued about everything. In the end, when he finally listened to me, the police caught the killers, and I was off the hook. Thank goodness!

Then, a week after Thanksgiving, a man turned up dead on the railroad tracks in a dodgy part of town. Tom and Danny were called to the scene, and they found one of my old business cards in the victim's pocket. Long story short, the decedent was a childhood friend who discovered some things about the ugly underbelly of our little town. I couldn't believe it! Who would have thought that Creekwood had one? With the help of Carl Parkins, a couple of DEA agents and, of course, the detectives, the case was closed in time for a quiet Christmas Eve.

The calm didn't last long, though. On Christmas Day, I received a nasty threat, and I worried for the people I love, so I disappeared with my Border Collies to keep everyone safe.

The rumor mill tells me I'm in the doghouse. Ha! It wouldn't be the first time.

Oh! Before I go. Let me be the first to welcome you to Creekwood, where the holidays are murder.

Warmest,

Marnie

PS: Shari added a novella called The Island at the end of Fatal Vow. It provides interesting insight into me when I was five years old. My best friend, my mother, father, and brother are also in the story. Family dynamics are interesting, don't you think? Read it now. Read it later. You'll be happy you did.

-*Chapter 1*-

Creekwood, New York

Paige Reynolds' long auburn hair ruffled in the breeze as she lay across a carpet of last autumn's leaves. Dried blood smeared her forehead—the by-product of the three-inch gash on her temple suffered when she stumbled over a tree stump onto a granite boulder protruding from the forest floor. Scraped hands rested on her chest, just above the neckline of her azure tank top. Fear contorted her once pretty face as her body gave one last shudder and her blue eyes clouded with death.

First day of summer

Chirping cicadas and tree toads masked the footfalls of the weary travelers on the long driveway leading to the cabin. Thick with heat and humidity, the air swarmed with mosquitoes and black flies eager for sustenance. Beyond the cabin, a rippling lake conjured a memory of a frigid winter's night, and an icy battle that ended the life of a wannabe ninja. The stillness of the day, standing here under a canopy of pines and leafy green maples, was soothing in contrast to the recollection. The trio crept into the shadowy forest, biding their time as they waited and watched an oddly handsome man as he worked.

Detective Danny Gregg chopped logs at the edge of the deer run. His skin, bronzed by the sun, glistened with perspiration. His light gray T-shirt clung to his chest and back and his defined muscles pulsed with every movement. He laid down his ax, took off his shirt, and wiped the sweat from his face and neck. The scar on his back, a reminder of an incident involving an icicle last winter, glowed shiny and white in contrast to his tan. He'd lost weight, and his oddly handsome face was thinner and drawn. He tossed the sweaty garment into a wheelbarrow, took a drink from a water bottle, then doused his head, back, and chest with the rest. Glancing into the woods, he squinted his steely blue eyes and quirked up the side of his mouth. He ran his fingers through his sandy brown hair, picked up the ax, and got back to work.

"Quiet. Sit. Shush ... shh..."

They slunk deeper into the trees at the approaching sound of a truck kicking up gravel. The crunch of the tires caught Danny's attention, and he turned toward the path's break in the foliage. He swung the ax—embedding it into the log, pulled on his T-shirt and walked to the truck that had come to a stop. Detective Tom Keller and his black Labrador Gus stepped from the vehicle.

"Shush. Sit. Stay."

Their voices were low and hard to hear over the chirps and buzzes of the native fauna. Tom said the name "Marnie," and then shrugged and handed Danny a file, who flipped through the pages. This was a familiar scene—the detectives working a case—discussing leads and next steps. Tom glanced up. His violet eyes surveyed the woods—a stormy expression clouding his face.

She had remained in this spot for what seemed like ages, clutching tightly to the leashes of her Border Collies. Weary and apprehensive, she stood beneath the trees, patiently awaiting the perfect opportunity—or the courage to approach Danny and inform him of her return to Creekwood, but she couldn't find the words. What could she possibly say? Merely apologizing for her sudden departure, leaving him with nothing but a letter, didn't feel sufficient. On the drive to Creekwood, she had mulled over the conversation with her dogs.

"I left because I love you and couldn't bear anything bad happening to you again. There is a deranged murderer on the loose. I had to protect you and Tom, Gram, and Hannah, and everybody!"

Although that explanation sounded feeble, it was the truth. That was the speech she had prepared until she spotted him. At that instant, her heart leaped into her throat, and the dread of rejection seeped in, leaving her frozen with uncertainty.

"Come on, Reilly," she muttered to herself. "Suck it up! One foot in front of the other. Move it!"

Distracted by her daydreams of what once was, Marnie's hold on Tater's and Dickens' leads slackened. Tater leaped forward, freeing himself from her grasp, and Dickens bounded after him—as he always did. Excited to see the detectives, Tater barked, Dickens yelped, and both made a beeline for Danny and Tom. Mouth agape, she froze, watching in horror as her Border Collies revealed her presence. With resignation, she took one step forward. She had no choice but to step into the sunshine, lighting the path to Danny Gregg's cabin.

The two men turned in tandem when they heard the familiar barks of Tater and Dickens. Danny kneeled on the path and held out his arms, which Tater ran into, squiggling and whimpering. Dickens joined in and bumped Danny's chin with his nose. Gus barked and leaped about, excited to be reunited with his friends.

Angry eyes fixed on the trail, Tom charged forward, coming face-to-face with his childhood friend. Her strawberry blonde hair was lighter—bleached and highlighted by the sun. It had grown past the middle of her back and hung loose—her signature ponytail forgotten. A smattering of freckles dotted her sun kissed nose. She appeared tired but fit, standing there in her tan cargo shorts, white tank top, and hiking boots.

The dogs broke away from Danny, waggled their tails with excitement, and ran to Tom—Tater nearly knocking him over with a friendly nudge. Tom ignored them—he stood there, staring into Marnie's face. His stern gaze shocked her. Tears welled up in her aquamarine eyes, and her bottom lip trembled. She didn't know whether Tom was going to hug her or throttle her.

"Where in the hell have you been?" Tom demanded, throwing his hands in the air. "For fuck's sake, Marnie, we've been going crazy here! We didn't know if you were hurt or worse, dead! You take off without any notice, and leave a letter for us—with Carl? What in the hell were you thinkin'?" His jaw clenched, and his hands rolled into frustrated fists.

"Hey! Take it easy!" Danny walked the distance between the woodpile and the path.

Tater and Dickens trotted behind Danny—tongues out—silly Border Collie smiles on their faces. Gus ran to Marnie, sat, and then leaned on her leg. She scratched the top of his head and gently tugged his ear.

Tom wheeled around, glaring at his partner. "No! I don't think I will take it easy. She took off and didn't think to get in touch. What the fuck is that?" He reeled back around—angry eyes focused on Marnie.

Tater stopped next to Tom, nudged his hand with his nose, and then reached out a paw and placed it on his knee. Tom glanced down. The Border Collie smiled at him. Then Dickens pushed his head between his knees, sat, and let out a soft *woof.*

"C'mon, Tommy. Let's be calm and rational." Danny stopped and stared into his runaway girlfriend's face.

She saw the hurt in his eyes. Rather than hold his gaze, she bent, grabbed hold of Tater's and Dicken's leads, and broke the awkward silence.

"Danny? Could I get water for the knuckleheads? We've been on the road since early this morning."

"Uh ... Yeah. Sure. You must be hungry, too. Can I get you something?"

She gave a curt nod and trudged up the path to the cabin.

Tom stomped behind them with a huff. "Are you freakin' serious? You're gonna feed her?"

-*Chapter 2*-

A blanket of dry pine needles snapped underfoot as Sam Reilly and a man he called Pigeon crept up a steep bank behind Danny Gregg's cabin. They had tracked Marnie since 3:00 AM. The journey began in a small village on the St. Lawrence River in Northern New York, and traveled through the Adirondack Mountains to Creekwood, New York. Sam knew exactly where his sister was going as soon as they hit the town limits. He had taken a different route to the cabin, worried her uncanny sixth sense would tell her to look in her rearview mirror.

Sam's original plan was to grab her at a rest stop, where she pulled over to walk the dogs. But even in the early morning hours, too many eyes were watching. A woman screaming and kicking, and two dogs barking would call attention to the fugitives. They had new clothes with thanks to people who hung laundry on clotheslines. But Sam was infamous. His picture had featured on the front page of newspapers and online news sites. He even made the evening news often in the past six months. A manhunt was afoot, and he would be damned they would catch him before taking care of his sister.

"Taking care of Marnie" had been a niggling thought for years. He would be happy to see her suffer and delighted to see her sad and broken. The thought of her begging for her life or the lives of the boring people she loved produced in him a twisted and sick form of joy. But seeing her dead was the peace he longed for since he was sixteen years old. Sam vowed last year his sister wouldn't see another Christmas, and he promised himself he would take out anyone who got in his way.

"But why?" crept into his thoughts.

Sam swatted away a deerfly, and a frown creased his forehead as he tried to make sense of his goal. Then he turned to see what his travel mate was up to.

With an impish sneer, Pigeon said, "I've been behind bars for twenty-eight years. Let me take care of your sister. Do a pal a solid. Remember, you wouldn't have busted out without me. You owe me."

"You are not my pal and you will not touch my sister! If not for my plan, you would still be in your cell. I helped you. Got it?" With a jab of his index finger into his companion's sternum, Sam locked a piercing gaze onto the man's eyes, who gave a stiff nod.

Sam wheeled around, focusing his attention on voices up ahead. "Besides, she's all mine," he snarled. "But I will gladly hand over Kate Parish. I know where she is. It may be time to pay her a visit and wring her pretty neck."

Pigeon scratched his chin, glanced off into the distance and considered the offer. "You mean that little bitch who double-crossed you? Yeah. She'll do."

Both men peered over the firewood stacked at the rear of the cabin. A hundred yards ahead, Danny Gregg kneeled on the ground, petting Marnie's dogs, with Tom Keller standing to his right. The top of Marnie's head was visible beyond Tom's left shoulder.

"We will wait until tonight to grab her. The detective will swing his doors open wide and welcome her back." Sam turned his back to the woodpile, stretched, and surveyed their surroundings. "We better go. There is a big black bear roaming these woods. I had a run-in with him last year." He scanned the forest, eyes intent—searching. "We will come back after twilight and wait for Marnie to take out the dogs before bed."

"We could pop the detectives now and take her," Pigeon suggested, spreading his arms to his sides. "Out here, who the hell would even know? It could be days before anyone knew, and by then, that bear would have picked their bones clean. The rest of the scavengers would take what's left."

Sam rolled his eyes—a sigh of derision followed. "We are not killing cops. If Gregg gets in our way tonight ... No! That is not part of my plan."

"You're scared of killing cops? Tough guy like you? Story around the yard is that you offed a few. That's not true? You made that story up to make a rep for yourself?" Pigeon twisted his mouth into an evil smirk.

Sam pursed his lips and leaned close. Through gritted teeth, he hissed, "Back off, Pigeon! Killing a cop is not a problem *if* it is necessary. But I will not do it for sport, and if you do, you can shove off. I don't need you. I never did."

Sam turned his back, but hearing a faint grunt of expelled energy behind him, he reeled around as Pigeon hefted a log to his shoulder like a baseball bat. He swung at Sam's head, but Sam ducked, sprang forward, darted left, then kicked his attacker's legs from under him. Eyes bulging and gasping for breath, Pigeon found himself flat on his back on the forest floor.

Sam placed a boot-clad foot on the silly man's chest. "I told you to back off! I'm ten steps ahead of you. Do not forget it! The only reason you are still with me is because you strike me as a snitch." Sam pressed his foot hard, applying enough pressure for Pigeon to gasp in pain. "I don't like snitches. They have a nasty way of turning up dead."

With one last jab, Sam turned and headed to the path they had traveled earlier. Pigeon struggled to his feet, placed his hand on his chest, drew in a jagged breath, and stumbled along the uneven path, mumbling to himself.

"I'll kill you, Sam Reilly, and your sister."

Sam glanced back; his jaw tight—his right eyebrow raised. "No, you will not."

-*Chapter 3*-

Danny's cabin was exactly as Marnie remembered—except it wasn't winter, and no fire crackled and danced in the fieldstone fireplace. Instead, a warm breeze off the lake billowed through the curtains of the open windows. She'd never been to the cabin in the summer, but this place with vaulted ceilings and comfortable furniture had been her home. From Thanksgiving to Valentine's Day, she'd felt protected behind the large, bulletproof windows. Her eyes traveled to the wide plank floor, expertly planed by Danny. Then she spied the plug patch in the board where Hannah Patterson, Danny's twin sister, had fired a warning shot into the floor last winter. And then there was the smell—she stopped inside the front door and closed her eyes. *Deep inhale.* Pine. Cedar. Lemon Pledge. It smelled like home—but not *her* home. Danny's home.

The clatter of dog nails brought her back to the present when the Lab and Border Collies scooted around her, making a beeline for the kitchen. Tom stopped short in the doorway. She turned and stared up into his brooding face.

"C'mon, Marnie! Move it!" Tom placed a firm grip on her shoulders, moved her aside, and stalked past her in a huff in pursuit of the dogs.

She stumbled sideways—taken aback by Tom's use of her full name—and not so much by the unceremonious way he had moved her aside. Marnie turned to Danny. If she was hoping for sympathy, she didn't get it.

His steely blue eyes were icy and his dimples hid beneath deep lines of anger—hurt—or both.

"He's pissed off. So am I. You don't know…" He leaned close, and through gritted teeth, he scolded, "You have no idea how *we've* been feeling. Did you even care? You could have picked up a phone and called the station. Any *untraceable* phone would have worked."

He stopped—backed up a step, tossed up his hands, then turned away and sucked in a breath. Running a hand through his unruly hair, he looked back at her. "But we'll talk about that later. Let's get Tater and Dickens some water." He strode off to the kitchen without a backward glance.

His words stung, but she knew she had earned his and Tom's ire. Marnie stood at the entryway and slumped her shoulders. "Well, that could have gone better," she mumbled. She pushed back her shoulders, swallowed the lump growing in her throat, and followed Danny.

The dogs slopped up water from mixing bowls filled for them by Tom, who sat at the counter, picking at the label on a beer bottle, his jaw taut and his cheeks still burning with anger. Finished with their drinks, the Border Collies joined Gus at the windows overlooking the deer run. Danny handed Marnie a glass of water and turned to the refrigerator.

"I don't have much, but I can make you a bologna or … Uh… Nope. I don't have bread." He shut the fridge and opened the cupboard. "Soup? I have chicken noodle."

"That's okay. We all ate in the car earlier. Tater and Dickens had kibble, and I had breakfast a few hours ago. The water is great," she replied, taking a drink. "We should probably be on our way. I'm sorry to have troubled you, but I wanted to see you and talk…" She stared at her feet and fiddled with the snap on the pocket of her shorts, then glanced back up. "Perhaps I should have called first, and now I'm rambling. Sorry."

Marnie turned before Danny and Tom could see the tears welling up in her eyes. They didn't need to *see* the tears; they heard them in her trembling voice.

The two men exchanged glances—each motioning for the other to do something. Tater ran to Tom and bumped him with his nose. Tom looked down as the dog rested his head on his knee and stared at him with soulful eyes. He scratched the bridge of the Border Collie's snout and said, "No."

"Tater! Dickens! Come! C'mon, boys!" Marnie ordered as she crossed into the living room.

Tater let out a whine and nosed Tom while Dickens raced after his mistress. Tater nudged Tom again, his intelligent eyes pleading, and then he ran to Danny, putting his paw on the detective's knee with a whimper.

Rolling his eyes, Tom called out, "Marnie! Marn! Get back here!" He was out of his chair and halfway to the living room when she appeared in the doorway, a stream of tears pouring from her eyes. He reached out, grabbed her arm, and pulled her into a hug. She reciprocated and bawled.

Through her tears, she explained, "I'm so sorry I left and didn't let you know where I was going. Sam is out there, and I thought if I wasn't here, he wouldn't hurt you—any of you! But it's even worse now because he has someone with him. Someone scarier. Someone..." Marnie dropped back a step back and looked up at Tom. Her tears dried up and anger took over. "Thomas Keller! We made a pinky swear when we were 8 years old. We promised to look out for each other!" She turned to Danny. "And I promised myself that I would never let Sam hurt you. You've had enough loss and heartache in your life! He's my brother! I need to figure out a way to stop him. It's these damn premonitions! They show me bits and pieces, but I don't know *how* to stop them!"

Tom side-eyed Danny, who shrugged, and pulled out a seat at the kitchen table.

"Marnie, why don't you sit and tell us about the man with Sam?"

She sighed. "You're never going to believe me."

"Of course, we'll believe you," Tom replied—his tone softening. "C'mon, Marn. Sit. Tell us what you've seen."

-Chapter 4-

Margaret "Gram" Ryan rushed through Albany International Airport to baggage claim to pick up her suitcases. One floor below, Hannah Patterson leaned impatiently on a luggage cart by the carousel, awaiting her grandmother's arrival. She checked her phone. The flight had indeed arrived on time.

It was unlike Gram to leave Ireland early, and it was unusual for her to ask Hannah to pick her up. She normally asked Danny to collect her when she returned from her annual trip to visit her sons, Fionn and Liam. Hannah checked her phone again and then turned to see her grandmother jogging merrily through the terminal.

Hand over her head, Gram waved and shouted, "Hannah! Hannah, love! IIere I am!"

Hannah waved a hand in response—then scrunched her shoulders, trying to make herself smaller so as not to be noticed. Reserved in her nature, Hannah didn't like attention being drawn to her—and as a special agent with the DEA; she loathed it.

Gram reached her, dropped a kiss on her cheek and hugged her granddaughter warmly.

"It's lovely to see you, lass! Thank you for collectin' me," Gram said as she stood back and examined her. "Why the long face, dear? You've lost weight. You're thin as a rail."

"Everything is fine, Grandmother. How many bags do you have?" Hannah replied with a roll of her eyes.

"I checked three bags. Can you believe they charged me extra for the third? Goodness! Why are airlines so feckin' greedy?"

Gram watched the carousel and then glanced back. "Hannah, how's Tom?"

"I wouldn't know. I haven't spoken to him in months. He and Daniel are probably off chasing more leads in their silly quest to find Marnie Reilly. I've told them both that if she wanted to be found, she would be. They don't listen!"

"They're worried about her, dear."

"You're not worried, though, are you?" Hannah appraised her grandmother through her rimless glasses. Her cool gray eyes were astute at picking up body language.

The older woman shook her head. "Marnie can take care of herself, and I'm certain she, Tater and Dickens are home safe and sound."

Hannah scrunched her brow. "Hmm. I guess we'll find out soon enough. Daniel invited us to dinner."

Gram looked over her granddaughter's head, thoughtful eyes scanning the crowd. "No. We won't find her at the cabin. Marnie has other plans."

Hannah squinched her eyes. "Have you been speaking with her?"

Gram's bright blue eyes twinkled. "I suppose I have. I've never lost track of Marnie. Remember, we share a gift. She and I are always in contact—one way or another."

Hannah snorted in disgust and rolled her eyes. "Well, it would have been nice if you had let Daniel know she was okay. He and Tom are obsessed with finding her."

"Hannah, dear, I did. Now, enough of that, here are my bags." Gram hurried to the carousel, hauling a vintage turquoise Samsonite hard case to the floor.

She reached for the next, but Hannah retrieved one larger bag and a cosmetic tote, then placed all the matching cases on the luggage cart.

"Shall I take you home or straight to the cabin?" she asked.

Gram thought for a second. "Hmm ... take me home. I'll meet you at Danny's at 6:30 for dinner. I want to pick up Jack, unpack, and have a shower to wash away the day."

"Okay. Let's go. I'm parked in the short-term lot." Hannah led the way out of the airport, but stopped short when her grandmother wasn't beside her.

"What's wrong?"

Gram stood in the thoroughfare, and with a shiver, she turned to see who was behind them—but no one was. With a cautious step forward, she said, "I don't know. There's somethin' in the air. Ya know, that static electricity feelin' before a thunder and lightnin' storm?"

-Chapter 5-

Danny placed a cup of tea on the table in front of Marnie. She glanced up and thanked him with a strained smile. He crossed back to the fridge and grabbed beers for Tom and himself, twisting off the caps and tossing them in the garbage. The canines sprawled in varying locations around the kitchen floor. Tater's legs and ears twitched as he dreamed. Dickens's tongue lolled out of one side of his mouth, and Gus sighed and grumbled every few minutes.

"I'm sorry Lilly isn't with you anymore, Danny. I asked Ellie if she might find you another shepherd before I left. I guess she couldn't find one, huh?" Marnie's gaze shifted to the dogs. She thought of the Australian Shepherd she had given Danny for Christmas last year. Ellie Nikol, Marnie's friend and Tater and Dickens' vet, ran a rescue shelter. Tom's Labrador Gus and Gram's Jack Russell Jack had been gifts, too. Hannah received a Belgian Shepherd named Sophie, who was training to be a sniffer dog for the DEA.

Danny pushed out his chair and rose from the table. "No. Well, yes, she did. I told her I wasn't interested. I don't understand how people can abandon a dog, change their minds, and then take the dog away from the person who has been caring for her for months. It's just wrong. Anyway, I don't want another shepherd." He crossed to the window and brooded.

"Well, I'm still sorry. Ellie believed Lilly was..."

He cut her off. "It doesn't matter. It's in the past. Let's leave it there, huh?"

Marnie nodded. The hush that followed was heavy.

Tom broke the silence in the only way he knew how—abruptly. "Okay, Ms. Reilly! Where the hell have you been?"

Marnie straightened her shoulders and glared at him.

Danny turned from the window and echoed Tom's question.

"North!" she replied tightly.

Tom scowled. Danny raised an eyebrow. Both men waited for her to elaborate. She didn't.

"Marn, that isn't an answer," Tom replied.

"Yes, it is," she retorted, tossing her head.

Danny crossed the room, stood opposite her, placed both of his hands flat on the table, and began his interrogation.

"Okay, Ms. Reilly. Let's try that again. Where *north* were you?" he growled.

With a look of indignation, she stood, dropped her hands to the table, and growled back.

"North. Of. Here, Detective Gregg!"

The two leaned nose to nose across the table, scowling at one another. Tom stood and placed his arms between them and pushed them apart. Danny took one step back and blew out a disgusted breath. Marnie brushed off Tom's arm and dropped back into her chair—her bottom lip protruding in a childish pout.

"Okay. This isn't getting us anywhere!" Color rose in Tom's cheeks. He moved around the table, picked up his beer bottle, and rolled it between his hands.

As she opened her mouth to answer, Tater warned the trio with a long howl. They all turned to the glass doors at the rear of the kitchen to see the dogs—scruffs bristled—staring intently into the woods. Tater stretched out his front legs up onto the window and growled. Letting out a mournful *ah-roo*, Dickens bounced left to right, and Gus grumbled, cocking his large head.

Danny glanced at his watch. "It's too early for the deer to be running. The sun's too high."

"Didn't you put posted signs up everywhere?" Tom asked, crossing to the windows.

Danny snorted. "Yeah. All the good that will do me. Posted signs, like locks, only keep the honest people out."

"Maybe it's Percy," Marnie suggested the black bear who lived in the woods around Danny's cabin.

Danny said, "It's too early in the afternoon for Percy. He's out first thing before the sun gets too high, and then after the sun sets."

Tater dropped his front paws to the floor and paced in front of the window—a low growl rumbling as he walked.

"His ears are back. That's never a good sign," Tom commented as he picked up a pair of binoculars hanging on the wall and inspected the woods. With a chuckle, he hung them back up. "There's a flock of wild turkeys in the brush."

"Ah. Geez. That's good!" Marnie said with a nervous giggle. She rested against the wall and drew in a long breath.

"You thought it was Sam, didn't you?" asked Danny. "Has he been trailing you? Did he follow you from ... north?" He raised an inquisitive eyebrow.

Marnie wrinkled her nose and threw back her head. "Pfft! I told you! I only returned because I knew he was on the way here! If he had stayed put, I would have, too! I guess he figured I would return. I knew he was coming here, but I didn't realize he was following me until I hit the town limits and his car veered off into the woods."

Anger grew in Danny's face. "Jesus, Marnie, he could have killed you!" His face stony, he turned away, gathered a modicum of composure, and spun back around. "You're telling me you would have stayed if you thought Sam wasn't here? Abandoning your friends— everyone you say you love—if your *voodoo* magic hadn't told you your psycho brother was coming to Creekwood?"

Marnie tipped her head and gazed up at Danny, a smirk creeping onto her lips. She had never seen Danny so angry or animated. She shouldn't find it funny, but she did.

"Yes," she replied—her smirk still in place.

Danny took a step back and narrowed his eyes. "*Yes!* That's all you're going to say?" With a disgusted grunt, he turned away.

"I know you are all in danger. Sam is traveling with a treacherous man."

Tom huffed out an angry breath. He scrunched up his face and snorted. "He escaped with his *cellmate*, Madame Séance. Leo Scrud is hardly a dangerous man. He's an embezzler, but he isn't dangerous."

Marnie frowned and put her hand to her mouth in thought, and then absently ran her fingers through her long locks. Her aquamarine eyes widened and focused on the windows, mesmerized by something the detectives couldn't see. Danny and Tom watched her in silence.

Finally, she shook her head. "No. That's not right. That's not the man with Sam. Leo Scrud is dead. I'm certain of it. He died in that fire. He is not the man with my brother."

Marnie lifted her head in resolve; she knew something that neither Tom nor Danny knew. Her visions had become stronger since leaving Creekwood. She had clarity. She was seeing things as clearly as she had when she was a child—perhaps clearer. Her gaze caught Danny's and then Tom's who cocked his head. He recognized the look in her eyes. He hadn't seen it in a long time, but he knew Marnie was right. Leo Scrud was, in fact, dead.

Danny disappeared into his office and returned with a file. He opened it and flipped through the pages of reports.

"Marnie, three men died in the fire your brother started. A corrections officer named Gordon Hayes, a thug named Paulie Piccione, and a guy named Jed Rawlins. The last two were in the cell next to Sam's. They left Bayview in body bags. More likely in zip-lock bags. There wasn't much left of them."

"Why was Rawlins there? What was his crime?" she asked.

Danny flipped another page, read, and glanced up. "Assault with a deadly weapon."

Marnie nodded. She focused on the windows again. "An ax wouldn't have been his weapon of choice, would it have?"

Danny raised an eyebrow, then looked at the file. He chewed his cheek as he scanned the pages. His eyebrows shot up and he looked at her. "How did you know?"

She shrugged. "Clarity. I've got clarity."

Danny scowled. "What the hell does that mean?"

"She's seeing stuff better. The fog has lifted, so to speak," Tom replied with an upward wave of his hand and a slight catch in his voice.

Danny turned to Tom, who was staring at Marnie. He glanced back at her and he saw it too. Her eyes were the most brilliant shade of aquamarine he had ever seen.

Marnie cleared her throat and took a sip of tea. "By the way, that report is wrong. Sam did not start that fire. Jed Rawlins did."

Danny raised an eyebrow. "Okay. I'll bite. Who told you that?"

"Isn't it obvious?"

"No!" Danny and Tom responded in unison.

"Leo Scrud told me," Marnie replied with a chin nod toward the windows. She pointed to the report in Danny's hands. "And by the way, Paulie Piccione, also known as Pigeon, is not dead. He's with my brother. You better make sure you have the latest copy of that report, because Jed Rawlins is also very much alive."

Sam Reilly sat on a tree stump, massaging the nape of his neck to ease a booming headache. Not wanting to show weakness, he told Pigeon he needed to get his bearings and figure out the best plan for the night. It had been four months since they escaped from Bayview and the pain in his head worsened. Even the extra strength Tylenol he liberated from random pharmacies hadn't helped. He wondered if he hadn't left Bayview, if the headaches could have subsided. Dr. Miller suggested surgery to remove the sliver of shrapnel that lodged in Sam's brain when he ran out of an exploding building. The doc also recommended psychotherapy to treat his PTSD, a condition he didn't realize he suffered.

Then he thought about the undercover work he had done while working with the FBI. It was near the top of his list of regrets. But listening to Kate Parish crowned that list. He frowned, closed his eyes, allowing his damaged brain to defragment his memories.

Sam was working on a joint task force with the DEA. Things had gone haywire, and people assumed he had gone rogue. He hadn't. He *had* gone off the grid to protect an undercover junior agent who had been "found out" by a nasty cartel leader. That's about all he remembered. He could see the agent's face, and he had a feeling he knew him well, but he didn't know why. So much of the past was now a blur. Like old Polaroids, his memories faded away bit by bit. Some memories from childhood would burst through the fog and remind him of happier days. Others of Marnie and him when they were kids.

Sam pushed the recollections back into their not-so tidy compartments, he mustered his strength to keep moving. A nagging thought popped into his head. *Why do I want to kill my sister?* The question conjured a vivid childhood memory:

Sam, sleeping bag and pillow in hand, stood in the doorway of Marnie's bedroom. She was five years old—Sam was twelve.

"Hey, Squirt, do you mind if I crash in here with you tonight?" he asked.

Marnie sat up and patted the side of her bed, inviting him into her room. "Sure! We can have a slumber party! Are you scared?"

"Nope. Are you?"

"Nah! You won't let anything get me, will you?"

"I'll always protect you. Always!"

"Cross your heart?" she asked.

"And hope to die."

The memory haunted him. When did everything change? What flipped that switch in his brain? When did Marnie become his enemy?

Sam had felt a lot of things over the years—rage, resentment, hate, exhaustion, perhaps even fear, but how he was feeling right now terrified him. At this very moment, he felt sad, lonely, and lost. He considered calling Kate, but remembered he always felt worse after speaking with her. He knew where she was, but it probably wasn't wise. No. It was a terrible idea. She was the last person he should call. She was the reason people died last Thanksgiving. Her actions had put him in Bayview Correctional. He considered the carnage last Christmas. While Erin Matthews was responsible for that body count, Kate had played a role in it, too. Palms sweating, he took a calming breath and then another, regretting the respective days he had met either.

Sam turned to see what Pigeon was doing, but he was nowhere in sight. He heard an awful squawking and screeching of an animal in pain and scanned the woods.

A moment later, the convict emerged from the brush, grasping a dead turkey with one hand and a bloody ax in the other. He held it up like a trophy and announced, "Dinner!"

"Okay, Marn. What aren't you telling us?" asked Tom.

"You know, guys, I'm tired. I want to have a shower, feed the boys, have something to eat myself, and get much-needed sleep. Tomorrow I will answer your questions," she replied with a sigh and a glance out the windows. "Someone *is* out there. I've got goosebumps. Danny, you better lock things up tight and make sure the skylight is closed."

He followed Marnie's gaze to the windows. "I'll lock up. I know what your brother can do."

"It's not my brother you should be worried about."

The guys stared at her. She glanced between the two, saying nothing. When she didn't provide further information, Tom shrugged, got up, and walked to the windows.

Danny reached out and brushed the back of Marnie's hand with his fingertips. "You're welcome to stay with me, if you're comfortable with that."

She smiled. "I think tonight I will crash at Tom's, but we'll talk soon. I'm so sorry about the way I left. It was a terrible thing to do, but it has nothing to do with the way I feel about you. Well, it has a lot to do with it. I didn't want anyone else to die. I thought I could keep you safe if I wasn't here, and if you weren't trying to protect me." Her eyes filled with tears.

Danny placed his hand on the side of her face, tracing her cheek with his thumb. "I know, but please don't ever do that again. We've been crazy with worry."

Marnie nodded, took his hand in hers and pressed a kiss into his palm. "I'm sorry." She stood and joined Tom and the dogs. Tree branches swayed gently in the breeze as a chipmunk dashed under a log, and a family of squirrels played chase in an old hickory. Tater's ears twitched and a low grumble grew in his throat. She tugged one of his ears, then bent to give him a hug.

She whispered, "I know, buddy. I know he's out there. It's okay. Everything is going to be all right."

The dog rewarded his mistress with a gentle nose bump under her chin. He stared into her face with intelligent eyes and then leaned against her leg.

"We better get going," Marnie announced, as she straightened and turned to Tom. "Can we crash with you tonight? I've got an early start in the morning, and you are closer to where that start is located."

Tom cocked his head and wrinkled his brow. "Oh really? And what would that be?"

"While I was away, a property that I have always loved and dreamed of owning came up for sale, so I bought it," she replied.

Tom's eyes nearly popped out of his head. "You didn't!"

Marnie shrugged her shoulders, grinned, and nodded.

"You bought the Billingsly's ranch?" he asked.

Danny frowned. "I've never heard of it."

"It's an old homestead about fifteen minutes from Marnie's house and only a few minutes farther away from mine. We spent a lot of time there when we were kids."

Marnie beamed. "It's breathtaking, Danny! There's an apple orchard, vegetable gardens, horses, cows—beef and dairy. Oh! Chickens. There are even goats! Not the fainting kind, but there are goats!"

Her animated counting of the critters on the ranch made the detectives chuckle.

"Ha-ha! Goats too, huh? How did you hear it was for sale?" asked Tom.

"David Bennett. As my lawyer, I *had* to speak with him about finalizing Ken's estate, and while we were speaking, he told me the ranch was up for sale. Jonas Billingsly wanted to keep it when his folks died, but his wife has always hated it. She put her foot down, told him to sell it, and build them the house she wants. You remember Lanie Howard, don't you, Tom?"

Tom curled his lip and then turned to Danny. "In the dictionary under princess, you will find a picture of Lanie Howard-Billingsly."

Danny put up a hand. "Hang on! Marnie, how in the hell are you going to run a ranch? Do you know anything about livestock?"

Marnie said, "No. I'm not going to run it. Jonas will manage it, and I'll oversee a mental health wellness program for veterans. We'll work with children too, but we don't have approval for that yet. The ranch is all about giving back."

"Wow! You've thought this through!" Danny replied.

"I have! I needed to get perspective. All that money Ken left me is going to do so many things to help others. I didn't know it, but it's exactly what I needed to get focused! There is a lot to do, but I'm excited!"

"I can see that," Danny said with a grin. "So, veterans will work on the ranch? Like work therapy?"

"Yes! They'll have a job, a place to stay, and get the help they need."

Danny frowned. "What do you mean, a place to stay?"

With excitement, Marnie grabbed his arm. "I forgot to mention! The old bunkhouses are still on the property. Those are under renovation right now. They housed the farmhands who worked the land back then. When the Billingslys downsized, they didn't have staff living on the property anymore. Jonas and his father did most of the work, but they had a few part-time and seasonal hands. From the information I have gotten from David, the Billingslys wanted to give the ranch to Jonas, but Lanie wouldn't hear of it. Anyway, David worked with Jonas to have an inspection done; they gave me a list of what needed repair, and Stu, David's brother, has been working through the list for the past few months. He finished the house last week. I'm going to see it in the morning. Want to come with me?"

Both men nodded.

Tom asked, "Will Jonas continue to live at the ranch? Don't he and Lanie live in the caretaker's cottage?"

"Yes, they will stay until their house is completed. Lanie's parents bought them a plot of land on Croft Mills Road near the old flour mill."

Tom whistled. "That land would have set them back a fair bit!"

"Yup! Lanie wanted to live in the most exclusive neighborhood money can buy. Should we tell her that gated communities aren't always as safe as they seem?" Marnie thought back to her ex, Ken Wilder, whose murder had occurred within the same community last fall.

Tom blinked in disbelief. "I don't see how they could afford to live there. The HOA fees and taxes alone are more than either of them would make in a year!"

Marnie shrugged. "Maybe Lanie's parents will help with the bills. Like Kate's parents, Lanie's have always given her everything she wanted."

Tom nodded. "True. I'm sure the rumor mill will inform soon enough." He laughed and then spun back toward the windows.

Danny jerked his head. "Did you see something?"

"Hmm ... It could be my imagination, but I thought I saw someone walk around the back of that dead hickory."

Marnie glanced out the windows. An icy chill ran up her spine and she shivered. "Someone is out there, Danny. I'm not so sure you should stay here alone. You should come with us."

"I'll be fine. My gun will be on the nightstand and I'll lock up. Besides, I don't sleep soundly with mosquitoes buzzing around my room. I like fall and winter. No bugs."

"Not to change the subject, but have either of you kept up to date with what's happening with Kate?" asked Marnie.

Kate Parish was a childhood friend of Marnie's and Tom's. If choosing one word to describe Kate, it would be treacherous. If choosing more than one word ... manipulative, narcissistic, murderous and cruel would explain her. Last Thanksgiving, Kate and Sam colluded to murder Marnie's ex, Ken Wilder. Making matters more precarious, they had tried to kill her when plans hadn't worked out the way they wanted. The collateral damage was two dead police officers, two wounded officers, and losing her home. Well, the house wasn't lost, but she couldn't bear the thought of living there with all that spilled blood and death on her doorstep. She was thankful that Danny had given her and Tater a place to call home while she searched for a new house.

Kate's involvement had been a hard pill to swallow. Marnie and she had been friends since grade school, making the woman's betrayal almost worse than her brother's treachery. Marnie and Sam weren't close. The sibling rivalry created by him years earlier left Marnie marginally unsurprised by his actions, but Kate was different. The bond they shared had been strong—some would say sisterly. Marnie had believed that Kate always had her back until recently.

Exchanging glances, Danny nodded for Tom to take the lead.

"She's locked up at Pine Ridge Mental Hospital. She's not doin' well, from what I have heard. I check in once a month to make sure she's still there. Harry Carlisle has done his best to get her out, but the doctors aren't cooperating. They believe she's *deeply troubled*. Pfft! They don't know the half of it! I ran into her parents in Town Square last month. Her father asked after you. I told him you were out of town. Her mother got all huffy and said you and I should burn in hell for what we did to their daughter. I told her that had she not spoiled Kate rotten, she may not have turned out to be such a murderous bitch, and then I walked away."

"You didn't say that!" Marnie shouted and shoved him.

"I really did," he replied with a wry smile.

She laughed. "Yay for you! I've wanted to tell that woman what I think of her for a long time. She always told me not to worry—that I would grow into my looks someday. She was so nasty to me."

Danny scowled. "Grow into your looks? What a horrible thing to say to a child!"

"It was the long arms and legs, freckles, and strawberry blonde hair; I was a bit gawky," Marnie replied with a shrug.

Tom nodded and patted her on the shoulder. "The boys always thought she was cool because she could run really fast, *and* she wouldn't hesitate to race her bike up a ramp. Marn was fun. Kate wasn't. Lanie Howard wasn't either."

"Thank you, Tom! I was a tomboy, and there is nothing wrong with that," she said.

Danny smirked. "*Was*? Ha-ha! You still are!"

"She grew into her legs and arms, which is all that matters," Tom replied with a chuckle.

She waved off his comment. "Whatever! We have to go! I'm starving!"

"Yeah. Let's get movin'. Where's your car? I didn't see it in the driveway."

Marnie blushed. "I parked at the top of the road—in the tall grass."

Danny's eyebrows shot up. "Trying to sneak up on me?"

"Yes! I wasn't sure what to say."

Danny pulled her into a hug. "Well, I'm happy you're back in one piece. But we still need to talk."

"We will. I promise!" She gave him a tight hug to confirm. "We'll see you tomorrow?"

Danny nodded. "Yeah. I'll come to Tom's around 8:00, with coffees."

Tom shot him a look of indignation. "Hey! I have a machine!"

Danny snorted. "No. You have a dirty water maker. I'll pick up some on my way."

Marnie laughed. "We'll see you at 8:00 with coffee!"

As she bent to put leashes on Tater and Dickens, she noticed in her periphery, the men motioning to one another. She turned to see what they were doing, and the two stood still. Tom made a quick exit.

"C'mon, Gus!" he shouted, opening the front door.

Before she could follow Tom, Danny grabbed her hand. She stopped and gazed up into his blue eyes—happy to see the ice had thawed.

He cocked his head and smiled. "Are we okay?"

She quirked up the corners of her mouth. "I think that's up to you, Detective Gregg."

He nodded. "Come here, Ms. Reilly," he murmured, pulling her close for a long kiss.

Danny cleaned up the dishes and went back outside to chop wood before Gram and Hannah arrived. It was 3:00 and the groceries would come around 5:00, and his family would be over at 6:30. There was still time to get work done before showering and changing for dinner. He glanced out the windows into the woods and wished that Tater was there to alert him to anyone lurking around on his property. He shook away the thought, returning to the tasks of chopping and stacking wood.

As he rounded the corner of the cabin, he heard laughter. He stopped and listened carefully. A scan of the woods didn't reveal trespassers, so he thought it to be a raven or a crow. Then a familiar scent wafted around him. He sniffed the air. *Hmm ... who is cooking turkey?* He frowned. There wasn't another house for at least five miles. A chill ran down his spine. Something felt wrong. He continued around the exterior of the garage to the woodpile and stopped dead in his tracks. His ax, which he had left in a large log, was missing, as were kindling and firewood. He raced into the garage to find that someone had broken into and searched the cupboards that lined the far wall. Danny ran a hand through his unruly hair and growled.

"Son of a bitch! Dammit!" He kicked the tire on his Jeep.

He did a quick inventory, noting the missing items as a hunting knife; two LED lanterns; waterproof matches; one sleeping bag; a large backpack; a hatchet; camp dishes; cookware; utensils; and a tarp. He rushed to a large steel cabinet and held his breath as he tried the handle. It didn't open. He breathed out a sigh of relief. Reaching into his pocket, he took out a keyring, found the right key, unlocked the cabinet, and pulled open the door. Staring back at him were rifles and shotguns of several makes and models. The shelf above housed ammunition. He pulled out a Mossberg Maverick, loaded it with buckshot, and walked outside.

Boom! Danny fired one shot above the lake, and shouted, "Don't fuck with us! I will turn in my badge, hunt you down and kill you!"

Boom! Boom! He fired off two more shots, picked up the shell casings and stormed back to the garage. He pulled two large gun totes from the cabinet, put the shotguns into one, the rifles into the other, and split the boxes of ammo between them. Zipping the bags, he slung each over a shoulder and carried them into the cabin. With the firearms secure, he snatched up the garage door remote and the Mossberg, and returned to the garage, securing it. He checked for intruders, and when he found none, he pressed the remote and lowered the door.

Upon returning to the cabin, Danny called his sister, Hannah.

"Hi, Daniel," she answered.

"I need to cancel dinner tonight."

"Because Marnie is back in town?" she replied, sounding miffed.

"What? How did you know she's back?"

"Grandmother told me."

"Ah. Okay. Well, no. This isn't about Marnie. It has to do with … uh…"

Hannah growled, "Out with it, Daniel! What's wrong?"

"Someone broke into the cupboards in my garage. They stole camping equipment, my ax, and a few other things. I think Sam Reilly is hanging out behind the cabin, waiting for Marnie to return."

"I'll speak with Grandmother, and tell her you've been called into work, and that tomorrow night will be better after she has settled in."

"Thank you! I owe you one, sis."

"I, on the other hand, will see you A.S.A.P. *after* I make a call to the US Marshal and FBI."

"You've got people you trust?"

"I do. This is federal, and you must stay out of it. You know that. That's why you called me," she said before disconnecting.

Danny nodded, scratched his forehead, and then set his phone on the coffee table. He glanced around the cabin, listening to the tick of the clock on the mantle. *Should I call Marnie and Tom?* He rubbed the stubble on his chin across his shoulder, deciding she should have a calm first night back in Creekwood.

Remembering Hannah's order, he went to the kitchen and grabbed the binoculars. He pulled the rubber covers off the lenses, checked that Tom hadn't inked the rims again, and then held them up to his eyes. He scanned the woods left to right and back again, adjusting the lenses as needed. There was no unusual movement—squirrels played chase, chipmunks darted between hiding spots in logs, and a bobcat sat aloft a branch overseeing the activity of the wild turkeys darting through the brush. Nothing worrisome stood out until he spotted smoke rising about a mile into the woods.

"Son of a bitch!"

The detective hung up the binoculars, stalked into his living room, retrieved a long-range rifle with a scope and loaded it. He glanced back at the coat rack in search of his hunting vest. It wasn't there, but he knew exactly where he would find it and raced upstairs to the bedroom Marnie stayed in last November and early December. He opened the closet to find her plaid flannel bathrobe there. Technically, it wasn't hers, but she had rescued it from the back of his closet. A chuckle bubbled up at the memory of her commandeering the garment. She told him it was "comfier" than her own. He didn't mind; he had several bathrobes his grandmother had given him over the years. Besides, his bathrobe looked great on her. He stood with his thoughts for a moment, then located his vest, pulling it on as he ran downstairs. With two boxes of shells in his pockets, he reached for the door, but stopped when the phone rang. It was Hannah.

"Hello."

"Daniel, there are field agents on the way to the cabin now. I've given them your coordinates. They will be there in twenty minutes. Stay inside, lock the doors and wait! Do not go all Rambo and go off into the woods on your own!"

"Hey! I saw smoke a few minutes ago, so I'm going out to have a peek..." Hannah cut him off.

"Daniel, I am five minutes away. Do not go out there alone!"

He rolled his eyes. "Yeah. Okay. I'll wait."

He stared at his phone, shrugged and left the cabin, ensuring to lock the door. It was eerily quiet—no chirping birds—no rustling leaves. He peered out over the lake. Dark clouds were moving in, and a thunderhead reared its ugly head in the north. With a laugh, he threw back his head and spoke to the clouds. "Marnie Reilly, do storms follow you everywhere you go?"

The crunch of Hannah's tires alerted him to her arrival. She was going faster than she should and skidded sideways when she stopped. Danny watched her toss her seatbelt aside and throw open the car door.

Pointing a finger at him, she stormed across the driveway; her face was red with anger. "Daniel Gregg, I told you to stay inside! What are you doing out here? Get back in the cabin, now!"

Danny did the one thing Hannah wasn't expecting. He laughed, which made her furious. At five-feet-five inches, Hannah weighed one-hundred and ten pounds soaking wet. At six-feet-five inches, Danny towered over his twin sister. Closing the distance between them, Hannah grabbed Danny's pinky finger and twisted hard. He stopped laughing.

"Get inside now!"

"Geez! What's with the pinky finger? Why do you always do that?" He winced in pain and fidgeted to get away from her.

"Because I am half your size, and it is the only way I have ever been able to stop you from being a stupid head! Get inside, now!" Still holding his finger, she dragged him to the cabin. Danny had no choice but to follow her.

-*Chapter 6*-

Marnie leaned back in a sky-blue Adirondack chair, munching on the cheeseburger and fries she and Tom picked up on the drive to his house. Stretching out her long, tanned legs, she sighed. Her back ached from driving, and her shoulders and arms were tight from gripping the steering wheel. The thought of seeing Danny and Tom had tied her in knots.

Tom pulled two icy cold beers from the cooler, opened both, and handed one to Marnie. She accepted the frosty bottle, took a long drink, and settled back into her chair again. Glad to see the end of a day filled with emotion, she rested her eyes. Childhood memories flooded in and her tension eased. When she opened her eyes, she was delighted to see lightning bugs flickering in the distance, keeping time with the chirps of the crickets.

"What's that smile for?" asked Tom, offering his beer to her for a clink.

Leaning forward, she tapped her bottle on his. "I was thinking about the island." She popped the last bite of burger into her mouth and chewed thoughtfully.

A cloud of disbelief shrouded his face as he eased into a chair. "Uh ... and you were smiling?" he asked.

Marnie realized Tom was referring to the *last* time they had been on the island. The night in November when they apprehended Sam. The same night her brother tried to kill her and Tater.

She giggled. "No. Not that time. I was thinking of the trip we took when we were five. Don't you remember? That horrible man ... what was his name?" She snapped her fingers as if it would magically bring the memory closer to the surface.

Tom's jaw dropped, and his head bobbed up and down. "Wow! Yes! I remember that day. The thing I remember most was having a huge bump on my head and you having a fat lip. Geez! I haven't thought about that in a long time."

"Well, I was thinking about the treasure we left behind. You must remember when we climbed into the coal bin and then peeked up its chute. You remember, right?" She grinned and took a long drink of beer. "We should go get it!"

Tom laughed. "Go get the treasure? It probably isn't there anymore, Marn. How many years has it been?"

She stared up at the stars and recalled a game she and Sam had played as children. "Goin' on a treasure hunt. X marks the spot..." She smirked and side-eyed him.

"You're serious! You think we should go to the island and search for that stupid treasure?" He chuckled.

"I do. We should grab a couple of flashlights and go get what we should have taken when we were five. Geez, Tom! You ended up with a concussion, me a fat lip—we earned that treasure!"

He stood and stretched. With a grin on his face, he sang, "Goin' on a treasure hunt..."

Marnie sat up—eyes wide. "Really? You want to go?"

He held out a hand, and when she took it, he pulled her to her feet.

"Is the old boat gassed up?" he asked.

Marnie shrugged. "I don't know. Have you got a gas can?"

Tom nodded. "Yeah. I've got two in the shed."

"We'll fill them up along the way, and we'll get an ice cream cone at the truck stop. Should we bring the boofheads with us?" Marnie nodded toward Gus, Dickens, and Tater, who lay stretched across the grass and were sound asleep.

"Nah. Let's put Gus and Dickens inside. We'll take Tater with us. He's the only one who will behave in the boat."

She frowned. "Gus won't mind? Dickens will not be happy. You might come home to shredded shoes."

"I've got a couple of peanut butter filled Kongs in the freezer. They'll be fine," he reassured her.

She threw up her hands. "Okay! They're your shoes!"

He glanced between Gus and Dickens. "You may be right. We better bring them."

She nodded. "That would be the safest option for your shoes."

He laughed.

"Hey, Tom."

"Hmm…"

"Bring your gun."

"I always do."

"I like your new ride, Marn. This is pretty cool," Tom commented as he glanced around the interior of her new Jeep.

"I like it. My old car was 12 years old. It was time for something a bit more reliable," she said.

"Hmm … This is quite the upgrade!" he said sarcastically.

"Yup. Well, I've worked hard. I deserve a new car." She got quiet for a moment and then got angry because she realized he was pushing her buttons. "Don't try to make me feel bad, Thomas Keller! You know I always feel guilty when I buy something for myself."

He held up his hands. "Hey, it's a great vehicle, and I'm really glad that you have a reliable car. I won't spend so much time helpin' you dig out your car come winter."

"I asked once last year!" she barked, holding up a finger. "Once!"

"Ha-ha! I know. It's nice to have you back, Marn. I missed razzing you."

She glanced sideways at him, and asked, "Tom, where's Hannah?"

He rubbed his face with both hands and shook his head. "Ah! Geez! Why'd you bring that up?"

"What happened? Did you get all commitment-phoby again?" she teased.

He curled up his lip and glared at her. "No! I didn't! Hannah dumped me because, in her addled brain, she thinks I'm in love with *you!*"

Marnie's jaw dropped. "She what?!"

Tom frowned. "Yeah! Because Danny and I were worried and kept lookin' for you, she put two and two together and came up with a bazillion! Apparently, I'm obsessed with you!"

Marnie sat slack-jawed for a moment—eyes focused on the road. Then she turned to her friend. "What. The. Fuck. How could she think that? We've been best friends since we were five—of course you would worry about me."

"Watch the road, Marn!" he warned.

Eyes ahead, she said, "I am seriously stunned that she would think that. Everything was great between you two when I left, wasn't it?"

He shrugged a shoulder. "Eh! It was okay."

"What's that mean? Didn't you two have big Valentine's Day plans? You went skiing in Lake Placid and spent the night, didn't you?"

He shrugged again.

"What happened?"

"She didn't like skiing, the lodge, or the restaurant, and she was pissed off that I only booked one room," Tom confessed. "I offered to sleep on the couch, but she said that I would have to get another room. Anyway, I couldn't get another one—because, well, Valentine's Day. They didn't have any left. I ended up sleeping in the truck, and then it ran out of gas. I had to call a friend in Placid to bring me some so I could get to a service station."

Marnie made a face. "Wow! That sucks! I helped you organize the ski lodge and the restaurant. *And* it's the Valentine's Day trip that Danny and I would have taken if he hadn't gotten such a nasty cold. What's this bit about her not liking to ski? She told me she loves it when I told her that Danny and I were planning to go. She said she hadn't been in a long time, and that she would love to take a trip to the mountains! That's why I suggested it to you! Was she pissed off because that's where we were going? She may have wanted to get away from Danny and me. I'm really sorry!"

"Marn, it wasn't your fault. I think she simply didn't want to go away with me. I surprised her, and I don't think she liked not havin' control of the situation. She made a comment about me not including her in the plans. Dunno. I mean, you don't like surprises much, do you?"

"Hmm ... No, but that was a nice surprise. Didn't you tell her you were going to the mountains and to pack accordingly?"

He nodded. "Yeah. I did."

"Well, she could have been dealing with other things she wasn't ready to discuss," she suggested, giving Hannah the benefit of the doubt.

"Maybe Hannah decided Patrick was a better option," he grumped.

"Ah. Are they seeing each other?"

"Don't know. Don't care."

"What does Danny say?" she pushed.

"He doesn't. We don't talk about it." He turned to look out the window.

Marnie took that as a sign that the conversation was finished.

-*Chapter 7*-

Danny and Hannah crouched behind a felled hickory tree. The rifle leaned against the trunk. Through binoculars, they watched as Sam Reilly and his cohort paced around a crudely built rotisserie.

Danny whispered, "Okay. I'll go around the other side, and we'll..." A low, resonating growl interrupted him.

"Shh!" Hannah said. "What was that?"

"It sounded like Percy," he replied, crouching lower and twisting around so his back rested against the tree. "I don't see him."

Sam Reilly heard the growl. He stood motionless and moved only his eyes left to right.

Pigeon jerked with fear, turned in a circle and squatted into a wrestler's stance. "What the fuck was that?"

"A bear," Sam replied calmly. "Don't make any sudden moves. Be calm."

"Fuck that! We need to kill it!" Picking up the ax, Pigeon readied for the bear to attack.

Sam chuckled. "Do you know the size and strength of a black bear?"

Pigeon shook his head.

"They can be 7 feet tall when standing and weigh around 500 pounds. One of his paws would crush your skull with one swipe.

Simmer down. Wait and see why he's growling. It may not be us." Sam stood calmly scanning the woods.

Percy ambled through the trees and brush. He stopped and raised his nose in the air, sniffing.

Sam eased away from the rotisserie. "He smells the turkey. Stay still. Let him take it. Don't move."

"That's our dinner!"

"No. It's the bear's dinner. Better he eats the turkey than one of us, don't you think?"

Danny had his binoculars trained on Sam, and Hannah focused hers on the black bear.

"Is Percy going to kill them?" she asked nervously.

"No. He wants the turkey. Bears don't wanna deal with people—he only came out because he smells food. It probably woke him up from a nap."

Hannah checked her watch. "Where in the hell are the field agents? They should have been here half an hour ago."

He shrugged. "Hey, doesn't Sam seem a bit too calm? I mean, there's a bear standing a few feet away from him and he doesn't appear in the least bit frightened."

"You've read his profile. Sam Reilly is a survivor. Percy is a threat, but no worse than the criminal masterminds he dealt with when he was in the FBI. Besides, he grew up hunting and fishing. The wildlife here is not alien to him," Hannah reasoned.

"Yeah. Marnie is pretty adept at being in the woods, too. She knows how to mark trails, loves ice fishing, but I'm not sure she hunts. She might. I've never asked."

Hannah scowled.

He poked her with his elbow. "What's that face about?"

"I hope your precious Marnie doesn't tumble off that gilded pedestal you and Tom have her perched upon. It would be a nasty fall."

The detective screwed up his face. "What? We don't have her on a pedestal."

"Bullshit! You and Tom think she can do no wrong. It's disgusting. I'll bet that neither of you gave her hell for taking off."

"Uh, *yeah*, we did. Let's talk about it when this is over." He glanced back. "Where are those agents? Do you think they took one of the old service roads? We would have heard them if they were coming this way."

"I don't know. I gave them coordinates. They may have consulted a map." Her shoulders tensed, and she hip-nudged Danny.

He turned his attention to Sam and the other man, now racing their way, with a fire-roasted turkey cradled in his arms like a football. Percy, in hot pursuit of the turkey, was gaining on him.

Hannah leaped to her feet, pistol drawn. Danny grabbed her belt and yanked her behind the log.

"Get down!" he growled.

"Percy is going to kill him!"

"No, he won't! He'll rough the guy up a bit, but Percy doesn't want him—he wants the turkey."

He popped up his head as the black bear pounced, propelling his full weight into the man's back. Pigeon screamed. The bird flew out of his arms, shot through the air, and plunked to the ground between Hannah and Danny.

The detective sprang into action, grabbed his sister's arm, and pulled her awkwardly to her feet. He pushed her ahead of him, only turning his head to see if the bear was coming after them or the turkey. Then halted and chuckled at the sight of the bear sitting serenely, munching on the rotisserie bird. Percy stopped eating long enough to look up and lick turkey grease off his paw as the detective and the agent ducked out of sight behind a stand of pines.

"We better make tracks in case he's still hungry when he finishes," said Hannah.

"Afraid not, sis! We've got a couple of bad guys to catch." Danny took her by the shoulders and turned her around. "Let's go to the other side of the trail and see if we can cut them off."

-*Chapter 8*-

"I love twilight," said Marnie as they got out of her Jeep. "I remember when we were little—twilight was that magical time between sunset and dusk when everyone in the neighborhood was in their front yard or on their veranda having a chat."

Tom stretched his arms over his head. "Yup. We'd be over there in the field playin' frozen tag and What Time is it Mr. Fox? And then there was my favorite, kissing tag." He wrapped an arm around Marnie's shoulders and sang, "Marnie and Stuart sittin' in a tree!"

"Ha-ha! It was more like, 'Tom and Katie sittin' in a tree', pal!" she laughed, and playfully elbowed his ribs.

"You know, I never did like her. When we were kids, it was you who I liked," he admitted.

She side-eyed him and grinned. "I know."

"Marnie Reilly! You're b-b-back!" Patrick Kowalski shouted from the front porch of her old house. He hopped off the front steps, meeting them with a warm smile on the sidewalk.

Last December, Patrick, working undercover, played an integral role in solving a murder and breaking up a drug trafficking scheme. He also saved Marnie's life—twice. Once when he dove onto a burning parade float to guide her to safety, and again when he fired the shot that stopped Erin Matthews from shooting a deadly arrow into Marnie's heart. His tragic childhood and his time in the military in a bomb squad both contributed to his PTSD and a stutter that worsened with stress.

"Patrick! Hello!" She crossed the front lawn and threw her arms around the DEA agent for a hug. His face reddened as he returned the embrace.

"Hey, T-T-Tom!" Patrick held out his hand. "Long t-t-time, n-n-no see. How are you?"

Reluctantly Tom reached out for his extended hand. "Good. You?"

"Yeah, just exhausted. I've been working doubles the last two weeks. My b-boss threw me out of the office t-today. Told me t-t-to take five days off or else. It's been crazy. I was planning to come over to the station this w-week to discuss a joint t-task force with your department. Is Mac Gregg still filling in for Captain Sterling?"

Tom nodded. "He's traveling between here and home. He did mention that he and your boss talked about it. Danny is assisting where he can, but we've been busy, too. You should catch up with him."

Sensing her friend's anger, Marnie made an excuse to exit the fray. "I'm going to get the knuckleheads out of the truck. Back in a tick."

"I heard about those murders out on Hudson Pass," Patrick said. "Any closer to figuring it out?"

"Nah. We're thinkin' it's got something to do with the drugs you and your guys are chasing. It can't be a coincidence that we've got teenagers and twenty-somethings droppin' like flies because of fentanyl overdoses and two small-time dealers with bullets in the back of their heads. As I said, the Chief and your boss discussed it, and again, you should talk to Danny."

Squinting into the sun, Patrick frowned. "Yeah. I'll d-d-drop in tomorrow."

"Danny's off this weekend," Tom said curtly.

When he lifted his head, the friendly smile was gone. "Hey, T-T-Tom. Have I d-d-done something to p-p-piss you off?"

"I don't know. Have ya?" He raised an eyebrow and crossed his arms.

"Listen, if I've upset you, t-t-tell me."

"Have you been seein' Hannah?"

"What?" Patrick pulled a face. "No! Shit, Hannah and I work together! No way!"

Satisfied, Tom nodded "Okay."

"Hey, Patrick! Have you taken the boat out recently?" Marnie called out from the Jeep.

"Uh ... only the skiff," he replied.

"I left you a message last week about my father's boat. Was it delivered?" she asked.

"Yeah. They put it in the boathouse last Thursday. I haven't checked on it, but I did clear the skiff out so that they could put it away."

"Thanks for that!" she said, returning with Tater and Gus off lead, but Dickens wasn't as well-trained and needed restraint. Tater sniffed the grass, then wandered to Patrick, sat, put a paw up onto his knee, and smiled.

"Hey, Tater! How are you, buddy?" asked Patrick stooping to pat Border Collie. He nodded toward Marnie's new Jeep. "Nice wheels!"

She beamed. "Thanks! I figured it was time to get a new one. I don't want issues like I had last year."

Patrick laughed. Between Tom, Danny, and Patrick, there had been a dozen calls for help to jump-start Marnie's old car and a few occasions when she needed help to get out of the parking lot at her office.

"We're going out to the island. You're welcome to join," she said.

"Thanks, but no. I am g-g-going to sit out on the back p-p-porch with a beer and listen to the crickets. I am wiped out!"

"Well, if you hear any screams, Marnie's or mine, get in the skiff and get over to the island fast. Our last few trips out there have been eventful." Tom chuckled.

Patrick furrowed his brow. "I'm sure that's a story I will hear at some point."

"Over a beer," Tom replied.

"You can leave the knuckleheads with me," Patrick offered.

"Uh, maybe." Tom turned to Marnie.

"I think we better take Tater with us. He's an excellent guard dog," she replied, bobbing her head. "We'll take Gus and Dickens out on the boat the next time."

Tom agreed. "Good plan. Let's get the gas cans and bags out of the truck and shove off, Captain!"

Danny and Hannah doubled-back, running to the lakeside of the cabin and then to the shoreline. The latter called the field agents as they ran.

"Dammit! They got hung up on I-87. A tractor-trailer jackknifed. They are trying to get to an exit to take Route 9. They say the traffic is crawling—they're turning on their lights and going up the shoulder. They're still going to be awhile," Hannah relayed the information to Danny as she spoke with agents. "Look, guys, we've got an opportunity to apprehend two escapees. We're taking it. My brother is a police detective, and I'm an agent. We're fully equipped, and we *are* going after them. We'll see you when you get here." She hung up before they could argue.

The siblings stopped to catch a breath and used the time to discuss a strategy.

"Okay. How do you want to handle this?" asked Danny.

"Me?" Hannah's eyebrows shot up. "Don't you have a plan?"

Danny responded in a snotty tone. "Well, I do, but I'm not *Special Agent* Patterson of the *DEA*. I deferred to you because it's *federal*."

"Yeah. Well, my field experience may not be as extensive as yours," she admitted.

"Ah!" Danny stopped himself from razzing her and took the win like a grownup. It wasn't often she admitted her lack of field experience. "Okay. I think you should take the trail that goes around the lake. I'll go up through the woods, and then we ... Actually, let's stick together. We'll get to the deer run where it meets the lake. They're probably sticking to the trail. It's easier to navigate."

"You don't think Sam would think about that?"

The detective narrowed his eyes and scanned the trees. "Good point. You go around the lake. I'll go through the woods." He turned back to Hannah, his face lined with determination. "We have to get them. This has to end!"

"Tonight!" said his twin, completing his thought.

Danny gave a brisk nod and disappeared into the woods.

Arriving at the island, they pulled up to the pier. Tom's eyes widened at the sight of a new dock.

"Hey! That's new. The last time we were here, the dock was falling apart. I'm surprised it didn't dump us all in the pond."

"Hmm ... Someone must be looking after the place," she said, hiding a grin.

"Hey! Look up there on the beach. Those 'No Trespass' signs are new too." He glanced at Marnie.

She nodded and focused on docking the boat. Tom threw the bumpers over the side and then jumped out with the bowline in his hand. Nudging the boat forward, she then cut the engine and threw the stern line to Tom. Tater sat in the boat waiting for his mistress to tell him to "come". Grabbing the backpack full of flashlights, sweatshirts, a couple of small bags of chips, and a few other items, she stepped onto the dock. Tom took the bag and opened it before she could stop him.

"Whoa! What's this?" Tom, eyebrows raised, pulled a pistol out of the bag.

Marnie shrugged a shoulder. "It's mine. All licensed and everything."

"This is a concealed weapon when you're carryin' it in a bag. You know that's not legal, right? Not without a permit, anyway."

"I've got that too." She took the pistol and the bag away from him. "Tater! Come!"

The dog hopped off the boat, ran to his mistress's side, and sat.

"Who did you use for references?"

"Sergeant Beaumont, Ellie, Patrick, and Rick Price," she replied.

"Marnie Reilly, what else aren't you tellin' me?" he asked, eyebrows arched.

"Well, when I spoke with David Bennett about the Billingsly homestead, he told me that this island could be snatched up reasonably. All that was needed was for the back taxes to be paid."

Tom laughed and turned his eyes skyward. "Let me guess! You paid the back taxes?"

"Yeah! I own the island and everything on it—including the creepy house!"

"Wow, Marn, that's crazy. What are you gonna do with an island?"

"Once they repair the bridge and clean-up has happened, I thought it would make a great events venue. We could add a pavilion or two. Anyway, the money from the sale of Ken's house will pay for all of that."

"I keep forgetting that you're an heiress." Tom bent and gave Tater's head a scratch. "I guess you can have all the tuna you want, buddy."

"Ken Wilder's money is going to do good things for Creekwood. David has lined up charities for me to consider. The estate is too large for one person. Anyway, I can't put all that money in the bank. I have to make sure it works for me and as many other people as possible."

Tom nodded. "An events venue, huh? Hey! You and Danny could get married here."

Marnie rolled her eyes. "Ha-ha! Come on! We've got a treasure to get!"

She tossed her bag over her shoulder and led the way to old man Barnes's house—where the treasure awaited them—she hoped.

-*Chapter 9*-

"**W**ait!" shouted Pigeon, eyes wide as he scrambled to his feet. Sam stopped, turned and watched the escaped convict stumble across the overgrown path. "Pick up your feet! Thanks to you, we've got a cop on our tails!"

"What do ya mean? I had nothin' to do with that bear comin' after us!" Pigeon argued, brushing dirt from his stolen clothes.

Sam hung his head. *"I shouldn't have let him talk me into cooking that turkey. That was amateur!"*

His head shot up—anger contorting his face. Pigeon puffed out his chest in false bravado, challenging him.

"From here on, *Pigeon*, we do things my way and my way only! Got it!" Spittle flew with each enunciation as he jabbed his index finger into the other man's chest.

"Hey! Fuck you!" He wiped spit from his face and then, with both hands flat out, he shoved Sam. "You're the one who brought us here before stopping for food! I'm hungry! I want food—now!"

Stumbling back, he quickly regained his footing, charged forward and stood toe-to-toe with Pigeon. "The next time you shove me will be your last!" He took two steps back. "Now, get your stupid ass moving. We have to go. That cop is coming after us. Stick to the woods—not the path!"

Sam grabbed up his backpack and shot off into the trees. He didn't look back, nor did he care if Pigeon was with him or not. He needed to get ahead of Detective Gregg and the woman with him. She didn't look like a cop—she looked more like an accountant. It didn't matter—he needed to put as much distance between himself and them as possible.

Hannah navigated the ragged ground with ease. It was the mosquitos and black flies that slowed her pace when she stopped to swat away the bugs from her face, neck, and limbs. She paused again when the voices of men arguing cut through the quiet evening air. *"They couldn't have been dumb enough to come this way?"* she thought. Her phone buzzed in her pocket. She thought about answering it—then considered against it. The field agents would find them when they arrived. She poked along, trying not to break an ankle or fall into the lake.

Danny bobbed and weaved around boulders, trees, and overgrowth. He could hear Sam's voice off in the distance, but the sound carried funny out here—the lake and mountains muddled from which direction the voices actually came. The convicts were ahead of him. But where? With the hem of his T-shirt, he wiped sweat out of his eyes, then smacked a deerfly who was making a dinner of his arm. He cocked his head, listened, turned to his right and set his steely blue eyes on a thick grouping of trees.

"Gotcha!" he whispered.

Sam stopped behind a stand of pines to catch his breath. His eyes scanned the landscape, searching for a ridge up ahead. He knew it dropped off sharply, but he couldn't remember at which point it plunged into the ravine or into the lake.

"When I catch up to you, Sam Reilly, I'm gonna kill you, and then I'm gonna find your sister..." Pigeon's rant halted abruptly.

"Federal agent! Don't move!" Special Agent Hannah Patterson stood on the trail two yards away—shoulders taut—feet planted, her pistol in her right hand, and her badge in the other. "Get down on your knees. Put your hands on top of your head and then lie on your stomach. If you don't follow my directions, I *will* shoot you!"

Pigeon smirked.

"Down! Now!"

Grinning widely, he scoffed and took a step forward. "Who you kiddin'? Ha! You ain't gonna shoot me."

Hannah pulled the trigger and shot him in his left thigh. "Drop! Now!"

Pigeon howled and dropped to his knees. He clutched his thigh and dared a peek to assess the damage. Blood spotted his hand as he pulled it away from his leg. He leaned left, then right, glanced up at her—his eyes glassy, skin pasty and beaded with perspiration. "You shot me," he muttered, and then he toppled forward onto the mossy path.

Twigs snapped with every step Danny took as he crept toward the stand of pines. It was nearly impossible to be stealthy—they hadn't seen rain in Creekwood in weeks and the temps had been hot. Danny suddenly remembered the campfire. Was it still burning? He turned to see if he could see smoke rising into the air, and while he didn't, that didn't mean it wasn't smoldering. He glanced toward the pine trees and then back at his cabin. *Get Sam Reilly—then put out the fire.* Decision made, he eased forward. As he reached the trees, he could see Sam standing in a small clearing; he appeared to be alone, and his back was to him. Danny pushed quietly through the foliage with his pistol aimed at Sam.

"Federal agents! Put down your weapon, get on your knees and place your hands on top of your head! Now!"

Sam turned, spying the agents. Danny spun around to see two FBI field officers dressed in khakis, hiking boots, blue t-shirts, ball caps, and FBI vests stepping into the clearing. One agent was tall and pale, with a slight paunch. The other was compact, sturdily built with the pasty pallor of a desk jockey.

"Put your weapon down now! Get down on your knees, hands on top of your head," said the paunchy guy.

Danny shouted, "I'm Lieutenant Daniel Gregg with Creekwood PD! Special Agent Hannah Patterson of the DEA called you! Sam Reilly is right there!" He wagged his chin in Sam's direction.

"Put down your weapon! Kick it over here! We will not ask you again!"

He rolled his head back, bent, laid down his pistol, kicked it lightly across the clearing; he dropped to his knees and put his hands on top of his head. Pistol still drawn, the paunchy agent ran toward him.

The convict and the detective stared into one another's eyes. Sam gave a nod of recognition, then disappeared into the trees with the pasty agent trailing him.

"You won't die. The bullet only grazed you. Stop whining and stand up!" ordered Hannah, pulling on Pigeon's arm.

He struggled to his feet; his hands now cuffed behind his back. "You shot me!" he whimpered.

"It's a graze. There's barely any blood. You'll be fine. Now, get moving!" Hannah nudged him ahead of her on the rugged path, keeping her distance in case he stumbled backward or turned quickly to kick her.

"I'm gonna fall. Take the cuffs off!"

"The path gets easier up ahead." She rolled her eyes and under her breath said, "What a wuss!"

"What did you say?"

"I said you're a wuss!"

As they reached the top of the path, she pushed the convict into a clearing. The scene she came upon brought a smile to her face— for there in the clearing she saw Danny on his knees, hands cuffed behind him, with an FBI agent yelling at him.

She pulled her badge off her belt and held it up. "Federal agent! I am Special Agent Hannah Patterson of the DEA! I am escorting a suspect. That man on his knees is Detective Daniel Gregg of Creekwood PD." She worked hard to hide a smirk that was bursting to the surface.

Danny jerked his arms. "Get the cuffs off me now!" he growled between clenched teeth.

The field agent glanced at the two. "Agent Patterson, he doesn't have identification."

"It is Special Agent! Take the cuffs off him." She scanned the area before turning back. "Where is Sam Reilly?"

The federal agent fumbled with the cuffs. "He took off into the woods. My partner's tracking."

Danny rubbed his freed wrists and sniggered. "You idiot! Your guy will never catch him. Sam Reilly knows these woods like the back of his hand. He grew up here. The man is a survivor, and a pencil pusher will not catch him."

Pigeon snickered, but dropped his chin to his chest when he spied a glower from Hannah.

"What's your name?" she demanded.

The man scowled. "Agent Andrew Harding." He showed Hannah and Danny his credentials.

"Who's tracking Reilly?" asked the detective.

"Agent Dobbs. Derek Dobbs, and he's not a pencil pusher; nor am I."

Hannah said, "No need to be surly with us, Harding. You and Dobbs are the ones who apprehended a cop, and then let Reilly get away."

He scoffed. "He had no ID!"

"I told you I was from Creekwood PD," retorted Danny, as he crossed to the crude spit and kicked dirt onto the convicts' campfire.

Hannah raised an eyebrow. "And I told you over the phone who I was working with. Didn't you bother to look up either of us? Did you actually walk into this without viewing our profiles?"

"We were called in last minute. We didn't have time..."

"That's crap! You were stuck in traffic for well over an hour!"

Gunfire echoing in the woods saved Agent Harding from an uncomfortable response. *Bang! Bang! Bang!* A muffled *bang* followed. They all pivoted—their attention focused on a spot where the open field met the forest.

Agent Dobbs ran out of the trees, his pasty face splattered with blood, and a splotch of red seeping through his shirt. His chest heaved as he caught his breath. Harding jogged to his partner's side.

Harding asked, "Where's Reilly?"

Bent at the waist with his hands on his knees, Dobbs breathed deeply, then pointed into the woods. "He ambushed me! He ... he took my gun! I shot him! I know I did!"

Hannah and Danny exchanged glances.

"Are you sure?" asked the detective.

Dobbs nodded assuredly. "Yeah! I felt the spray of blood on my face."

"That's your blood. Your shoulder is bleeding," said Hannah.

Dobbs drew himself up to his full and compact five-foot five inches. "Pfft! I'm not bleeding." He looked at his left shoulder, and then his right—and fainted.

Sam crashed through trees and brush—branches tearing at his clothing, backpack, and skin. He spotted the ridge up ahead and rocketed forward, saying a prayer as he soared over the ledge. He didn't look down. What was the point? It was going to be a painful and deadly landing or not. He held his breath as his stomach did that strange flip-flop it does when falling in a dream. When his feet found water, he celebrated his luck, thankful for the soft landing. Submerged in the cool water, he propelled himself to the surface, treaded water and searched the shore. While not a religious man, he turned his face skyward and said another prayer, thankful someone was watching over him. Clouds gathered, moving swiftly overhead, and big drops of rain fell. Before lightning could find him, he swam into a reedy cove, threw his backpack ashore, and then pulled himself up onto the rocks and crawled up the bank. He laid back onto the peaty ground, the canopy of the trees keeping most of the rain off him. A raindrop trickled to a leaf, splattering his nose.

He thought it strange that his life hadn't flashed before his eyes as he hurled himself into the unknown. "Hmm ... maybe mine hasn't been a great one," he thought. He sat up, pulled up his shirtsleeve to assess the damage the bullet had done to his left arm, and breathed a sigh of relief. "Okay. I've had worse."

The elliptical, raw wound was approximately two-and-a-half inches long. It seeped minimal blood—possibly lessened by his recent "swim" in the lake. He dug through his backpack looking for his first-aid kit, thankful he'd had the sense to put everything into Ziploc bags. Once he smeared his wound with an antibacterial ointment and dressed it, he pulled down his sleeve.

"Where to now, Reilly?" he asked himself. A low rumble in the pit of his stomach told him his next stop needed to include food.

-*Chapter 10*-

"What's that smell?" Nose scrunched up, Marnie glanced around, searching for the offending odor. "Can you smell that? Gawd! It's disgusting!"

The corners of Tom's mouth dropped, and he gagged. "Blah! It smells like something died!"

Tater, mouth closed, sniffed the air, relishing the thought of rolling in something so delightfully stinky.

The trio paused on the path to get their bearings, but nothing looked familiar. Marnie's shoulders stiffened as a telltale tingle prickled her scalp.

"Uh-oh. That's never good," she muttered under her breath, running a hand over her head.

"What?" he asked.

"Nothing," she lied.

"Marn, didn't you think to come have a look before you bought this place? I mean, this is ... Phwaw!" he pulled up the neck of his shirt to cover his nose.

"It was cheap, Tom! How was I to know it was going to smell like ... like... What is that smell? Ugh! Do you think it's a dead deer?" She shivered, even though the evening air was warm.

"It's probably a dead turtle. Buzzard puke and dead turtles are vile!" Tom stuck out his tongue and shuddered. "Hey! Did you feel that? Was that rain?" He glanced up. "We better get a move on. Those clouds are about to dump on us!"

"Buzzard puke? Ick!" She rolled up her lip. "Let's get to the Barnes house, if it's still standing. I asked Paige Reynolds to do a recon before I got back into town, but I haven't heard from her." She hiked up the backpack onto her shoulder and jogged. Tater trotted happily beside her, with Tom close on their heels.

Paige Reynolds was in school with Marnie and Tom. A few years back, she was driving home from a party when a child ran onto the road and Paige accidentally hit him. The child had not survived, and while Kate Parish had taken up Paige's defense, she went to prison for vehicular manslaughter. Then, six months before her release, an inmate stabbed her in the chest with a shiv.

"Is Paige doin' the landscaping?" asked Tom.

Marnie nodded. "Yeah. It would be nice to throw her more work. She's always been a sweetie. David tells me the gardens at the ranch are spectacular. I guess we'll see tomorrow."

Tom grunted in agreement and looked up again. Thunder rumbled and flashes of heat lightning backlit the clouds. Marnie picked up the pace. Tater and Tom followed her lead, nearly slamming into her as she came to an abrupt halt when the old Barnes house came into view.

"Wow, Tom! It's scarier than I remembered."

They stood five yards away from the front door. Grape vines and Virginia Creeper encapsulated the building and weeds tufted up around the foundation.

"It looks like someone was here recently. The grass around the front steps is flat, like it's been walked on." Tom approached the house with caution.

"Maybe Paige or the contractor David hired has been out here. They came out to do an estimate on the bridge. Stu came out to see about demolishing the house and clearing the brush and dead trees."

Tom's jaw tightened as his keen eyes surveyed the lay of the land. "Yeah. That could be it."

"What aren't you saying?" She nudged him with her elbow.

"I'm remembering the last time we were in the house. Papa Jack wouldn't be hanging around, would he?" He was referring to Marnie's grandfather, who spoke with her often when she was a child.

"Uh-uh. He hasn't been in touch since Dad died. Anyone on the other side of the veil can talk to me whenever they want, but I don't like to bother them."

Tom nodded. "Yeah. I thought he might be around."

Marnie pushed out a determined breath. "Okay! Let's go get that treasure!"

Tom grinned. "You go first, Madame Séance."

She glanced at him over her shoulder with a smirk. "Chicken!"

"Yep!" he agreed.

Dilapidated steps greeted them. The risers leaned left, and the steps were rotten. The front door stood closed—remarkably, the window in the door remained in one piece.

"Hmm ... We'll have to step directly onto the porch," said Marnie.

She took a big step over the stairs and gingerly placed a foot on the old decking. Tom held her elbow, and she took another step up. Tater leaped over the stairs and stood next to her. Tom stepped up and tested the decking by jumping up and down.

Marnie glared at him. "Seriously? Why would you do that?"

He shrugged. "I'm a man."

"You're an ass! You could have gone through the decking and hurt yourself!"

"Pfft! Chill, Marn! The deck is solid." He took a step, the decking split and one of his legs dropped through to the ground beneath. "Son of a bitch!"

She laughed and then went to help him. "Are you hurt? Is your leg scrubbed?"

He placed a hand on her shoulder and pulled himself out of the hole. His shin oozed with blood.

"Geez! That hurts!" He sucked in a breath and held it, bent at the waist, and tried to breathe normally. "Shit! That fucking hurts!"

"Let me see," she said, kneeling and pushing away his hand. "It doesn't look terrible, but it is going to hurt tomorrow!" She stood and took gentle steps across the deck to the door. "You know, your sheets are going to stick to that when you sleep."

"This is one of those occasions when I should look for sympathy in the dictionary between shit and syphilis, huh?"

Marnie giggled. "Only true friends laugh, then make sure you're okay."

"Gee, thanks! Have you got a first-aid kit in that bag of tricks?"

She dug through her backpack and handed him a plastic bag filled with first-aid supplies, then she turned back to the door. Peering through the dusty window, she couldn't make out much of anything. She tried the doorknob, but it didn't turn. "I think it's locked."

Tom sat on the deck with an antibacterial wipe in one hand and a tube of antibiotic cream in the other. He glanced up. "You own everything on the island, right?"

"Yeah."

"Give me a sec. I'll get it open."

"Do you want help with that?"

"No. You'll make it hurt more, like my mother always did," he said, scowling.

Marnie laughed and watched him clean his shin and then apply the cream. He searched through the bag and pulled out an elastic bandage to wrap his leg.

"That's not overkill?"

"No! I don't want anything to get into it. I'd like to keep my leg, thanks very much." He pushed himself up and joined her at the door, picking up an old clay flowerpot along the way.

She grabbed his arm. "Hey! Don't break the window!"

If looks could kill, Marnie Reilly would have dropped dead at that very moment.

"Aren't they going to tear the house down? What the hell difference does it make if I break the window?" Tom fumed.

"History. If I don't raze the house, it would be nice for the glass to be intact. I'd like that choice." She looked up at the window, twisting her lips to one side in thought.

Tom rolled his eyes, put down the flowerpot, and pulled a knife out of his pocket. He inserted it between the door and the jam and jiggled it. The door popped open; he gave the door a push with his toe and bowed dramatically. "After you, Ms. Reilly."

"Coward," she replied as she walked through the open door.

"Yes, I am!" Tom followed—somewhat reluctantly, with Tater at his side.

Dust motes floated through the air, and the smell of dank enveloped them.

Marnie screwed up her face. "Eww! This is disgusting!"

Tom's expression resembled Marnie's with an added measure of fear. *Scratch. Scratch. Scratch.* Tater's ears perked up—he tipped his head, and then crept toward the fireplace, snuffling the floor along the way.

Tom jerked around, searching for the culprit of the scratching. "Is that a rat?"

Marnie's senses tingled as she surveyed the room. "This house has been empty for nearly 30 years. I would guess that a few critters have taken up residence. Tom! Watch out!"

Too late. He walked through a huge cobweb.

"Argh!" Arms flailing—body convulsing—long legs kicking, he frantically brushed away the silvery threads. With a shudder, he gulped out, "Cobweb cooters! For fuck's sake!" He pulled the sticky strands of webbing from his face and shuddered again.

Marnie raced to his side and brushed at his arms. "Lean over and let me get them out of your hair."

"Where's the spider?" He jerked from side to side—running his hands up and down his body and through his hair. "It feels like it's crawling on me! Where's the damn spider?" He yanked his shirt off over his head and shook it violently. "Is it gone?"

"Stand still!" she shouted. She reached up, plucked a house spider from his hair, carried it to the door and then set it on the deck.

He held up his hands. "I am out! Get the damn treasure yourself!" He stormed off toward the door.

Marnie grabbed his arm and threw in a foot stamp for effect. "Thomas Keller, get back here! We have a treasure to find!"

He tossed back his head and turned around. Tom knew he was beaten as soon as he saw her face—it reminded him of five-year-old Marnie, determined and fearless. He hung his head and shook it. A huge sigh of resignation followed. When he lifted his head, he saw little girl Marnie was still glaring at him. He threw up his hands. "Fine! You win!"

With a grin, she searched through her bag, and presented him with a bottle of tequila. "Liquid courage, my friend!"

He snatched it from her and held it up. "Nectar of the cowardly!" He pulled off the top and took an impressive guzzle. "Ahh! That should help."

As he handed it back, he saw movement in his periphery. "Did you see that?"

Tater's eyes focused on an area of the room where evening shadows danced up the wall, compliments of a light breeze and tree branches outside the window. He whimpered softly and cocked his head.

"See what?" she asked.

"You didn't see somethin' move over there?" He pointed to the far-left corner of the living room.

"Nope." Even if she had seen something, she would not admit it. Tom would scarper out the door, and they would never get the treasure.

"Huh. Okay," he replied, not buying it. "You saw it, didn't you, Tater?"

The Border Collie looked up at him and smiled.

He shivered and said, "This place gives me the willies. Let's get this over with and get the hell out of here."

Marnie and Tater followed him to the cellar door, and he squeaked it open.

"What have you talked me into?" he asked, peering into the darkness.

Marnie flashed him a cheesy smile. "Childhood goals sometimes have to wait until adulthood." She gave him a nudge. "C'mon. Let's do this!"

"You go first! I'm not having a face-off with Mr. Barnes. Living or dead—he's a cranky bastard."

"Fine! Get out of my way!"

"No! I'll go." He eased his gun out of its holster and warily descended the stairs into the place that had terrorized them as children.

Marnie dug a flashlight out of her bag and followed. Tater scooted around them and raced downstairs. He skidded to a halt at the bottom—his scruff stood on end and he growled. Tom stopped short. Marnie bumped into him, and a snarling Tater sprang forward into the darkness.

-Chapter 11-

Kate Parish rested comfortably on a chaise lounge in her suite of rooms at Pine Ridge Mental Hospital. Her shoulder-length raven hair had nearly recovered from the hatchet job executed last year by Erin Matthews. Equally recovered was her forehead—the plastic surgery performed to remove the brand of the Eye of Providence had been a success.

"Daddy, you must figure out a way to get me out of here! I can't possibly stay cooped up any longer!" She threw back her head into the cushions of the lounge, a sullen expression marring her outer beauty.

Lawrence Parish stood next to an iron-grated window looking out on the Hudson River and the sanitarium's immaculate gardens. He was a man of average height and build, with snow-white hair and manicured nails. His navy-blue suit, crisp white shirt, silk gray striped tie and polished Italian loafers gave him a businesslike air. His amber eyes revealed boredom.

"Katie, we have been over this repeatedly. You don't have a choice. Either you stay here or stand trial for the nonsense Sam Reilly dragged you into last year. You must understand, darling. My hands are tied."

She jolted upright, her indigo eyes flashing with anger. "You haven't tried hard enough, Daddy! Why can't I go home with you and Mother? Couldn't you have a nurse take care of me at home? This is so unfair! I feel like a caged animal! You don't care if they keep me until the day I die!" She flopped back abruptly and whimpered. "You would get me released if you loved me."

Lawrence glanced at her mother, Kitty, who sat on a chair beside her daughter's chaise lounge. She reached out a delicate hand and placed it on Kate's arm.

"Katie, darling, Daddy has done everything he can. We are both doing our best. You have the nicest suite of rooms here," she soothed.

Swiping away her mother's touch, she swung her legs off the lounge and walked purposefully to the window, glancing wistfully at the flowing river. She smoothed her hands down her legs and frowned at the wrinkles in her blue linen slacks and white linen tank top. The frown deepened when she noticed gray scuffs on her white kicks. She knew her parents, especially her father, were easily manipulated, so she turned on the waterworks—an art she practiced often in the bathroom mirror.

Adding a quivering bottom lip to break them, she said, "I would like you to bring me a new wardrobe—summery things. I'm stuck in here and I'm sick of the clothes I have with me. Mother, please bring me a pretty dress. Daddy, please!" Kate sashayed to her father's side, taking one of his hands and twirling into his arms. "Please, Daddy! Just a few new things."

Lawrence warmly patted her arm. "Of course, Katie Kat! Your mother and I will go out tomorrow and buy you a summer wardrobe."

"Could I please have a pair of running shoes? I'd like to go to the gym."

"Of course, dear. We've been hoping you would find an activity to enjoy. The facilities here are wonderful," her mother said.

"The facilities are average, Mother. Nothing here is wonderful." Kate tossed her head, adding a loud sigh for effect.

Lawrence moved the discussion to another topic before his daughter could launch into an unpleasant tirade. "We see you had a visitor. Did you and Paige have a pleasant visit?"

"A pleasant visit? No, Father, we did not! She came here to gloat. She's out of prison, and I'm locked up for no reason. I saw her smirking. Paige Reynolds is a horrible person! I did everything I could to help her and she repays me by celebrating my incarceration!"

Kitty sat forward, lifting her handbag into her lap as women do when readying their departure. "Come now, Katie. I'm sure Paige didn't come here to gloat. That poor girl has been through a terrible ordeal. Killing a child and then the stabbing..."

Kate spun around, eyes blazing. "Poor girl? That 'poor girl' killed a child! That 'poor girl' ruined my career as a defense attorney! She is the reason they relegated me to paper-pusher!"

"Enough. Your mother didn't mean to upset you, did you?" Lawrence shot his wife a warning glance.

Kitty set her handbag on the floor, their exit likely delayed by her daughter's outburst.

"Darling, it's only that Paige nearly died when she was attacked in prison. If not for a brilliant surgeon and a pacemaker, she wouldn't be alive today. She didn't deserve a death sentence. The child's death was an accident. Why the jury and the judge didn't take that into consideration..."

"How dare you!" Kate seethed, her eyes burning with fury. "How dare you blame me for her sentence?"

Hands covering her face, Kitty recoiled. "Katie, I didn't blame you..."

Lawrence stepped between his daughter and wife. "That's enough, ladies. Kate, your mother didn't mean to imply you were at fault. You did the best you could. Isn't that right, Kitty?"

Lifting a hand to fluff her perfectly coiffed hair, Mrs. Parish's eyes flashed with contempt for her husband. "Why do you pander to her so, Lawrence?"

He lifted an eyebrow. "Apologize for upsetting our daughter so that we can move on from this tedious topic."

Kitty lifted her handbag once again and set it beside her in the chair. "I didn't mean to upset you, Kate. I am sorry if my choice of words affected you."

Eyes narrowed, Kate curled up a corner of her mouth. "You almost sound like you meant that, Mother."

With a toss of her hair, she flitted back to the window, staring out at a woman weeding the flowerbeds.

"I've been thinking about writing a book. An account of my side of the story." Kate pivoted back to her parents—eyes wide and innocent. She explained, "If I could write about my feelings and what I've been through, and all that nasty business with Ken, Sam, and Erin. Of course, I'll include how hateful Marnie Reilly was to me. Anyway, I thought it would make me feel better. We could give it to the judge or the director here at Pine Ridge. They may understand the ghastly duress I was experiencing."

She sashayed back to the chaise and flopped down dramatically. "I'm certain I would feel better if I could put my words on paper. Don't you agree?"

Her father nodded. "Writing can be cathartic. I think it's a wonderful idea, don't you, Kitty?"

Kate's mother agreed with a vigorous nod. "Yes, it's a positive step. I'll bring you new notebooks and pens tomorrow."

Kate wrinkled her nose and wailed, "Notebooks and pens? Why would you bring me notebooks and pens? I want a laptop!"

Lawrence sighed, shaking his head. "You can't have a laptop; no electronics, Katie. You know the rules."

"I don't care about the rules!" she hissed, leaping to her feet, arms raised dramatically. "I've been following orders for months! I haven't gotten credit for doing as I'm told! I've done everything they have asked of me! Why are you two telling me I can't have a laptop? Get me one! Get. Me. A. Laptop! Now!" Kate hovered menacingly over her mother, who had remained seated. Kitty turned to her husband, jerking her head toward the door.

Lawrence hurried to the door, knocked, and a steward's face appeared in the wire-meshed window. The door unlocked with a heavy clunk, and Dalton Hooley, a baby-faced man built like a linebacker, entered. He was a hulk of a man—six feet, eight inches tall, short cropped jet-black hair, and kind brown eyes.

"Everything okay, Mr. Parish?" Dalton asked, his voice a melodious, deep baritone.

"I'm afraid we've upset Kate. We think it is best Mrs. Parish and I leave. Can you please help us?"

"Yes, sir. I'll take it from here. You and the missus step out."

Kitty rose from her chair, handbag clutched under her arm. Not meeting her daughter's eyes, she said, "We'll see you tomorrow, dear."

In response, Kate threw one of her white kicks at her mother's head, which was caught mid-air by her steward.

"Miss Kate, don't make me write you up. Apologize to your mama."

"Make me!"

The big man shrugged his beefy shoulders. "Fine by me. I'll write up a report and you won't be getting your meals delivered to your room anymore. You'll be eating in the dining hall with everybody else. Doesn't bother me. I won't have to clean up after you, and you'll have to schlep your own dishes to the bussing station."

Kate closed her eyes, and with a pained expression, she apologized. "I'm sorry I threw my sneaker at you, Mother."

"That wasn't convincing, but it was a good try. Now, pick up your shoe and put it on. I need to take you out for your exercise."

Lawrence and Kitty Parish slipped out the door while Dalton Hooley distracted their daughter.

-*Chapter 12*-

"If he jumped into the ravine here, he probably didn't make it," Danny commented gravely, glancing over the side. "Do you know if he jumped right here or was it further down?"

Agent Harding held up his partner while they awaited the ambulance. Agent Dobbs mashed his lips together and shrugged a shoulder. "I don't know where he jumped."

Hannah raised an eyebrow. "You told us two minutes ago that you saw him race off and then you said that he jumped. Was it here or there?" She turned and pointed to her right.

"It all happened so fast, he ambushed me and he shot me and…" Dobbs stumbled over his words.

Harding frowned. "Take it easy on him! He's got a bullet in his shoulder!"

Danny pulled a face. "Hang on! You said you shot him. You were certain of it. Did he shoot you and take your gun, or didn't he?"

Pigeon stood beside Hannah. He coughed and then obnoxiously cleared his throat.

Hannah swung around. "Have you got something to say?"

The felon smirked—his left shoulder lifting ever so slightly.

Danny scowled and waved away his smarmy expression. "Ignore him. He knows nothing."

"Yeah, I do!"

The detective turned his back—dismissing him.

"Sam told me he wasn't gonna kill no cops. He said it today!"

"Is that right?" Danny eyed the convict and took two large steps toward him. "What exactly did he say?" he asked, standing nose to forehead with the annoying little man.

Intimidated under the detective's height, Pigeon raised his shoulders up, hoping to appear bigger. "He said killin' a cop is no problem, he just don't want it to be a sport or somethin' like that. He said if you got in his way, he might think about it."

Danny shot him a dirty look, then walked back toward the ridge.

"Hey, his beef ain't with you! It's with his sister! He's got no problem killin' her!"

The bristling comment drew no verbal response. The detective's shoulders tensed and his fists clenched—but he continued to the ridge.

"Wanna know what he said about your girlfriend?" The singsong tone of the convict's words did nothing to halt the detective.

"He said I could have fun with her before he killed her. Owooo!" Pigeon's animalistic howl was his undoing.

Hannah cringed. "That wasn't very bright," she said dryly.

She sidestepped away from the convict as Danny steamed forward, grabbing the front of Pigeon's T-shirt, pulling him up to eye level. The two FBI agents glanced at one another and then turned away.

"If you ever lay a hand on Marnie Reilly, I will break every bone in your body, you worthless piece of shit!"

An ugly sneer appeared on the felon's face in response to the threat. The sneer dissolved as a forceful head-butt connected with his brow bone with a sickening *thunk*. Pigeon staggered back, landing hard in the dirt, his hands still cuffed behind him. He rolled to his side and tucked his knees up to his chin, readying for a kick to his ribcage. When moments passed and the kick didn't come, he struggled to sit up. He glanced around uncomfortably, but the detective was gone. Only Hannah was there, glaring at him.

"Keep your mouth shut! If you don't, I'll be more than happy to shut it for you!" she warned. Turning her back to him, she called out to the FBI agents. "He's all yours."

Pigeon struggled to his knees, still dazed from the head-butt. "You can't threaten me! That's police brutality! I know my rights!"

Harding approached. "Uncuff him, Agent Patterson."

Hannah narrowed her eyes. "It's Special Agent, and not on your life! If you want that scum uncuffed, you do it!" She tossed the key to him.

Harding caught it and bent to uncuff Pigeon. He glanced up at her and asked, "Is Marnie Reilly Sam Reilly's sister?"

"Yes. Why?"

"We should probably speak with her. She may know where her brother would go—that is, if he survived."

She dismissed his thought. "I'm quite certain Marnie wouldn't. They aren't close."

"Sometimes things aren't as they appear, *Special Agent* Patterson."

"What's that supposed to mean?" She scowled.

"He escaped back in March. How has he survived all those months without help?" Harding asked. "People don't escape and run for that long without someone assisting them."

"It's been only a few months. The weather has been agreeable. IIe would be fine. He can kill and cook his own food. Fruits and vegetables from the market stalls are easy enough to steal around here. He is neither a stupid nor an unskilled man, Agent Harding. After all, he outsmarted Dobbs, didn't he?" She sucked in her cheeks and raised an eyebrow. "Rethink your assumptions. You may have him pegged all wrong. Have you read his file? Are you a profiler? Do you have that skill? No? Then shut up!"

As the wail of sirens screamed closer, she stalked off to join Danny's search for the convict.

-*Chapter 13*-

"Tater! Come!" said Marnie as she and Tom reached the bottom of the stairs.

Tater growled in response. She narrowed her eyes and pushed in front of Tom, coming face-to-face with the grotesque, translucent, gray man standing across from her.

"You don't scare me, Mr. Barnes! This is my house now. I own it and the land. Get out! It's time for you to leave!" she shouted.

Tom stiffened. He leaned forward and whispered, "Mr. Barnes is here?"

She nodded and pointed beyond Tater. "Yeah. He's right there at the end of the workbench, and he looks *pissed*!" she whispered. "Let me handle him."

Tom placed a hand on each of her shoulders and gave her a gentle shove forward. "He's all yours!"

"Get out, Mr. Barnes! You aren't welcome here. This isn't your house. Do not make me remove you! You won't like where you end up."

Marnie crossed her arms in front of herself, challenging the ghastly spirit of the murderous man who had attacked her and Tom when they were five years old.

Tater bounced forward with a deep growl.

"Is he still there?" Tom asked with a shiver.

"Yup! He's trying to throw something at us."

"What?" he asked, his voice cracking.

"He's trying to throw that circular saw at us—but he can't. I'm not giving him any power like I did when we were little. Don't be afraid of him. He can't hurt us. Don't give him your power."

The ghost shooed a bluish-gray hand at Tater, who stood his ground—growling and snarling.

"Mr. Barnes, I warned you!" Marnie dug into her bag and took out a bundle of white sage and a lighter. Setting her bag on the floor, she lit the sage and blew on it until it began billowing smoke. "Bye-bye, Mr. Barnes!" She whispered as she waved the sage and meandered through the cellar with a trail of white smoke wisping around her.

"Hello, my name is Marnie; this is my space now and I promise to be respectful to those of you who are respectful to my family, my friends and me. I thank all the gentle and good spirits who live in the house and on this land, and ask for your help to bring peace by ridding this space of negative energies and entities. I acknowledge the first people of the land and state my intention to care for this land; and I encourage all peaceful and positive spirits to remain. Those who intend to do harm, be damned!"

Marnie turned back to where the ghost of Mr. Barnes had been to see the space empty. Tater was no longer growling, but was standing beside Tom with a big smile.

"Is he gone?" Tom asked with a wary glance about the room.

"Nah! He'll hang around for a while. We'll let the others take care of him."

Tom gulped. "Others? How many others are here?"

"Enough positive spirits to push his sorry ass out! C'mon! Let's get the treasure and get outta here! He'll be back once the smoke has cleared." Marnie bent and rubbed the sage onto the cement floor and shoved it back into her backpack once she was sure it was no longer burning.

"It was up inside the coal chute, right?" asked Tom, crossing the cellar.

"Yup. It was on the left side, and I remember it was in leather or oilcloth, and was really heavy." She followed him to the chute while Tater sat near the stairs—alert—ears up, listening.

"Hmm. I don't think the old bin will hold my weight," said Tom.

"Here," she said, holding out her hand. "If you'll steady me, I'll get in and grab the treasure."

She climbed over the side with his help, opened the chute's door and eased her hand up inside.

"Careful, Marn. There could be a critter up there."

"Geez, Tom, you are such a scaredy cat. I'm going to feel around and see if I can ... Oh! Got it!"

"Seriously? It's still there?"

"Yeah, but it's stuck on something. I'll take a peek."

She peered up and jerked backward, shocked to see Paige Reynolds staring at her.

"Holy crap, Paige! I didn't expect to see you up there. Gosh! Give us a minute and we'll be right out."

Marnie ducked back out of the chute, put her hand up inside once again, and gave the leather bundle a yank. Whatever held the treasure released it and she pulled it out of the chute, holding it up for Tom to see.

"Here it is! Look at this! I can't believe it's been up there all this time." She put a hand on Tom's shoulder and jumped out of the bin, cradling the treasure under her arm.

"Did you say Paige is up there?"

"Yeah. Kinda late for her to be out here, isn't it? Anyway ... Let's go see what Paige is up to and then head home to open the treasure."

"I wonder where she got to. I said we'd be right up." Marnie set her bag on the ground, her eyes on the horizon, searching for Paige.

"Maybe she's waiting on the dock rather than hanging around here gettin' eaten up by mosquitoes," Tom suggested.

His ears twitching away gnats and mosquitoes, Tater meandered around a mound of sagebrush with his nose in the air.

"Hey. Remember when we were kids, and the top of my head would tingle?" asked Marnie.

"Yeah." He looked sideways at her.

"Well, it happened when we first arrived, and it's doing it again."

"That can't be good."

"No, not usually. Anyway, I'll call Paige and let her know we're on our way to the dock." She rummaged through her bag for her phone.

"What's up with him?" Tom asked, nodding a chin toward the Border Collie, who stood stock-still—eyes on a stand of natty pines.

She shrugged. "Probably a squirrel or possum. Who knows? It could be another ghost." With a snicker, she held her phone up to her ear.

"Ha-ha. That was so funny." Tom sighed. "Got phone service?"

"Surprisingly, yeah, but Paige mustn't. Her phone keeps cutting to voicemail."

With a shrill yip, Tater bolted off, kicking up a flurry of dirt and pine needles.

"Tater! Come!" Marnie called, then threw up her arms. "Geez! That's all we need. Him off chasing woodland creatures."

Tom checked the sky. "We're burnin' daylight and there's more rain on the way. We better go find him."

"Yeah. This isn't the most hospitable place during the day, and I'm not keen on it at night. Let's go get the knucklehead."

Both broke into a jog, following the dog's course through the pines. He crashed through brush and bushes ahead of them, his shrill 'follow me' yips keeping them on the right path.

"That weird yip is new. When did he start that?" asked Tom, stopping to wipe sweat from his brow with his shirt.

Marnie stopped beside him, retrieved bottled water from her oversized bag, and passed it to him. He took a swallow and handed back the bottle. She took a drink and dropped it back into the bag.

"That started two months ago while we were out for a hike. I slipped on a wet rock and fell into the river. Anyway, I sprained my ankle, so I sent Tater back to the camp to get help. He yipped the entire way. Ever since then, he's been doing it when something is urgent to him."

"Good to know. We better make tracks, then."

Tater made the sound again, adding in his signature *ah-roo* for good measure.

-Chapter 14-

A dazzling display of lightning bugs sparkled on the horizon as Danny and Hannah stepped to the precipice of the ridge. The detective shined a flashlight below. Calm water glistened, lapping gently to the left. Jagged rocks and trees jutted up to the right.

"Why didn't they call in a search party to locate Sam? If you ask me, they were unprepared for the operation. Two guys. They sent two guys to catch a couple of escaped convicts."

Hannah let out a long sigh. "Good question. I reported to my office about Pigeon. I told them what had transpired, but they informed me that no one was available to assist. It doesn't seem they are taking it seriously. Perhaps they don't think Sam Reilly is a threat, or maybe they don't care. All they cared about is my report being completed before morning."

"Well, the Sheriff's office wasn't much help either. I called, but no one has called me back." The creases on Danny's face deepened. "It's you and me, kid. Let's take the safe route into the ravine."

"There's a safe route?" Hannah's eyebrows shot up.

"Yeah. Come on. We'll hop in the canoe and go via the lake. We can pull it up on the rocks and see if Sam is alive."

Hannah peered over the edge. "He'd be fortunate to have survived that drop."

"Hmm ... For Marnie's sake, I hope he did. That sounds strange, doesn't it?"

"No, not really. He *is* her only living relative, even if he is a murderous asshole." Hannah turned and walked off toward the dock.

"Tater! Come!" Marnie stopped, bent her knees and peeked through a scrub of dead trees. Tater stopped—his snout in the air—his eyes focused on a granite boulder. "C'mon, Tater! Let's go to the boat!"

Another yip and he was racing in tight circles around the big rock.

"What's gotten in to him? He usually listens," asked Tom.

"I don't know. I guess being away from a normal routine messed us up. You know how he is. He's regimented—follows a schedule." She shrugged.

Tater sprinted past them, turned back sharply, jumped and grabbed Marnie's bag in his teeth on his way back around, pulling her with him.

"Whoa! Mister OCD, your retraining starts as soon as we move into the new house," she mumbled as she crashed through the pile of limbs and crunchy leaves.

The Border Collie halted a few feet steps from the granite boulder his mistress had seen through the scrub. Marnie stopped short, clambering sideways to avoid stumbling over him. Tom stalked through the brush, twisting and snapping dead limbs to clear the path.

"Geez! Tater! What the hell is so damn urgent?" he said, picking leaves and twigs from the sleeve of his T-shirt.

The dog ran to Tom, and jumped up, putting his front paws on Tom's waist, and then poked him in the stomach with his snout. The shrill yip that followed pierced the evening air. Tater raced off again, skidding to a stop on the far side of the boulder.

They followed him, encouraged along by the dog's grumbles of 'rah-row-rah' and his herding stance.

"What is it, buddy? What's wrong?" Marnie stepped around the boulder, lurched back into Tom's arms, and screamed. "Paige! Oh my god, no!"

"He was here, that's for sure. Look there. Blood." Danny squatted in a bed of river pebbles near the shore. He looked up at the ridge, stood, walked a yard away and stopped, pointing to his right. "He must have jumped there."

Hannah stood beside him, tilting her head back to see a narrow clearing in the trees above. "How can you be sure?"

"If he'd jumped from a few feet either way, he'd still be here—probably dead or badly injured." Glancing to his left, he explained, "Over there, he would have hit the pebbles or the rocks." Danny turned to his right. "This way, the water would have been too shallow. But right here, there's a drop off."

"How deep is it?"

"I dunno. Deep enough, obviously."

Hannah scanned the area, her eyes returning to the ridge. "Well, he couldn't have gotten far. He's injured, and it's doubtful he has a means of transportation."

"Sam would have had a first-aid kit in his backpack. I'm missing one, but he wouldn't be out in the woods without one. He's a woodsman. I bet he stopped over there, treated his wounds, and headed off through the ravine. That landscape wouldn't stop him from getting wherever it is he's headed." Danny took a step toward the rocks. "You wanna go for a hike?"

"No. Not really, but what choice do we have? Reilly is out there, and if he has murder on his mind, he'll be going after Marnie."

"Which means both Marnie and Tom are in danger." Danny frowned, stooped, picked up a pebble and skipped it across the lake—watching it bounce along the water's surface. "Six."

"What's the record?" asked Hannah.

"Dad holds the record here on the lake at twelve. The world record is eighty-eight."

She smirked. "So you have a ways to go?"

"Yeah. Let's get moving. Maybe we'll get lucky and find him passed out up ahead." Danny turned away, his boots crunching through the pebbles.

With a hesitant step forward, Hannah absently touched her sidearm. "Or he'll find us."

"Shit, Tom! This is all my fault! I shouldn't have sent her out here on her own," said Marnie, shaking her fists. "I should have told her to wait until I was back. We should have focused on the ranch and then come here together. What was I thinking?" Tears streaming down her face, she looked at her dead friend—waves of regret overwhelming her.

Tom grabbed her shoulders and moved her away from the corpse. "Marn, you couldn't have known. Don't you always say, 'don't should on yourself'? Isn't that it? Stop it. Paige is an adult. Hang on." He moved toward the body, bent and picked up Paige's hand from where it lay across her chest, revealing two red burns about two inches apart. His memory drifted back to Christmas, and the marks left on his back when Sam and Kate attacked him on the bridle trail near Marnie's house. "Hey. When you saw Paige looking at us through the coal chute, real or not real? Take your time. Think about it."

Fingers to her temples, Marnie recalled the encounter. "Geez, Tom, I should have seen it. Her eyes. Her eyes should have told me. I saw her spirit, not her..."

"Thought so. She's been here a while. I'm gonna call Danny and Rick and get them out here. Is there another place she might have docked a boat or beached a Zodiac?"

She nodded, glancing to the opposite side of the island where they had docked. "Yeah. She could have beached a smaller craft on the other side, which makes sense. Her parents live over that way."

Tater leaped past his mistress, planted his feet and snarled. Marnie and Tom swung around to see what the fuss was about. Tom saw nothing, but Marnie scowled and threw up her arms.

"Mr. Barnes, go away! Get off my island! Did you do this? Did you scare Paige? Is that why she fell onto this boulder?"

The specter shook his head and faded away.

Tater circled the spot where the spirit stood, sniffed, and then leaned against Marnie's leg. He looked up into her face, lifted a paw, and woofed.

"Good boy! Thanks for warning us," she said, bending to scratch the dog's head.

"Okay. I need to call the guys. Wow! You're back, what, not even ten hours and already we've got a corpse. Way to go, Marn!" Tom blew out a loud breath and trudged away to make a call.

"Hey, that's not fair! January, February, and March were all quiet!" She laced her hands together over her head and paced. "I can't believe this is happening. Paige, what happened? Talk to me!"

Tom strode back a moment later, fingers fiddling with the damp curls brushing his neck. He stopped to gather his thoughts, then decided it was best to pull off the proverbial Band-Aid quickly. "I got hold of Danny. He isn't coming. He and Hannah are..." He hesitated. Telling her that his partner and his partner's sister were tracking her brother wasn't an easy conversation. "Look, it's like this. Sam was at the cabin with that escapee, Paulie Piccione. It's a long story, but they captured Piccione. Unfortunately, your brother jumped off the ridge."

Marnie gasped, her eyes stinging with tears.

"They think he survived. Danny believes he hit the lake at the drop-off. Now, they've found blood, but that's because an FBI agent shot him. But they aren't sure. They're going to search for shell casings when they get back up to the ridge. They're hiking into the ravine now."

Marnie crossed her ankles and sunk to the ground. She pulled Tater into her lap and hugged him.

Tom kicked a stone with the toe of his sneaker, sending it into the undergrowth. "Rick is on his way with his team, and he'll call Dr. Markson and bring him if he's available."

Rick Price was Creekwood's forensics doctor extraordinaire. He had connections throughout the intelligence agencies in the US and abroad. If Rick couldn't find information, there was likely nothing to find. Dr. Giles Markson was Creekwood's medical examiner and Marnie's godfather. Since his goddaughter's parents passed away, Giles doted on her and provided fatherly advice when needed—or not.

A low rumble of thunder echoed above them as large drops of rain dotted the crime scene.

Tom asked, "I don't suppose you've got a tarp in the boat to cover up Paige?"

Marnie searched her bag and pulled out two garbage bags, handing them to him. "Here. Use these. I'll run to the boat and get a tarp."

Tom accepted the bags with a confused expression. "Do you always carry around garbage bags?"

"I've been on the road a lot. You never know when you'll need one," she said, pulling out a third bag. "You better cover up that boulder, too. There's blood on it. Back in a sec."

"Hang on! I'll come with you after I cover up Paige. Your brother is on the loose, and we know where that can end." Tom laid the bags over Paige, placing rocks on the corners to hold them; he then placed one over the boulder.

She waved him off. "I'll be fine. Sam hasn't had time to make it this far." As she walked away, she caught a flutter of energy to her left. It was Paige Reynolds. Marnie welcomed her to join in the trek to the boat. "C'mon! Keep me company, and then you need to get on your way. I don't want you hanging around down here any longer than necessary. Walk with me, Paige, and tell me how this happened."

-*Chapter 15*-

"We should head back. Searching for Sam in the dark is not only futile, it's dangerous. It's blacker than pitch out here. I'm afraid one of us is going to sprain an ankle, or worse." Hannah removed her glasses and wiped sweat and rain from her forehead with her forearm. Realizing her arm was equally wet, she gave up and then smeared the rain around her glasses with the hem of her shirt before putting them back on.

Danny agreed, "Yeah. This isn't getting us anywhere. He's probably holed up in a cave by now. Let's go back and get something to eat."

"Ha! Screw food! I need a drink," said Hannah, making a move to return to the pebbled shore, but a howl made her jerk forward. She lost her footing, and with a ghastly shriek, tumbled sideways into a shallow crevice. Her flashlight flew out of her hand; landing in the bushy branches of a white pine, its beam casting a ghostly shadow on the granite walls of the ravine as the tree swayed from the impact.

"Oh shit! Hannah!" Danny weaved his way through the treacherous path to the place where his sister disappeared.

"Argh! Son of a biscuit! I can't find my glasses and I think I broke my ankle." Hannah tried without luck to pull herself up from the rocks that held her hostage. "Danny, I need help."

"I'm comin', but I'm being careful. If I break *my* ankle, we're screwed. Hang on! I'm nearly there." He picked his way over the rocks and through the foliage, his flashlight trained on the ground.

When he reached her, he held out his hands to pull her up. She grabbed hold, but she wouldn't budge.

"Ow! Stop! My foot's wedged," she cried.

He kneeled and shined his flashlight into the crevice.

"Try wrapping your arms around my neck and I'll lift you carefully."

She did and screeched with pain. "Danny, stop!"

"Okay. I'm heading to the cabin to get something to dig your foot out. I'll grab the first-aid kit and call Patrick along the way. He's always great in an emergency. Will you be okay for a few minutes?"

"No! You can't leave me here. What about the bear?"

"Huh! I'd be more worried about snakes, but don't worry. You'll be fine." He turned, walking away.

"Daniel Gregg! Do not leave me here!"

"I won't be long!" he called over his shoulder. "I'm calling Patrick! Don't worry! Everything's gonna be fine!"

"Daniel!"

A note on the door told Marnie and Tom that Dickens and Gus were inside on the sun porch with popsicles. Patrick had had to leave to help Danny with a situation.

"That's strange. Why did Danny call Patrick and not me?" Tom frowned.

"Because you had your hands full on the island. Besides, isn't Hannah with him? Maybe he's had enough awkward for one day," Marnie suggested.

"Yeah. That's probably it." He bent and searched under the doormat for a key. "Doesn't he have a key stashed?"

"Ha-ha! No. He knows that I still have a key for emergencies." Marnie dug a ring of keys from her bag and unlocked the door.

They walked through the house to the sunporch, to the whimpering and whining of Dickens and Gus. When the dogs saw their owners, their bodies wagged. A purple stain circled the white fur around Dickens' mouth, and Gus had a bright orange tongue.

Marnie clipped on Dickens' lead and turned to Tom. "Let's go get it over with, huh?"

He stuck out his bottom lip and blew raspberries. "Yeah. I hate notifications, but better coming from me than a stranger. Do ya know where the Reynolds live?"

"Yup. Let's drop the knuckleheads at your house before we go. Tater will keep an eye on Dickens. Your shoes will be safe."

Sam jolted awake, wincing with pain. He sat up groggily, searching the darkness—certain he heard a scream for help. The chilly dampness of the cave made him shiver, and he reached for his backpack.

"I better put on my sweatshirt," he said, unzipping the bag and pulling out the hoodie. "I don't want to catch my death of foolishness." He smiled sadly, hearing his mother's words come out of his mouth.

Another scream echoed, assuring him the first hadn't been a part of his nightmare.

"What the hell is going on out there?" He eased the shirt over his head, and when he tried to put his left arm through the sleeve, he cringed as a wave of nausea moved over him. "Suck it up, Reilly!" He held his breath and tried again with pain-filled success.

As he ducked to go out into the night, rain trickled from the top of the cave's wide opening and down his neck and back. Another shiver and he was on his way—backpack slung over his right shoulder with the flashlight in his right hand. Then he heard it again—a cry for help.

"Hurry! How long does it take to get help?"

Sam followed the cries and when he came upon the source of the shrieks, he pulled his hood up over his head, hoping to hide his face.

The woman whose head poked up through the ground was the one he had seen with Detective Gregg today.

"Shit! They must have been searching for me," he muttered.

Not saying a word, he rushed to Hannah's side.

"Who the fuck are you?" her head whipped around and she glared at him. "What are you doing?"

Sam turned his head away and shined the light into the crevice, took Hannah's sidearm from its holster, and set it out of her reach.

"What are you doing?" she shouted. "That's *my* gun!"

Ignoring her, he pulled her shoulder holster over her head and tossed it across the rocks near her gun.

"Hey!" She grabbed the front of his sweatshirt and shoved him back, jarring his shoulder.

Sam squeezed shut his eyes and drew in a big breath. "Please don't do that. I'm trying to help."

Hannah froze. The huskiness of his voice—she had heard it before when Marnie had received a call from her brother. He rifled through his backpack, drew out a hunting knife, and showed it to her.

"I need you to wrap your arms around my neck and pull yourself up. Your shoelace is stuck on a jagged rock. I need to cut it so that we can get you out of there."

She found her courage. "I will not! I am not touching you! My brother will be back soon, and he can cut me loose."

Sam sat back on his heels, his head tipped to one side. "Okay. You can stay here. I'm sure the snakes will be thankful for a warm body to curl around until your brother gets back."

"Don't you dare try to scare me! There are no snakes out here."

He rested his right elbow on his knee, dropped his chin into his palm, and stared past her. "There *are* snakes out here and there are a couple right behind you. They aren't venomous, but I don't believe you would enjoy having them wind themselves around you. Now, will you do as I ask?"

Hannah nodded tightly and when Sam kneeled again, she put her arms around his neck. He clamped the flashlight between his teeth, and holding the knife in his right hand, he reached into the crevice and cut her shoelace. He tossed his knife onto the ground, and awkwardly wrapped his right arm around Hannah and lifted her out.

"Are you hurt? Do you need first aid?" he asked.

Stunned by his kindness, she stared blankly at the fugitive. He got a bottle of water out of his bag, loosened the cap, and offered it to her. She accepted it and took a gulp, easing her dry throat.

"I thought you might be thirsty with all that screaming you were doing. Let me check your ankle."

She flinched, but he didn't notice and kneeled again. He held the flashlight with his mouth and examined her ankle. Her forehead creased, wondering how this purportedly violent man could be so gentle.

He glanced up, his gray-blue eyes meeting her icy-gray gaze. "It looks like a sprain. Would you like me to wrap it?"

"No, thank you. My brother is bringing a first-aid kit back with him. He can wrap it."

"Okay." Sam stood, gathered up his knife, and put it in his backpack. As he turned to leave, he caught a glint on the ground near the crevice. "Are these yours?" he asked, bending to scoop up her glasses.

She nodded, and he handed them to her.

"I hope your brother gets here soon."

"Stop! You can't leave. You're under arrest," she said, grabbing at his pant leg.

He sidestepped her and said, "Sorry. That won't work for me."

"No? You can't believe that I will allow you to walk away." She scooted on her backside toward her gun, but she knew she would never make it to her sidearm in time. He would either run off or kill her first. She settled back, hoping Danny and Patrick would arrive before he scarpered again.

He dug his hands into his pockets and stared up into the drizzling night sky with a lopsided grin that took the edge off his imposing presence. "Well, that's how it's going to be. It's been nice meeting you. What's your name?"

"Special Agent Hannah Patterson," she said.

"Well, Special Agent Hannah Patterson, I am, as you guessed, the infamous Sam Reilly. I'll see you around. I hope your ankle feels better real soon." With a salute, he, with his uneven gait, disappeared into the darkness of the ravine.

-*Chapter 16*-

"Well, that was the worst death notification of my career," Tom said, climbing into the Jeep. "Thanks for coming with me, Marn."

"I wouldn't have been anywhere else. The Reynolds are lovely people. After everything Paige has been through…" Marnie slammed her door, dropped scrunched up tissues into the console, and put the key into the ignition. "I don't know how they've done it. How they have remained so positive and kind. First the prison sentence, then the stabbing, and now this. We'll have to drop in on them in a few days to see how they're doing."

"Yeah. Let's wait until after Rick and Dr. Markson have finished their reports and the autopsy. Having answers for them is important." He snapped his seatbelt in place, then reached across and patted Marnie's shoulder.

She sniffled and reached for a tissue. "I still can't believe there were electrical burns on her chest."

"Right over her pacemaker," Tom added, clearing his throat.

She frowned. "Sam didn't do it. I know he didn't."

"I didn't say he did, but you have to remember what happened to me and what happened to Ken last Christmas. We got tasered. Well, in reality, we didn't. It was a stun gun. But that doesn't matter. What does matter is I was luckier than Ken, but it could have ended differently if Kate hadn't intervened."

"Yes, but the marks you had didn't look like Paige's, and I don't believe for one minute Kate intervened. Something is brewing. I don't know what yet, but I feel something explosive is about to happen."

"Thanks for the warning, Great Oracle of the North. Why do you say that?" Tom leaned forward in his seat and stared at her profile.

She shrugged a shoulder. "The air is prickly. As soon as I drove into the town limits, the hair on the back of my neck stood on end. I can't explain it."

"Somethin's afoot, eh?" Tom smirked.

"Zip it, Sherlock! Laugh at me all you like. I'll bet Gram will back me up. She's back from Ireland today."

"Have you spoken?" he asked.

"No. But I can feel her energy. I'll bet she knows I'm home, too."

"Okay! Okay. You're creepin' me out! Let's get movin' and remind me to call Danny when we get back to my house."

She turned the key, and the engine purred to life. It was comforting to have a new vehicle that didn't cough when started.

"You haven't heard from him?" she asked, pulling away from the curb.

Tom gave her a dirty look. "You know, signal lights aren't painted on! Use your dang signal! And no, I haven't heard from him."

"Geez, Mr. Traffic Cop, I'm sorry! I always use my blinker. I don't know why I didn't just then."

"Yeah, well, be careful. That's a great way to get sideswiped." He turned in his seat and stared out the window.

The dogs raced out the back door when Marnie and Tom returned to the house. Tater gave chase, herding the Labrador and his brother into a corner. Dickens circled Tater, sniffing his mouth and backside as dogs often do.

Marnie sat on the back stoop, watching them play while Tom went inside to call Danny. When he joined her on the back step, she knew instantly something was wrong.

"What's happened?" she asked.

Tom stood on the step, his eyes scanning the night. Marnie noticed he was still wearing his sidearm.

"Why didn't you lock up your gun when we got back? That's the first thing you do when you get home."

He gave her shoulder a gentle tap. "C'mon. Let's get the dogs inside and have a drink. Danny's on his way."

Marnie tipped back her head so she could read his expression. He dragged a tanned hand across his whiskers, lines creasing his forehead.

"I told you the air is prickly," she said.

"Yeah. You did. C'mon. Let's get the knuckleheads inside, especially Tater."

Danny pulled open the screen door. He, too, wore his sidearm and a grave countenance. "Are all the windows locked? Upstairs and down? Did you check the attic? The cellar?"

Tom nodded. "Yeah. We're locked up tight."

Danny pointed to the front door. "Really? You tellin' me I magically unlocked the door when I touched it?"

Tom sighed. "We knew you were on the way, and I'm standin' right here!"

"I don't like this. You two should come back to the cabin with me." He stormed to the kitchen to check the back door.

"Hey! I can take care of Marnie and me. Plus, we've got three dogs who will alert us if anyone gets near the house. Do you truly believe Tater will let Sam Reilly get within six yards of this place?"

Danny scratched his head, mussing his hair. "No." His hand moved to his forehead and then he dropped his arm to his side. "Look, Hannah had an accident while we were out looking for Sam. We were in the ravine and she fell into a crevice."

"Oh no! Is she okay?" Marnie crossed to him, placing a hand on his shoulder.

"Was she hurt? Is she at home?" asked Tom, his face tightening.

Danny waved them off. "Yeah, she's fine. I dropped her off at the emergency room. We think it's a sprain, but want to make sure her ankle isn't broken."

"I'm here if she needs anything. I'll call her in the morning," said Marnie.

"Tell her I'm around, too." Tom's cheeks reddened. "I know she doesn't want to hear from me, but I'm here."

Danny gave a tight nod. "Will do. Gram took her to the hospital and will take her home when the doctor finishes. Anyway, the three of us, uh, six of us, should stick together, like we always have. Sam is out there somewhere and we've already got one body in the morgue."

Marnie stepped away from the detective, her expression sour. "Hang on! Sam did not kill Paige, and there is zero proof or evidence he did. Tom and I both saw the blood on the boulder. She could have tripped on a stump and cracked her temple. You're getting accusations ahead of the autopsy, Detective Gregg."

Frustrated, Danny dragged his hand over his face. "Well, tell me, Ms. Reilly, how do you know your brother isn't good for it?"

"Paige told me he didn't do it." She tossed her head and dropped onto the closest overstuffed chair.

"Ah! Madam Séance has it all figured out!" Danny closed his eyes and rolled back his head. "Tell me, Ghost Whisperer, while you were interrogating the spirit, did you happen to record the conversation and have her sign a statement so that we can get it into evidence?"

Her bottom lip pushed out and her eyebrows knitted together. "No! Ghosts can't hold a pen, but if I had had a recorder, I might have gotten an excellent EVP."

Danny screwed up his face. "EVP? What the hell is an EVP?"

"Electronic Voice Phenomenon." She kicked out her legs and got to her feet. "I need a beer!"

Tom called out, "Grab me one too! Danny? Want a beer?"

Scratching the side of his head, Danny said, "Yeah. Thanks."

"Marn! Make that two!"

She returned with three Saranac Summer Ales, handing one to each of them. Slipping the bottle opener out of her side pocket, she popped the top off her bottle, pocketing the cap, and then handed the opener to Tom.

He looked at his bottle and back at her. "Did you shake my beer?"

She rolled her eyes. "What am I? Four?"

Tom popped the top without a cascade of beer flowing over, then passed the opener to Danny, who frowned and looked at Marnie—eyebrows raised.

"No, Detective, I did not shake it! What is wrong with you two?" She flopped into the chair and set her beer on a coaster on the coffee table.

Danny sat in a chair opposite her and Tom sprawled on the couch.

"We need to talk," he said, inspecting the label on his bottle.

Tom sat up. "What's goin' on?"

Danny took a swig of his beer and set it on the floor next to him. He sat forward, resting his elbows on his knees. "When Hannah fell into the crevice, I couldn't get her out. I had to go home to get my hiking pack. So I left her there."

Tom asked, "Are you feeling guilty for leaving her?"

Danny grimaced. "Only because Sam is on the loose. She was in danger and I left her because I fucked up and forgot to get my pack before leaving the cabin. Why am I so obsessed with catching him?" His face burned with anger.

Marnie sat forward and picked up her beer. "Did my brother hurt Hannah?"

"You know, Marnie, every time you call him your brother, I want to scream. You couldn't be more different, and yet you never disown him."

Angry tears brimming her bottom lids, she said, "As inconvenient as it is for you, Sam is my brother and once upon a time, he wasn't a horrible person. I still have good memories of him. He's the only family I've got, Danny, and whether he's a murderer or not, he is still *my* family!"

"Loyalty. It's a wonderful trait until it gets you killed." Danny stood, guzzled his beer, and went into the kitchen. Marnie and Tom heard the bottle drop into the empties bin on the back porch. Danny returned with bottled water and sat.

"While Hannah was screaming for me to hurry up and struggling to free herself, Sam appeared from whatever hidey-hole he'd been camping in. He cut her shoelace loose from a rock that was holding her in the crevice, pulled her to safety, and left. She said he was polite, kind, and comforting. He gave her water, examined her ankle, offered to wrap it for her, and he found her glasses and gave them to her. He left her there unharmed and hydrated. Does that sound like your brother?"

Tears welled up in Marnie's eyes; she caught a sob and buried her face in her hands.

Tom leaned over, rubbed her shoulder, and looked up at Danny. "That sounds like the guy we knew when we were little."

Marnie threw her arms around Tom's neck and sobbed. Between hiccups, she mumbled, "That sounds like my Sammy Bear."

Stunned, Tom looked at Danny, held up one hand and mouthed, "What the fuck?" Then he patted Marnie's back and said, "Yes, it does, Marn. It does."

-*Chapter 17*-

D alton Hooley entered the suite, clipboard in hand. "Miss Kate, it's ten o'clock. Lights out."

Post-it notes and scraps of paper lay scattered on her oval faux Edwardian coffee table, a black crayon in her hand. "I can't wait until Daddy brings me proper notebooks and pens tomorrow." She swirled around, producing the fat crayon. "I am not a child! Do not treat me like one."

The large man eased across the room, stared at the papers scattering the table and frowned. He saw names, places, and dates. "Miss Kate, what's all this?"

She leaned over, her arms circling the scraps, and with a childish flair, scooped the papers to herself. Each scrap she purposefully placed into a tattered cigar box, which contained the remaining crayons from an eight-pack. "Horrible people," she muttered, dropping the black crayon into the box with the others.

Dalton moved closer. "Beg your pardon? I didn't hear you."

Lifting her face to him, she smiled sweetly. "These are the people who have ruined my life."

He took a step back. "Why's my name in there?"

The sweet smile faded in an instant, replaced by a sneer. "You make me follow the rules, and I hate rules."

He fiddled with the clipboard, tapping it against his leg. "That's my job. I'm here to protect you."

"Ha! You're here to protect others from me! Don't lie to me, Dalton!" She snatched up the black crayon and flung it at him.

He caught it mid-air. "Kate, it's time to turn out the lights." His face stony and unflinching, he put the crayon into the cigar box and closed the lid.

"Oh! Now you're cross with me!" she cried, throwing herself back into the couch cushions.

"I'm not cross, but I am disappointed by your ungrateful display of hostility toward me. I have helped you, protected you, listened to you, and I have been there when your parents were too busy." He picked up the box, carried it to the desk, and placed it in a drawer.

Next to a block of fluorescent post-it notes, he spotted a coil of wire and took it out of the drawer. He held it up. "What is this?"

"It's a G-string," she said, adding a coquettish smile.

"Where did you get it?" He kept his tone even and relaxed.

"The conservatory."

"How?"

With a wave of her hand, she dismissed him.

His shoulders tensed, as did his tone. "I asked you a question. How did you get the piano wire?"

She laughed. "The piano tuner was here yesterday. He left bits and pieces lying around while he worked on the Bluthner. I showed an interest. He was nice to me, and I slipped it into my pocket when he wasn't looking. No big deal."

"It is a big deal!" The big man's jaw clenched. "Do you realize the trouble you're in?" He waggled the coil at her. "This is a murder weapon. This is what the Creekwood Strangler used! You were with him when he killed those cops and Mr. Wilder! This is a big fucking deal! Do you *want* to go to prison?"

She smoothed her hands over her hair and the sweet smile returned. "Don't worry, Dalton. Daddy will take care of it. Could you please turn out my light as you leave?" Gracefully rising from the couch, she slipped her silky robe over her perfect shoulders, lay it across the foot of her bed, kicked off her slippers, and climbed into her down-turned nest, pulling the duvet up to her chin. "Good night, Dalton. Sweet dreams."

"Guys, I can't talk anymore. It's been a long day and I've got a longer one tomorrow," said Marnie, getting up from her chair and collecting empty beer bottles and caps. On her way to the kitchen, she stopped and scratched Dickens' tummy, who was lying on his back, legs in the air.

Danny checked his watch and whistled. "Yeah. It's late. Can I crash on your couch?"

"Why don't you take the downstairs bedroom? It's more comfortable," said Tom, knowing his partner wanted one of them on each floor of the house.

"Thanks."

Tom picked up a bag of chips and an empty bottle and headed for the kitchen. Over his shoulder, he said, "Safety in numbers is a good credo."

Marnie met him in the doorway. "What's that?"

"I said we should stick together."

She returned to find Danny scratching Tater's neck. The Border Collie, with a look of contentment, leaned against the detective's leg.

"I missed you, buddy," he said. When he looked up, his eyes appeared to be teary.

"He missed you, too. Look at that smile." Marnie stooped and tugged one of Tater's ears.

"Did his mom miss me?"

"She did," she whispered, then cleared her throat and fidgeted with the zip on her pocket. "She needed time to clear her head. The end of last year was ... Um... Challenging. Then Sam escaped, and I was sure he was coming for me. I couldn't put all of you in danger again."

"You could have told me what you were going through." Danny cocked his head, his blue eyes searching her face.

"I could have, but you would have taken me in your arms, kissed me, and told me that everything would be okay."

"Gee! That would have been horrible!" he said, louder and harsher than he had intended.

"No. It would have been lovely, but I needed to work through things on my own. My head was spinning, Danny. Not only did I find out that my dead brother is actually alive, I found out that he is a cold-blooded murderer and he was involved with Kate—someone I believed was my friend, but wasn't." She shrugged. "I don't like it when my senses fail me."

"So you were worried that I wasn't what I seemed?" he asked, a pained expression lining his face.

"Uh-uh. You, I was sure about. You're one of the good guys." She crossed the few feet between them and wrapped her arms around his waist. "I'm sorry I hurt you, but I'm not sorry I left. You deserve me to be at my best, not worst, and I am telling you right now, I was not at my best."

He kissed her forehead and hugged her. "I'll take the good, the bad, the bat shit crazy…"

Tom stepped into the room. "Are you two done with your sappy reunion? I wanna go upstairs."

"Bat shit crazy? Huh. We will pick up that conversation later." Marnie snatched up her bag and headed for the stairs. "Tater! Dickens! Come!"

Tom quirked up the corner of his mouth and watched Marnie clomp up the stairs, the Border Collies on her heels. "What was that about?"

"You walk in at the most inopportune moments, Tommy." Danny hung his head for a beat and then stared at the ceiling—Marnie's loud footsteps telling him *bat shit crazy* was a poor choice of words. "I was trying to tell her she's perfect as she is. Then you walk in and mess it up."

Tom shrugged, heading for the stairs. "Talk to her in the morning. Make her a cup of tea and apologize for whatever you said. We don't need her running on coffee and anger." He stopped on the landing and turned to face his partner.

Danny stretched, a long yawn escaping as he reached to the ceiling. "Yeah. I'll do that. Any idea what time she needs to be out of here in the morning?"

"The moving company will be at the ranch by 11:00, so she'll probably be outta here by 7:00 to figure out where everything goes. You're going with her, right?" asked Tom.

"Are you?"

"No, I gotta go finish my reports. I told her I would meet her there at 10:30."

"If she's not pissed at me in the morning, I'll go with her." Danny rubbed his hand across his chin.

"You have to go with her regardless of her mood. We don't know where Sam is."

Danny gazed off toward the kitchen. "Yeah. I know." He stalked off with a wave and a goodnight.

The tick-tick-tick of the grandfather clock downstairs in the living room counted the hours until Marnie could see her new home. She tossed, turned and tossed again, a grumble and mumble from the Border Collies her castigation for disturbing their slumber. Tater slept with his head on the pillow next to her while Dickens sprawled at the foot. She didn't need to look at her watch to know what time it was. The Westminster chimes echoed through the stairwell and a single bong told her it was one o'clock.

Marnie's head tingled, and she rolled over to face the door. A soft nightlight from the main bathroom cast a creamy glow in the hallway, and she watched a tall shadow drift down the hall. She propped herself up on her elbow and chewed her bottom lip.

"Mom?" she whispered.

A moment later, a calming energy entered her room. Tater and Dickens both sat up on the bed and smiled as a gentle breeze ruffled their fluffy coats. Marnie's mother appeared before them, a grim expression lining her pretty face.

Marnie got to her knees, tears stinging the back of her eyes, and patted the bed, welcoming her mother to sit. "What is it, Mom?"

Sophia Reilly sat and explained to her daughter the reason for her visit, and what Marnie's mother shared changed everything. When the spirit dissipated, Marnie tapped out a quick text message to Mr. Lewis, the owner of the moving company. She asked him to bring the steamer trunk from the attic of her old home. If her mother was right, her brother's journals were still in the trunk, and many questions would have answers. Before falling asleep, Marnie said a prayer, figuring it couldn't hurt.

-Chapter 18-

The percolator bubbling on the back of the stove filled the house with the rich aroma of coffee, while an old, blue-enameled teapot sat on the table, steam rising from its spout as it steeped Marnie's favorite English breakfast tea.

The grandfather clock bonged five times as Marnie skipped into the kitchen. She opened the back door for Tater and Dickens, stepped out onto the stoop, and then went back inside, searching for whomever had made the tea and coffee. The downstairs bedroom door creaked open, and Danny appeared, hair damp from the shower, dressed in yesterday's clothes. He startled when he saw her.

"Geez! I didn't think anyone else was up yet," he said.

Tom traipsed into the kitchen with Gus trailing. "C'mon, Gustifer, let's go out." He opened the back door so the lab could join his friends. "Argh! I've got reports to write. I don't want to be stuck in the office all weekend. It looks like you have a nice day to move, Marn."

She rifled through the cupboard, searching for a china cup. Tom reached over her head and handed her what she was looking for. "There you go, Miss Fussypants." He retrieved a mug for himself.

She tossed her hair over a shoulder with the flip of her hand and wrinkled up her nose. "Thank you!" she said, opening the fridge and taking out a quart of half-and-half.

"Thanks for making the coffee, whoever made it," said Tom, pouring himself a large mug before settling into a chair.

"I did while you two were snoozing." Danny took a mug from the cupboard and poured a coffee for himself. "When did you get the percolator?"

Tom shrugged. "My mother bought it for me for Christmas and taught me how to use it. It's pretty good, if you ask me."

Danny took a sip. "Yeah. Not bad. I could have made it stronger, though."

"Did you put cinnamon in it?" asked Tom.

"Nope. I only do that in winter." Danny opened the screen door and stepped out onto the stoop to play fetch with the knuckleheads.

Tom reached for the cinnamon in the lazy Susan, sprinkled it into his coffee, stirred with his finger, and took another sip. A satisfied smile lit up his face. "How'd you sleep?" he asked Marnie.

"It took me a while to get used to the grandfather clock ticking away, but I slept pretty well. The excitement of seeing the ranch kept me awake." She paused, knowing her next statement would send her friend into a tizzy. "And Mom came to see me last night."

He looked up—his expression calm.

"Huh! You didn't freak out," she said, grinning.

"Yeah, well, I saw a shadow moving down the hall toward the spare room, and since I checked the entire house before going to sleep, I knew it wasn't a bogeyman. I figured you had a visitor of the ghostly variety. Besides, I can be brave."

"No, you can't! I'll bet you pulled the covers up over your head and nearly suffocated."

He yawned and scratched his chest. "Nearly, but when I didn't hear you yell, I figured it was someone you knew, so I didn't worry. What did she want?"

"I'm not a hundred percent sure, but I know I need to read Sam's journals. She told me she was wrong. About what, I'm uncertain, but I understood her when she told me to read his journals. The books are in the attic in Papa Jack's steamer trunk."

Tom crinkled his forehead. "So, when she talks to you, it isn't like you and I having a conversation?"

Marnie said, "No. It's more images than sentences or words. I don't know how to explain it. Some messages are clear and words do pop into my head, but it's not always exact."

"Content and context are like a puzzle for you to put together to get the real meaning, then?" he asked.

"Something like that, yeah."

"Okay. Kinda like when Hannah and I have a conversation. Let me know if you find anything interesting in those journals, huh?" He stood, topped up his coffee, and joined Danny on the back stoop.

"Do you wanna stop at the diner for breakfast before heading to the ranch?" asked Danny, folding his long legs into his Jeep, keeping the door ajar, before starting the engine and rolling down the window.

Marnie's eyebrows shot up. "You're coming with me? I thought you would head home first."

"Nope. I had a shower and put these clothes on last night before I came over and I've got a change of clothes in the back for after we move your couch around fifty times."

"Ha-ha! Good point," she said, settling the Border Collies into her backseat, then set her bags in the cargo. "The diner sounds like a plan. I'll meet you there."

"Good stuff! By the way, nice wheels." He grinned and waved as he pulled away.

Marnie gave a thumbs up and climbed into her Jeep. She reached for the stick shift, but stopped, sucking in a shaky breath. Leaning between the shift and the dash sat a book.

"I really need to lock my car," she said to herself. Her curiosity got the better of her, and she picked it up. Eyebrows drawn together, she studied the cover's tatty brown paper jacket, which read "A Boy's Will by Robert Frost," and then opened the cover, which again revealed the book's title, as well as New York, Henry Holt and Company, 1915.

"Huh. I wonder if this is a first edition?" she pondered, pulling out her phone to investigate. A quick search delivered an affirmative on her suspicion. "Where did you find this, Sam?" She flipped through the book, knowing her brother would have left a threatening message for her somewhere within the pages, and then she saw it, a few thin strands of auburn hair, roots attached, pressed between the leaves of a poem. Marnie wrinkled her nose and muttered, "Ah, geez! Why did you have to do that?"

As she read the first three stanzas, she realized it was unfamiliar to her.

Two fairies it was
On a still summer day
Came forth in the woods
With the flowers to play.

The flowers they plucked
They cast on the ground
For others, and those
For still others they found.

Flower-guided it was
That they came as they ran
On something that lay
In the shape of a man.

She read enough and snapped shut the book. "I don't remember reading 'Spoils of the Dead'." The book sat in her lap, and she glanced again at the cover, and then looked out the window. "This isn't right. Who left this for me?" she said, searching the street for answers.

Tom's red-brick Dutch Colonial home sat at 88 Hudson Hill Road in a quiet bit of Creekwood. The rolling front lawns, abundance of old-growth trees, under pruned shrubs, and a lack of streetlights would have made it easy for anyone to leave something in her Jeep under the cover of night. She scanned the neighborhood, wondering if anyone had security cameras. Most were elderly, but you never know. Stuffing the book into the console, she made a mental note to speak with the detectives about it when they were all together later today.

Marnie pulled up out front of Ryan's Diner to find Danny chatting with Theodora "Teddy" Jones. Teddy, a Creekwood native, was a classmate Marnie never quite trusted since the day Teddy broke Tom's heart when they were in eleventh grade. Marnie bristled when the other woman ran a hand flirtatiously across Danny's chest.

"Good morning, Theodora!" Marnie waved as she sauntered to Danny's side. Tater and Dickens bumped the detective with their noses, and he squatted to give them both a hug.

"Hi, Marnie. I hear from Lanie that you bought the Billingsly's old ranch. You sure have your work cut out for you. From what Lanie tells me, the place is a dump." Teddy's amber eyes mocked as she ran fingers through her shoulder-length cappuccino waves.

Marnie's eyebrows shot up, although not surprised at all by Teddy's comment. "Well, we both know Lanie exaggerates. Besides, I've had a great crew working on renovations for weeks now. They finished yesterday." She dangled the house keys in Teddy's face.

Teddy dropped her voice to a small-town whisper, grabbed Marnie's hand and glanced sideways to see who might be eavesdropping. "Did you hear about Paige Reynolds? Can you believe that somebody from our class is dead?"

Danny wrapped a protective arm around Marnie's shoulders as sadness overtook her and tears flowed.

"Yes, I heard." She squeezed Teddy's hand warmly and leaned into Danny, whose arm tightened around her.

Teddy dropped Marnie's hand and her eyes grew wide as she looked around cautiously, drawing up her shoulders as if to protect her neck from a lurking vampire. "I hear she visited Kate Parish in the looney bin last week. My source tells me they had an argument and I hear Kate threw her out of her room!" Giddy with gossip, Teddy bounced on her toes.

Danny heaved a sigh. "Teddy, you wanna tell me who your source is?" he said with mild irritation.

Teddy's head jerked from Marnie to Danny, whose steely stare caught her by surprise. She softened her posture, her right hip tilting toward him, and brushed her fingers up the detective's arm. "Gosh, Danny, I forget you're a cop." When her batting eyelashes did nothing to ease his glower, she stiffened.

"Yeah. Well, I am. Who's your source?" he said gruffly.

Teddy retreated, waving away the building tension. "Let's forget I mentioned it. I don't want to cause problems for anyone."

With a roll of her eyes, Marnie said, "Pfft! That's *exactly* what you were doing." She wanted to say more, but knew she shouldn't so she held up her hands and turned to leave. "Danny, we'll see you inside."

He sent her a distracted wave, his eyes never leaving Teddy's. "Be there in a sec," he said. "Now, Teddy, who is your source? You can tell me here or at the station. Your choice."

She shifted uncomfortably and heaved a sigh. "Well, if you must know, go over to Drake's Drug Store and listen to the coffee klatch. They have the inside scoop on everything that happens in Creekwood, not me."

Danny's dimples deepened, and a smirk appeared on his rugged face as he imagined Corinne Hooper, Irene Hazelton, Carol Chadwick, and Susanne Connor all sitting at the lunch counter, sipping their morning coffee, eating pastries, and yattering on and on about town gossip.

"Ha! Not knowing doesn't stop you from repeating what you hear, though, does it? Stop doing that. It'll get you into trouble." Without another word, Danny strode off to join Marnie and the knuckleheads.

Red-faced and flustered, Teddy tramped up the street to Drake's so she could tell the coffee klatch what she knew, which wasn't much, but that didn't matter. She could now confirm Marnie Reilly's return to Creekwood and that she was having breakfast at the diner with Danny Gregg right this very minute.

The detective found Marnie sitting at the booth his grandmother always kept reserved for him. As he approached, he saw Tater and Dickens sitting under the table with a bowl of water. He slid into the opposite seat, tapping the edge of his wallet on the table and glancing around for Gram.

"She'll be back. There's something upstairs she needed to get." Marnie looked out the window, rolled her eyes, and slouched in her seat. "Geez! Here comes Lanie Howard-Billingsly," she whispered.

The detective laughed. "You really don't like her."

"I don't dislike her, but she's not my favorite person. I don't know. She always has something snarky to say about Jonas."

Danny frowned. "Didn't you say Jonas is her husband?"

She nodded and pursed her lips. "Yeah. You know, he's a sweet guy, really mellow and kind, and he would do anything for her. I think she takes advantage, but hey, I don't have to live with her. If *he's* happy, that's all that matters."

"But you don't think he is."

She shrugged and sat up. "He wanted to keep the ranch. Anyway, he's staying on to run it so that I can focus on what I do best."

"Speaking of ... Have you seen Carl?"

"Not yet. I think he's coming out to the ranch sometime today. He texted me this morning with great news. He's been working on the paperwork we need for licensing the ranch as a mental health rehabilitation facility, and we have an inspection scheduled for next week. As long as the bunkhouses and cabins receive certification, we should be good to go. Carl has interviewed counselors, social workers, registered nurses, and other support staff, too. We need another psychiatrist, but we can sort that out later. For now, we have Carl. We'll go through all the applicants next week."

"Hang on! Carl is a psychiatrist?" Danny asked, pulling a face.

"Yeah, of course he is."

"I didn't know that. You've never said."

"He's a medical doctor with a specialty in psychiatry."

"You're kidding?"

"Well, if you weren't so suspicious of him, he would have told you. Actually, I'm surprised you never did a background check on him."

Her arched eyebrow made him laugh.

"Ha-ha! I thought it best to not poke the bear, and by bear, I mean you."

"Grr!"

Lanie Howard-Billingsly schoolgirl's shriek clipped Marnie's next words off.

"Marnie Reilly!" Lanie flounced to the booth, her manicured hands extended, her bejeweled flip-flops slapping the floor.

Marnie squirmed in her seat. Her deadpan expression told Danny everything he needed to know about the woman waggling her bling-adorned fingers in his girlfriend's face.

"Hi, Lanie. How are you?" asked Marnie flatly.

"I heard you were back in town. Everyone is locking their doors and windows in case you brought your psycho brother with you. Ha-ha! Oo! Who is this handsome man?" Lanie pointed to the detective.

Danny turned to see a woman of average looks, weight, and height stuffed into a lemon-yellow sundress a size too small. Her nutmeg-brown hair with blonde highlights curled in thick layers, framing her round face. Hazel eyes made up with powdery blue eyeshadow, clumped mascara and outlined with thick slashes of black eyeliner assessed him. He involuntarily wrinkled his nose at the sight of her heavy foundation and ruddy blusher. He turned to Marnie, who smirked.

"This is Detective Danny Gregg. Danny, meet Lanie Billingsly."

"Hello, Danny. It's lovely to meet you. I'm Lanie *Howard*-Billingsly. Marnie always forgets that my last name has a hyphen."

Marnie grinned. "I don't forget. I just like watching your face turn red when I don't use it."

Danny stood and shook the woman's hand. "It's nice to meet you, Lanie."

The top of Lanie's head barely met the detective's shoulder. She tipped back her head, staring up at him in awe. "You have the most interesting face."

"Uh. Thank you ... I think."

Lanie whipped her head around, her attention back on Marnie. "Jonas tells me you made a lot of changes to the farm. It's nice of you to keep him on. It's not like he could find a job anywhere else, and it's not as if you had a choice, since you know nothing about farming."

Marnie huffed out a snort. "That's a record. You've insulted your husband and me in under a minute."

Tater and Dickens sat up, low grumbles escaping from their throats.

Lanie took a surprised step back. "Why are they growling at me?"

Marnie said, "They aren't. They're talking."

Lanie pulled her hands to her hips and frowned. "Dogs don't talk. Will they bite?"

"Only if you bite first." Danny snickered and slid back into his seat.

The woman's eyebrows shot up. "I would never bite a dog. Who told you that?"

Danny's face registered a "you can't be serious?" expression before he said, "Uh, I was joking."

Marnie dropped her head to cover a giggle.

Lanie smiled weakly and fluffed her hair. "Oh. Well, I don't like dogs. I prefer cats. Dogs are unpredictable. You never know when they'll turn ugly." She took another step back, pulling a face at the Border Collies, who mumbled something to one another, then lay back down.

Marnie and Danny didn't take the bait, other than to pass a knowing look between themselves.

"I ran in to Paige when I left the cottage a few days ago. She'd obviously tended to your gardens. The smell of fertilizer was atrocious. Anyway, she said she was going home to shower before visiting Kate. I'm going over to see her later today. Care to join me?" asked Lanie, a smug smile drawing up the corners of her gooey lip-glossed mouth.

Marnie looked up—her expression blank. "She doesn't want to see me anymore than I want to see her, and you know that, and I'm almost certain you aren't on her visitor list either. Going over there to tell her I bought the ranch and to gloat about the new house your parents are building for you is cruel." Marnie scoped out the diner, looking for Gram to save them from this irksome woman. "If you want to stir shit, Lanie, go to Drake's lunch counter. I hear they're looking for another gossip since Mr. Drake's unfortunate incarceration."

Lanie stood for a second with her mouth open, before shouting, "Marnie Reilly, you are a horrible person! How dare you call me a gossip?"

"Well, if the bedazzled flip-flops fit," said Marnie, glancing at the woman's feet. "I don't have time to visit with toxic people. That statement pertains to Kate Parish and you. Why don't you expel your pent-up energy on counting your blessings instead of relishing in other people's misery?"

Eyes bugged, Lanie stood speechless before snatching up a sugar packet and throwing it at Marnie, who laughed. Danny jumped to his feet and escorted a hysterical Lanie Howard-Billingsly out of the diner. Every set of eyes in the place followed them to the door, before turning to Marnie, who smiled and waved at the gawkers.

When Danny returned, he slid into his seat. "Well, you've certainly made a smooth re-entry."

-*Chapter 19*-

Whispers around Creekwood Police Department's coffee pot included the news of Marnie Reilly's return, the death of Paige Reynolds out on the creepy island in the middle of Perch Pond, Hudson Bay Police Department's capture of a drug dealer, and the shooting of an FBI agent at the hands of Sam Reilly. Tom felt a throng of energy bouncing through the building as soon as he opened the front door.

"Mornin', Beau!" he said to Sergeant Lou Beaumont as he entered.

"I notice you didn't say 'good'," said the sergeant with a chuckle.

"What's good about fillin' out reports on a day off? I haven't had time off since the first of June. I've been itchin' to get some fishing in, but something always comes up," he griped.

"Hey, how's Gregg feeling now that his girlfriend's back? Is his mood better?"

"It's improved marginally, but it isn't gonna be better until Sam Reilly is behind bars," he said, before taking the stairs to the squad room three at a time.

He pushed open the doors to find detectives and officers crowded around the coffee station.

"What's goin' on?" he asked.

"We were discussing this morning's briefing," replied Officer Cheryl Garcia.

"Uh-huh. Gossiping is more like it."

"We weren't gossiping!" said Officer Pete Connor.

Tom glanced up, checking the duty roster. "Looks like you've all got a full day. Better get to it."

Tom's desk sat nearest the door, and it was littered with empty takeaway coffee cups and cellophane wrappers. He frowned, scooped up the trash and deposited it in the nearest wastebasket.

"I would appreciate a little respect, guys! How about throwin' your junk into the garbage instead of on my desk?" He pulled out his chair, noticing that someone had adjusted the seat height. "And stop messin' with my chair! Sit at your own desks!"

"Sounds like you need another coffee," said Rick Price, as he presented Tom with a steaming takeaway cup.

Tom rubbed his forehead, then reached for the coffee. "Thanks, Rick. What are you doin' over here on a Saturday morning?"

"Giles and I worked late on the Reynolds case. Here are your reports." Rick dropped a thick envelope into the detective's inbox.

"Thanks! I was getting myself organized to do my report. Should I read this first?"

"Wouldn't hurt," said Rick, his expression grave. "I found no alcohol or unprescribed drugs in her system, and the blunt force trauma to her head is not the cause of death. It was 'the electrical current' applied directly over her pacemaker that did the trick." Rick gestured imaginary quotation marks around 'the electrical current,' and then continued. "Whoever did this knew what they were doing. We suspect her pacemaker was faulty."

"I guess those quotes you threw up mean something, but I didn't think stun guns would affect a pacemaker."

"It isn't your average stun gun. Giles and I agree."

"So, somebody rigged a taser to pack a bigger charge?" asked the detective.

Out of patience, Rick's mouth tightened. "It's one possibility. Besides, it is not completely unheard of for a stun gun or a TASER to stop a pacemaker. They aren't supposed to, but a fault in the unit could have a deadly result. It is unusual, but possible. And let's get something clear, even though I have explained it before. A stun gun and a TASER are two different things. One is traceable. The other is not. I don't know why you guys keep confusing them. Second, it wasn't a run-of-the-mill TASER or a standard stun gun that killed Paige Reynolds." He took a drink of his coffee, waiting for Tom's reaction.

The detective thought back to the marks he had seen last night. "We should check in with Paige's doc, then?"

"That, Detective, is an excellent idea! That's why Giles is doing it." Rick clapped him on the back. "I am heading home to my pillow. Call me if you have questions, but wait until *after* noon, huh?"

Tom dropped into his chair, his chin smacking the edge of his desk. "Who the fu..." He cut short his tirade when Chief Mac Gregg pushed through the door. "Chief, we weren't expecting you today." He scrambled to lift his chair, but the hydraulics failed, so he jumped to his feet.

"You okay, Keller?" Amusement played at the corners of the chief's mouth.

"Yes, sir. My chair's broken."

"Well, get one out of my office until we get you a new one. Where's Daniel?" The chief scanned the squad room, looking for his son.

"Uh, he's keeping an eye on Marnie. She returned yesterday, and I'm guessing you know Sam Reilly is back in town, right?"

Mac ran a hand through his thick white hair, a pained grimace stretching across his haggard face. "Yeah. I heard. Where are Daniel and Marnie now?"

"They were heading out to Marnie's new house. It's the old Billingsly ranch. Do you know it?"

The chief stared over Tom's head, his steely blue eyes searching for a memory. "That's out there in Spooky Hollow, right?"

Tom pulled a face. "Spooky Hollow, sir?"

"Yeah. That's what we used to call it. The ranch is on one side of the road and the founders' cemetery is on the other. Is that the place?"

The detective shrugged. "I've never heard it called that, but yeah, there's a cemetery up there."

"You need to bone up on your local history, Keller," said Mac, disappearing into his office. He reappeared a moment later and scooted a chair across the floor. "That should do," he said before disappearing again and slamming the door.

A plain white murder book sat on the corner of Tom's desk; the buzzing fluorescent light above distorting it to bluish gray. He gazed at the binder and gave an involuntary shudder; the color reminded him of Paige's eyes in death. A glance to his left brought a frown to his face as he stood up and approached a yellowing investigative board sitting on an easel next to his desk. The crime scene photos loomed before him, and a hint of acid filled his mouth. It didn't matter how many homicides he investigated, they all made him feel sick, but this one more than others. The victim was his friend. He pushed the rising bile back down into his gut, picked up a black dry erase marker—its mashed felt tip barely usable—and got back to work.

A droning buzz of voices filled the staircase outside the squad room. Tom looked up as Officers Pete Connor, Tony Tartetto, and Cheryl Garcia entered.

"What's the word?" asked Tom.

Garcia sucked down the last of her iced coffee, tossing the plastic cup into the trash. "I spoke with Stu Bennett." She pulled her notebook out of her breast pocket and flipped through the pages. "He said he and his crew left the island around 3:30 yesterday afternoon. He remembered the time because he had to pick his kids up at day camp. They all returned to the dock near his folks' house around

3:45. Caleb Bennett, Drew Garrison, Allison Bobb, and Joe Holcomb traveled back on his pontoon. Pat Farley, John Nguyen, and Cassie Eldridge followed in Pat's boat. No one stayed behind. As far as they know, Paige Reynolds was not on the island while they were there." She unfolded a piece of paper and set it on the corner of his desk. "Here's the inventory of what they left in the storage shed, and here's the extra key for the padlock."

The detective glanced at the inventory. "Thanks. You told them not to go back until we give the okay, right?"

"Yeah. They need their tools, though. Stu was real upset about that. He said if he can't work on the island, he needs to take care of other projects while he waits," she said, studying the murder board. "Is that all we've got?"

Tom glowered. "No. I haven't put everything up. The prying eyes of the public and all."

"Sorry, but it looked like a lot of white up there," she apologized.

"We need another room we can lock," said Tartetto.

Tom huffed. "We need a lot of things we ain't gonna get. What did you find out?" He raised an eyebrow at the patrolmen.

"We checked Paige Reynolds' movements yesterday. She visited the garden center, Marnie Reilly's house, and she stopped for gas on Station Road. Word is she also had a meetup with Kate Parish at the looney bin. Can we get your okay to go check on that?" Connor picked up the murder book and waggled it. "Can we look?"

"Yeah, you can look at it. Don't repeat anything to anybody from the autopsy report, though." Tom rubbed his jaw as he contemplated Paige's visit to the sanitarium. He blew out a breath before responding. "I'll take care of Kate Parish. I know her tells. She's a liar, a master manipulator, and I know when she's playing games."

"Keller, why don't you take me along?" Chief Gregg stood in the open doorway of his office. "I haven't been in the field lately. Why don't you arrange a meeting with the infamous Ms. Parish on Monday morning? Make sure the administrator knows we're coming, but let's keep it a surprise for Kate."

The detective spun around. "You wanna go with me?"

The officers scattered to their desks, still wary of the chief's booming voice and commanding presence.

Mac jerked out a nod. "Yeah. I haven't been out to Pine Ridge in a long time. I had a young guy put away there twenty-five or thirty years ago. He's long gone from there now—but it was an interesting case. We apprehended him on that island in Perch Pond. You're probably too young to remember."

Tom studied the chief's face. "Are you talkin' about Jethro Barnes?"

"That's him. You've read the case file?"

"No, sir. I'm *in* the case file. Marnie and Sam Reilly, too. Barnes was the center of nightmares for all of us."

"Hang on! That was you? You were the little guy with the bump on your head?"

"Yes, sir. Marnie got the worst of it. Barnes knocked her around and split her lip."

Mac nodded. "Yeah. I hadn't put it together, but then, I haven't thought about that case in years." Thinking back, he chuckled. "Oh, she sure gave Pete Sterling a run for his money that day!"

"Captain Sterling was there?"

"He was. Lou Beaumont, too. They were both patrolmen back then. I was on loan to Creekwood PD because their detective was away on vacation." He raked his fingers through his hair, his eyes lost in thought. "Isn't that something? Sam was the young guy who gave Barnes what for. Brave kid protecting his sister like that. Barnes was a psycho. It's strange how our lives connect, huh? It's funny. I knew Marnie was familiar. Who could forget those eyes of hers or that sassy mouth?" He chuckled again.

"Hey, Chief, you okay if head out for the day? It's my day off, and I'm supposed to help Marnie move." Tom grabbed up the padlock key. "I'll drop this off to forensics first so they can check out the tools the construction crew left on the island."

Mac waved him off. "Go! I don't need the mayor giving me grief about overtime. How Sterling has managed him all these years, I will never know."

"Any word on when the captain will be back?"

Mac pushed out his bottom lip and gave his head a tight shake. "I wouldn't bet on him returning before the end of the year."

"He's not comin' back, is he?" Tom asked.

"You'll make a good detective someday, Keller," the chief replied with a wink. "Are you interested in his job?"

Tom made a face. "No! Besides, isn't Danny next in line?"

"Yeah," said the chief, disappearing into his office and closing the door. He stood before Captain Sterling's desk, a grave expression on his face. "I don't think my son is cut out for your job, Pete. Not yet, anyway," he said to the captain's empty chair.

-Chapter 20-

G ray granite headstones and obelisks set a dull scene on the left side of Hallowed Hills Road. Danny squinted up at the old signpost straddling the driveway leading into the cemetery. "Hallowed Hills Memorial," he said to himself. "Pfft. Leave it to Marnie to buy a house across the road from a graveyard."

Turning on her right signal light at the last minute, she swerved into a driveway hidden behind a red maple tree.

"Dammit!" Danny hit his brakes, cranked the steering wheel and followed, a cloud of dust kicking up around him. His phone rang, and he thumbed a button on the steering wheel to answer. "You tryin' to kill me?"

"Ha-ha! No! Sorry about that! I nearly missed the turn. We're taking the back road into the property," she said. "Carl and Tom are both on the way. They'll meet us at the homestead, but I wanted to come this way so you could see the property before them."

"Hey, are you aware there's a graveyard across the road?"

"Of course. That's the founders' cemetery," she said.

"It won't bother you living so close to all those dead people?"

"No! I'll seal the house with sea salt before I go to bed tonight."

Her nonchalant response made him smile. "Well, as long as you've got it under control, I won't worry."

"I'm hanging up now. If I lose you, stay on this road."

"If you lose me?" he asked, but she didn't answer as she sped off toward her new home.

Danny looked out across an open field. The grass was greener than any he remembered seeing. "Wow! This is beautiful!" He slowed to a stop and rolled down the window to take in the country air and the property. A big red barn appeared in the distance, a family of goats romped merrily through a paddock surrounded by a wooden split-rail fence, and cows dotted a field beyond the barn. A row of freshly whitewashed bunkhouses sat on a hill to the right of the barn, and he watched a man wearing a windbreaker slip between the buildings and head toward the muddy dam. He wondered if the man was a farmhand, or the inspector Marnie mentioned at breakfast.

Danny kept the window open to enjoy the early summer breeze and crept up the road. Wildflowers sprouted up in the shallow gulley, and the distinct honk of geese filled the air. "Geese? I hate geese," he said, pulling up out front of a stone and timber homestead with red clapboard gables, white shutters, and a wrap-around veranda.

"Nice digs, Ms. Reilly," he said, unbuckling his seatbelt and opening the car door. As he stepped onto the driveway, a gaggle of white geese raced out from behind a garden shed at the far corner of the house, honking wildly and heading straight at him. Danny took one look at their stretched-out necks and beady black eyes and scrambled back into the vehicle.

Marnie appeared on the veranda, tea towel in hand, and raced down the steps. She waved the towel at the geese and shooed them away from her visitor.

"It's safe to come out now," she said. "He-he! I guess I should have warned you about the geese. Jonas shooed them away when I arrived."

Danny looked up to see a man descending the steps of Marnie's veranda. The fellow was average in every way—height, weight, and looks. The detective exited his Jeep and held out his hand to the man.

"Hi. I'm Jonas. Nice to meet you," he said, shaking the detective's hand.

"I'm Danny. Good to meet you," the detective replied.

"I'll get the geese settled in their pen so they won't chase your other visitors. Don't worry. They'll get used to people coming and going in no time, but we better keep them locked up for now. They'll do damage if they have a mind to." Jonas pulled a faded red ball cap out of his back pocket and clamped it on his head. "I'll be back to lend a hand when the moving van arrives," he said, then strode off to tend to the flock.

Marnie reached out her hand and wrapped it around one of Danny's. "What do you think?"

"I'm not keen on the geese, but the rest of the place looks amazing!" he said with a laugh. "Where are the knuckleheads?"

"They're in the house chasing ghosts. The Billingslys had cats, and a few are still here."

"Ghost cats?"

"Yeah. I've seen three so far. I asked Jonas how many to expect, and he said at least eight that he can remember. Ha-ha! Tater and Dickens are going to be busy."

"So Jonas knows about your clairvoyance?"

"Most people around here do, especially those I went to school with. They called me Ghost Girl or 'that spooky chick' or Tom's favorite, 'Good Witch of the North'."

"Ha-ha! I've heard him call you that."

Marnie glowered. "Well, it beats 'Madam Séance'. Anyone who knows me, knows I would never hold one of those." She finished her sentence with a toss of her head.

"Oh, hey, I think I saw your inspector by the bunkhouses. I hope that goes well."

She furrowed her brow and took her phone from her pocket, checking the screen for missed calls. "Huh. He's not supposed to be here until next week. I'm sure that's what Carl told me."

Danny shrugged. "Is he a farmhand? Or..." His face lost all color, and he smacked himself in the forehead. "What is wrong with me? It's..."

Marnie held up a hand to stop him. "No! Don't say it! Sam couldn't … Dammit! Gossiping gossips in this town!"

Jonas returned, carrying a bundle of chicken wire. "Those are the faces of a bull staring down the business end of a cattle prod! Everything okay?"

"Yes!" shouted Marnie. "Sorry. I didn't mean to yell."

Danny whispered, "We better tell him. We all have to be on the lookout."

She drew in a deep breath and relented. "Jonas, I thought you should know, my brother is back in Creekwood. I don't think he knows I bought the ranch. Danny saw someone around the bunkhouses. Do we have anyone working out there today?"

"Yeah. Elk is tidying up the paint and such. He'll lock things up tight when he's done." Jonas looked out onto the green meadow and sucked on his bottom lip. "I always got along with Sam. Things can change, but there was a time when he was a good friend to have. I think … Never mind. None of my business. If I see him, I'll tell ya."

"What were you going to say?" asked Danny.

Jonas adjusted his faded cap, looked at his scuffed boots, and raised his head slowly. "I guess I would ask myself what flipped the switch in Sam's head. It doesn't make sense to me is all."

"I've been asking myself that same question," said Marnie. "It's hard when you know who he was. Danny's never seen the guy we knew."

The detective chewed the inside of his cheek and considered what they said. "Look, I saw the guy who tried to kill you and Tater last year, and the same guy killed two cops. I can't forget about that."

Jonas kicked a stone down the path, turned to walk away, then stopped and glanced back. "It's like a magic show. You can't see what makes the illusion, but you know there's a trick to it. A misdirection. Who's the magician in Sam's show, Detective?"

Danny pulled a face as Jonas ambled away, then turned to Marnie. "What's that supposed to mean?"

She shrugged. "I've been wondering about that myself."

"What?" he asked again.

"I don't know, but I am going to dig into Sam's diaries tonight."

Danny frowned. "You've lost me."

"My mother visited me last night. She told me she got it wrong, and that I should read my brother's diaries."

"What did she get wrong?"

Palms up, Marnie said, "Exactly!"

The detective did a double-take, curling his lip. "I am completely lost! What the hell are you and Jonas talking about?"

She lifted an eyebrow. "Isn't it clear? Things aren't always as they seem."

He opened his mouth to ask another question when Carl pulled up. Through his open window, he called out, "Those are serious faces. What's up?"

Danny threw up a hand, a befuddled look on his face. "I wish I knew."

-*Chapter 21*-

"Hello, Lanie. You're looking as dreadful as ever. Is there a banana convention in town? Does that explain the yellow get-up you're wearing? And those flip-flops! My God! Do you still bedazzle everything like you did in high school?" Kate led the way to an outdoor table, prancing her way across the grounds like a model on a catwalk. She pivoted gracefully and took a seat on a wrought-iron chair. "And what's with your makeup? It's so ... so... clown-like." With a look of distaste and a dismissive wave, she pointed to a chair. "You may as well sit. You look awkward standing there gawking at me."

Lanie plopped into a chair, tucking her feet beneath it. "Why do you have to be so horrible?" she hissed, pasting on a smile. "People are staring at us."

"They aren't staring because of what I said. They're ogling us because you look so ordinary. These people are wondering why I would take time out of my day to visit with a swamp creature." Kate tossed her head and peered down her nose at her visitor. "Why are you here? Bored with your moronic husband?"

"I have news you might be interested in. But if you don't want to hear about Marnie Reilly, I'll go." Lanie sat forward to get up, but Kate slammed a hand onto one of hers.

"Wait! Paige Reynolds told me Marnie was returning. Is she in Creekwood?" Kate's indigo eyes dilated as adrenaline raced through her.

"You spoke with Paige? When?"

"She was here a few days ago. Something about forgiving me. Why would I need or want her forgiveness? She's the one who killed a child, not me." Kate glanced away with boredom.

"It was an accident. She didn't hit the child on purpose. We both know Paige wouldn't ... couldn't hurt a fly." Lanie tried to pull away her hand, but Kate held tight. "You know she's dead, right? They found her out on the island last night."

"Really? Huh. Well, you know what they say. If you can't be fabulous, you're better off dead."

Lanie scowled. "I've never heard that! You made that up! That's a horrible thing to say! Paige was nice. Her life was finally coming together, and then she dies. How can you be so mean?"

"Anyway, enough about Paige. Tell me about Marnie." Kate leaned closer, her hand still clasping her visitor's.

Lanie yanked away her a hand and pouted. "Why should I tell you anything? All you've done is insult me since I arrived."

Kate rolled her eyes. "Boohoo! Poor little Lanie. Everyone picks on me." Her eyes flashed with anger. "Stop whining and tell me what you know!"

Lanie pulled her chair closer and tipped her head to the side. "Well, Marnie was at the diner with that sexy detective. What's his name? Danny?"

Kate blew out an annoyed breath. "Yes. Danny Gregg. What about him?"

"Oh, nothing about him, but he is quite attractive, isn't he?"

"He's okay, but he's a cop. What could he possibly offer? He's in a dead-end job that will never be enough."

"Enough for who?"

"Whom, and I suppose Marnie."

"Ha! She doesn't need a man to take care of her. She has Ken Wilder's money. All of it!"

Kate bristled. "Well, we'll see. That money is rightfully mine, and it will be once I'm out of here."

"Don't be silly. You're never getting out of here. Everyone knows that but you. And if you do get out, you'll go straight to prison. No passing Go. No collecting Ken's millions."

"I will never go to prison, and I will leave this wretched place!" Kate's nostrils flared and her perfect alabaster complexion reddened.

Lanie giggled. "You *are* crazy. That's the buzz around town, but I can see it's true. Geez, Kate, you are certifiable."

Dalton Hooley approached the table. "Is everything okay?"

Kate composed herself and smiled sweetly at her ward. "Yes. Everything is fine. We're having a private conversation. Go away, please."

He nodded and backed away. "You need anything. Let me know." He turned back and added, "Either of you."

Once he turned his back, Kate clamped her hand around one of Lanie's and narrowed her eyes. "Don't you dare call me crazy! I will leave Pine Ridge sooner than you think." She gave her company's hand a tight squeeze, digging in her nails, then released her. "Now, tell me what Marnie is doing with my money."

Lanie stared at the red crescents on her hand. A trickle of blood seeped from one. She fought back tears and steadied her nerves, then lifted mocking eyes to Kate. "Marnie bought Billingsly Acres, and she has a new car, and Jonas is working for her. She gave him a hefty raise. Such a nice raise that Jonas and I are building a house on Croft Mills Road. We'll stay at the cottage until our new house is complete. It really isn't terrible. Marnie paid Stu Bennett handsomely to renovate it. It has a brand-new kitchen and two new bathrooms. It's quite charming, really. And you should see what she's done with that drab old farmhouse. It is absolutely stunning! Marnie has everything she could ever want—including your money." She stood and stepped away from the table so Kate couldn't reach her without causing a scene. "See you later, Kate. I hope they keep you locked in here until you are old and gray."

Kate leaped from her chair, but Dalton grabbed her before she could reach Lanie.

"C'mon. We'll get you back to your suite. Never mind her."

Kate swung around wildly. "Did you hear what she said to me? Can you believe she spoke to me like that?"

Dalton patted her hand, then guided her toward the building. "I did, Miss Kate. I heard everything, and so did everyone else. You gotta let go of your thoughts of leaving Pine Ridge. They will never let you out if you continue to fight with your visitors."

"Lawrence, you must stop spoiling her so. You have given that child everything. Since she was a tiny baby, you have spared no expense. This wardrobe is far too extravagant for someone locked in a sanitarium." Kitty Parish held a strapless evening gown of midnight blue silk in front of herself. "When will Kate ever wear this?"

"It doesn't matter when she will wear it. This elegant garment hanging in her closet will make her happy," said Lawrence, caressing the luxurious fabric. "We must keep her hopes up or she will go mad."

Kitty scoffed. "I've got news for you. Our daughter is well past mad, dear. She hasn't a snowball's chance in hell of leaving Pine Ridge in our lifetime."

Lawrence picked up a dainty cup from its saucer and sipped his tea before dropping it onto the plate. "I can't drink this dirty dishwater any longer. I need a cup of espresso."

His wife shot him a disapproving glance. "Your doctor…"

"I don't care. I am also a doctor and I plan to self-medicate with a strong cup of coffee," he said, getting to his feet as a phone rang in the distance.

Kitty waved her hand dismissively. "Do as you please. You always do."

He returned a moment later with the phone pressed to his ear, his coffee fix forgotten.

"They don't know where he is? No? Well, this is good news. Thank you for keeping me informed."

"Who was that, dear?" Kitty looked up from the stack of journals and pens she was packing for her daughter.

He stared out the window, bouncing the phone against his chin. "That was, well, never mind who it was. It is what they said that is important." He set the phone on an end table and turned around with a smug smile. "Sam Reilly has returned to Creekwood."

"Have they arrested him?" She crossed the room and grasped her husband's arm.

"They have not. He is out there somewhere, though. I wonder if he knows where Kate is? We should advise the administrator of his return. He won't stay away from Kate for long. He will have to see her."

"You don't seem concerned," she said.

"He would never harm our daughter; of that, I am certain."

"What about his sister? Will he harm Marnie?"

Lawrence straightened his sports jacket and nodded. "Yes. I am confident he will."

-*Chapter 22-*

“Marn, you’re gonna have to get a four-wheeler and a snowmobile. This place is bigger than I remember!” Tom gazed across the property, teetering on the edge of envy. “If you weren’t my best friend, I might be jealous. But since I can come visit any time I want, I’m good. Ha-ha!”

“So, how many acres are there?” asked Danny.

“Five-hundred-sixty-three acres, including the creek and that bit of land over there,” she said, pointing to a wooded area.

“That’s a good chunk of real estate. How much livestock?” he asked.

“Um, you’ll have to get the correct count from Jonas, but I think we have a hundred and twenty-eight dairy cows, one bull, twelve goats, five horses, heaps of chickens, two roosters, a gaggle of geese, ducks, and turkeys, and that’s it.” Her eyes danced as she counted off on her fingers.

Carl tapped her elbow. “Don’t forget about the ponds and the dam.”

She nodded. “I won’t. There are two natural ponds—one is okay for swimming, the other one is muddy, and then there’s the creek. It has white water way down there.” She pointed beyond the red barn Danny had seen earlier.

“It flows into the Hudson River?” he asked.

She glanced at Carl, who nodded.

"David dropped off the deed yesterday," Carl said, leaning into his car and then handing her a folder. "Make sure you lock that up."

"Yeah. I'll take it to the bank Monday morning, but I want to read through it before I do that. David said it's interesting." She turned to Tom. "Did you know the original name of the property was Wild Creek Ranch?"

"Nope, but that would make sense, since it sits next to Wild Creek."

The crunch of gravel alerted them to company.

"The moving van is here! Yay!" Marnie whooped.

"How did you get these boxes labeled?" asked Danny, cutting open a carton.

Marnie blushed. "I didn't label. Carl was kind enough to go over to the house with Mr. and Mrs. Lewis to give them a list of what was to stay and what was to come here, and then Mr. Lewis and his team packed everything for me. I felt guilty, but they offered. They said it's not unusual to pack and unpack for people."

Tom and Danny exchanged angry glances.

"You could have called us," said Danny, the lines in his face deep.

"What the heck, Marn?" griped Tom.

"Can we please let it go? You guys are busy enough without having to pack my stuff. Besides, Mrs. Lewis said she had nothing in her schedule, and it allowed her to give her team extra hours."

A knock at the back door saved her from explaining further.

"Hello!" Ellie Nikol, Tater's, Dickens' and Gus' veterinarian, opened the screen door and entered.

Marnie met her friend at the door and gave her a warm hug. "Hey, Ellie! Where's Julie and the kids?"

"Home! We thought about all of us coming out, then changed our minds. You have enough going on without two bored kids moping around. Besides, she's dropping the kids at their father's house soon. She'll drive out afterward." She glanced around the room, searching. "Speaking of kids, where are Tater and Dickens?"

"Upstairs. The Billingslys left behind a clowder of cats."

Ellie's eyebrows shot up. "Oh, no! Do you need me to find them homes?"

Marnie giggled. "No. I doubt anyone wants ghost cats."

"Ha! No, probably not."

Tater, Gus, and Dickens raced into the kitchen, a clatter of nails clicking across the floorboards. Tater and Gus stopped short, but in pursuit of a spirited feline, Dickens ran straight into the closed pantry door and dropped to the floor with a frustrated woof.

Ellie kneeled and called over the dogs, who covered her with licks and gave her warm nose bumps. "Wow! You two look great!" She looked up at Marnie. "How do you think Tater will feel when Dickens is bigger than him? I can't believe how much he has grown!"

"Ha-ha! As long as he's the boss, he won't care," she said, reaching out a hand to ruffle Tater's fur.

"How about I stay here in the kitchen and get your cupboards organized? I've known you long enough to know where you'll put things." Ellie got up and surveyed the cupboards and drawers.

"That's perfect! Thanks so much! There's a pantry over there. Geez! I'll have to go grocery shopping to fill up the larder."

"Marnie Reilly with an empty fridge and bare cupboards. That's so wrong," said Tom with a chuckle. "Does that mean you have nothing for lunch? I'm starving!"

She rolled her eyes. "You're always starving. I've got pizza, wings, and salad arriving soon."

"Hey, Marnie, can you and Tom come into the living room for a sec?" Danny called from the doorway, motioning with his head for them to join him. As they entered the room, he pointed a thumb over his shoulder at the mantel. "Did you see this?" he asked.

A tatty scrap of paper leaned upright on the mantel and Marnie crept closer to read it and her eyes teared when she recognized the perfect penmanship and precise wording.

She read aloud the hand-written note. "'Home is the place where, when you have to go there,

they have to take you in.'"

"Do you recognize the writing?" asked Danny.

She nodded, and so did Tom.

"That's Sam's writing," she said.

Danny stared at the paper, doubt creasing his forehead. "Marnie, I have studied the inscriptions he has written in other books. That's nothing like the others."

Tom edged closer to the fireplace, eyes scanning the words. "When we were little, Sam sent us on treasure hunts…"

"Tom! The treasure!" Marnie grabbed his arm, her eyes wide with the realization that, in the commotion and tragedy of last night's events, they had forgotten to open the leather satchel.

Eyes popping, he refocused and brushed away her hand, but not before giving it a tight squeeze. "As I was sayin', he wrote us little notes and drew maps for us to follow. This is definitely Sam's writing. I could never forget it. His penmanship is perfect. Why didn't we see this before? The other notes were … um…what's the right word?" He snapped his fingers, turning to Marnie.

"Manic?" she suggested.

"Yeah. That's as good a word as any."

"Let's get Carl. He's in the library unpacking books," said Danny.

A blaze of anger rose on Marnie's cheeks. "We don't need Carl to answer this question. I am a psychologist, and I can tell you that yes, a person's handwriting can change with varying degrees of psychosis."

Danny grimaced. "Sorry. I forget sometimes, but for the spooky stuff, I always call you."

She cut him off with the wave of a dismissive hand. "Forget it," she snapped, before stepping closer to the note. "I've read this before, but I can't recall … Oh! Wait!" She pulled out her phone and typed in the words and stared at the screen. "It is Frost," she said, and continued to read, her head bobbing in time with the cadence of the verse. Without looking up, she said, "It's from *The Death of the Hired Man*."

"Shit! That can't be good," said Tom. "We better warn Jonas."

Marnie shook her head, eyes still glued to the screen. "He won't kill Jonas. This is about *his* death. Sam's death. He's come home to die."

"Marn..." Tom began, but she stopped him.

"I'll be right back. There's something I need to show you."

Marnie returned and set a book on the mantel. "I found this propped up between the seats when I got into my car this morning. Be careful though. There are strands of hair marking a passage. I think it's Paige's."

"Why didn't you tell me about this at the diner?" asked Danny.

"You mean between Teddy flirting with you, Lanie bugging us, and every busybody in Creekwood stopping at our table to find out the latest about Paige?"

He frowned. "I wasn't flirting with Teddy."

"I didn't say *you* were. I said *she* was. We didn't even have time to chat with Gram. Did you eat your breakfast? I didn't, other than a forkful of eggs and a bite of toast."

"I'm sorry," he said. "We had a busy morning." He picked up the book, opening the passage marked by the hair. He glanced at the page, then looked up. "*Spoils of the Dead*?" he said, screwing up his face. "Tell me again why you are such a fan of Robert Frost? This is morbid."

Marnie shrugged. "Yes, some of his poems are, but not all of them. It's emotive though, isn't it?" She turned to Tom. "Do your neighbors have security cameras we could check? The person who left the book could be on video."

"Nah. Sorry. I've been thinkin' about getting cameras for a while, and no one else has them. There was a break-in two doors down last week. I canvased without luck."

Danny took care in turning the pages, searching for an inscription. "There's no note."

Tom looked over his partner's shoulder. "Maybe the hair is his note," he suggested.

Marnie scrunched her face. "That doesn't make sense. Why would he do that if he planned to leave that on my mantel," she said, pointing at the scrap.

Danny closed the book and set it next to the tatty note. "He wouldn't. So, who put this in your car? It would have to be someone who knew you were back or when you planned to return and who knew you got a new car?"

"Carl did. Patrick too, and he saw my car last night. Um … David, Paige, Jonas. I don't think Jonas was aware of my new car, though, until today. Mrs. Henry at the bank, but she wouldn't tell anyone. She's not a gossipmonger."

"When did you tell Paige?" asked Tom.

"Hmm … I mentioned it while I was driving the other day. She had trouble hearing me because I had the roof off."

"Would she have shared it with anyone?" asked Danny.

Marnie quirked up the corner of her mouth. "Well, this morning Lanie said Paige planned to visit Kate. Paige may have said something if Kate was throwing barbs at me. It may have been a throwaway comment to shut Kate up."

Tom agreed, "Yeah. I can see Paige doing that. Anything that's good in your world would send Kate over the edge. She may have told her about the ranch, too. She'd throw out everything that would stick in Kate's craw."

"Yeah … Wouldn't we all. We're horrible people," she said with an impish grin.

"Not as horrible as your brother or the person who left that book in your car. It takes a sick mind to leave a bookmark like that.

Anyway, I better call it in. Your ranch is going to get busy real soon." Danny stepped away to make the call.

"What's goin' on Marn? You've got that spooky look in your eyes. They've gone from normal green to the eerie ghost detector green," Tom said, bending and leaning closer to study her eyes.

"Hmm ... Nothing. I was thinking about a conversation Sam and I had a long time ago. Tom, have you seen an old steamer trunk kicking around? The last time I saw it, it was on the truck."

"Yeah. Danny and I carried it up to your room."

She squeezed his arm as she passed. "Thanks. I think the pizza guy is here."

-*Chapter 23*-

"**O**h, Daddy! This is divine!" Kate waltzed around the room, holding the silk ball gown in front of her.

Lawrence beamed. "I knew you would love it, darling. And the color complements your eyes brilliantly! Look how beautiful she is, Kitty!"

"It's lovely, dear," she said, unpacking clothes onto the bed. "Kate, here are the workout clothes you requested. Could you please try on the sneakers to see if they fit?"

Kate danced to her mother's side, flinging the gown onto the bed. "Where are my notebooks and pens?"

"Dalton has them. The wards have to be ... uh... You can... Lawrence, help me out? This type of news is always better coming from you." Kitty glanced at her husband and mouthed, "You tell her."

"Come sit, Kate," Lawrence said, taking a seat. "We need to talk."

"Please don't tell me I can't have my pens and notebooks. I've had enough horrible news today," Kate said, her indigo eyes leaking crocodile tears.

"No, no, darling, you can have them, but with supervision. When you wish to write, your ward will take you to the conservatory. The hospital won't allow you to have a pen in your room. They worry you might hurt yourself."

She ran to her father, kneeled at his feet, and grasped his hands. "Tell them I won't, Daddy. Make them listen!"

"I tried, Katie, but my biased opinion doesn't count. I'm your father, and I think you are perfect." He squeezed his daughter's hands and kissed the top of her head. "Now, we have a whole new wardrobe for you over there on the bed. How about a fashion show?" He stood, clapping his hands with encouragement.

Kate rose gracefully to her feet, glancing toward the new clothes. She fixed a threatening glare on her mother—and added a mocking sneer to unnerve Kitty. When she turned back to her father, tears rolled down her cheeks and her bottom lip protruded. "I don't feel like trying anything on today. You can return everything—including the evening gown. I have nothing to look forward to because I am going to die here!" She broke into a sob and threw herself onto the chaise lounge. "Go away! Just leave me here to die!"

Kitty marched to her daughter and yanked her upright. "That is enough! I have had enough of your tantrums, young lady! Stop this nonsense, right now!" She spun around, facing her husband, pointed an accusing finger and warned. "Don't you dare butt in. You created this monster!" She turned back to her daughter, whose tears had dried up—her face turned to stone. "Don't you look at me like that! You sit here day after day, scheming up ways to twirl your father around your finger. Take responsibility for your actions. What were you thinking? It is your fault you are here. Not Marnie's. Not Sam's, and not Erin's. The legal system is not conspiring against you. It is you! This is your own damn fault, you spoiled brat!"

Dalton appeared in the window of Kate's door and knocked before entering. "Everything okay in here?"

"No, it is not!" shouted Kitty, her face a mottled red—wet with angry tears. She rushed across the room, gathered up her handbag and cardigan, and stormed past the ward.

Dalton cast his eyes out the door, watching as Kitty rushed down the hallway and into a restroom. "Miss Kate, go into the bathroom and splash water on your face," he instructed. Once he heard the water running, he turned to Lawrence. "Sir, we need to talk."

Lawrence drove his Ermine White 1964 Corvette Stingray convertible through the front gates of Pine Ridge and turned left onto the highway toward home. He tapped his fingers on the steering wheel, searching for words that would not stir another outburst.

"Dalton advised me Lanie Howard visited Kate this morning. It seems she brought news of Paige Reynolds' death. The wretch also shared gossip about Marnie Reilly's inheritance and her purchase of Billingsly Acres."

Kitty shot him a disdainful glance. "What of it? Lanie and Marnie have nothing to do with Kate's behavior. Kate never liked Paige—not even when they were children. The only reason she defended her was because it was her job. I often wonder if she wasn't somehow responsible for that poor girl's conviction. I am sorry, dear, but our daughter has been an envious brat since she was a small child. Whatever Marnie Reilly had, Kate wanted three. She was jealous of Marnie's relationship with Sam and did everything she could to turn him against his sister. Ken Wilder presented her with another opportunity to take someone away. You witnessed it and so did I, and it irks her she has never broken the bond Marnie shares with Tom Keller. She tried, but Tom saw through her."

Lawrence chuckled. "Our daughter has a complex personality; I will give you that."

Kitty scoffed. "Complex? There is nothing complex about her. Five words describe our daughter: pampered, vindictive, treacherous, brat, and coquette!"

"Kitty!" Lawrence slammed his hand on the steering wheel, his face purple with anger.

"Don't you *Kitty* me! I've gone along to get along for too many years, and I will not take part in this sick game any longer. I will no longer be unkind to Marnie to appease our daughter. She's locked away, and can no longer harm me when I do something that displeases her. You haven't forgotten the depilatory cream in my shampoo or the drain cleaner in my mouthwash, have you? How about the razor blades she tucked neatly into the mattress on my side of the bed? Or how she turned all the sharp knife blades up in the drawer? Or the radio she threw into my bathtub? Thank goodness she didn't plug it in."

"Of course, I haven't. Those were only the childish games of a girl who wanted her mother's attention. Kate didn't want to share you."

"My God, Lawrence, you can't honestly believe that, can you? The signs our daughter is dangerous have stared you in the face since she strangled her hamster when she was three years old. You were a noted psychiatrist until..."

"Stop it! Our daughter will not die in that hospital!" He gripped the steering wheel, shaking with anger.

Kitty's mocking eyes assessed her husband. "I will make sure she never steps one foot out of Pine Ridge, or I will die trying."

Lawrence slammed on the brakes to the blare of horns and screeching tires behind him. His head slammed into the steering wheel and while the car stood stationary, his wife continued on the car's set course, hurling forward through the windshield. Before losing consciousness, he lifted his head, and with little regret, he watched Kitty's crumpled body slip down the bloodied hood of his classic car to the gray asphalt below.

-*Chapter 24*-

S am flinched with pain as he pulled his sweatshirt and T-shirt over his head and stared at the dry, bloody splotches on his clothes. He searched through his backpack for Tylenol, a bandage, and salve while thinking of Marnie.

I wonder if she found the note, he thought, hoping she had, and knowing the detectives would call the feds if they found it first. It was a calculated risk, he knew, but he had to leave a message for her. Besides, if the agents were as useless as the two sent last night, he had little to worry about. Although, the drumming of helicopters above told him they were searching the land around the ranch.

"They won't find me in here," he said aloud, scanning the tidy room. "I doubt she knows this place even exists. I wonder if Jonas has mentioned it. Why would he? He's a smart guy, but he doesn't have a sneaky bone in his body. He doesn't think the way I do. God help anyone who does."

Sam tended to his wounded shoulder, bunched up his sweatshirt using it as a pillow, and lay back on an old army cot. He pulled a scratchy wool blanket to his chin as thoughts of doubt took over his tired and damaged brain.

"Maybe I shouldn't have left the note. Why did I leave it? Am I warning her or simply letting her know I am here?" he thought as he popped four Tylenol tablets into his mouth and chewed. He shut his eyes and wished away the thumping in his head, the throbbing of his shoulder, and the foreboding lump of doom settling in his throat.

"I'm sorry you can't stay for lunch," Marnie said to Carl.

"I'll come out tomorrow. We can drink coffee, and catch up," he said. "The study is half unpacked. It shouldn't take us long to organize."

"How about just catching up and coffee? I'll finish the study when I finish it?" she said.

"Good deal. See you later!" he said, disappearing out the door.

Marnie placed a stack of paper napkins and plates into the middle of the long trestle table, which sat amongst the unpacked boxes in her kitchen. "Does everyone have a plate?"

Tom folded a slice of pizza in half and said, "Who needs a plate? I've got two hands." He winked and took a big bite.

Danny chucked napkins at him and chuckled. "You also have pizza grease running down your arm."

"Ha-ha! We can't take you anywhere, Keller," Marnie said before folding her own pizza and taking a healthy bite. She dropped her slice onto a plate, wiped her mouth with a napkin, and jumped up from her seat when two car doors slammed. "Oh! Gram and Jack are here! Looks like Hannah is with her, too!"

Tater and Gus abandoned their cozy cabin underneath the table and ambled to the door. Dickens poked out his head—a rim of red stained his white muzzle.

Marnie sighed. "Who fed Dickens pizza?"

Ellie's right hand shot up. "Guilty! I fed them all a teeny-tiny piece of crust. It won't hurt. I should know. I'm their vet." Her left hand held a napkin to her mouth, covering a sheepish grin.

Marnie wagged a finger but couldn't help but smile, knowing she would have done the same before lunch was over.

"Bless this house and all who enter!" Gram said as she crossed the threshold. She carried a large basket over one arm, and her dog Jack in the other. She handed the pup to Hannah, who grimaced and held him out as if he were a diseased creature. The older woman clucked her tongue. "He won't hurt you, love, but set him down before you give the poor lad a complex."

Hannah set the Jack Russell on the floor, then slid onto the bench next to Ellie before Marnie could hug her.

Gram embraced Marnie with her free arm, kissed her cheek, and whispered, "Thanks for stayin' in touch, love. It's good to see you lookin' fit and well."

Marnie gave Danny's and Hannah's grandmother a tight squeeze. "It's great to see you! How was Ireland?"

"It was magic, as always. Now, I have a small token here for you and the wee ones. It's not much, but it's tradition." Gram set the overflowing basket on the table and began pulling out items—holding up each as she explained the significance.

"Here's a cricket for your hearth. This little fellow will bring you luck and protection. And don't we all know who much you need that these days." She set a wrought iron cricket on the table. "He also doubles as a bootjack, farm girl." Gram tittered as her hand dove into the basket, producing a brass acorn. "This is for your mantle. An acorn holds great meaning to our ancestors. They bring good health, wisdom, and a big dollop of perseverance. Did ya know that acorns have a time of dormancy before they grow? There is a time for growth and a time for rest. Have ya rested enough?" she asked, her blue eyes staring over her glasses.

Marnie gave a half smile, knowing rest rarely came to those who speak with the dead. "Rested as I'll ever be," she said.

The older woman patted her arm. "I know that feelin'." Hand back in the basket, she produced a bottle of wine. "Wine to fill your days with joy and prosperity. I know ya will enjoy this one. I had Danny choose it."

Next, she handed Marnie a pouch of Celtic Sea salt. "This is a promise of flavor in your life. Take that anyway ya like." She winked and continued, "Of course, the bread is so there's never hunger, which I know isn't a problem in your home." She looked upon the table covered with food and laughed. "Just one more thing," she said, removing a bag from the basket. "Irish kelp and salmon dog biscuits for the boys."

"Thank you so much, Gram! This is so lovely. I'll bet the knuckleheads wouldn't mind one of those healthy treats now." Marnie turned to Ellie and shook her finger. "Ha-ha! Their diet has been good, but not as good as it should be. I must admit to feeding them chicken burgers recently."

"Shall we get to unpackin'?" Gram asked as she slipped off her light cardigan and hung it on a coat rack behind the door.

"Thank you. Let's finish lunch first. Anyone who has had enough of this rat race, please don't feel you have to stay. It's been a busy morning." Marnie took another bite of pizza, before reaching into the fridge and getting a can of soda. "Water? Wine? Beer?" she asked.

The detectives said beer. Ellie and Gram requested water, and Hannah declined.

After Marnie had doled out the drinks, she turned to Danny's sister. "Hey, Hannah. Can you and I have a chat?"

"If we must," she replied, her hands wringing together.

"C'mon! We'll go into the study."

Hannah limped after her, a sour look on her face.

Once they were both in the room, Marnie closed the door. "I understand you had a run-in with my brother last night. Danny said he was helpful. Did you feel threatened in any way?"

Hannah jerked her head tightly from left to right. "Uh ... He was okay."

Marnie nodded, looked out the window and murmured something inaudible before getting to her other points of concern. "Look, I didn't leave to hurt any of you. I left to protect everyone from Sam. I also know you believe Tom has feelings for me, but Hannah, that couldn't be further from the truth. He and I are friends—best friends, but there could never be more than that between us. Tom is like my brother, and I know he thinks of me as a sister. There has been nothing between us except once in college, and that was only a kiss. We decided it wouldn't work, plus we didn't want to ruin our friendship."

Hannah rolled her eyes. "Tom told you that, did he?"

"Yeah. Isn't that what you told him?"

Hannah groaned and dropped into a chintz-covered club chair. "I did. Truth is, it was an excuse. He and Danny were obsessing over you. It drove me nuts! My brother was a mess. He really loves you, you know."

"I do, and I never meant to hurt him. I thought he would understand, but I handled it badly. I messed up. Anyway, you said it was an excuse. Why would you need an excuse?"

Hannah stared up at the ceiling, tears brimming over her bottom lids. Her steely gray eyes softened, and she gulped back a sob. "He was getting too serious too fast, and I could see it falling apart, like you and Danny."

"Danny and I didn't fall apart. I left. Big difference. He and I will work things out, but he knows I am working through things. So much has happened—from the day we met, our lives and homes ... Geez! Ken, Sam, Erin Matthews, The Collective, and Grace! Plus, he has been dealing with the deaths of Officers Webb and Weaver and Captain Sterling's attack. All of that hit him harder than he lets on. It has been a lot to take in, and then Sam escaped and is back in Creekwood. We saw six murders in a one-month period, and of course, Patrick shot Erin at the lake, but that's fair. She was planning to kill me."

Marnie took a breath and, emotionally exhausted, slumped onto the edge of a coffee table, and looked at her friend with remorse. "I'm sorry for leaving the way I did."

Hannah squeezed Marnie's knee. "I'm sorry for suggesting you and Tom are more than friends. It was overwhelming. Do you think that what happened last Christmas simply caught up with each of us in different ways?"

"Yeah, I do. Everyone manages stress in their own way. Tom makes jokes. Danny chops wood. I run away, and you pull away from the people closest to you. It's all normal as far as normal goes."

Hannah smirked. "Aren't you a therapist? Shouldn't you know better?"

"Ha-ha! Yes, I should, but that's life. No one is perfect and we don't always use logic when we're afraid."

"I suppose not," Hannah replied. "I accused Danny and Tom of putting you on a pedestal. Truth be told, they didn't put you there. I did. After what happened with Erin, and how brave you were to confront her by yourself..."

Marnie interrupted. "I wasn't alone. You, Tater, and Patrick were looking out for me. I was never alone."

"But you didn't know Patrick was there. None of us did. Frankly, we weren't even sure if he was a good guy," argued Hannah.

"The way he saved those children was courageous, and then he dove into a fire to save me ... Well, I had little doubt about him, and don't forget, I am clairvoyant. I know things without really knowing."

"Hmm ... there is that!" Hannah laughed before the lines in her forehead deepened and sadness filled her eyes. "For a few months I had a sister, and I loved that. Then you were gone. I was angry."

"Yep. I abandoned all of you. I am sorry about that, but in my head, it was better than everyone being killed." Marnie stood and held out her arms. "How about a welcome home hug?"

Hannah quirked up a corner of her mouth and got to her feet. "I suppose it won't kill me."

As they were leaving the study, Hannah stopped and called out. "Marnie, last night ... your brother was not what I expected. There was a calm and measured approach to his actions. He took my gun out of its holster, placed it out of my reach, and pulled me from the crevice. Then, he offered me water and first aid *and* he found and returned my glasses. I did not see the maniacal madman I have heard through your phone." She pushed up her glasses with a finger and thought of Sam's behavior. "I am convinced he caught a bullet last night. He favored his left arm. But that's a different topic. My point is, he had my gun. He could have killed me or forced me to go with him. Why didn't he? I could have been a bargaining chip."

Marnie stood in the hall, glancing back at Hannah. "I don't know," she said with half a shrug and turned to leave the room. "C'mon! Let's have wine."

"I don't think Sam killed your ex, or those cops." Hannah covered her mouth with her hands, surprised she had blurted out her suspicion.

Equally stunned by Hannah's epiphany, Marnie stopped and returned to the doorway. Leaning against the doorjamb, a pensive smile slipped across her face. "Neither do I," she said, before turning away again and returning to the kitchen with a determined stride.

-Chapter 25-

“How’s your partner?” Danny asked Agent Andrew Harding, who stood inside Marnie’s kitchen door.

“Fine,” Harding said, suspicious eyes surveying the people sitting around the table. “Have any of you seen Reilly? We’ve searched every outbuilding and the ranch from the air. There is no sign of him.” He turned to Danny. “You saw a man enter a bunkhouse. Right?”

Danny nodded. “Yeah, but that was a few hours ago. He could be anywhere by now.”

“We want to search the house. Make sure that his sister isn’t hiding him.”

Eyes flashing with anger, Hannah shot to her feet from her seat on a bench. “We have searched the house. He is not here.”

Harding smirked. “Take it easy, *Special* Agent. We’re gonna take another look around if it’s all the same to you.”

Marnie grabbed Hannah’s arm, pulling her back into her seat. “It’s okay. They won’t find my Sam here.”

Harding narrowed his eyes. “You sure, Ms. Reilly? If we find him, life will get complicated for you and everyone here.” He glanced around the table, then he saw Tom leering at him from the doorway of the summer kitchen. “Who are you?”

“Ms. Reilly’s best friend, and I don’t appreciate the way you insinuated she’s hiding a felon in her home.” Tom’s cheeks burned with the ruddy glow of anger.

The agent scoffed, "Yeah, okay." He turned to Marnie. "That note he left. What's the significance? Is it a secret message telling you where he is? It's not unusual for siblings to protect each other. Where are you hiding your brother, Ms. Reilly?"

Laughing, a sardonic grin eased across Marnie's face. "Search the house. Explore the outbuildings again. You won't find my brother. He's not stupid. If he was here, he would have left when he heard the helicopters."

Harding edged by Danny, and loomed over Marnie, who remained seated. "Do I need to remind you that the man is a felon?"

"You don't need to remind me. I know who my brother is, and I know what he is capable of. What you don't know is that before this is over, Sam Reilly will turn himself over to Detectives Gregg and Keller. But by all means, search the house—if you have a warrant." Marnie pushed herself up, and snatching up her phone, she disappeared to the other room.

Danny, Tom, and Hannah followed, but she was on the phone when they reached her.

"Thanks, David. I appreciate it. See you soon." Marnie turned around, she raised a hand to her hip and scowled. "What? Do you think I should let him search my home and go through everything? That is not going to happen. If they want to search for Sam, that's fine. But they are not going through my belongings. I called David. He can handle this." She walked to the front of the house and stared out the window, watching two crows peck at bugs in the grass.

Crossing the few steps between them, Danny gave her shoulder a reassuring squeeze. "Marnie, we think calling David was the right thing to do. We support you. We've searched the house and we know Sam isn't here. By the way, what did you mean when you said he will turn himself over to us?"

She stretched her back, then turned to face them. "I had a premonition or a feeling, I guess. What I'm saying may not seem clear, but it will. My brother is going to cooperate with you and Tom.

He has something to do first." Eyebrows knitted, she glanced between the detectives. "You have to trust me. Please."

The detectives' phones chirped, and they pulled them from their pockets, then looked at one another.

Tom clenched his jaw. "Shit. We have to go. There's been an accident on the freeway. The chief is callin' it suspicious based on witness accounts and the people involved. We'll be back as soon as we can." He chucked Marnie under the chin with a knuckle and grinned. "I trust ya, Marn."

Danny kissed her forehead. "I trust you, too. We'll see you later."

The door slammed, and Marnie turned to Hannah. "Does Gram have to go back to the diner?"

"Yes. She won't want to miss the dinner shift, and I must go too. I have a meeting in Hudson regarding my behavior last night. Agent Harding reported me for being disrespectful to him and his partner."

"Oh, no! Are you in trouble?"

Hannah shrugged. "I doubt it. My superiors read my report. It's protocol."

"Is your ankle okay to drive?"

"It's sore, but yes."

"Are you going to tell them of your run-in with Sam?" Marnie looked over Hannah's head into the kitchen, watching to see what Harding was up to, but he wasn't doing anything untoward—other than fussing over Dickens and not Tater.

She shook her head. "No. I think it best not to create another layer of questioning. I don't have the energy. If they ask, I injured my ankle while hiking with my brother."

"Yeah. It's probably for the best. We'll have dinner soon, huh?"

"If you're cooking, I'll be there."

When they returned to the kitchen, Harding's restlessness earned the group a glare. Marnie had kept him waiting on purpose. She didn't like his attitude.

"My lawyer will be along shortly, Agent Harding. Take a seat while you wait."

"Why are you being difficult? We just want to look around." The agent's whiny tone grated like the proverbial fingernails.

"You don't have a warrant. I gave you permission to search my land and outbuildings, but my home is different. You won't take the word of two police officers and a DEA Special Agent that my brother isn't here. Why is that?"

"I don't trust them. They're your friends, right?"

"Yup, but not one of them would break the law to protect my brother. If they found him in my house, he would be in custody. Would the agents you work with protect your brother under similar circumstances? Is that why you're so untrusting?"

Before Harding could answer, Marnie's lawyer arrived.

"Knock! Knock!" David Bennett called out as he walked through the back door, bringing with him his brother Stu and another man. "Marn, you remember my paralegal Oscar, don't you?"

"Yes, of course. It's good to see you again." She reached out her hand and he shook hers firmly. "Hi, Stu. Thanks so much! The house looks fabulous!" Then she turned to David. "This is Agent Harding. He's the one I told you about," she said, glaring at the agent.

The men shook hands. "Marnie tells me you've searched the grounds and outbuildings, and that Detectives Gregg and Keller, and Agent...uh...Special Agent Patterson searched the house. Why do you feel a need to search the house again? Don't you trust other branches of law enforcement?"

The agent's face hardened. "No! I don't. If Sam Reilly, a known felon, is in this house, I will find him—not the detectives, not the DEA agent. Me!"

Hannah scoffed. "There is nothing worse than an inadequate cop. I did my research, Harding. I know you have fucked up many times, so now you're overcompensating. First, you report me for being mean to you, and now you are questioning two cops *and* a federal agent."

A look of amusement appeared on the lawyer's face. "Agent Harding, my brother, here, and my paralegal are Notary Publics. The three of us will join you in your search for your suspect. We will then provide you with an affidavit of our findings. Different to how you are used to working, but effective. You can open closets and cupboards, and look under beds and behind curtains, but you will not go through Ms. Reilly's belongings. There are four floors to search: the cellar, the ground floor, the second floor, and the attic. My brother is the contractor who renovated the house. He brought along the plans he obtained from town records. We don't want to miss any hidey-holes, do we?"

Harding let out an exasperated breath, but finally agreed with a hesitant nod.

Gram stood and cleared her throat. "Marnie. I'm sorry, love. I have to be gettin' back to the diner. But I'll be back tomorrow so we can have a proper visit."

Ellie jumped to her feet. "I'll be heading out too, but we'll talk later."

"Of course! I understand. I'll walk you out," said Marnie. "The knuckleheads need to go out, too." She turned to David; her eyebrows raised. "I will leave it with you?"

"Yeah. We've got this. Take the fur kids for a walk, and I'll be here when you get back. We'll toast your new house," he said, pulling a bottle of red wine from his satchel.

Tom recognized Lawrence Parish's white convertible as soon as he pulled up to the scene of the accident. He rolled down his window and stared out at the shattered windshield and the trail of dried blood that streaked its hood. Officers Cheryl Garcia and Drew Kriss sidled up beside his truck, both wearing grim features.

"Oh, God! Did Kitty Parish survive?" asked Tom.

Garcia nodded. "Barely. She was unresponsive when we arrived, but the paramedics did their magic. She's critical, but breathing."

Kriss rested his elbow on the truck's mirror. "The doc isn't in great shape either. His head and chest took the impact. Well, no impact. They didn't hit anything. Folks say he just slammed on his brakes. Nobody saw anything dart across the road in front of them. Might have been a bee in the car, but we don't know. The people passing them a mile up on the opposite side of the road thought they were fighting."

Tom rubbed his hands over his face. "Someone's gonna have to tell Kate. I'm thinkin' a psychiatrist would be best, cause I sure as hell don't want to witness that meltdown."

"Did you call Mr. Parish 'doc'? I thought he was in IT?" Garcia looked up into Kriss's face.

"Yeah. He was my mother's psychiatrist when I was nine or ten, then she started seeing Doc Ellis instead."

Lost in a memory, Tom thought of a time when his parents discussed Lawrence Parish in hushed tones in the kitchen. Did they mention Sophia Reilly or had they said Judge Reilly? He shook himself out of the past and joined the conversation. "I remember somethin' about that. I'll call my parents and see what they can tell me."

Danny and Chief Gregg approached Tom's truck.

The chief knocked on the roof. "One of you has to tell Kate Parish about her folks, and since she's your childhood friend, I have appointed you the deliverer of bad news."

"I thought as much. I'm takin' Carl Parkins with me though." Tom nodded. "If she flips out, I want someone who can talk her down."

"Fair point. I'll call her doctor and let them know you'll be coming out," said the chief, as he stepped away from the truck to make the call.

Danny jogged his shoulders up and down. "It beats moving Marnie's couch one more time," he said, trying to make light. "Hey, what do you know about Kate's parents? Good marriage?"

Shaking his head, Tom said, "No idea. I haven't spent time with them in fifteen years. I never liked them much. Phony baloney, batshit crazy family, if you ask me."

Chief Gregg returned, shaking his head. "The supervisor on duty says it's not a good idea to visit Kate today. She flipped out when her parents left the hospital a while ago. She smashed up everything she could get her hands on, including her ward. They've got her heavily sedated and restrained."

Glancing back at the white Corvette, Danny asked, "Since this isn't a homicide, do you need me? I'd like to get back to Marnie, if that's okay."

"Nah. Go on. You can help her hang pictures," said the chief with a snicker. His phone chirped, and he walked away to answer it.

Danny turned to Tom. "You comin'?"

"Yeah. I'm gonna run home first to pick up Gus' food. He doesn't like tuna, do you, pal?" He scratched the Lab's neck and turned the key in the ignition. "I'll see you soon."

"Hold on!" The chief raced back to the detectives and officers. "Lawrence Parish is dead. I've got Connor and Tartetto over at the hospital. They tell me the wife is awake sporadically. Danny, I need you to go to the hospital." He stopped to catch his breath. "Tom, this may be premature, but you have to chat up that judge who's always flirting with you. See what we can do to get a warrant to search their house?"

Tom curled his lip. "Ah. Really?"

"Look. I'm callin' this an attempted homicide. We have witness accounts saying the Parishes were arguing, and anyone who knows anything about cars knows a 1964 Stingray doesn't have seatbelts, but Parish had a custom seatbelt on the driver's side." Mac hooked his thumb back. "Your pal Rick, over there, told me the seatbelt is faulty. Whoever installed it didn't do it right. Maybe Mr. Parish believed he'd be fine to slam on the brakes. Maybe not, but let's have a look, huh? And decide amongst yourselves which of you will go to Pine Ridge. We need to find out what happened out there today. What pushed Kate over the edge?"

"Ha! It wouldn't take much for her to flip out. Anyway, I'll go to the station, call the D.A. and then call Judge Lawrence. Then I'll take a drive out to the looney bin." Tom's tires spit back gravel as he sped off toward the station.

"What do you reckon, Gus? Should we call Marnie?"

Gus thumped his tail, then jumped into the backseat.

"That's a no, then?" Tom asked. "You're probably right. She's got enough goin' on without this drama."

David retrieved his satchel from the coat rack. "Well, now that we've christened your new home, I better be on my way. If you have more trouble with the feds, you call me, right?"

Marnie raised her wineglass to her friend. "Cheers to you! Thank you so much for rescuing me. I wish Stu and Oliver could have stayed for a drink. I'll invite them when I throw a proper housewarming."

"Just let us know when, and we'll be here with our feedbags on." David chuckled and reached for the door. He turned back—his face serious. "Lock up tight, Marn. If Sam's still in town, he will be back."

"Don't worry. Danny and Tom shouldn't be long. Tomorrow will be a fluster of friends dropping in and out, so I don't need to worry about being alone."

He gave a satisfied head jerk. "Good. I'll drop by for a tour of the ranch."

"Done. We can have lunch and relax a bit more than we did today," she said.

"See you later, knuckleheads," David said.

Tater and Dickens poked their noses from under the table and flashed smiles at the lawyer.

"Ha-ha! Those two crack me up. See ya!" David stepped outside and moments later, Marnie heard his car start and the crunching of his tires down the driveway as a message bleeped on her phone. She picked up her phone as another message landed.

"Well, boys, we're on our own tonight. Danny and Tom have to work. How about I fix you two dinner? Want some tuna?"

The dogs raced out from under the table, Dickens spun in circles and Tater nudged Marnie toward their bowls, which someone had thoughtfully placed under a window by the back door.

"Who did that? Was it Tom? Or Danny?"

Tater barked and hit his food dish with a paw, sending it skittering across the kitchen floor.

-*Chapter 26*-

A warm evening breeze carrying the scent of lavender, sweet petunias, and peppery nasturtiums drifted through the open casement windows of the master bedroom. Her mind wandering, Marnie hefted a cardboard box up onto a deep windowsill and began unpacking.

The familiarity of the old ranch house was a comfort. A feeling of displacement had haunted her following the murders at her childhood home last Thanksgiving. Danny had certainly welcomed her into his cabin, but death found her there, too.

"Geez! The last three houses I've lived in have had death on the doorstep. Ken's, Mom and Dad's, and Danny's ... Huh! That's a thought that's going to fester." Tossing a sweatshirt onto the sill, she scolded herself. "Stop it! Let it go, Reilly!"

The French doors opening to the balcony were ajar, and a breeze brushed across her. Right eyebrow raised, she spotted a familiar face near the muntins bay window. She relaxed and smiled warmly.

"Mrs. Billingsly, I wasn't expecting to see you. Do you approve of the changes I've made?"

The spirit held out her arms, and Marnie knew she was home.

Tater barked in the distance. She crossed to the door and cocked her head. It was strange; she'd never heard this tone.

"Boys! Come!"

The Border Collie let out a howl mixed with a trilling whine; a moment later, his canine companion joined the chorus.

"Ah, geez! What has gotten into them?" Marnie jogged down the hall, stopping on the top step. "Tater! Dickens! Come!"

The dogs ignored her and continued their song, but it was the repeated thunk of a melon being whacked with a wooden spoon and the drumming of paws on timber flooring that sent her racing downstairs. Tater stood with his snout in the air, hackles raised—a mournful strain of his wails filling the room. Dickens scratched and bounced at the floorboards beneath the trestle table, his head connecting with the underside of the table each time he sprang up.

"Guys! Knock it off! We have ghosts. Get used to it." Marnie clapped her hands, hoping to pull the pups out of their current obsession. Both turned and assessed her, then continued with the racket. She crossed her ankles, sunk to the floor, and held out her arms. "Come here. Come get a cuddle."

The Border Collies ambled to her side; their scruffs standing at attention. Dickens stretched his neck over her right shoulder and placed a paw on her leg. Tater curled awkwardly into her lap, rested his head on her knee and glanced back at her.

"What's all the fuss about? You've been around spirits before," she said calmly. "Let's go upstairs. You can help me unpack."

Once she made a quick pass through the house to confirm she had locked all the doors and windows, they went upstairs to her bedroom. She organized their beds, so that Tater was closest to the door, and Dickens' mat was under the casement window.

"You two will keep out the bogeyman, huh?"

Both looked up at her with curiosity, then settled into their beds, grumbling to one another, while she continued her task.

Tom sat on a bar stool in the kitchen of his parent's summer home, allowing his mother to fuss over him.

"Thanks, Mom. Coffee would be great. I've got a long night ahead of me."

His sister Annie died as a child, the result of having run into the road and being hit by a car. Ever since that day, Abigael Keller had coddled her boy.

"Everything all right, dear? You look worried," she said.

"Yeah. I've got to go to Pine Ridge tomorrow to tell Kate about her parents. Her father died a few hours ago and her mother is barely hanging on."

Abigael's hand flew to her mouth. "Goodness! What on earth happened?"

Tom's father, Declan, came into the room as he continued.

"We're not sure yet, but the unofficial account is that Lawrence Parish slammed on his brakes on the freeway. Kitty flew through the windshield and his seatbelt failed."

"Oh, dear God! How dreadful!" His mother moved around the island and sat next to him, enveloping one of his hands in both of hers.

"Lawrence always drove that Corvette with reckless abandon," said Declan, taking a seat across from his son.

Tom nodded, remembering the many speeding tickets he had given the man. "Witnesses in oncoming traffic said they were fighting. We don't know if that's accurate, or if a bee was in the car, or what other hundred things could have happened. Anyway, I've gotta tell Kate, and I am not lookin' forward to it."

Abigael asked, "Will Marnie go with you?"

Tom stared at his mother, not believing what she had said. "Hell, no! I don't even wanna think about the storm that scenario would create."

His mother bobbed her head. "True. That pot would surely boil over."

"Ya think?" said Tom with a choppy laugh. "But, hey, I had a question. I remember you talking about Lawrence Parish when I was a kid. You guys were in the kitchen whispering about him, and I think I remember you mentioning Marnie's mother."

Declan and Abigael exchanged glances.

"You heard that?" asked his father. "And here we thought we were being quiet. What else did you overhear that you shouldn't have?"

"Plenty, but I remembered that conversation today when speaking with a few officers. One of the guys, his mother, anyway, had been a patient of Lawrence's."

Abigael said, "As I remember, Sophia Reilly filed a formal complaint against Lawrence about the way he treated Sam. I don't know if you remember, but Sam went to see Lawrence after that incident on that dreadful island. Colin and Sophia spoke with us often about him not sleeping and having horrific dreams."

"I didn't know about that," said Tom.

"Well, you wouldn't. You and Marnie saw Doctor Powell. We thought he would be better for you both. He specialized in children, but Sam was older. Sophia got Lawrence's details from a colleague who used him as an expert in court cases," said Declan as he got up to fill a coffee cup to which he added two heaping teaspoons of sugar from the bowl on the counter. "The Reillys became concerned when Sam's behavior changed, especially toward Marnie. Lawrence told them he blamed his sister for what happened that day."

Abigael put the lid back on the sugar bowl and shot her husband a disproving look for the unhealthy dose of sugar he added to his coffee. "It surprised us all. He was always so protective of her. That Sam could blame her for what that man did seemed odd."

Tom leaned back on his stool, clasping his hands in his lap. He stretched and said, "Jethro Barnes. Marnie and I were talkin' about him last night."

His mother gasped. "Why on earth would you two speak of him? Do you know how many sessions it took for you to forget him?"

"Nope. But I do remember it was fun goin' to Doctor Powell's office to color." Tom winked at his father, who grinned. "Mom, Marn and I are fine. We're all grown up. The bogeyman doesn't scare us anymore."

"No, but Sam Reilly does. I heard through the grapevine he's back in town. Are you two being careful?" she asked.

"Yes, Mom," he replied, trying hard to not roll his eyes. He sipped his now cooled coffee and steered the conversation back on topic. "Back to Mrs. Reilly. Tell me what happened."

Abigael looked at her husband, wondering where to start. "Well, Sophia asked Lawrence for the tapes and files from Sam's sessions. He refused, claiming patient confidentiality. Sophia, being a judge, knew she could have what she requested. When the person is a minor and the parents request the information, the doctor must give it. Doctor Powell shared progress reports with us all the time."

Declan added, "Colin went to Parish's office and told him to hand over the tapes and files or there would be consequences. He refused again. So Sophia put on her lawyer hat. When he finally handed over the files and tapes, several sessions were missing. He claimed water damage when his cellar flooded, but we knew better. In the end, the Reillys listened to the tapes and were appalled by Lawrence's method. They gave everything to Doctor Powell, and he suggested they take action. They did. Lawrence lost his license, and that is that."

Tom snickered and said, "Well, that explains Kitty's hatred for Marn."

His mother waggled her hand back and forth. "Hmm... I'm not sure Kitty is capable of hate. I think she would put on a show for her husband and daughter, though."

"Your mother's right. We went to school with Kitty. She hasn't a mean bone in her body. Quite the opposite. We jokingly called her Lin, short for linoleum, because people walked all over her."

Bottom lip out, Tom considered the new information. "That search warrant may help me find those lost tapes and files. I'll bet he's got them stashed in a hidey-hole."

"You're searching their house?" asked Declan.

"Yeah, once I get Judge Lawrence to sign the warrant."

-*Chapter 27*-

The whirs, beeps, and whooshes of medical equipment pulsed in the background as Danny patiently waited for Kitty Parish to wake up again. He had made brief eye contact with her once, taken aback by Kate's likeness to her mother, the same indigo eyes and raven hair. The horrid discoloration, lacerations and swollen features made him wonder if this was the karma doled out to a person who had been cruel to a child.

At the sound of a groan, Danny looked up to see Kitty staring at him. He saw fear in her eyes and he got up and went to the side of her bed. She reached out, and he gently took it.

"Kate," she muttered hoarsely, and then her eyes widened with recognition, and she squeezed his hand. "Marnie. I. Sorry."

"Shh. I'll get the doctor," he said.

Pine Ridge's supervisor sent Dalton Hooley home after the doctor in residence patched up his broken nose, put a dislocated thumb back in place, and cleaned the scratches and bites on his arms and neck. They told him to stay home for a few days to recover from the injuries he sustained, trying to restrain Kate Parish, who was now locked in the infirmary with injuries of her own. The super-sized ward had accidentally cracked three of her ribs in the frenzied throw of calming the manic woman.

"If she could break Dalton's nose and cause that much damage to a man three times her size, what could she do to us?" asked a petite nurse, who looked through the observation window of the infirmary.

A doctor in a white jacket and jeans standing next to her pressed his face to the glass, studying the patient. "Three and a half times her size, and I don't plan to find out. She's one-hundred and ten pounds, and lethal."

The nurse shivered. "Did you see Dalton's neck? She sunk her teeth in. Imagine if she had bitten into his carotid? Gawd!"

"I don't believe she could have done that. Dalton's neck is a mass of muscle. Although, if she'd had a knife, he would be in the morgue."

"Doctor, why does she have a private suite? I don't understand why she isn't in the maximum-security wing."

"Ah. That's easy. Money and influence will buy the finest suite of rooms. The powers-that-be here at Pine Ridge reprimanded me for my diagnosis of Kate Parish. I spent twelve weeks working with her. My findings are not wrong." He dimmed the lights and backed away from the glass.

The nurse joined him at the desk and asked, "What was your diagnosis?"

He paused, then decided the truth was always best. "She is a fucking psychopath. Be careful."

Danny returned to Kitty's room, having excused himself for the nurses and doctor to administer care. He carried a steaming cup of bad hospital coffee and pushed the door open to find a man standing over the patient's bed. "Pardon me. Sorry. I didn't know Mrs. Parish had company. I'll come back," he said.

The man didn't acknowledge the detective, so Danny stepped into the hall and leaned against the wall to drink his coffee. When thirty minutes passed and the man had not come out of the room, Danny peered through the window, but there was no one in the room—other than Kitty Parish.

"Well, that's weird." He raked his fingers through his unruly hair, wondering how someone could have gotten by him. He hadn't dozed off, and he hadn't walked away or spoken with anyone. Another peek through the window confirmed the man was gone, and when he entered, the bathroom door stood open—it was empty.

"Lawrence? Is that you?" Kitty mumbled.

The detective went to her bedside and looked into her searching eyes. "No. It's Detective Gregg. Was Lawrence here?"

"Yes," she said, before closing her eyes.

Danny dropped into a chair moments before a nurse came into the room.

"Detective, she won't be answering questions tonight. Go home and we'll call as soon as she comes around."

He rose to his feet. "Yeah. I that's a good idea. I'm so tired, I'm seeing things," he said, laughing.

"That happens here all the time. Don't you know? Hospitals are notoriously haunted," she said.

"So I've heard." He pulled out his card, handing it to the nurse. "I'd appreciate that call. Have a good night."

He called Marnie when he got to his car and explained what had happened. She wasn't surprised, but her exuberance about his reemerging gift sent shivers up his spine.

"Yeah. Let's not celebrate, huh? It's not a gift I care to nurture. I'll see you tomorrow. I've got to find Tom and give him a hand searching the Parish abode. The feds and our guys are still watching your house, but lock up tight and set the alarm. If we finish early, we'll be over."

They said their goodbyes, and he called Tom to tell him he was on the way.

-Chapter 28-

F resh from the shower and wearing pajama shorts, a tank top, and flip-flops, Marnie carried a cup of tea to her bedroom. She eyed the steamer chest holding Sam's journals sitting in one corner of her bedroom and decided now was good a time for answers.

She kneeled down in front of it and pulled up the hasp, revealing a treasure trove of childhood memories.

"Oh! We forgot about the treasure again!" She leaped to her feet and dashed down the stairs, through the living room to the study—the Border Collies close on her heels.

With a flick of the light switch, she took in the room. The built-in mahogany bookcases on the back wall were full of books and knick-knacks, broken down boxes lay stacked in the center of the room, a garbage bag of discarded packing tape hung from the knob of one French door, and several dozen cartons were yet to be opened. She walked through the piles, searching for her duffel bag, finally finding it tucked beneath the desk.

Tater scratched the floor and whimpered, then sat and stared at her.

"What's up, buddy?" She grabbed the duffel and crossed the room, inspecting a box near the spot the dog had scratched. "Ah! That's where the treats were hiding. Good boy! You can have one in the morning. You've had enough today."

Dickens followed his brother's lead and bounced, adding a whine for effect. Marnie gave in and handed them each half a peanut butter biscuit, but neither satisfied, they carried on whining.

"No. That's enough. Upstairs! Now!" She clapped her hands and led the way back upstairs.

Once in her room, she tossed the duffel on the bed and closed the door so the Border Collies couldn't escape. Now they knew where their treats were, they would be obsessed until they had a full biscuit. Dogs are smart and don't appreciate being jipped.

She considered the treasure, then the trunk and decided it was unfair to open the treasure without Tom. So, she sank to her knees beside the chest and rifled through to find Sam's journals. The books sat at the bottom, each in a Ziploc bag, each numbered, starting with one and ending with twenty-three. At a glance, the journals each had a hand-written message on the front cover. Number one's message read:

Dear Marnie,
Do not open! If you do, I will hide Mr. Monkey and you will never see him again.
Love,
Sam

She laughed and returned to the trunk to search for Mr. Monkey, her childhood friend and confidante, who she found tucked into a bag, which would have horrified younger Marnie. How could he breathe in a bag? She freed the stuffed animal from his plastic prison and thought back to a time when Sam had gone away to baseball camp. The pint-sized toy had hitched a ride in his knapsack, compliments of a little sister who didn't want her brother to be lonely. But all it did was anger him for the teasing he had received from the other boys and make her miss her brother and nighttime buddy.

Gathering up the journals and the monkey, she got up and set them on her nightstand. As she passed by the window to retrieve her teacup, she stopped to look at the view. It was 8:00 PM and still light, a lovely gift of summer. In the fading light, the figure of a man darted into the shadow of a big maple tree. Whoever it was, they weren't inconspicuous. She watched for a moment, but didn't worry. The custom security system installed after the house inspection was top-notch. If someone tried to break in, they would have a hard time achieving their goal, and they would be in for a terrible surprise. A blaring siren, an electric shock, and a cloud of pepper spray would make them think twice. Was the system legal? Probably not, but she and her dogs were safe, and that was what mattered.

"Let them try, huh, boys?" she said to the Border Collies, who curled their noses into their fluffy tails and grumbled.

Tom sat in his truck outside Kitty and Lawrence's Gothic Revival-style villa at 103 Palter Boulevard in a swanky section of Creekwood. Here the homes wore brass plaques detailing the year of construction. The Parishes said eighteen thirty-six. Headlights flashed behind him and he looked up. His partner had arrived; the search for Sam Reilly's files and other incriminating information could begin. They gathered evidence boxes, a camera, and a duffel bag from the back of Danny's Jeep and trudged up the flagstone path to the house.

"You should take that nice judge out to dinner," Danny said with a smirk as he and Tom entered the Parishes house.

"Nah! I don't wanna be the talk of the town. Stephanie's nice, but she is way too high profile."

"Ha-ha! And what? You're not? Geez, Tom, we're cops. Everybody in town knows who we are."

"Yeah, but we don't have to attend fancy dinners with muckety-mucks?"

"Hmm ... There is that," said Danny as he switched on the light in a grand foyer. "Where should we start?"

Tom glanced down the hall and pointed to the end. "Lawrence's study is as good as any."

"Okay. You take the downstairs and I'll go upstairs."

With a teacup in one hand and a journal in the other, Marnie read her brother's journals. On the one hand, she felt like she was invading his privacy, but on the other, she knew her mother had done this years ago, and with good reason. Books one through five were the ramblings of a pre-teen. Topics like baseball and girls were prominent, but so were activities their family had shared. He wrote about the adventures he got up to with his friends, and silly anecdotes about her. She set aside her teacup and rested her head against her pillows, trying to recall last night's conversation with her mother. The number twelve popped into her head, so she followed the advice and searched through the stack. The note to her on the cover differed from the books already read, and she teared up as she pulled the twelfth journal out of its bag.

Marnie,
Touch this and die!
Sam

The handwriting had changed too. She stood and set the books in order on top of the duvet, studying the change in her brother's penmanship. Journals one through nine were similar, but ten through twenty-three saw his writing degrade further with each one, and the messages to her grew more violent in ascending order.

"What the hell happened to you, Sam?" she asked, blowing out a breath. "Well, let's see if I can't figure out how to help you."

As Marnie tore through Sam's journals on one side of town, Tom popped off the false back of a bookcase in Lawrence's study on the other.

"Bingo!" He stared at a second set of shelves holding folders and VCR tapes. "Shit! Where the hell am I going to find a VCR?" he said to himself.

"Right there," replied Danny, pointing to a built-in television cabinet on the opposite wall.

Tom leaped, banging his head on a shelf. "Jesus! You scared me!"

"Come upstairs for a sec. I've gotta show you something." Danny disappeared out the door. "It'll only take a minute."

Rubbing his head, he muttered, "First it's a sec, then it's a minute." He skulked after his partner and raced up the stairs two at a time. "Whatcha got?" he said when he reached the top.

"You are not gonna believe this! Look!"

Danny was in the master bedroom, standing in the open doorway of a closet. Tom peered around the door and wrinkled his nose. "Geez! Like I needed to see that!"

"Who'd a thunk it. An entire room dedicated to their fetishes. But, hey, let's not judge. Gawd! It's gonna be difficult for me to question Kitty without my mind wondering which one is in charge."

"Yeah, and it's not like you can ask. Have you checked out the princess's room?"

"Not yet. You know where it is?"

"It's way down the end of that hall. I think they used to call it the south wing," Tom replied dryly.

"Where did their money come from? Was Lawrence pulling in big bucks from IT sales?" Danny asked as they made their way to Kate's room.

"Nah. Kitty's family is wealthy. They own the timber mill out on Loomis Road. Her brother, Preston Belmont, runs it now, but I'm not sure if she still has an interest. I know Lawrence and Mr. Belmont were at odds for a long time. They had a punch up at the county fair years ago. Lawrence took the first swing, but he didn't win, I can tell you that."

"We better call her brother. Things were easier when Captain Sterling was around. He knows everybody, and everybody knows him. He used to take care of all this stuff."

Tom asked, "You think he'll be back?"

"The chief says no, but it's only been six months. I wouldn't count him out."

Captain Pete Sterling had been the victim of a home attack last Christmas. Erin Matthews, a crazed confidential informant of Sam Reilly, had pushed him down his stairs, leaving him a broken man, literally.

"Well, here's Kate's room—at least it was when we were kids."

Danny opened the door to reveal a beautifully appointed room of soft raspberry with white ruffles, fluffy pillows, and dolls of every shape, size, and type. He spotted a curio cabinet of porcelain dolls and shivered. "Dolls are so frigging creepy. Why are there so many?"

"Ha-ha! Come on, I'll help you look around, and then I gotta get back downstairs to those videos."

"This doesn't look like a teenager's room, does it? I mean, would this have been the way Kate left it when she went off to college?" Danny opened a dresser drawer and searched through the contents. "These are kid's clothes." He held up a white T-shirt with baby pink polka dots. "There's no way she was wearing this in high school."

They opened the wardrobe to find the same thing. Then they opened the nightstand drawers which revealed stacks of crayon drawings and childish mementos of a Slinky, packets of bubblegum, and hair bobbles. The toy box held board games including Candyland, Monopoly, Trouble, Pickup Stix, and Barrel of Monkeys.

"This isn't right. She must've moved into another room at some point." Danny turned to Tom, who shrugged.

"This is the only room I was ever in. We didn't come here often. We spent most of our time at the Reillys or we were outside."

"Okay. I'll keep searching up here, and shout if I find anything."

"Same, but I'll be in the study watching TV," said Tom.

The deeper Marnie dove into Sam's journals, the sicker she felt, and she wondered who this 'Doctor L' was that he continuously referred to in his entries. She didn't even know her brother had been under a psychiatrist's care. Her parents and Tom's had taken them to see Dr. Powell after the incident on the island. But she couldn't remember Sam ever attending therapy. As an adult, it made sense, but how could she not know?

Her tea had long grown cold and her shoulders ached. "I'm going downstairs to get a refill. Do you two need to go outside?" she asked the dogs.

Dickens rolled to his back with a yawn, his front paws sticking in the air. Tater grumbled and curled his nose further under his tail.

"Okay. I'll be back in a jiff."

When she returned with a hot cup of tea, she found Tater at the casement window, his front paws on the sill. He mumbled a low growl, then turned to look at her.

"What's the matter, bud?"

His ears twitched, and he whimpered as Marnie joined him, looking out into the yard. The same figure stood to the left of the garden shed, looking up. She leaped back from the window and then calmed herself. "It's definitely not Sam. I would know him—even in the dark. It has to be a fed keeping an eye on me." She returned to the window and waved, then pulled Tater to the floor and closed it. "At least they know I know they are there. C'mon, Tater, hop up and keep me company while I read this last journal," she said, crossing back to her bed.

The clock read eleven-thirty when she slammed closed the cover of the last book. A wave of emotions moved over her; sadness rose to the surface and tears trickled down her cheeks.

"Mom was right. Sam's journals explain so much. Whoever this 'Doctor L' is, I am going to find him and make him pay for what he did to my brother."

As anger overtook sadness, her feet hit the floor, and she stomped over to the chest. "What else have you got in here, Mom?"

-Chapter 29-

"Holy fuck! You sick bastard!" Tom pushed himself up from a black leather recliner and jammed his finger onto the eject button.

It was 3:00 AM when the detectives had their fill of Lawrence Parish's twisted games.

Tom pulled every file and tape from the hidey-hole, chucking them into an evidence box that sat on the glass and steel desk. "I'm havin' a hard time processing this. What the hell did we just watch?"

Danny dragged a thumb over the five o'clock shadow on his chin. "That was disturbing, disgusting, abhorrent, vile ... Lawrence was a sick piece of shit." He stood and paced the room, then paused, locking eyes with his partner. "How are we gonna tell Marnie? All this time, we've believed Sam is a psychopath."

"I think it's a good thing Lawrence died today. If not, I would help Marnie kill him. And with a clear conscience." Tom clenched his fists, then in a frenzy of anger, swept everything off the desktop and onto the floor, before heaving the plush swivel chair out a window. "Fuck!"

"C'mon, Tommy," said Danny, moving to his partner's side. He clapped a hand on his friend's shoulder and bent to clean up the mess. "Let's get these files and tapes to the station. There's an old VCR in the captain's office, and I want the chief to watch this shit."

Tom snatched up a family picture of the Parishes and stared at Lawrence's face, then his gaze moved to Kate's mother. "There's no way Kitty didn't know about this. That fucking piece of shit filmed his sessions in this room. Look!" he said, pointing to the built-in, and the reupholstered sofa. "Same bookcase, same couch! How could she have allowed it to happen, for fuck's sake?" His violet eyes flashed with anger, and the muscles in his jaw bulged. "These people live in our town. How could this have happened? How could anyone brainwash and manipulate a kid like that?"

"Tommy, I'm not gonna tell you to calm down, but man, you gotta know we'll figure this out. We'll set the record straight. It's all we can do." Danny sealed the lid on the evidence box, wrote out a receipt, and pulled out his phone to place a call to the duty sergeant. "Yeah, this is Detective Gregg. I need a window boarded up at 103 Palter Boulevard. Can you get somebody over here now? Thanks, Sarge." After he hung up, he turned to his partner, who was still fuming. "They'll be here soon. Let's get this stuff back to the station and call it a night, huh?"

Tears of frustration teetered precariously on Tom's lower lid. Feeling a fool, he groaned, "Jesus! He was my friend, Danny. Sam was a good guy until that sick fuck played with his head and turned him into a psycho. I think we should go out to Marnie's and make sure she's okay. I've got a funny feeling."

"It's 3:30, and if Marnie needed us, we would have heard. Her place is crawling with cops, her alarm's set, and if it wasn't, we'd know. She put that app on our phones this morning so we could disarm the system in an emergency."

Tom opened the app and nodded. "Yeah. It's set." He glanced around the room. "We're coming back tomorrow with a team, and we are going to rip this place apart. How many other kids did that monster mess with?"

"You and I should step away from it for a day. We can have a team come through, but we shouldn't be involved. We are both too emotionally attached. Let's focus on Paige and let this go until Monday."

"Gonna question Kitty?" asked Tom, the storm in his eyes still brewing.

"Yeah. I'm waiting for the hospital to call." Danny glanced out the window and saw the team arrive who would board up the window. "C'mon. Let's get outta here."

Tom agreed and gathered up the evidence box, holding onto it like his life depended on it.

Officers Moretti and Stewart walked up the footpath as the detectives stepped onto the small veranda.

"I hate these houses up here. They're all creepy. I expect Dracula and Frankenstein's monster to come walkin' out of the fog," Moretti said, glancing up at the architecture. "It's like a scene out of a Lon Chaney flick."

"That's Glenn Strange you're thinkin' of. Lon Chaney played the Wolfman. Glenn Strange was the monster," corrected Stewart.

"The monster is dead," snarled Tom, pushing past the officers on his way to his truck.

Moretti hooked back a thumb and scowled. "What's eatin' him? He's usually the first to make a joke?"

Danny's eyes followed his partner to his vehicle. "It's been a long night. Could you guys go around the side of the house, get the office chair and then board up the window? Don't ask questions."

"Is Keller okay?" asked Stewart.

"Uh-uh! No questions." Danny wagged a finger. "Text me when you're done. Here's the key. Leave it in the top drawer of my desk when you're done. Don't check out the house. Don't use the bathrooms. Get the chair, fix the window and get out. We'll do a full search tomorrow." He walked off to his Jeep.

"You gonna tell us what's goin' on?" asked Moretti. "Do we need to keep an eye on the neighborhood for Break and Enters, or are you keepin' us in the dark?"

The detective stopped, pivoting back. "Don't worry about monitoring the neighborhood. It was not a B&E."

Once Danny was in his vehicle, Moretti nudged Stewart. "Five bucks it was Gregg who chucked the chair."

Stewart said, "Nah! Ten it was Keller. Did you see how red his face was? It looked like a smacked ass."

Sleep didn't come easy for Marnie. She tossed and turned. Her racing mind dragged her through myriad scenarios involving her brother, the mysterious 'Doctor L' mentioned in Sam's journals and the thick file of notes in her mother's handwriting she found in the false bottom of the trunk.

She pulled the soft cotton sheet over her shoulder as Tater sighed and nuzzled into her neck, breathing deeply in his sleep. Dickens lolled on his back at the foot of the bed, grumbling and mumbling each time she moved her restless feet. Tonight, she broke her 'no dogs on the bed' rule. The boys seemed unsettled after months of travel and the events of the day, so she rationalized a bit of rule breaking was in order.

Dickens jerked to his feet—his mouth closed tight—eyes trained on the bedroom door. Tater's head snapped up, his ears twitching. The Border Collies locked eyes, each letting out a hushed 'a-rooh'. Tater nose-nudged his mistress, who jolted up and listened.

Marnie slid open the top drawer of the bedside table and took out a canister of pepper spray. She swung her feet off the bed, pressing a finger against her lips as she tiptoed to the bedroom door.

"Shh," she whispered.

Both dogs cocked their heads in response and sat back on their haunches. She pressed her ear to the door. Soft footfalls creaked on the old oak flooring, causing goosebumps to prickle her skin. Her eyes widened as a sliver of light shone under the door and she stepped back, holding the pepper spray at what she hoped was eye-level.

The Border Collies growled and slunk off the bed when the doorknob turned. They positioned themselves between Marnie and the door.

"I have a weapon! If you open that door, I will use it!" she shouted.

The door opened a crack, and a gravelly throat cleared on the other side. Tater and Dickens snarled and lurched forward against the door, slamming it shut.

"I am not kidding! I will shoot!" she yelled, trying not to sound frightened.

"I promise not to hurt you. Please, Squirt, open the door. It's me. Sam."

Her mouth dropped open, and she backed away from the door. Hands trembling, she held up the pepper spray.

"Get. Out. Of. My. House!"

"Please, I'm hurt and I need to speak with you. I didn't kill Mom. Believe me. Please!" His words trailed off with a faint groan, followed by a sick thud.

With a deep breath in, Marnie closed her eyes. She focused on her brother, hoping to tap into his energy. Eyes wet with tears, she brought a hand to her mouth to stop herself from crying out. Her eyes popped open, and she rushed to her door, yanking it open to find her brother collapsed in the hallway, blood seeping through his sweatshirt. The dogs raced around her, sitting between her and her brother, but she scooted around them and told them to back up and stay.

Sam's flashlight rolled back and forth on the floor beside him, casting eerie shadows across his pale face. Marnie dropped to her knees and took his head in her hands.

"Sam! Wake up!" she said, patting his face, and when he didn't respond, she lay her head on his chest—searching for the thumping of his heart.

His hand weakly eased up and caressed her back. "I'm awake," he croaked. "Could I please have water?"

She bolted upright and tossed her blood-soaked hair behind her shoulder. "Sam Reilly, how dare you scare me like that!" As her face fumed with fury, a weak smirk slid across his lips.

"Water, please," he croaked again. "Then you can yell at me."

She jumped up and ran into her bathroom, catching sight of the blood on her cheek in the mirror. "Eww!" she said, grabbing a washcloth, wiping it away.

When she returned, Sam sat upright against the wall with both Border Collies growling into his face.

"Tater! Dickens! Come!"

The dogs obeyed and sat at her feet, but glanced back, keeping their eyes on the intruder. She went to his side and handed the glass to Sam. "Do you need a painkiller?"

He nodded, and she disappeared into her bathroom again, returning moments later.

Two bottles in hand, she said, "I've got Tylenol and naproxen." She waggled the bottles. "Which do you want?"

"Naproxen," he said, holding up his palm.

"You're getting blood all over my wall," she said and dumped two gel caplets into his hand.

"So, sue me," he replied, popping the pills and drinking the entire glass of water. "Can you help me stand up?"

"Why should I? You break into my house at night, mess with my alarm system, and scare us half to death?"

Shaking his head, he laughed. "I didn't break into your house, and I didn't mess with your alarm. The door was unlocked when I got here this morning. I left the poem on the mantel and hid in the bunker under the study until everyone left. Sorry if I dozed off because I feel like shit on account of the bullet hole in my shoulder."

"There's a bunker below the study?" Marnie gasped, then she offered a hand to help him stand. "You're not gonna kill me, then?"

"Not today. I'm too tired," he said, accepting her help and struggling to his feet.

"We'll leave the lights off, huh? There are feds crawling around, and I don't want them to come knocking."

"It's probably better if you turn them on. They'll think you're hiding something if they see activity in the kitchen and no lights."

Marnie pulled a face. "Why would there be activity in the kitchen?"

"Because you're going to fix me something to eat. I'm hungry."

The microwave clock read 5:15 when Marnie placed a plate of bacon and eggs and a glass of orange juice down in front of Sam.

"Thank you," he said, picking up a fork and diving in. "This is great."

"You're lucky my friends were kind enough to bring me groceries. Otherwise, you'd be eating cold pizza and drinking beer." She sat across from him, sipping coffee and watching him eat.

Tater's intense gaze followed Sam's every move. With the occasional rapid glance at his mistress, and his mouth closed, he assessed any danger this man may pose. Marnie saw his trepidation in having her brother here in their home, and fair enough. The last time the dog had seen Sam, he tried to choke the life out of him. But Border Collies have a capacity to reason, and they have compassion. The wounded man sitting here showed no signs of violence; he appeared calm, and his mistress didn't seem panicked. Tater bounced forward and looked up into Sam's face, who slowly lay out a hand for the dogs to sniff, which both did, and received a gentle ear scratch as a trust pact.

As the dogs settled, Marnie turned her attention back to her brother.

"I read your journals."

"Yeah. Where did you find those?" he asked.

"Mom had them sealed in Ziploc bags in a steamer trunk at the house. She said she was wrong, and I should read them."

"Wrong about what?"

"I wasn't sure, but now I think it was about you killing her."

"Does that mean you aren't afraid of me?" he asked.

"No. I have pepper spray in my pocket and two dogs ready to attack you at a moment's notice."

Sam looked down at the Border Collies, who sat gawking at him—both with drool running from their mouths.

"Ha! I reckon I could win them over with a piece of bacon."

"Sam, who killed Mom?"

His eyes met his sister's, and his right shoulder lifted. "I don't know. You and Dad thought I did it, but I swear to God, Marnie, it wasn't me. I was on the road, heading back to DC."

"Why were you angry when Mom gave me her car?"

"I don't know." He set down his fork and knife, looked over her head out the window. "There is something wrong with my brain. I have dribbles of happy memories, but violent recollections too. I have a small piece of shrapnel lodged up here," he said, touching his head. "Dr. Miller at Bayview said they could remove it, and the headaches might stop. He also told me I have PTSD, which I didn't realize. We were working on that." Sam picked up his fork and took a mouthful of eggs.

"Who is Doctor L? You wrote about him in your journals."

Sam looked up at her, finished chewing his food, and said, "You know, you still ask a lot of annoying questions." He picked up a piece of bacon with his fingers, broke it in half, handed a piece to each of the dogs, and then wiped his hands on a napkin. "Doctor L? That's Kate's father. Lawrence Parish."

Marnie's face contorted with disbelief. "Are you fucking kidding me?!"

"Don't cuss, and no, I am not kidding you. He's been my psychiatrist for years until last year when Bayview became my primary residence. Dr. Miller asked me to stop speaking with him. Why?"

A knock at the front door made them both bolt up from the table. The dogs barked and darted to the entryway, then turned back, awaiting a command from their mistress. The siblings stared at each other before racing to the study, where the trap door lay open.

"Hide. I'll get rid of whomever it is."

Sam scurried down the steps and pulled the door into place. Marnie kicked boxes over the hatch before walking to the front door with Tater and Dickens on either side. She peered through the curtain, shocked to see who was outside.

With a scowl on her face, she disarmed, unlocked, and opened the door.

"Ransom Elliot. What are you doing here?"

A strikingly handsome man of five-foot-eleven, with pale gray eyes, a sinewy build and short cropped blonde hair, stood on the veranda.

"Ha-ha! Marnie Reilly! You are a hard lady to find, and as gorgeous as ever!"

He reached out to hug her. She pushed him away, rolling her eyes.

"Pfft! I find it hard to believe that you couldn't find me. What is it these days? Secret Service? FBI? CIA? Mercenary?" she scoffed, backing away from her first true love.

Before she could stop him, he wrapped his arms around her, smashing his cheek against hers, his lips brushing her ear. "Play along with me, kid. I'm trying to save your ass."

The scent of citrus and spice hit her nose and then the warmth of his embrace dulled her senses to everything but the moment. It's funny how the olfactory senses work. Good and bad memories often come wrapped in the fragrance of a flower, the aroma of hearty stew, or the scent of a man's luxury cologne.

"Hug me back, Reilly," he whispered, and she did. "Now invite me inside."

She pasted on a smile, dropped her arms, and waved him into the house, then peeked into the early morning before shutting the door and turning the lock.

"What are you doing here?" she demanded, eyes blazing and fists clenched at her sides.

He moved swiftly through the downstairs, peering into each room with the skill of a seasoned agent. "Where is he? Where is Sam?"

"Tchah! What? Sam?" She dropped onto the couch and waved a hand. "Go ahead. Look for him all you like. He isn't here."

On his way upstairs, he doubled-back, and shoulders raised he studied her. His gray eyes read her expression and he pivoted back to the study. "Give it up, Reilly! I know you too well."

"Dammit!" she said, jumping up from the couch.

Ransom slid boxes away from the bookcase and pulled books from the shelves. "Which one opens the bookcase?"

Marnie laughed. "I haven't a clue."

"Bullshit. You know as well as I do you're hiding your brother. Where is he?" He continued pulling books, and then he turned around, his shrewd eyes inspecting the room. "Over here, perhaps," he said, stalking across the study and nearly running Marnie over. She stepped to the side at the same time he did, and did it again, getting in his path a second time—an awkward dance ensued. Finally, he grabbed her shoulders, picked her up and moved her out of his way, but not before planting an unsuspected kiss on her lips.

"Hey!" she protested, wiping the back of her hand across her mouth, before spinning around and growling at his back.

Behind the desk, a built-in bookcase stood empty, and he felt along the shelves until setting his eyes on the fireplace along the outside wall.

Marnie watched with amusement as he pulled, poked, and twisted the ornamental rosettes carved into the mahogany woodwork. Then her eyes widened, and she let out a gasp as the bookcase on the far wall sprang open.

Ransom heard her surprise. "You didn't know this was here?"

She scowled. "Does this look like the face of a person who knew there was a secret room in her house?"

"I suppose not," he said, crossing the study and disappearing behind the bookcase.

He came back a minute later, swearing under his breath. "Marnie, where is your brother? Look, I'll level with you. I know he's hurt. Let me help him and you."

Sam had his ear to the trapdoor, straining to hear the conversation. The voice was familiar, but he couldn't be sure. He closed his eyes, hoping his message would reach his sister. "Who is it, Squirt? Say his name."

Marnie shivered as imaginary pins pricked her scalp. "Ransom Elliot, get out of my house!"

"Huh! It still works. Thanks, sis." Sam smiled and pushed the trapdoor open.

Ransom, hearing the creaking hinge behind him, swung around and lifted the door.

"Am I glad to see you!" he said, holding a hand out to Sam, who accepted his help. "What are you doing here? I asked you to meet me at the old ranger station."

"It was crawling with tourists. I didn't want anyone to recognize me. Anyway, I was in a gas station up the road, and I heard a couple of women saying Marnie bought the old Billingsly place, so I came here."

Marnie's mouth popped open. "Wait! What?"

Ransom waved her off. "We'll explain later. We have to scram while it's still dark."

"Oh, no, you don't! The last time you rushed out the door, it took you ten years to come back. I want answers from both of you." A hand on her hip, she glared at her old flame and her brother.

Sam leaned against the desk. "Danny and Tom will be back before long, and you will have a never-ending group of friends trailing through today. I will come back. I promise."

She narrowed her eyes, not knowing if she could trust him. But he was right. Danny and Tom would arrive early, wanting coffee. "Fine. Go!"

Ransom tapped her elbow. "Hey, kid, I hate to ask, but do you have any cash? I prefer to not use my cards, and I didn't have time to withdraw money before coming here."

Her cheeks bloomed crimson, and she reeled around, thundered through the living room and up the stairs.

"She'll get over it," said Ransom.

Sam snorted. "Who are you kidding?"

"Does that room down there have another exit?"

"Yes. It has two. One comes out at the cemetery, near the back of the mausoleum, and the other exit is in a paddock. I don't remember which one, though."

"Okay. I'll meet you at the mausoleum in one hour. Does that give you enough time to get there?"

Sam scratched his forehead. "If I can get more painkillers in me, yes. I'm moving slower than usual these days."

"Slow for you is speedy for most. Don't worry. I'll wait for you."

Marnie returned with a wad of cash, a bottle of naproxen, and a first-aid kit. She handed half the cash to Ransom and half to her brother. "Sam, do you have a backpack? Do you need something to carry these in?" she asked, shoving the painkillers and first-aid kit at him.

"I'm all set, thanks. My backpack is in the bunker." He stared down at his feet, then looked at his sister. "I am sorry for what you've been through, especially for my part in it. I'm not taking medication prescribed by Lawrence, and I am not speaking with him or Kate, but you should know your name is a trigger."

"I figured as much. Remember, I read your journals. Do you need anything? Water? Cold pizza, perhaps?" She summoned a smile, though she didn't feel happy.

"Both, please. I never know when my next meal will be."

Marnie pulled bottles of water out of the cupboard and wrapped leftover pizza in foil. She placed the items in a cotton tote before returning to the study and handing the bag to him. "After I get groceries, I'll leave food and water in the bunker for you."

"Thanks." Sam turned to descend the bunker steps, but pivoted back, wrapping an arm around his sister. "I truly am sorry, Squirt," he whispered before leaving.

Ransom closed the hatch, then turned to Marnie. "That's a lot to take in, huh?"

"You should leave," she said, walking to the kitchen. "I don't want you here when Danny and Tom arrive."

"Ha-ha! Are you and Keller a thing, or is it Danny?" he asked.

"It's none of your business!" She whirled around. "My personal life has little to do with you. Please go!"

He reached out and gripped her elbow. "Hey! I'm not the enemy. My life was complicated back then, and you knew it before we got involved. I never made promises, and I didn't pretend to be anyone other than myself."

"Pfft! This isn't about you disappearing back then. This is about you hiding information about my brother. You knew he was psychologically flawed. Why didn't you call me? Why didn't you tell me he wasn't himself?"

"Ha! This isn't about me! It's about you, a psychologist, not realizing a sick shrink played Manchurian Candidate with your brother. Besides, I didn't know until recently. I visited Bayview when Sam escaped and spoke with Dr. Miller, someone you should call after all this crap plays out."

"Who are you with, Ransom?"

"I'm with you and your brother. I owe him. He protected me and Billy and got blown up. Sam wasn't a rogue agent. He knew who was, though, but wouldn't tell us."

"Billy?"

"Yeah. He got mixed up in some nasty shit. Apparently, he was a friend when you were kids. Billy Williams? You remember him?"

With a palm smack to her forehead, she said, "That's how he got my business card. Sam must have given it to him!"

"What?" Ransom pulled a face.

"He was murdered last year, and the detectives found my business card in his pocket. Maybe Sam gave it to him."

"Billy's dead? Shit!" Ransom brushed a hand through his short spikes. "I didn't know. Sam didn't mention it."

"Anyway, we can discuss it later. You need to leave before the detectives arrive. I don't feel like answering questions or lying to Tom and Danny to cover up why you're here." Marnie pushed Ransom toward the front door, as tires crunched in the driveway. "Shit! That sounds like Tom's truck. Go!"

"I'm parked at the top of your drive. Whoever it is, already knows you have company."

"I thought you didn't want anyone to know you're here?" she said.

"No. I didn't say that. I said I didn't want to use my cards. A digital footprint is what I'm avoiding."

The alarm beeped, and keys jiggled in the lock of the kitchen door. Marnie swung around, glaring at Ransom.

"If you stop looking like the kid who got caught with her hand in the cookie jar, everything will go smoothly. Leave it to me." Ransom left her standing with her mouth open as he made his way to the kitchen.

-*Chapter 30*-

"She's not out of the woods yet, Detective, but she is responsive. She might be capable of answering questions, but I'm not sure," said the nurse.

"Thanks for calling me and letting me in outside of visitor hours," said Danny. "I appreciate it when people work with the police."

"Well, don't upset her, if you can help it." The nurse opened Kitty Parish's door and left the detective to get on with his questions.

"Lawrence. Is that you?"

"Uh. No, ma'am. It's Detective Gregg. I was here last night."

"Oh. Where's my husband?"

Oh, shit! They haven't told her, Danny thought.

"I'm not sure," said the detective. It was all he could muster. Technically, he didn't know if Lawrence was in the morgue or autopsy. What he knew was Lawrence Parish was probably burning in Hell, or he was stuck in the in-between, as Marnie called it.

"Mrs. Parish. Kitty. I need to ask you some questions about the accident. Do you feel up to it?"

"Does my daughter know I'm here?".

"Not yet, ma'am. Detective Keller will see her today."

"Tom?"

"Yes, ma'am."

"He's a good boy, isn't he? Do you know his friend Marnie?"

"Yes, I do."

"Could you please tell her I'm sorry?"

"Sorry for what?" Danny eased closer to the bed. Kitty looked up at him, her eyes vague and watery.

"For so many things," she said through a sob, before covering her face with her bandaged hands.

"Ransom Elliot! What are you doin' here?" asked Tom, patting the Border Collies who met him at the door with waggly tails and smiles.

Ransom held out his hand. "I'm checking in on Marnie. I heard her brother made his way back to Creekwood. Why are you here so early?"

Tom shook his hand and glanced at the microwave clock, which read 6:15 AM. "It's not early for a cop. Truth is, I haven't really been to bed yet."

"Where's Danny?" asked Marnie from the doorway.

"Don't worry, Marn. He isn't gonna catch you dressed like that with your old boyfriend here."

Tom held up a brown paper-wrapped package and dropped it on the trestle table. "This was on the back step."

She glanced down at her pajamas. "Get yourself a coffee. I'll be right back."

After he heard her feet on the stairs, he turned to Ransom. "What are you really doin' here?"

"Like all those poor dopes out there on stakeout, I'm looking for Sam. I figured showing up early would catch him off guard if he was in the neighborhood."

"Uh-huh." Tom scratched his head and shuffled to the cupboard to find a coffee mug.

"What are you doing here so early?" asked Ransom, a hint of defensiveness creeping into his usual even tone.

"She makes great coffee. Her secret is Saigon cinnamon. Besides, she's my best friend. I don't need an excuse."

Marnie returned to a tension-filled kitchen and slipped her feet into a pair of flip-flops she had kicked off last night near the back door. She felt less vulnerable, having swapped her pajamas for denim shorts and a light sweatshirt.

"Did I walk in on something?" she asked.

Tom shook his head. "Nah. Just catchin' up. How'd you sleep?"

She went to the coffee pot and filled her mug. "Not great. I read Sam's journals last night. There's so much I want to share with you and Danny."

"Yeah? We've got things to share with you, too."

They paused when the power flickered, heads turned, and all eyes focused on the overhead light.

"What the heck? I just had the house rewired," said Marnie.

"Maybe a squirrel got fried on the line," suggested Tom.

"Well, that's not a nice thought," she said, crinkling her nose. "I'm taking my coffee out to the veranda. The dogs need a run."

They stepped outside, and the Border Collies darted past them, racing to the grassy lawn.

"This is a nice piece of land, Marn. I'm glad you bought it," said Tom.

"When David called me, I couldn't believe it. I've never decided on something so fast, but the price was right."

"It was a great decision. Look how happy the knuckleheads are." Tom laughed and sat on the railing. "You should have a housewarming party for the Fourth of July. Ransom, you gonna be in town long?"

"I'm not sure, but I can always change my plans for a party," he said, smirking.

Marnie stared at him. "I haven't even planned a party. Tom's spit balling."

"Don't worry, kid. I won't spoil your plans. I'll be out of here in a few days." Ransom sat on a porch swing and winked at her.

"Don't leave on my account." She rolled her eyes and sat on the railing next to Tom. "Any idea what time we'll see Danny? I need to go for groceries."

"Order them online. It's easier," he suggested.

She turned and looked at him. "Oh! That is an excellent idea."

"I have an account," he said, pulling his phone from his pocket. "Order it through my app and have it delivered here. It'll save you the setup time."

"Thanks, Tom! You know, there are so many reasons you are my best friend."

"Ha! But this means you have to cook me dinner. You know that, right?"

"I better order raspberries then." She laughed and started filling out the list.

"By the way, Marn. Did you hear about Lawrence Parish?" he asked.

Her expression soured. "Just what I read in Sam's journals last night."

"Ah! Well, this news might give you weird and morbid joy, then. He's dead."

Without lifting her head, she said, "That's a shame. Did Kitty join him on his excursion to the in-between?"

"No. She's in ICU. Danny's there now, questioning her."

She paused a beat before responding. "Hmm ... She's relieved. Happy he's dead."

"How do you know that?" he asked.

"Clarity," she said.

Tom let her reply hang out there and turned his attention to her visitor.

"So, Ransom, where have you been the last few years?"

"Here and there. Mostly there." Ransom took a sip from his mug. "Yum. Cinnamon really is quite tasty in coffee."

"Uh-huh. And what agency are you with now?" Tom looked at him over his shoulder.

"I'm not with any one agency," he said, staring across the lawn.

"Ah! So you don't have a badge anymore?"

Ransome pushed himself to his feet. "I've got credentials."

"Are they valid in New York State?" asked Tom. "How about that gun under your jacket? You got a concealed permit for that?"

"Yes and yes," he replied stiffly.

"A New York State permit?"

"Correct." Ransom stalked across the deck and nudged Tom. "Hey! I'm not your enemy. I'm here for the same reason you are."

"Yeah. Well, when I get to the station later, I'll be checkin' on that license and permit."

"You do that." Ransom walked down the steps, picked up a stick and threw it for the dogs, who ignored him and romped across the lawn after a ghost cat.

"There! Groceries will arrive at 9:00 AM. Thanks," said Marnie, handing back the phone.

She brushed a hand over her head and shivered.

Tom saw the movement and her expression. "What's goin' on?"

"Don't know, but I think Jonas does," she said, pointing to the man running across the field, arms waving and a look of panic in his eyes.

Marnie and Tom stood in the bathroom of the caretaker's cottage, staring down into a water-filled bathtub. Lanie Howard-Billingsly lay in the tub, submerged and lifeless.

"Geez! This is not what I was expecting when Jonas said she got hurt in the bathroom." Tom rubbed his hands over his face and swallowed the bile rising in his throat.

Marnie stared down at the woman, who appeared to be enjoying the luxury of a lavender-scented bath. With her face scrubbed clean of the gaudy makeup, she was remarkably attractive, considering the circumstances.

Tom slung an arm around her shoulder. "Marn, are you okay?" he asked, resting his head against hers.

"Yeah," she said as the numbness of self-preservation set in. "Oddly, death becomes her. That's the calmest I have ever seen her."

"I don't get it. People who get electrocuted don't usually look that way," he said.

"What if she didn't die in the tub? Someone could have killed her and put her in there, then thrown in the radio," she suggested.

"Is she tellin' you that?"

"No. I haven't seen her yet. She may not even realize she's dead." Marnie glanced around the room but didn't see or sense Lanie.

"I'll call Rick. You take care of Jonas, okay?"

"Yeah. I'll take him to my house. He doesn't need to be here for this."

"Good idea. Shit, Marn. That's two from our class in under forty-eight hours. I hope there isn't a connection."

"Did you have to put that thought in my head? Geez!"

"Mrs. Parish, what happened yesterday?" asked Danny.

"Lawrence was angry with me. Kate and I had an argument, and he always took her side. We were having a heated discussion about her behavior. The last thing I remember is telling him I would never allow our daughter to leave Pine Ridge. I don't remember the accident. Did we hurt anyone? Was anyone killed?"

"Why would you want Kate to stay in the sanitarium?"

"Detective, I want to speak to my husband. I won't answer your questions until I speak with him."

"Mrs. Parish, I regret to inform you, your husband is dead. He died yesterday when he slammed on the brakes on the freeway, his seatbelt failed, and the steering wheel crushed his skull and chest on impact."

With a sudden pang of guilt for the unsympathetic way he blurted out Lawrence's death notification, the detective placed his hand over

Kitty's which clutched the bed rail. Her mouth opened, but no sound came out. A wave of relief appeared to wash over her.

"Mrs. Parish, can I call someone for you?"

With a hint of a smile, her eyes brightened.

"No. Everything will be fine. Kate will never leave Pine Ridge, now."

"Mrs. Parish, I'll ask again. Why do you Kate to stay in Pine Ridge?"

Her gaze met the detectives. The pause that followed made him uneasy; she stared into his eyes, as if looking for something.

"My daughter is a monster. She always has been."

"A monster?"

"I'll make it easy for you and give you the clinical diagnosis. Kate is a psychopath. I don't want her to leave Pine Ridge for one simple reason. She will kill me."

"Is that right? Why didn't your husband have her committed years ago?"

"That's an excellent question. Perhaps Marnie could ask him."

Kitty has certainly found strength in her husband's death. Maybe she's a psychopath too, thought Danny before he said, "Yeah. I'll do that. I'll ask Marnie to whip out her Ouija board to consult with a dead guy."

"Isn't that the sort of thing she does?" she said. Not expecting a reply, she continued, "Could you please contact my brother and ask him to visit me? Tom will know how to reach him."

"I'll do what I can."

"My husband was here last night, wasn't he?"

"In a sense, yes."

Kitty peered closely at Danny, seeing the same haunted look Marnie's eyes held.

"I suppose you see them too?"

Danny lifted a shoulder. "Not on purpose. I'm not like Marnie."

She continued to gaze into his eyes. "Oh, I think you are. Tell me, is my husband here now?"

"No, ma'am, not that I can see."

"Good. I don't need that man haunting me the rest of my days."

"Mrs. Parish, what can you tell me about your husband's practice?"

"He hasn't practiced in years."

"Are you certain of that?"

"No. I suppose he has spoken to some of his past patients."

"How about Sam Reilly? When did he speak to him last?"

"Last year. Lawrence called him at Bayview last year, but he wasn't on the call list. He wrote to Sam, but never received a reply. Why?"

"Did you know your husband brainwashed Sam?"

She waved a hand dismissively. "Don't be absurd."

"Kitty, we found the tapes tucked in a false-backed cupboard in his office."

Her eyes darted away from his. "Oh."

-*Chapter 31*-

Thunderheads roiled above as big drops of rain slid down the windshield. Danny flicked on the wipers and glanced out the windshield at downtown Creekwood. The little town was awake and shoppers dashed under awnings to escape the rain. Others pulled umbrellas from their bags and continued about their business.

He parked out front of the station and scrolled through his phone to return Tom's call, when a knock at his window jolted him. Teddy Jones waved, motioning for him to roll down his window, which he did. With her tote bag over her head, she asked him if the rumor was true.

"What rumor?" he asked.

"We heard that Lanie Howard is dead," she said.

"What did I tell you about repeating gossip?"

The woman took a step back, feeling Danny's steely blue eyes burning holes into her forehead.

She tossed her head. "It's not gossip. We heard it on Mrs. Drake's scanner." She pushed out an indignant lip and turned her head.

The detective slammed his palm into the steering wheel. "Dammit! Teddy, I cannot confirm or deny activity at the ranch. Let's leave it at that. Please move. I have to get into the station."

Danny shoved open the door, nearly sending Teddy into oncoming traffic.

"You were much nicer to talk to before Marnie came back!" she shouted.

With an expression of disgust, the detective moved around her. "Grow up, Teddy. The real world doesn't revolve around gossip, and Marnie's not the cause of my current mood. I'm pissed because I live in a town filled with nattering busybodies. Go home. Lock your doors. Mind your own business and stop running your mouth."

The station lobby smelled like French fries cooked in old oil and dirty socks. Danny grimaced and searched for the origins of the stench. Behind the desk, the duty sergeant munched on French fries, but that didn't explain the socks.

"Geez, Halp, what stinks in here?" he asked.

"It's a bunch of teenagers waitin' for their parents to come pick'em up. We caught'em ferryin' drugs and tossed'em in lock-up. Why do teenage boys stink so freakin' bad? It's like old cheese."

Danny laughed. "I have no idea. Is the chief in?"

"Yeah. He and Cap are upstairs havin' a pow-wow."

"Cap's here? That's interesting."

"Nah. He brought over a VCR he had at home. The one upstairs is wonky."

"Ah. Okay. Well, I hope the kids get picked up soon. How can you eat with the stink hanging in the air?"

"Smells better than when drunks puke or shit themselves."

"Ha-ha! I suppose it does. See ya!" Danny ran up the stairs and entered the squad room to find his father's door shut. He stood for a moment, then knocked twice.

"Yeah!" boomed the chief.

"Got a minute?" he asked.

The door swung open, and Captain Sterling appeared. Dressed in cargo shorts, a Creekwood Police Department T-shirt, and walking shoes—he looked the picture of health.

"Cap! You look well. Good to see you, sir," said Danny, shaking Sterling's bear paw hand.

Sterling clapped him on the back. "You look like shit, Gregg."

"Yeah. We've got a lot of balls in the air."

"Don't drop them and get some sleep. Mac, I'll talk to you later. Let me know what you find on those tapes, huh?"

Mac stood behind his desk. "Don't you want to stick around to see what the guys found?"

Sterling half-shrugged. "I do, if I won't step on your toes. You're in charge."

"I think you should both watch them," said Danny. "The contents are disturbing, but it will go a long way to understanding Sam Reilly."

Mac's eyebrows shot up. "Is that right?"

Sterling huffed out a breath. "Will it explain why he murdered Officers Webb and Weaver? Or Ken Wilder? Or why he shot Jalnack and whacked Keller on the noggin?"

"We may need to take another look at that, sir."

"Why would we do that?" asked Mac.

"Just watch the tapes. You'll understand."

"Pete, wanna cup of coffee?" asked Mac.

"No, thank you. I can't drink that swill. How about the diner?"

"Great idea! I'll join you. We'll get coffee, have one of Margaret's cinnamon rolls, then come back and have a look."

"Ryan's Diner it is. It will be good to see your mother-in-law."

"Daniel, you want us to bring back anything?" asked Mac.

"No, thanks. I have to head out to the ranch. Give Gram a hug from me."

"Ha! That's not gonna happen," said Mac with an eye roll. "I don't need a frying pan to the side of my head."

Danny called Hannah on his way to the ranch, asking her if she wanted to meet him there. She confirmed, but it would be about an hour before she could get away. Next, he called Tom.

"Hey! What's happening? You didn't leave a message," said Danny.

"You got me on speaker?" asked Tom.

"Yeah, but I'm alone."

"Good. Lanie Howard's dead. The old radio in the bathtub trick. Well, that's not accurate. Blunt force trauma to the back of the head. Then the killer positioned her and the radio in the tub."

"Where's Jonas?"

"He's with Marn at her house. Rick's here now, but he can't tell us anything but what I've already told you."

"What do Paige and Lanie have in common?" asked Danny.

"Other than they both graduated with me and Marn? Nothin' that I know of."

"That sounds ominous." After a long pause, Danny said, "You goin' to see Kate?"

"Yeah, but not today. I called Pine Ridge, and the administrator said she can't have visitors."

"They know the situation, though, right?"

"Yeah. After her meltdown yesterday, they don't believe it's in anyone's best interest to break the news to her until they have her stable—whatever that means."

"Okay. Well, I'm on my way. See you in about fifteen."

"Yup."

"Jonas, are you sure I can't get you anything?" asked Marnie as she made herself a cup of tea.

"No." He sat at the trestle table, rocking his head back and forth in his hands.

"Do you want to talk? Being a psychologist, I'm a good listener."

Jonas' raised his head, his cheeks still wet with tears. "I want you to tell me who did this to my wife. Ask her who did this."

Marnie sat down opposite her friend and searched for the right words to explain how her gift works. "Jonas, I can't ask her. She's not here and I don't feel her around us. I didn't sense her or see her at the carriage house, either."

"Can't you call out to her? Use a Ouija board or a crystal ball?"

"No, I can't. Her spirit has to come to me, and it probably will when she's ready."

He buried his face in his hands and screamed. "I didn't mean it! I shouldn't have said it!"

Marnie shot up from her bench seat and raced around the table, placing her arms around Jonas. "It's okay. Take a breath."

He shrugged away from her and looked up into her eyes. "It's not okay! I have wished her dead so many times. She was horrible to me, Marnie! Every chance she got, she put me down and insulted me in front of our friends. I was never good enough—for her or her parents. That damn monstrosity of a house they're building ... I hate it. I never wanted to leave the ranch."

Marnie took the seat opposite again and looked him in the eyes. "Jonas, what you've just said to me, repeat it to no one. Not Tom. Not Danny. No one."

"I didn't kill her," he said.

"That outburst would certainly make you the prime suspect. You are anyway because you're her husband, but don't hand them a reason to arrest you, huh?"

He nodded and wiped his arm across his eyes.

Marnie held out her hand. "Give me a dollar."

"What?" He screwed up his face and dug a hand into his pocket, pulling out a crumpled twenty-dollar bill. "That's all I've got on me."

Marnie snatched it out of his hand. "Now tell me you need me to be your therapist."

 A light switched on and Jonas understood. "I want you to be my therapist."

She reached across the table and squeezed his hand. "Now that we have client confidentiality out of the way, where were you this morning? What time did you leave the house?"

"Same as every morning. I was milkin' cows at 4:00 AM. Scraped down the barn at 5:00. Fed the horses and chickens at 5:30. Then I jumped on the tractor and dumped feed in the pasture and checked the troughs. I was in the maintenance shed when the lights flickered. I knew somethin' was up. Your lights were on, so I checked on Lanie first. She freaks out when the power goes off."

"Can anyone confirm you were milking at 4:00?"

"Yeah, of course. Arnie and Elk were with me."

Marnie frowned. "I didn't hear any vehicles come up the driveway until Tom arrived."

"This time of year, they ride their four-wheelers over every morning. They cut across and check the fences along the way. In the winter, they come over on the snowmobiles."

With a light rap on the back door, Tom walked into the kitchen, wiping mud from his feet on the mat. Tater and Dickens appeared from beneath the table and greeted him with murmured trills and nose bumps.

"Geez! That rain's comin' down. Hey, Jonas. How are you holdin' up?" He squeezed the man's shoulder and searched the counter for the mug he used earlier.

Marnie pointed to the cupboard. "Get a clean one. I put the mugs from earlier in the dishwasher."

"Like the pans you used for the bacon and eggs?" He flashed her his *I know everything* look.

"No, smarty-pants. I washed the pans by hand and put them away," she said, avoiding eye contact.

"Jonas, can you excuse us for a sec? I gotta talk to Marn about somethin' in the other room."

"What's up?" she asked.

"Come here, please." He motioned for her to join him, a stern expression coaxing her along.

She left her bench once again, patted Jonas' arm on her way past, and joined Tom in the living room.

"What?" Hands clenched at her sides, green eyes challenged him.

"I know you didn't cook breakfast for old lover boy this morning. What time did Sam knock on your door?"

"He didn't. He was already in the house. After he left that slip of paper on the mantel, he hid."

Tom leaned forward, mouth open. "And you didn't think to tell me? Jesus, Marnie!"

His cheeks burned red, and she grimaced at his use of her full name.

"I didn't have time. Ransom was here."

"He helped Sam get out unnoticed while we were at the cottage, didn't he?"

"Not exactly."

"Then what exactly?"

"Come here," she said, grabbing his hand and dragging him into the study, where she pushed away boxes and lifted the hatch. "Look, Sam didn't hurt me. He's injured and needed help and painkillers for his shoulder."

"So he came to the one person he's been tryin' to kill for how long now?" He glanced out the French doors of the study, trying to gain his composure, when what he really wanted to do was throttle her. With a big breath in, he placed both hands on her shoulders. "I want you to listen to me. Paige is dead. Lanie is dead, and we graduated with both of them. I'm not sayin' there's a connection, but for God's sake, don't be stupid. Our friends are droppin' like flies."

"First, Lanie was never a friend. Second, Sam killed neither of them, and you know it."

"Marn, your brother is a fugitive. You should have called me or Danny, or even Hannah ... You don't make the guy breakfast."

"I read his journals, Tom. Lawrence Parish turned him into a madman. Did you know my name is a trigger word for him? That bastard brainwashed my brother to hate his family."

Tom put a hand over his mouth and calmed himself. "Yeah. I know. Danny and I watched the session tapes last night. They were behind a bookshelf in Lawrence's office." He looked away, the thought of the tapes fueling his anger.

"So you know, Lawrence was a monster." Marnie cupped Tom's chin in her hand and turned his head so she could see his eyes.

He stared at her and nodded. "Yeah. I know. Hell, I threw his cushy, pretentious chair through a window and shoved everything off his desk," he said, grinning.

Marnie held up her hand for a high-five and he obliged.

"Ha-ha! You know, if Sam showed any signs of violence or irrationality, I would have shot him, right?"

"Yeah," he said, giving her back a pat. "C'mon. You need to check on Jonas and I gotta go pick up Gus before he eats my kitchen."

-*Chapter 32-*

By 3:00 PM the rain had subsided and a steamy late afternoon brought out mosquitoes, black flies, and a rousing chorus from tree toads, whose rustic melody grew sweeter as the jug-o-rum of bullfrogs, birdsong, and distant moos of a cow joined in. Tom didn't notice nature's song—he was busy getting bad news from the sanitarium.

"Whaddya mean you can't find her? Have you called the sheriff and state police?" he asked, playing through the ramifications of Kate escaping in his mind. He listened to Pine Ridge's administrator explain to him that Kate Parish was no longer in the secure ward of the hospital and they have notified all local law enforcement. "Yeah, well, keep me posted and make damn sure your security team can handle her. By the way, can you tell me who's visited her over the last week or so?"

He heard the ruffling of pages and the tap of a keyboard before the administrator provided him with the names as requested, to which he mouthed, *Fuck!*

"Do you think you could text that list to me? Yeah? Great."

When he disconnected the call, he slouched onto the porch swing, stared at the rain dripping from the gutters, and made another call, but received voicemail rather than a person.

"Hey, Rick. It's Tom. Can you do me a favor when you have a minute? Check into a concealed carry permit for a guy by the name of Ransom Elliot. Can you see if you can find him in local, state, or federal law enforcement too? Whatever you can find is great. I wouldn't bother you, but you're better connected than I am."

Five honking white geese raced around the corner of the veranda. Their necks were outstretched threateningly as Danny drove into the yard.

He parked, opened his window, and yelled, "Get Marnie! Those damn things hate me."

"Ha-ha! Hang on!" Tom got up from the swing and called through the screen. "Hey, Marn! Danny's here and the geese won't let him out of his car!"

Marnie hurried to the kitchen with the dogs on her heels, grabbed a tea towel, and rushed through the door. The Border Collies and Labrador slipped past her and gave chase. One goose flapped and snapped its beak at Dickens and then Gus, but Tater nipped its tail-feathers and all the geese, deciding the cunning canine outmatched them, scurried back to their pen.

"Sorry. I didn't realize they were out." Marnie turned to Tom and grinned.

Danny emerged from the Jeep and gave Tater an extra pat for saving his life.

"Go ahead! Laugh! I hate geese! Those beady eyes creep me out!" he said with a dramatic shiver.

"You should feed them. That won over Tater," suggested Marnie.

"Yeah. Maybe." He stalked to the veranda, carrying three grocery bags, glancing back warily to see where the geese had gotten to. "I bring steaks, wine, and stuff to make salad," he said, holding up the groceries like a trophy.

"Are you cooking?" asked Marnie hopefully.

"Sure. Where's the grill?" he asked, looking around in search of the barbecue.

"I don't have one yet. I didn't have the heart to take the one at the house away from Patrick. But my gas stove has a grill."

"That'll work."

"Hey! We gotta problem," said Tom, standing on the top step.

Danny dropped his arm and halted—his expression clouded. "What now?"

"Kate's missing. Pine Ridge's administrator called to say they can't find her anywhere."

Danny cast questioning eyes at Marnie. "Have you had security cameras installed?"

"Not yet," she said. "The system I want is on back-order."

"Well, I suggest you install a system that will do in the meantime. I've got a guy. We'll get something installed tonight or tomorrow." He pulled out his phone and walked away.

Tom twisted his bottom lip in thought. "You don't suppose Sam sprung her from the hospital, do you?"

Marnie side-eyed him. "I wondered that, but if he's with Ransom, no way."

"Where's Jonas?"

"He drove over to Stu Bennett's. He's going to crash there for a few nights."

"Good, 'cause the three of us need to talk."

"Yeah, and Danny will not be happy." She looked across the driveway at the detective, who waved the bags of groceries around with every word he spoke.

"Did you hear that?" she asked Tom.

He paused and listened.

"Conk-la-ree! Conk-la-ree!"

He rolled his nose. "That's a Red-winged Blackbird, isn't it?"

"Yeah."

He glanced back over his shoulder and shivered. "Is that your brother?"

"Could be. I haven't seen one Red-winged blackbird on the property—yesterday or today. Have you?"

Tom said, "Not that I've noticed, but it has been raining and there's a swamp not far away, so..."

"What are you two gabbing about?" asked Danny.

"Red-winged blackbirds," replied Marnie, reaching out to relieve him of the grocery bags. "Let's go in and get a drink and leave the mosquitoes and black flies to chew on someone else."

The hum of the air conditioner grew louder by the moment. It didn't really, but the constant noise made it hard to concentrate on anything other than the mechanical thrum. Sam practiced breathing in and out until he found a relaxed rhythm. He popped more naproxen, but the headache persisted. *I am hungry*, he thought. Ransom would be back soon with food, drinks, and antibiotics if he could rustle up a contact willing to prescribe without a patient. He had a wide variety of contacts he could normally call upon for help, but there may be questions this time. Antibiotics usually meant someone didn't want to go to a hospital for varying reasons—most illegal.

Noise in the next room was driving him mad. The screech of children followed by the shouts of their mother telling them to stop jumping on the bed. Then the banging of the headboards into the wall. He counted backward from ten—then from a hundred, but the panic increased. He sat up, inhaled, exhaled and got up and went into the bathroom, where he splashed cold water on his face.

"Pull it together, Reilly," he said to himself, resting his elbows on the vanity—his head hanging over the sink.

In the mirror, he could see blood oozing through his T-shirt again. Ransom had done a decent job removing the bullet, but the bleeding continued. He checked the clock on the bedside table. It had only been a few hours since the bullet was dug out. Experience told him it could take a while for blood to stop. Until then, he would apply more antibiotic ointment and a clean dressing.

The beep of a card key in the lock announced Ransom's return, and Sam closed the bathroom door and waited to be sure.

"Hey! I'm back. I scored antibiotics from a lovely lady doctor who owes me a favor." Ransom set down a bag of takeaway burgers, drinks and pulled a prescription bottle from his pocket. "I'll be back in a sec. I've got other stuff in the car."

Sam stayed in the bathroom until he returned, on the off chance someone jumped Ransom and used the card to enter their room. The smell of hamburgers reached his nose—his stomach felt hollow and his mouth watered.

"Geez! I'm like a dog salivating over food. How did my life come to this? I want to sit in a café and have a cup of coffee and a piece of pie without looking over my shoulder." He looked in the mirror at a man he didn't recognize. "I need a shave, a haircut, and sleep."

The beep of the card in the lock brought him out of his self-pity, and he peered out the door. Ransom dumped shopping bags onto the queen-size bed closest to the door, then carried a grocery bag to the refrigerator.

"Thanks to your sister, you are all set. New jeans, cargo pants, shorts, T-shirts, a raincoat, sweatshirts, boots, socks ... You name it."

Sam stood in the bathroom's doorway, shaking his head. "I can't carry all that stuff when we leave here. My knapsack carries only what I need."

"You are staying right here until we have this mess sorted. Understand? You are not on your own anymore. Your sister will help. I'm going over to her place later tonight. I'll explain everything this time." He tossed the prescription bottle across the room, and Sam snatched it mid-air. "Well, your reflexes are still good. Take a double dose of those. Let's make sure gangrene doesn't kill you, huh?"

Ransom emptied the contents of the takeaway bag onto the dinette table. "C'mon. I got you a couple of bacon deluxe cheeseburgers, French fries, and a side of gravy. That's your favorite, right?"

Sam nodded, crossed the room, and pulled out a chair. "Yeah. Thanks. It smells good."

They ate in silence, savoring the comfort of the food and their friendship. As Sam's headache subsided, the flavor of the hamburger was better with each bite. He reached for his drink, took off the lid, and grinned.

"Is that a chocolate malted?"

"Yeah. I got strawberry. It's pretty good." Ransom sucked the drink through a straw and smacked his lips. "Right now, Sam, your life gets better."

"I sure as hell hope so."

"Oh! I forgot to tell you. Lawrence Parish is dead. I overheard Tom telling Marnie."

"Look at that. It's better already, but it is a shame. I would have liked to kill him myself."

"That's what your sister said."

"I wonder if the cops found Lawrence's session recordings. He keeps them in a false wall in his office and in a hidden room in his wine cellar.

"Want me to call Tom and ask?"

"Who's your source? That's what they will ask you," said Sam, popping the last bite of hamburger into his mouth.

"We could tell your sister and she could tell them she ... uh... divined the information."

"Ha! No. I don't think you should put her in the middle of it. She has been through enough without having to lie to the detectives more than she has." Sam wiped his mouth with his napkin and pushed his chair away from the table. "Thanks for that. Now, I need a shower. Did you get me razor blades?"

"In a bag over there. There's a set of clippers too."

"Why?" He reached up a hand and mussed his shaggy hair. "Do you think I need a haircut?" he asked with a laugh.

"I think changing the way you look would be a good idea."

"Hmm ... It's been a long time since my hair has seen a good old number three cut."

In search of the laundry room, Kate slipped quietly down the cool cement floor of a long, poorly lit hallway which led to the inner workings of the sanitarium. After all, she couldn't leave the hospital wearing an institutional blue nightie and cheap disposable slippers, and she certainly couldn't return to her suite. She needed something respectable and stylish. It was laundry day, so maybe she would find clothing of her own.

The *squish-squush* of rubber-soled footsteps alerted her there were others in the labyrinth the staff called "the dungeon" and she sidestepped into a doorway. A woman and man discussed her disappearance, hypothesizing where "that fucking psycho" could be hiding. The man suggested the air-duct system, but the woman thought the suggestion to be nonsense because they would hear her moving about.

Kate wrapped a nurse call button cord around her hands, readying a garrote in case they discovered her. Then she heard the man say he had release forms to sign upstairs, and the sound of his feet on the stairs. She tightened her grasp on the cord as the woman's footsteps grew louder—closer—then stopped. A phone rang, and the woman answered.

"Yes. Oh dear! I'll be right there."

Kate peered out in time to see the nurse race to the stairs at the opposite end of the hallway.

"Fucking psycho? They'll pay for that!" she said and resumed her search for the laundry room.

-*Chapter 33*-

Black flies and mosquitoes rallied around Tom's arms and neck, and one persistent gnat buzzed in his ear as he stood on the veranda, receiving an update from Rick Price.

"Okay. So I guess he *does* have credentials. I don't get why he couldn't tell me that instead of being a dick about it. Thanks, Rick. Anything new with Paige or Lanie?"

He listened, but the response wasn't helpful. Rick had nothing new to report. As the heat of the late afternoon sun eased, a balmy breeze blew across the pastures and the faint scent of clover danced in the wind. With a squeak, the screen door opened and three rambunctious dogs raced past him.

"Tater Reilly! You naughty pup!" Marnie pushed through the door, a tea towel wrapped around her waist. "God help us! He's learned how to unlatch the screen door."

"You gotta teach him how to make coffee next," said Tom with a wide grin.

"If he had thumbs, he would be dangerous," she said. "Come help me make a salad."

"I'll be there in a minute. I'm admiring the view. You know, I keep picturing it in the fall."

Marnie shoulder-nudged him. "Me too. It's our favorite season. Bonfires, mulled cider, comfort food," she said, daydreaming out loud.

He glanced down at her. "What's not to love about it? We should do a hay maze for Halloween and have Thanksgiving here this year."

"Sure. I think we will do something for the Fourth too. I know a guy who has a fireworks company. We can keep it simple and ask everyone to bring a dish to pass."

"I'll bring beer. You don't want me cookin'."

"Hey, there's Hannah," she said, waving to Danny's sister, who drove into the yard. "Huh. Gram isn't with her."

"Hello!" said Hannah, as she got out of her car. "Gram sends her apologies. She had an emergency at the diner. Dorie didn't make it in today. Something about receiving a terrible shock. I don't know."

"Oh, no! I hope she's okay," said Marnie.

Hannah shrugged. "I am sure we will all hear about it soon. I know I need a drink."

"Uh-oh! That's sounds ominous!" Marnie hugged Hannah as she reached the top step. "C'mon. We'll leave Mr. Keller to his daydreams of autumnal sunsets. Will you wrangle the pooches before you come in?"

Tom nodded. "Yeah, sure. I'll tell them it's dinnertime and they'll come runnin'.

Kate pawed through stacks of folded laundry, searching for a presentable ensemble befitting an escape. She grew bored with the selection on offer, then considered a pile of uniforms. Her eyebrows knit together as she pulled a doctor's white jacket from a hanger.

"This is a wonderful disguise," she said to herself as she eyed neatly laundered and folded blue hospital scrubs on a stainless-steel cart.

She quickly changed, leaving on her slippers, but hoped to find more suitable footwear. With her hair tucked up under a surgical cap, she peered out into the hall, then eased out the door and down the passage.

"There she is!" a voice shouted from behind her.

She whirled around to find two security guards running toward her, so she played possum, falling to the floor and curling into the fetal position. When they reached her, she whimpered and whined with all the sincerity of a spoiled two-year-old who didn't get their way in the grocery store.

"On your stomach, hands out in front of you, now!" yelled the larger of the two guards. She stood over Kate, gun drawn.

The second guard nudged her with the toe of his boot. "On your stomach." He turned to his partner. "Sheila, call upstairs. I don't have my radio."

Her gun still aimed at Kate, Sheila called for backup, which arrived quickly from all directions.

Six security guards stood around Kate waiting for her to roll over—none of them game to touch her after what she had done to Dalton Hooley.

"Guys, will one of you zip-tie her hands so we can get her upstairs?" said Sheila. At six-foot-three, she towered over the men, who had an average height of five-foot-ten.

"Oh, for fuck's sake, will one of you get a weapon on her? I'll deal with the ties." Sheila holstered her gun as two guards pulled their pistols.

With her knee pressing her full weight onto Kate's side, Sheila rolled her to her stomach, then positioned her knee on Kate's back.

"If you move; if you scratch, bite or spit on me, these guys are gonna shoot you. Understand? I won't put up with your crap," she said, grabbing Kate's left arm and pulling it behind her.

"One of you guys want to help me now?" she asked, looking up at her coworkers, her face pinched with impatience.

A stocky guard named Hank joined Sheila and reached in a jerking motion for Kate's right arm. "Ah, man. If she bites me..."

"I'll break her left arm if she tries. C'mon, now. Let's get her upstairs."

Hank grabbed Kate's arm and pulled it up and onto her back, and Sheila zip-tied the prisoner's wrists together. The guards got to their feet, and Sheila nudged Kate with her foot.

"Roll over, princess. You're going into a cell for the night."

Kate rolled herself into a ball and cried, so Sheila grabbed hold of one of her feet and dragged her down the corridor to the stairs.

"If I were you, I'd hustle to my feet because your head is about to be bounced up thirty cement steps. It's your choice, of course, but once I hit the stairs, I am not stopping."

The prisoner bucked, and Sheila let go.

Kate whined, "I need help to stand up."

"Nah. You can get up without help. Figure it out. You have five seconds."

Crocodile tears poured down Kate's cheeks as she scooted across the floor on her backside to the wall, then pushed herself up. She turned to the men, expecting one of them to help her, but they all backed away.

Sheila laughed. "After what you did to Dalton, don't plan on any of us helping you. If you were to fall down these stairs and break your neck, we'd celebrate your passing. Now, move it!"

"Oh, my gosh! This steak is so good!" said Marnie, running a piece of sirloin through the blood on her plate.

"I will never understand how you can eat it that rare," Danny said, his nose wrinkled in disgust.

She giggled. "Yeah, well, it's better than that hockey puck you're eating. Steak has no flavor if it's cooked too well."

"Tastes perfect to me," he said, chewing the well-done meat with gusto.

"Okay," said Tom, interrupting them. "Time to share between bites. What's everybody got?"

Hannah pushed a piece of red pepper aside with her fork and cleared her throat. "I've tried to reach the agents who were at the cabin the other night. Neither will return my calls."

Danny added, "Dobbs and Harding didn't seem all that switched on. I've never seen cops that unprepared or incapable. And I think Dobbs was covering up something. I think he shot Sam, but I think he lied about being ambushed. Why would Sam do that? He wanted to get away." He took another bite and watched the faces around the table.

"I agree with you, Daniel," said his sister.

Marnie wiped a napkin across her mouth, looked across the table at Tom, who nodded with encouragement.

"Well, I'll throw all my cards on the table. Sam was here last night. He's wounded, but he's okay, and he didn't even try to hurt me." Marnie took a big gulp of wine.

"He was here?" Danny's voice boomed through the kitchen, and the dogs fled to the other room. He dropped his fork and knife and flew to his feet. "Why didn't you call me?" he demanded before turning to Tom, pointing an accusing finger. "Did you know about this?"

Tom raised his hands in surrender. "Hey, I found out this morning."

"Danny, sit down, please. Sam didn't come here to hurt me. He needed help." Marnie took his hand and pulled him to the bench. "Please, let's talk it through. There wasn't time to tell you earlier. It's been kind of crazy."

"It's always crazy. Geez, Marnie, you had an escaped convict in your house and you let him get away. What the..." Danny stared down at her—his jaw muscles bulging; his blue eyes icy.

"Daniel, sit down. She is trying to tell you what happened, and I would think after my encounter with her brother, you would give him the benefit of the doubt." Hannah looked at him over the top of her rimless glasses.

"Yeah, but you aren't her," he said.

"Meaning what?"

"He didn't try to kill you. Look, we saw the tapes. We know what Lawrence Parish programmed him to do, and Marnie's name is a trigger!"

"Sam didn't use my name. He used my nickname." She reached for Danny's hand again. "Please, sit down."

"He called you Squirt?" Tom laughed, and Hannah and Danny joined in.

"Hey, it's no worse than Banana, Buck, or Gomer!"

"What?" Danny laughed and turned to Tom. "Who called you Gomer?"

Red-faced, Tom glared at Marnie. "A teacher who didn't like me very much," he said through gritted teeth.

"Ha-ha! I'm going to remember that one," said Danny.

"Let's get back on topic, please," said Hannah with a smirk.

Together, they reviewed through the pertinent details of Paige's and Lanie's murders, Lawrence Parish's tapes, Sam's journals, Sophia Reilly's paperwork and her visit to her daughter. Marnie also threw in an offhanded comment about the trapdoor and the bunker under the study.

They had very little to go on, but Marnie was sure of one thing: Kate Parish was behind it all.

"How can you say that?" asked Danny.

She shrugged. "Call it woman's intuition or whatever you like. She's up to something."

The chirp of Tom's phone interrupted their conversation, and Tom pulled it from his back pocket. He held up a finger. "Hang on. I gotta take this."

"Detective Keller," he said as he stepped out onto the veranda.

Danny nudged Marnie. "So, how long was your brother here?"

She jogged her head from side to side. "Hmm ... Not that long, really. I mean, if you consider how long he hid in the bunker, he was here all day. It should comfort you he had an entire day to do something sinister, but didn't."

"It doesn't," he said flatly.

Tom returned with a troubled expression. "They've got Kate locked up. I can speak with her in the morning, but Carl can't come. He has a conference in Hudson and he's on the road now." He ran his hand over his neck and glanced at Marnie. "Could you come with me?"

"No!" she said. "If I walk in there with you, she will implode."

"They said they'll cuff her to a metal desk."

"Oh. Well, I suppose that changes things, but I don't know how much we'll get out of her if I'm there. She might clam up."

"We don't need to get anything out of her. I have to notify her about her father's death."

Marnie cocked an eyebrow. "Don't you think it would be an excellent opportunity to make her admit she was the mastermind behind the Thanksgiving Massacre?"

"Ha! Is that what we're calling it now?" asked Danny.

"Well, that's what it was."

"And what about Christmas," said Tom. "After all, she was in cahoots with Grace Wilmot."

"We should dig into that a bit more," said Danny, thinking of the woman who they arrested last year for poisoning people, killing her husband, and trafficking drugs via a well-planned and diabolical scheme.

"Ugh! The last eighteen months have been a shitstorm," said Marnie, rubbing her temples.

"You think?" said Tom.

"For the fun of it, let's recap. Sam and Kate killed Ken Wilder and tried to frame me by stuffing his nearly decapitated body in my father's shed. When that didn't work, they killed Webb and Weaver, knocked out Tom, shot Jalnack and then Sam tried to strangle poor Tater. Enter Erin Matthews and the Christmas caper—bad name, but alliteration... Erin was definitely in cahoots with Grace, but she also claimed she was working with Sam. I don't think so and I believe if I can talk to my brother again, we will find out what happened.

He hadn't gone into Bayview yet, and he was still speaking with Lawrence. You guys should call Dr. Miller at Bayview and ask him about Sam. Kate's involved somehow. I know she is!"

Danny studied her. "Do you know where Sam is?"

"No," she said, looking him in the eyes.

Tom snapped his fingers. "But Ransom Elliot does."

Hannah frowned. "Who is Ransom Elliot?"

"Marnie's old flame. He was here this morning."

Danny angled his head and stared intently at his girlfriend, whose cheeks flamed crimson. "Is that right? What was he doing here?"

Tom dropped his friend in shit, and like a gentleman, he offered her a hand and pulled her out. "He's also the US Marshal who collected Sam. I'm not sure where he took him, but it can't be that hard to find out. By the way, both Paige and Lanie visited Kate recently."

Marnie sat back and steepled her fingers. "The plot thickens."

To which Tom added, "Mwahaha!"

Settled into her cell, Kate put a list together of the people she wanted to harm. Marnie was not at the tippy-top of her list, but the security guards, Sheila, and Hank, were. In her twisted mind, she exacted revenge, starting with a garrote and other grotesque murder methods, until ending with a twelve-inch blade slicing through their throats. Curled on her side with the covers pulled up snug, she fantasized about the remaining people on her long list.

"I'll keep you for last Marnie, your little dogs too," she whispered.

Danny handed a coffee to Tom. "Do you have the complete list of Kate's visitors?"

"Yeah. On my phone. I'll send it to you. We'll have to check in with everyone to see if they're okay."

Danny agreed. "We can have Garcia do welfare checks tomorrow."

Marnie got up from the table and said, "C'mon, knuckleheads. You haven't been out in a while. Let's get some air," she said, holding the door for the dogs.

Hannah glanced at her watch. "I better get moving."

They gathered on the veranda to say their goodnights to Hannah, and to wait while the dogs completed their nightly bathroom wander and dirt kicking. To the chirps of crickets and jug-o-rums of the bullfrogs, they sat and watched as twilight became night.

"Hey, Marnie, look over there," said Danny, pointing at the potting shed. "Do you see that? There's a woman over there. Real or not real?" he asked, squinting into the night.

She turned to the woman, then waved, and the woman waved back.

"Not real. See the faint cloudiness around her? It's not always there, but that's a sure sign it's a spirit."

"I see it!" he said, his face lit up. "Thanks! That's amazing."

Tom stared at them, his mouth askew. "Freaks," he said, and returned to the kitchen, slamming the screen door behind him.

Both chuckled, then turned back to the woman.

"Who is she?" asked Danny.

"I think her name is Elanor. She worked for the Billingslys taking care of the veggie patch and the cooking. She was lovely."

"Hey, I like this swing," said Danny, pushing back with his toes. "I bet I could build one for the lawn, if you wanted."

Marnie nodded and rested her head on his shoulder. "That would be nice. We could put a retractable sunshade over it, couldn't we?"

"Yeah. If I build a big enough stand, for sure."

"Are you staying here tonight?"

"If that's okay with you," he said, taking her hand.

"That's perfect for me. C'mon," she said, getting to her feet. "Let's get the kitchen cleaned up so we don't have to do it in the morning."

Sam lay on the comfy bed, pillows propped behind his head, watching the local news, surprised there was no mention of him. The beep of the keycard in the door caused him to leap to his feet and run to the safety of the bathroom.

Ransom called out, "Hey, I'm back."

Sam stuck his head out the door, a sheepish grin tugging at the corner of his mouth. "Every time I hear that keycard, I panic. Did you see my sister?"

"Nope. She's got company. Tom and another dude."

"Ha-ha! That other dude is Danny, her boyfriend."

"Yeah. I don't think I like him."

"You left her; she didn't leave you," said Sam.

Ransom sighed. "I know. Probably the dumbest thing I've ever done, but my career had to come first."

Sam shrugged. "Choices, my friend. Some drop you on a breezy path, some drop you in shit, others rip out your heart."

-*Chapter 34*-

"Gawd! I dread seeing Kate today!" Marnie whined to the dogs, who sat waiting for a morning treat.

The clock on the microwave read 5:00 AM as she handed over a peanut butter biscuit to each of her dogs. Tater patted her knee with his paw as a thank you; Dickens grumbled and nudged her with his nose. Gus asked for another, which Marnie agreed to after pouring herself a coffee.

The screen door squeaked open, and they all stepped out into the dewy morning. The dogs raced onto the lawn while Marnie curled up on the swing, feet tucked beneath her. Hands wrapped around her cup to chase away the morning chill, she rested her head against the seat back, closed her eyes, and breathed in the scent of lavender.

The door squawked open, Marnie opened her eyes, and Tom appeared, hair tousled, coffee in hand. He opted for a seat on the railing and leaned against a pillar.

"It's so quiet," he said. "You know, I'm gonna sell my house and move out here with you."

"Okay. We'll build you a nice place down by the creek where you can fish out your back door. How does that sound?"

"Like heaven," he said with a dreamy smile.

"Done. I'll talk to an architect and get plans drawn up."

"Ha-ha!"

"You think I'm kidding?" she asked, eyebrows raised.

"Nope. But do you really want me livin' in your backyard?" He scooted around so he could see the dogs.

"Why not? When you consider how often we see each other, living here makes sense. Think of all the gas money you could save."

"We gotta go see the princess today. I feel sick thinkin' about it. How are you feelin'?"

She scowled. "I'd rather be lit on fire."

Danny poked his head out the door, wagging the coffee pot. "Refill, anyone?"

"No, thanks," said Marnie and Tom in unison.

He joined them a moment later and sat with Marnie on the swing.

"What time are you seeing Kate?"

Tom said, "9:30."

Danny took a sip of coffee. "I'm going to see Rick about Paige and Lanie, and I'll talk to Garcia about the welfare checks. I guess we'll have her ask Kate's visitors if everything's okay and if they have anything out of the ordinary to report. Sound good?"

"Yeah, but we gotta be careful. We don't wanna scare people. We don't want Garcia sayin' anything about visiting Kate. That'll open a can of worms. I think we should focus on illegal drug activity in the neighborhood and kids actin' weird. That's all over the news, so it's a good cover."

"Works for me." Danny looked up at the sky and whistled. "Will you look at that sunrise?"

A palette of pinks, oranges, and flaming red spread across the horizon, the sun a stunning sphere of tangerine. Clouds plumed above, heavy with rain.

Marnie frowned. "Hmm ... A storm will probably kick up as we drive through the gates of Pine Ridge."

"Where are you going today?" asked Sam from the bathroom doorway.

Ransom sat at the dinette table, flipping through a file. He glanced up and, removing a pen from between his lips, he asked, "Should I pay a visit to Kate Parish? I'm asking because maybe she can answer some questions about last Christmas."

"She will tell you the same thing she has been telling anyone who will listen. I coerced her."

"How do you think it played out? You've never been the sort to blame others, so I'm curious."

Sam wiped his mouth on a napkin. "I think Lawrence Parish devised the entire plan."

"What makes you say that?"

"I have a cache of journals hidden in a cave near Danny Gregg's cabin. Some are from my time with the FBI. One is from a year ago. When I read them, I see many disturbing things. It is as if there are two versions of me. The person I am when I am seeking counsel from Lawrence, and who I am when I work through things on my own or with the help of others."

"Like Dr. Jekyll and Mr. Hyde?"

"No. We both know I can kill someone. My federal government training assured I could."

"Yeah. Okay."

"Killing someone for sport or because I want another man's money? Does that sound like the guy you worked with?"

"No, it doesn't. But that shrapnel in your brain might explain the mood swings."

"Dr. Miller said it wouldn't. He told me not to speak with Lawrence and to never again take any medication he gave me."

"Didn't Parish lose his medical license? How was he prescribing drugs?"

"He mailed them to me or we would meet up, or he would give them to Kate and she would pass them along."

"So you don't know what you were taking?"

"Nope. Silly me. Choices," said Sam, hanging his head.

"When did you start sessions with Lawrence?"

"When I was thirteen."

"And when did you stop?"

"Tenth grade, but I never stopped speaking with him. Lawrence has been in my life on and off for a long time, and when I wasn't talking to him, I was speaking with Kate."

"Let me ask this. Why does your face change when I say your sister's name?"

"Her name is a trigger. And so is my mother's name. Even saying 'mom' makes me feel like tearing this room apart. I won't, but I could. Dr. Miller helped me understand the programming of my mind."

"So, when you were in the FBI, you didn't have contact with him?"

Sam said, "Minimal. Only when I would go home to visit."

"What about college?"

"Same, although Kate would visit me and I would talk to her father on the phone."

"Huh. Dr. Frankenstein and his daughter created a monster?" suggested Ransom.

"I think the Doctor had a hand in his daughter's psychosis too."

"Pine Ridge is eerie when it rains," said Marnie, staring out at the slate-gray Federal-style hospital with outcroppings of newer architecture added to keep up with the growing numbers of patients and inmates.

As she predicted, the sky opened to a downpour of rain and flashes of lightning as they drove through the gates.

"Yeah. Like somethin' out of a horror movie," said Tom.

"It's hard to believe this was a hotel back in the 1800s. To think that it catered to the rich and fabulous back then and now it separates the criminally insane from the rest of us."

Marnie admired the perfectly manicured lawns, tidy garden beds, and walking paths.

"It beats me why they always use the prettiest chunks of real estate to house prisoners and loons," said Tom. "Look at all that waterfront wasted."

"Water is soothing. Just because they made mistakes doesn't mean they are irredeemable."

He shot her a dirty look. "You think Kate is redeemable?"

She twisted her mouth. "Well, maybe not her."

"What about your brother?"

"The jury is still out."

Tom parked the car in the visitor lot and they trudged up the footpath through the main door. After a series of checks, including a metal detector, they entered a long hallway and Marnie wrinkled her nose.

"I hate that smell," she said.

"I'm used to it. The lobby of the station ain't no bed of roses. But I hate coming to places like this. No phone. No gun. I feel naked."

Marnie laughed. "Thanks for that visual. Okay. We're supposed to go to the visitor's desk."

"Yeah. It's up here. Her ward will take us to her. How do you like that? Her ward makes it sound like she's a celebrity or somethin'."

When they reached the desk, Dalton Hooley stood to the left side, waiting to escort them to their meeting with Kate.

The big man offered a shovel sized hand to Tom. "I'm Dalton. I'll take you to Miss Kate."

At six-foot-five-and-a-half-inches tall, it was rare for Tom to look up to greet someone, but he did just that as he shook Dalton's hand.

"What did you do to yourself?" asked Tom.

"Ah, a minor accident. Please come this way," he said, completely ignoring Marnie.

"This is Marnie Reilly. She's a psychologist. I thought she would be helpful in understanding Kate's state of mind. You know why we're here?"

Dalton said, "Yeah. I know why you're here. You're going to tell Miss Kate her father died. But bringing her along wasn't a good idea. Miss Kate doesn't like her. It could create a problem."

Marnie's mouth dropped open. "Miss Kate tried to kill me."

"There are three sides to every story, ma'am. I'm not here to judge. I'm here to make sure Miss Kate remains in a supportive environment."

Tom said, "We'll do what we can to not upset her. Under the circumstances, though, that may be difficult."

"Understood. Should I remain in the room?"

Tom said, "No. I don't think that's necessary." Then he asked Marnie, "Do you?"

"We should be okay. Just don't use my name."

Tom nodded. "Could it trigger her?"

"Let's not find out, huh?"

"You got it."

When they reached the door, Dalton leaned on the door. "I'll be right outside. If I hear raised voices, I will enter and remove you. Do you understand?"

Tom stretched himself up to his full height. "Listen, Dalton, remember three things," he said, counting off the list on his fingers. "I'm a cop. Ms. Reilly is a psychologist. Kate Parish is the prisoner."

Dalton nodded. "I am aware."

Marnie looked up into the big man's broken and lacerated face. "Did Kate do that to you?"

Stone-faced, and without answering, he opened the door and stepped aside.

Tom peered inside to find Kate draped across a chaise lounge with her nose in a book. He stepped back into the hall, pulling the door closed behind him.

"Why isn't she restrained? They told me we would meet in the security wing."

"Under the circumstances, her doctor thought her suite would be a comfort," said Dalton.

Marnie wrapped a hand around Tom's wrist. "It'll be fine. We'll tell her about her father and leave."

Tom stretched his neck and back, allowing the feeling of dread to pass. "Yeah. Okay, but you stay next to me. Don't go near her, okay? And stay close to the door."

With a curt nod, she gave his arm a squeeze and followed him into the room.

Two coffees in hand, Danny walked into Rick Price's office. The latter sat with his feet on his desk, an open folder in his lap. He pulled off his glasses when he saw the detective.

"What's up, Danny?"

The detective held out a coffee and took a seat in the visitor's chair.

"Is coffee still the going rate for information?"

Rick laughed. "Yeah. That'll buy you what little I've got."

"Nothing new, forensically speaking, on Paige and Lanie?"

"Nope. Nothing new on either. Is Sam Reilly good for them?"

"That would make it easy, but no."

"Really? Huh. That's a surprise."

Danny drummed long fingers on his paper coffee cup, then asked, "If I needed information from Sam's doctor at the prison, could you get that for me?"

"Why don't you call?"

"Your MD status might get it quicker."

"What are you looking for?"

"Everything," said Danny, getting to his feet.

"Okay. Give me a couple of hours. I've got a few things to clear off my desk."

"I'll be back in three," he said and headed to the door.

"With coffee!" yelled Rick.

Danny sat in his Jeep, looking up at the storm clouds circling the town. A jagged streak of light pulsed across the sky, filling the air with the crackling electricity and the sweet scent of ozone. He usually loved a good summer storm, but chain lightning made him nervous for his home nestled amongst old-growth trees.

"Who killed Paige and Lanie?" he asked himself, pulling his notebook from the back pocket of his jeans, thinking through the events.

The detective believed that bad things happen threes and so he began a list of current catastrophes.

Lawrence, Paige, and Lanie. That's three. Do I count Lawrence? He did that to himself, so it shouldn't count. What about Sam and Dobbs getting shot?

His mind traveled back to last year. On Christmas Day, he had a count of two, then Sam broke out of prison, so that made three. Then Marnie left, and the cycle started again. Hannah broke up with Tom. That made two. Paige made three. A new cycle began with Lanie. Two more. Wait! Hannah's ankle. One more. Shit!

"Kate! We know you can hear us. Put down your book and pay attention," said Tom.

She turned another page and straightened a pink throw across her knees.

"This is good, Tom," said Marnie, nudging him with her shoulder. "Reading is cathartic for people in prison. You know, they need something to do so they don't go batshit crazy. Oh! Wait! Kate *is* batshit crazy."

Kate's gaze shifted to Marnie, a deep frown etching her face.

"Bait and hook. There you go, she can hear us." Marnie glanced up at Tom, who was trying not to react to his friend's childish, but effective, antics.

"What do you want?" demanded Kate.

Tom stepped forward, his eyes meeting the prisoner's. "Kate, I regret to inform you that your father died in a car accident two nights ago. Your mother was with him and remains in critical condition at the hospital."

If Kate registered what Tom had said, her face didn't show it. She set her book on her designer table and gracefully placed her feet on the floor.

"That would explain why I haven't seen them," she said matter-of-factly.

"Yes," said Tom.

"Why did you bring her with you?" she asked, wagging a finger at Marnie.

"Ma ... She's a psychologist and to be honest, I wasn't keen on being alone with you."

An evil sneer marred Kate's stunning face. "Are you afraid of me?"

"Nah. You're a liar and she's my witness."

Kate stood and slunk toward Marnie. "Well, now I know how you must have felt when your father died."

Marnie eased back a step. "I'm sorry for your loss. I know you were close to your father."

"What's the matter with you two? You act like I'm the bogeyman. Boo!" She leaped forward, hands clawed, then waved them off when they didn't flinch. "By the way, I heard from Lanie that Sam is in town. Let him know I would love to see him. I'll put him on my approved visitors list, which neither of you is on."

She pranced around the suite, straightening fluffy throws and looking at herself in the long windows.

"Isn't my new dress gorgeous? Father bought it for me before he died."

Tom and Marnie exchanged a wary glance.

"I see that you still have a poor sense of fashion, Marnie. What is that get-up? I think you take being a tomboy a bit too far."

"You are welcome to your opinion." Marnie kept her tone even and her expression blank. "My brother asked me to give you a message. He isn't interested in seeing you. After all, you tried to put all the blame on him when we all know it was you who killed Ken and the two cops."

"Darling Sam. I'm not surprised he told you that." Kate waltzed to the window and looked out at the river. She hummed, swaying to the tune. "I heard about Paige and Lanie. Are you investigating their deaths, Tom?"

"I am," he said, his back stiffening and his jaw tightening.

"Good luck with that," she said, whirling around, an evil glint in her eyes.

Tom's keen eyes scanned the room, searching for Kate's escape route.

He pushed Marnie toward the door. "We'll leave you to your book. Sorry for your loss, Kate."

As they turned to toward the door, Kate whispered, "'When you came on death, did you not come flower-guided like the elves in the wood?'"

Marnie froze, then glanced back. Tom took her hand and coaxed her to the door.

He whispered, "I caught it. C'mon. Let's get the hell outta here."

When they reached Tom's truck, they were both drenched. Marnie scrambled up into her seat and pulled a sweatshirt from her bag; after drying her arms and face, she tossed the shirt to Tom, who did the same.

"What the fuck was that?" he asked.

"I'm not sure, but my head feels like spiders are crawling all over it. Please tell me there aren't any," she said, tipping her head so he could see.

Tom ruffled her hair without looking. "No spiders, just a creepy web of delusions created by Kate."

"Do you think she's sneaking out of the hospital?"

"I'm gonna find out. Paige and Lanie were on her visitor list, and both are dead."

Marnie cast a sideways glance at him. "Well, that doesn't bode well for us, does it?"

Tom reached out and squeezed her arm. "I'll be stickin' to you like glue until we figure this out. Don't worry."

"Just like it's always been. I've got your back. You've got mine. Cross our hearts and hope to die, right?"

Tom nodded. "Yeah. I'll cross my heart, but that last part is off the table."

"I see your point." She gave a nervous giggle as he started the truck.

"Let's stop at my house so I can pack a bag. And then we'll check on that security system. Have you ever thought about a gate at the entrance?"

"What good would that do? If someone wants to kill me, they won't announce themself. They'll find another way onto the property, of which there are many."

"True," he said, pulling the truck onto the highway.

"Can we please stop at the drugstore? I gave Sam the last of my painkillers and my first-aid kit."

"Sure. We need to reach out to Teddy, too. She's on Kate's visitor list. Would you be okay for her to stay at the ranch?"

"She's annoying, but we can't lose another classmate, can we?"

"No, we can't."

Marnie turned in her seat so she could see Tom's expression. "You don't think Sam killed Ken, Webb, and Weaver, do you?"

He shook his head. "No. I think Kate Parish is the psychopath, not your brother."

"Sociopath sprang to mind today, but psychopath fits the behavior too. If Carl and I had access for a few weeks, we would have a better understanding. But making a snap diagnosis would be foolish. And dangerous."

"I'm gonna call Danny. I think the sooner we can get Teddy to the ranch, the better."

"He's going to want everyone at the cabin, you know that, right?" she said, pulling out a pack of gum from her bag and offering him a piece.

"Yup, but there are too many trees to hide behind there. Wide open spaces give us a better chance." He accepted the cinnamon stick and popped it into his mouth, chewing away the bitter taste of bile.

"Agreed."

-*Chapter 35*-

A call to Danny delivered a suggestion of lunch at the diner, which they agreed with wholeheartedly.

"We'll see you in about an hour," said Tom, hanging up and parking his truck in front of Drake's Drugstore.

"You need anything?" asked Marnie as she opened the door.

"Antacids," he answered flatly.

"Your stomach's bothering you?"

He took a deep breath and nodded. "Yeah; ever since we found Paige."

"Okay. Anything else?"

"A chocolate malted," he said.

"You got it!" She slammed the door and jogged across the footpath.

Marnie's eyes rolled back as she passed the yattering at the lunch counter. The harsh whispers of the coffee klatch told her their conversation focused on her.

"Good afternoon, ladies!" she said with a wave. "You know I can hear you, right?"

The hush that followed caused her to giggle, but the nattering began again as soon as she was out of sight. She gathered the items needed, then sauntered to the counter to order Tom's malted.

"Hi, Marnie!" A familiar voice and face greeted her.

"Alice! When did you start working here?"

"Three months ago. What can I get you?" asked Alice Wells, a long-time acquaintance and past nemesis of Marnie's. The two mended fences last year, and both were happier for it.

"Could I have a chocolate malted, please? Hmm ... Make that two."

"Is it good to be home?"

"Uh ... Yes. You'll have to come out to the house for tea and a catch up."

"That would be nice. I'll bring lavender shortbread."

"Yum," said Marnie, before turning to the gossips with boredom. "Go ahead. Ask whatever it is you want to know."

Susanne Connor leaned forward, half covering her mouth with her hand. "Is it true your brother is in town?"

"He was."

Corrine Hooper raised a suspicious eyebrow. "We hear he killed poor Paige."

"He didn't."

"What about Lanie?" asked Carol Chadwick, clutching at her faux pearls.

"Nope. Neither," she said, watching Alice put lids on the milkshakes.

Irene Hazelton cast an indignant glare at Marnie. "Well, he's back in town and suddenly two people are dead. Who else could have done it?"

Marnie winked at Alice before turning to face the women. "Don't you think it's odd that all of this happened as soon as I returned to Creekwood? It could be me. Have you thought about that?"

"Would you like me to ring up everything here?" asked Alice with a sly grin.

"Oh, yes, please."

"Marnie, why must you joke about something so dreadful?" asked Carol, twisting her pearls so tight the strand broke and scattered across the counter and onto the floor.

Marnie took her bag. "Am I joking?" She glanced at the beads skittering away. "Better pick those up before someone slips on them and breaks their neck. Have a nice day, ladies. Thanks, Alice!"

She trotted to the truck with a mischievous grin and opened the door. "Those women in there can't help themselves. They believe my brother murdered Paige and Lanie, but I guess that's what everyone in town believes, huh?"

Tom nodded. "Probably. Did you tell them he didn't?"

"Yeah. I suggested I did. He-he!"

"Why would you do that?" he asked, a smile playing at his lips.

"Because I'm evil," she said. "Here's your malted. Let's go get your bag and then lunch. I'm starving!"

"Hey! That's my line!"

"Do you wanna come in or stay in the truck?" asked Tom as he pulled into the driveway.

She looked out at the rain and said, "Nah. I'll wait here and call about fireworks."

"Okay. Back in a sec."

When he walked in the back door, he got an eerie feeling someone had been inside his house, but shook it off.

He checked the fridge and pulled out everything that could spoil over the next week, bagged up the contents, then ran upstairs to gather clothes and toiletries. The dark upstairs hallway was foreboding. He half expected Kate Parish to drop from the ceiling with a knife in her hand. Visions of horror movie possessions and a ghastly woman on all fours chasing him down the stairs crept into his mind.

"Geez! Stop creeping yourself out," he said to himself.

He double-timed his steps to his room, and bent to switch on the bedside lamp. With a click, a jolt slammed him into the wall as the snap, crackle, and pop of electricity burst from the light and the lampshade erupted into flames.

"Son of a bitch!"

He tore the blanket from the foot of his bed and threw it over the lamp, and pulled the plug from the socket, which delivered another shocking blow.

"God dammit!"

With the lamp wrapped in the blanket, he raced down the hall to the bathroom and tossed the smoldering bundle into the tub, then turned to go back to his room, but ran into Marnie at the top of the stairs.

"What the hell happened? I heard a boom!" she said, stumbling backward on the stairs as they collided.

Tom grabbed her forearm, pulling her to safety.

"My lamp exploded and burst into flames!"

"Want me to call the fire department?" she asked, phone in hand.

"No. Can you call your electrician, though?"

"Yeah."

"I don't get it. I've only had the lamp about a year," he mumbled on his way to the bathroom.

He removed the blanket and picked up the lamp to check the cord but set it back down, worried about wiping away fingerprints. Then, he called Rick.

"I've got bad news for you, Tom," said Stu. "Your electrical needs an upgrade."

"Yeah? That's what caused the lamp to burst into flames?"

"No, but I'll let your buddy explain that. You should replace everything, though. It's a mess."

"How much?" he asked through gritted teeth.

Stu glanced around the downstairs, adding in his head. "Well, the house is about two-thousand square feet and still has a fuse box.

I would say around ten thousand, give or take. I'll even throw in batteries for your smoke detectors for free."

"Great! There goes my hope for early retirement."

Rick walked into the kitchen, where Tom, Marnie, and Stu stood in the darkness. A random flash of lightning lit up the room as a wild wind whistled through the eaves.

"Who did you piss off, Keller?" he asked.

Tom scowled. "I'm a cop. It comes with the territory. Did you find somethin'?"

"The culprit took out a fuse and stuck a 1945 penny in its place. The year is important because between 1944 and 1946 pennies were made of ninety-five percent copper and only five percent zinc. Whomever did this has a decent understanding of electricity. A fuse will blow, but a penny allows for a constant flow of electricity through the circuit. They knew which fuse fueled your room, and they tampered with the lamp cord too. My guess is they thought you would turn it on tonight and it would blow up in your face. They believed the gunpowder in the light bulb would accomplish that. Thank God, it didn't."

"I have LED lightbulbs, though."

"Well, they brought along their own incandescent lightbulb, then. They probably have a stockpile of them."

"Lightbulb bombs?"

"Possibly. Back a few years ago, people bought up incandescent bulbs because they don't like LED. I'm one of those people. Whoever this guy or gal is, probably did that too."

"So that makes three people targeted on Kate's visitor list," said Tom, looking at Marnie, who pulled out a chair and sunk into it.

"I'm next," she said, resting her arms on the table.

A crack of thunder shook the house, and they all jumped when a lightning strike hit close by.

"Holy crap!" shouted Marnie. "Tom, go finish packing your things. Bring enough for the next few weeks until they can get your electrical problems fixed."

Rick cleared his throat and cocked his head to one side, peering at Marnie over his glasses. "I hate to bring it up, but does your brother know about this kind of stuff?"

"I'm sure he does, but he did not do this."

"Can you be sure?" asked Stu.

"As sure as I am that Danny Gregg is about to walk through that door," she said, hooking a thumb behind her.

A light tap at the window, and Danny walked into the kitchen.

"Everybody okay?" he asked, wrapping an arm around Marnie's shoulder.

"How did you do that?" asked Rick, staring at Marnie.

"She's a witch," said Tom.

At 2:00, the diner was quiet. Three regulars sat at the counter, while a couple sat at a booth drinking coffee. Tom, Marnie, and Danny trudged to their favorite booth and slid into their seats, and all turned to look for Gram, who appeared from the kitchen with a plate of meatloaf, mashed potatoes, and green peas. She set down the plate on the counter, filled a coffee cup, then rushed over to their table.

She slid into the seat next to Tom, patting his arm. "Are you okay, love? Danny told me what happened, then rushed out."

"I'm okay. Thanks for asking."

"Have ya called your parents

"No. They left for the Thousand Islands early this morning and won't be back until next weekend. It would ruin their vacation."

"Fair enough," she said. "Do ya fancy somethin' to eat?"

"That meatloaf looks pretty good. Got any left?"

"I do. Do you want gravy?"

"Yes, ma'am, and a ginger ale. Thank you." Tom squeezed Gram's hand, grateful for her kindness.

Gram looked at Marnie and Danny. "What can I get ya?"

"Make that two plates of meatloaf and gravy, but I'll have a glass of milk," said Danny.

"I'll have a hot pastrami and lemonade, please," said Marnie.

"Is Dorie back yet?" asked Danny.

Gram shook her head. "No. I expect her back tomorrow. She had a terrible electrical fire in her apartment two nights ago. She's fine, but she had quite a scare."

Tom and Marnie shared a glanced.

"Hey, Gram, what's Dorie's last name?" asked Tom.

"It's Haber, why?"

He took his notebook from his shirt pocket and flipped the pages. "Is her real name Doris?" he asked.

"That's right," said Gram, lines creasing her forehead. "Why?"

Tom said, "She's on Kate Parish's visitor list."

"Well, of course she is."

Marnie frowned. "Why would Dorie be on the list?"

Gram laughed. "She's Kate's auntie. Dorie and Kitty are sisters."

"Haber is her married name, then?" asked Tom.

"Yes. Her maiden name is Belmont, as is Kitty's. What's this about?"

"So, why does Dorie work here? Her family is wealthy," said Marnie.

"Because her father disowned her when she married Levi Haber. When Levi died during the war, Dorie needed a job, so I hired her. She's been with me for over twenty years."

Danny asked, "Which war?"

Gram waved a hand. "Does it matter?"

"Guess not," he said.

"Huh. Sisters. I would have never known," said Marnie.

"And you were Kate's best friend," said Danny.

"I was not!" she shouted, then apologized for her outburst. "I'm sorry."

"It's okay," he said, giving her a hug.

"Wow! I didn't realize how much it bothered me she and I were ever friends. How sad is that? Gawd!" She rested her forehead in her palms and rocked.

"Let me get your lunch and then you can be on your way. Marnie, I promise to visit soon," said Gram, leaving the three to chat.

"How did you go with your friend who installs security systems?" asked Tom.

"He's meeting me at the ranch at 5:00 to tell us what he can do. If it stops raining, he could get to work tomorrow, which I think would be best. Marnie? You okay with that?"

"Yes. We should put cameras in the secret room and the bunker, too."

"What secret room?" asked Tom.

Weary of the chatter, she sighed. "I'll show you later."

"Tommy's idea about wide open spaces is good. After we spoke earlier, I drove to the cabin and grabbed my things. We'll be camping at your place. Just like old times, huh?" said Danny, squeezing her hand.

But his attempt at levity fell flat and Marnie laid her head onto the table.

"All I wanted was a fresh start. A peaceful new home, unmarred by murder, and yet, here we are. With me topping another hit list."

"Better than dead," said Tom in a dry and even tone.

"There is that," she agreed, lifting her head. "*Not* dead is good."

Between bites, Marnie and Tom filled Danny in on their visit with Kate.

"She quoted the poem?" Danny choked on his meatloaf. "Jesus!"

Tom said, "We've gotta go over and search her room. She has to have an escape route."

"Perhaps the big dude is sneaking her out?" suggested Marnie. "He did seem overly protective." She rolled her eyes as she stuck her fork into Danny's potatoes and gravy, then savored the creamy and savory morsel with a contented smile.

"Dalton?" asked Tom.

"Yeah. What if Kate has worked her voodoo magic on him?" she added, dunking one of her French fries in Tom's gravy. She popped the fry into her mouth and had a sip of her lemonade.

"We should interview him, then. If he is chummy with Kate, she could manipulate him," said Danny.

Marnie shrugged. "I think she beat the crap out of him. Did you see his face and arms?"

Tom helped himself to one of Marnie's fries. "I did. He said he had a little accident."

"Kate's little," she replied.

"How big is this guy?" asked Danny.

"Taller than me, and bigger than a linebacker."

"Huh. Let's go see him in the morning."

"How was your morning, Detective Gregg?" asked Marnie.

"Well, Miss Reilly, I caught up with Rick. He's got nothing new on Paige and Lanie, but I asked him to reach out to Sam's doctor at Bayview. It's time we understand his state of mind when he escaped."

"What about the man who escaped with him?"

"Pigeon is back at Bayview," he said.

"No. Jed Rawlins. Have they found him?"

"Oh! No. That isn't in our hands, but I can check for you."

"I appreciate that. I can't shake the feeling he's lurking around town."

"The chief probably receives updates. I'll ask him."

"What did your father and Captain Sterling think of Lawrence Parish's tapes?" She pushed away her plate and leaned her elbows on the table, her chin resting in her palm.

"They're still ruminating."

Tom's face dropped. "Really? Didn't they see what we saw?"

Danny nodded. "Oh, yeah. They want Carl to review the tapes."

Marnie, forehead against the window, watched two crows pecking the grassy, rain-puddled verge, searching for worms.

"You know, we should give Carl the journals too," she said.

"Let's box them up and take them to him tomorrow," said Tom.

Danny agreed. "It could help put everything in context."

"Hmm ... I don't want my brother to die the bad guy," said Marnie.

The detectives watched her eyes change from aquamarine to a watery olivine, or creepy green, according to Tom.

"Why'd you say that?" Tom asked, chills trickling down his spine. "Clarity?"

She shrugged and went back to watching the crows.

-*Chapter 36*-

Teddy Jones tapped on the door and stood, shuffling her feet uncomfortably outside Marnie's kitchen.

Marnie waved and reached for a tea towel to dry her hands. "C'mon in and make yourself at home."

Teddy squeaked open the door and warily checked out the kitchen. She knew she wasn't one of Marnie's favorite people, so being in her home was weird. "I've only got one bag. Where should I put it?" she asked, hefting up a super-sized overnight bag as Tater, Dickens, and Gus milled around her, sniffing her toes.

"Sorry! I'll have to make up a room. I've just moved in and so much stuff is still in boxes. Would you prefer to be upstairs or downstairs?"

"If you're upstairs, that would feel safer."

"Good point. If you don't mind giving me a hand, we can put together a bed and then make it up. The guys are outside speaking with a security company, otherwise I would ask them to help."

"Sure. We can put it together between the two of us."

"Are the dogs making you uncomfortable?"

"No. I like dogs."

"Good. Let's go upstairs and find you a bedroom."

"That's a lot of cameras, Danny. You sure you want that many?" asked Mike Crump, the security technician.

"I know, but we want the property to be secure. You don't have to worry about the pastures, but all the outbuildings, the house, main walking paths, and the driveway are important. It sounds like overkill, but..."

"No! I get it. How about if we put up game cameras in the pastures? Those will connect to Marnie's phone. Then we'll light up everything and install cameras everywhere we can hard-wire them. The cameras all have a battery component, but I would suggest a generator in case the power goes out."

Tom said, "She told me she had new generators installed for the house and barn. A power outage won't be an issue."

"Great. I'll draw up the plans tonight, send you an estimate, and we can start in the morning. Will she be okay with that plan, or should I talk to her?" asked Mike.

"She trusts us. It'll be fine," said Danny.

Ransom sat in his car in the parking lot of the Bayview Correctional Facility, flipping through a copy of Sam Reilly's medical report. Doctor Miller was eager to share his diagnosis with a US Marshal as he felt his patient to be the victim in a madman's game.

Drug-induced psychosis, mind control, menticide, coercive persuasion, thought control, and thought reform were common words throughout Doctor Miller's notes following sessions with Sam.

The urine and blood tests Sam had taken on the day of his incarceration at the facility showed an absence of drugs, which was not unusual in his case. They had denied him visitors before his transfer. Ransom pumped a fist in the air when he saw the last page of notes the good doctor included in the report. Call lists from the county jail and from his time at Bayview. Only two names appeared. Names that confirmed his theory.

The room Marnie chose for Teddy was around the corner from the stairs, so the dogs wouldn't awaken her visitor in the morning. The bedroom windows opened to a rose garden which their recently departed friend, Paige Reynolds, transplanted from Marnie's mother's garden.

"I hope this is okay," said Marnie. "Sorry things are in a bit of an uproar around here."

Teddy asked, "Do you know why I'm here?"

Marnie glanced up from the slats she was setting on the bed frame. "Danny didn't tell you when he picked you up?"

"No. He told me to pack a bag, and he strongly recommended I stay here. When I asked why, he said he was being cautious." Teddy, eyebrows drawn together, sat down on a ladder-back chair, twisting the handle of her overnight bag.

Marnie scrunched up her face, wondering if the truth would freak out her old classmate, then decided knowledge of potential danger was better than dead because she didn't know.

"You know me. I'm blunt, so I will tell you what's going on. Don't freak out, okay?"

"Okay. Does this have something to do with Paige and Lanie?"

"Yes. You visited Kate a few days ago, right?"

Teddy nodded. "What's that got to do with anything? A lot of people have."

"And two of those people are dead. Did you piss her off? Did you go there to gloat or gossip? Tell me you didn't tell her about seeing me or about the ranch."

A sheepish grin and a sideways glance confirmed Marnie's fears.

"Well, I may have mentioned that you'd bought the ranch with Ken Wilder's money."

Marnie scowled. "Did you tell her about my new car, too?"

"No. Paige told her about that, and Kate told me."

"What else did you tell her?"

"Gawd! I don't remember! What difference does it make?" Teddy's shoulders dropped, and she sighed. "Lanie and I went over there to wind up Little Miss Perfect! We wanted to knock her down a few pegs, that's all."

Hands to her hips, Marnie scowled. "Wow! That's mature. She is off her pedestal. The woman is in a sanitarium for the criminally insane."

Teddy's bottom lip protruded, and her shoulders dropped in resignation. "Yeah! Okay!"

"Lanie visited her, and she's dead. Paige too. Tom and I paid her a visit, and a lamp caught fire at his house. That's why you're here."

Teddy's amber eyes widened, and she shrieked, "You think she's going to kill me?"

Marnie threw out her hands and pulled a face. "Who the fuck knows, but you are here until Tom and Danny catch Lanie's and Paige's killer. Don't think you're special. She wants me dead, too."

A Chinese takeout menu was on the kitchen table when the detectives returned from their meeting with the security technician.

"Guess Marnie doesn't plan to cook tonight," said Tom.

Danny flipped the menu around so he could read it. "She circled General Tso's Chicken, so I don't care if she cooks or not. She's trying to get Teddy settled, and she looked like she was up in her head earlier. I can't imagine what it's like to have dead people chattering at you all day. It must be exhausting."

"Yeah. She had that spooky look in her eyes. You know the one where her eyes change to that creepy green," said Tom, grabbing the pen and circling Orange Beef, pork egg rolls, and fried dumplings.

"Ha-ha! I don't think it's creepy, but I'm not afraid of the paranormal." Danny took another look at the menu and circled Salt and Pepper Calamari. "Want a beer?"

"Are we officially off the clock?" Tom checked the microwave. "It's 6:30. I'll take one to go. I'm goin' upstairs to change out of these wet clothes."

"That's the best plan I've heard all day," said Danny, taking two beers from the fridge and handing one to Tom. "Dry clothes, dinner, and an early night are on my agenda. How 'bout you?"

Tom twisted the cap off his beer and nodded as he took a swig. "Yeah. I'm beat. All I keep thinking about is Lawrence Parish and what he did to Sam. Well, that and our visit to Pine Ridge today and my lamp catching fire."

The dogs pranced into the room, with Teddy and Marnie not far behind.

"Chinese takeout is dinner tonight," said Marnie, picking up the menu. "Ah. The detectives discovered by well-placed clue and have circled their favorites. Teddy? What do you like?"

"I'm not fussy, but Szechuan is my favorite," she said.

"Okay. I'll order it and go pick it up." Marnie picked up her phone and punched in an online order.

"I'll go get it," said Danny.

A look of determination on her face, Marnie said, "No. I'm going—alone. I haven't had more than a few hours to myself since arriving in Creekwood."

"Marn, you shouldn't go out by yourself." Tom leaned against the counter and sent a "don't be stupid" look her way.

"Well, I am. End of discussion. Besides, you two should get out of your wet clothes before you catch colds. I'll be back in twenty, and do me a favor, please. Feed the knuckleheads." She grabbed up her bag and keys and dashed out the door before the detectives could stop her.

Tom laughed and mimicked her in a snotty tone. "Feed the knuckleheads. Change your clothes. Gawd! She's bossy."

"I'll feed the knuckleheads, if that means the dogs," said Teddy.

Danny said, "Thanks. Tater and Dickens get three-quarters of a cup of kibble and half a big can of tuna each." He pointed to the pantry door. "Everything is in there. Oh! Tater's is the blue bowl and Dickens' is red. Trust me. They know the difference."

"Ha-ha! Okay," she said. "Tom, what about Gus?"

"There's a shopping bag in the pantry with his food and bowls. He gets the same amount of kibble, but he gets a half-cup of beef and veggie mix that's in the fridge in a purple bowl."

"Do they all get along when they eat?" she asked.

Tom nodded. "Yeah. They're pretty good."

"Until they're not," said Danny with a chuckle.

Tom laughed. "We won't be long. Gotta get out of the wet clothes before Miss Bossy Boots returns."

They shared a laugh at Marnie's expense, then the detectives trudged upstairs to change while Teddy fed and watered the knuckleheads.

Not another car was in sight as Marnie made her way to the restaurant, which sat on the outskirts of town, a convenient four miles up the road. She peered into the cemetery, certain she had seen someone walking amongst the graves.

"Real or not real?" she wondered out loud. "Hmm... Not real. What sane, living person would roam the cemetery on a night like this?" Her sense of adventure almost saw her U-turn to investigate, but her better sense took over and she focused on the road, turning up the speed of her windshield wipers.

The buzz of her phone and a sideways glance at the infotainment screen alerted her to a call from a "private caller." She considered not answering it, but thinking it could be her brother, she accepted the call.

"Hello."

"Hey, kid, it's me Ransom. Can you talk?"

"I'm in the car by myself. Is Sam okay?"

"Yeah. He's fine, but he wanted to talk to you."

"Of course."

"Hi, Squirt. I need to see you. Will you be alone tonight?" asked Sam.

"No. Tom, Danny, and another friend are staying at the ranch. Is everything okay?"

"I want my journals. I have been trying to piece together my past, and I thought if I could read what I wrote back then, it would be helpful."

"Oh, shoot! That could be difficult. I gave them to Danny. They want my friend Carl Parkins to review the videos they found at the Parish house and the journals. He's a psychiatrist. Brainwashing is not something the guys come across often, but I think it could help them grasp the severity of what happened to you."

"Hmm."

"I was trying to help."

"Yes. I know. I would still like to see you, though. When would it be possible?"

"Well, I could meet you at the cemetery after everyone has gone to sleep. The guys will sleep like the dead tonight. If Ransom can send me his number, I can text you and meet you there. Are you staying nearby?"

"We will make it work."

"Okay. I'll see you tonight."

As she disconnected the call, she wondered if she was breaking the law by seeing her brother.

"Ransom is a US Marshal, so if Sam is in his custody, it must be okay," she rationalized. "Unless Ransom is not detaining him in an official capacity. Huh. Well, when you're skating on thin ice, you might as well tap dance," she said to herself before reaching for the radio and tuning in her favorite sixties through nineties music station.

To Steppenwolf's Born to Be Wild, she thought about her past relationship with Ransom, and wondered if he had gone rogue to help Sam. Ransom Elliot was a bit of a bad boy back then, and he loved breaking the rules. But would he sacrifice his career to repay her brother for protecting him? She decided yes, he would, because deep down, he was a good guy and he would try to do the right thing if he believed it to be the righteous path.

When Wild Cherry's Play That Funky Music rose out of the speakers, she cranked up the volume and sang along, tapping out the beat on the steering wheel. But as she pulled into the restaurant parking lot, she turned off the sound as Talking Heads' Psycho Killer burst into her happy bubble.

"We've had enough of psycho killers, thanks," she said and turned off the engine. "No more! You hear me, Universe? No more!"

A downpour of rain erupted when Marnie pulled her car into the yard and did a U-turn so that her door was closer to the veranda. She sat for a moment, thinking it would let up, then noticed Tom running through the rain with an open umbrella. He opened her door and held out his hand.

She gave him a funny look before saying, "Aren't you chivalrous!"

With an impish grin, he scoffed, "Gimme the food. I'm starving!"

"Ha-ha! You are such an ass!" She handed him the bag and stepped out of the car while he held the umbrella over them.

"Hey, is Jonas still working? I thought I saw his truck leave a few minutes ago."

"Yes. He wanted to keep busy. Lanie's parents have taken over the funeral planning, so he's feeling lost."

"The coroner hasn't released her or Paige, though," he said, wrinkling his brow.

"Don't know. That's what he told me. Anyway, let's get the food inside before the lightning starts again."

Around the kitchen table, dinner conversation remained light and away from topics like psycho killers and dead classmates.

"How's the Szechuan chicken, Teddy?" asked Marnie.

Chopsticks to her mouth, Teddy paused and replied, "It's so good. It's hotter than usual, but I love it!"

"I love it, too, but the guys always think it's too hot."

Danny laughed. "Your eyes tear up every time you take a bite."

"Yes, but I won't need an antihistamine for days."

Tom popped a dumpling into his mouth and chewed slowly, savoring the perfect pillow of goodness.

"I think dumplings are my favorite. I could eat all of them and then have a dozen more," he said.

Teddy poked him in the arm with her chopsticks. "I think you have eaten the whole carton. Can I have one if there is any left?"

He passed the dumplings, then reached for the General Tso's chicken.

"Thanks for feeding us, Marn."

"When don't I?"

"When you take off and leave us for months on end," said Danny, sounding snottier than intended.

"Well, I'm home now. Everyone will be fat and happy by Christmas," she said, fobbing off his snideness.

"I'm sorry. That came out wrong." He reached for her hand and gave it a squeeze.

"It's okay, but to apologize, you can peel the veggies for tomorrow night's pot roast."

"I'll do that!"

Teddy pushed away her plate. "I am so full! Thanks for dinner, Marnie."

"You won't be full in a few hours," said Tom. "Why am I always hungry, no matter how much Chinese food I eat?"

Marnie shrugged. "I don't know, but there are heaps left over if you get the midnight munchies."

Danny handed her a fortune cookie, but she didn't accept it.

"C'mon, Detective Gregg! You know I have to choose the cookie."

"Oh! Sorry, Miss Reilly. I forgot!" he said with a chuckle.

She plucked her own from the middle of the table, peeled off the cellophane and broke it in half. With the corner of her mouth quirked up, she raised an eyebrow.

"Three people can keep a secret if you get rid of two," she read. "That sounds ominous."

"It doesn't mean anything," said Danny, taking a cookie and opening it. "Huh. *Be cautious of walking in darkness alone.*"

Marnie shoulder-nudged him. "I think it's talking about that brass door stop in my room you stubbed your toe on last night."

"Ha-ha! I woke up in a daze and couldn't find the bathroom."

"I'll get a nightlight," she said with a laugh before turning to their guest. "Teddy, what does yours say?"

Teddy cracked the cookie and smirked. "Okay. This is good to know. *You don't have to be faster than the bear. You only have to be faster than the slowest person running from it.*"

"Ha-ha! That's something we all know living out here in the boonies," said Tom, choosing a cookie.

Marnie leaned across the table. "What's it say?"

He grimaced and dropped the fortune onto the table. "I think I want a different cookie."

Teddy snatched it up and read it aloud. *"Your heart will skip a beat."*

Tom turned away—storm clouds brewing his eyes.

"Let it go, Tommy. You know fortune cookies are a gimmick. Some believe they're an American invention," said Danny.

With a grim expression on his handsome face, Tom stood up, walked to the door, and bent to scratch Gus' neck. "Yeah, whatever."

"It could be talking about falling in love," offered Marnie.

He shrugged her off, still focused on his Labrador. "Hmm. No, thanks. That never works out. I'm gonna take the dogs out," he said, grabbing an umbrella and stepping out onto the veranda with the knuckleheads.

Danny and Teddy sat with their mouths open, but Marnie got to her feet.

"I'll go talk to him. The trauma from the stun gun, the blow to the head, Webb, Weaver, and that crap with Erin last year … Now Paige and Lanie. And losing his sister when they were kids. It's a lot to process." Marnie pulled on a rain slicker, turned to Danny and said, "You both need to set up appointments with Carl to talk through the last year and any other traumatic experience you've been through. It's important to have someone to confide in that isn't me. I would try to be objective, but I am not sure I would be, but he would."

Marnie stood on the top step and peered out into the rain. She caught sight of the two shepherd's lanterns of her Border Collies—the white fur at the tip of their tails. The night had turned steamy, the rain more of a fine mist than a sprinkle.

"Tom!" she shouted, walking down the stairs and onto the lawn. "Hey! I know you're not okay, so I won't ask. Is there anything I can do?"

"Go back inside," he said.

"Okay," she replied, turning to leave.

"Hey, Marn!" he called out.

She stopped and pivoted back to him. "Yeah?"

"When's it gonna be one of us?"

She tossed back her head and watched the falling rain. "I try not to think about it, but I have had a sense of something since returning to Creekwood. A sense of danger, and then when I saw Sam, I thought … uh…felt something bad was going to happen, and I still do. I lost my brother once. I can't to lose him again."

He crossed the lawn and looked down at her—his expression sad. "I don't want to lose you or Danny or anyone else. I know we joke about me being a scaredy cat, but I am scared."

Tears trickling down her cheeks, she hugged him. "I don't want to lose you or anyone else either."

He hugged her back, resting his chin on her head. "Is your head still giving off vibes?"

She nodded and squeezed him tighter.

"I love you, Marn," he said, choking back tears.

"I love you, too."

-Chapter 37-

Marnie lay awake, listening to Danny's soft snores—waiting for him to roll to his right side, away from her. The rain had stopped, and the moon bathed half of her room in a soft amber glow. She checked the clock on her bedside table. In bright green, it read 1:30, and she rolled to the floor. Tater and Dickens perked up their ears, but she held a finger up to her lips to shush them. With her hand flat on the floor, she mouthed "stay" so they wouldn't follow her downstairs.

The old oak floors creaked and popped with every step. Tense with the anticipation of being caught, she pulled up her shoulders and snuck to the stairs. When she reached them, she glanced at the banister, wondering if sliding down would make less noise. She thought better of it and carefully tiptoed down to the landing. The next six steps were the creakiest, so she slid down the short banister, and then eased herself onto the floor beneath.

She crept through a maze of boxes and furniture on her way to the pantry, where she had stashed shorts, a T-shirt and moccasins in the laundry room via the upstairs laundry chute before going to bed. She sent a text to Ransom, changed her clothes, and snatched up her bag and keys. With the alarm disarmed, she left the house, rearming it through an app once she was off the porch.

As she got into her car, she giggled because turning her car around earlier had served two purposes. One, she was close to the veranda, and two, she had placed the car in the perfect position to coast down the driveway in neutral. "I hope I remember how to pop a clutch," she said, giggling.

Her return trip would be more difficult, but she was quite certain if she came in via one of the rough service roads, she could coast quietly into the driveway—with her lights off, of course.

Tom flinched as an English ivy leaf brushed against his cheek. "Why did she come to the cemetery? Anywhere but a graveyard would have been fine," he said with a shiver.

Danny put a finger to his lips. "Shh! Where is she?"

Tom said, "Following her will not end well for either of us. You know that, right?"

"Yeah, I know." Danny dragged a hand down his face to wipe away the dirty look Marnie would give them when she found out. "She's gonna be pissed, standing there with her fists on her hips and those green eyes blazing."

"Yeah. Then her mouth is gonna get all tight before she blasts us." Tom winced at the thought.

They snuck along an unlit dirt path of Hallowed Hills Memorial, searching for her. Humidity hung in the air, and perspiration trickled down their backs as lightning bugs sparked in the darkness and an owl hooted above them, then flapped its wings, rustling the leaves of an old oak tree.

Dropping to his knees, Danny hid behind a huge family tombstone, Tom following suit. "She's right there," he hissed.

Marnie stood beside the headstone of her great-grandfather, Nolan Flannigan, ten yards from the detectives. Phone in her hands, she texted. She looked up and searched the grounds and then waved. Sam emerged from a wooded area, stepping briefly into the dull lights outside of the mausoleum.

Danny stood, but Tom pulled him back down.

"Wait a minute," he whispered.

When Sam reached his sister, he rested a hand gently against her cheek. Her hand closed over his as they stared at one another. The detectives couldn't hear the conversation, but Sam appeared humble, hanging his head and shrugging. Marnie spoke with considerable animation for several minutes, before her brother nodded his head in what appeared to be submission. Then she handed him an envelope, gave him a long hug, and disappeared behind the mausoleum. A moment later, she started her Jeep and drove out of the cemetery.

Shoving Tom, Danny said, "C'mon! Let's get him!"

But his partner grabbed his arm. "No, we have to talk to Marnie. She always has a reason for what she does."

Danny growled, "She is aiding and abetting a fugitive!"

"Not necessarily. Sam was with Ransom Elliot, a US Marshal. Maybe Ransom drove him here."

As if on cue, a car pulled up to Sam and Tom got a look at the driver.

"There you go. That's him, driving. Sam's in the custody of a federal officer."

"Yeah. We'll see about that!" barked Danny.

The Jeep coasted to a stop in the driveway, and Marnie opened the door and out. She crept to the veranda and covered her eyes as the outside light switched on. The detectives stood; arms crossed in front of them. Their scowling faces irritated rather than worried her.

"What the hell are you two doing out here?" she asked, her angry expression matching their own.

Danny narrowed his eyes. "No! What are you doing out here is the right question!"

Both eyebrows shot up and a condescending tone followed. "Excuse me, Detective? Last time I checked my birth certificate, I am old enough to be out at any hour I please."

Tom cocked his head, and his frown deepened. "Marn, you could have told us you were going out. You didn't have to sneak."

Her mouth dropped open. "I didn't sneak!"

"Then why did you coast out of here and pop the clutch at the bottom of the driveway? C'mon, Marn! We used to do that with your mother's VW. I'm not stupid."

"I didn't want to wake you."

"Bullshit!" said Danny.

She stalked across the driveway and clomped up the steps. "I can take care of myself! I don't need babysitters watching my every move!" She pushed between them, banged open the screen door, then spun around. "And I don't need your permission to leave my house."

Danny dropped his head to his chest before lifting his gaze to hers. "Marnie, you are aiding and abetting a fugitive. We should arrest you for that, you know!"

Her eyes widened with fury. "You followed me?!" Without another word, she slammed the door, set the lock, and armed the alarm.

Tom shouted, "We have keys! And the code!"

Ransom asked, "Are you sure that is wise?"

Sam stretched out on his bed, eyes closed, doing his best to rub away the headache that had been building up over the last hour.

"Yes. I think it makes sense. A meeting with my sister and the detectives could help us in the long run. Oh, the two FBI agents who were at Danny's house the other night were the men who tried to kill Billy. They are dirty. That is why Dobbs shot me. He was trying to eliminate a witness to his crimes."

Ransom's jaw dropped. "Are you sure?"

"Yes."

"There's no doubt they're the guys you were protecting us from?"

"Not one iota."

"Have you got proof?"

"I do. My parent's attic has a cubby under the eaves. There are three fireproof boxes and a couple of hunting rifles tucked away up there. Funny how easily I remember things when I am not under the influence of Lawrence Parish."

"Yeah. When did you speak with him last?"

"Never when I was at Bayview, but when I escaped, I called him once or twice. Please keep that between us."

Sam sat up and took a drink of water from a bottle on his bedside table. "I regret calling him. Each time we spoke..." He shook his head, as if the action would clear away the memory. "The signs were there that conversations with him were detrimental to my wellbeing. My headaches would ease, but I would not think straight for days."

Ransom twisted his mouth in thought. "They'd ease?"

"Yes. Why?"

"Do you think it's possible Lawrence controlled your headaches?"

"Anything is possible. That is why I want to read my journals. I began having headaches when I was fourteen or fifteen, but they became worse after the explosion. I ask myself often if it is the shrapnel, Lawrence's influence or a combination of both."

Ransom shot to his feet. "I need a drink."

The detectives disarmed the alarm and unlocked the back door. Danny stepped through first, shoulders and face tight with anger.

"Marnie! You can't lock us out and think this will all go away. What you did ... Going out there alone was stupid!"

"And dangerous," added Tom.

They stalked through the house, looking for her.

Tom scrunched his face and rolled his head, cracking his neck. "I told you this wouldn't end well for us."

Danny shot him a glare and stalked to the study, where he found Marnie unpacking boxes. She whirled around and pointed at the door.

"Go away, Detective!"

"Marnie, we gotta talk."

Tom leaned on the doorjamb, arms and ankles crossed, with mild amusement tugging at the corners of his mouth.

Hands to hips, she scowled at him. "Get that smug look off your face, Keller!"

He pushed himself off the jamb and, eyes blinking with innocence, he held out his hands. "That's my face. I wasn't goin' for smug."

She curled her lip and continued pulling items from a carton.

"Can we please talk?" asked Danny, touching her shoulder.

She shooed away his hand without answering.

"Marn, the silent treatment is an unhealthy way of dealing with anger. Haven't you told me that? Haven't you told me its emotional manipulation?" Tom crossed the room, dropped into an upholstered chair and rested his head on the stuffed back.

She cast him a sideways glare, then pushed away the box and turned to him. "If you had trusted me ... Grr! I was coming home to wake you up. Sam wants to meet with you. Both of you. I convinced him it was best for everyone."

Tom shot out of his chair. "Are you serious?"

"Yeah!"

"When? Where?" asked Danny.

"Here. Tomorrow morning at 6:00."

Tom asked, "Is Ransom coming with him?"

She gave a half shrug. "I guess. They're coming through the tunnel so the feds won't see them. If they are still watching the house."

"They would have followed you if they were," said Danny.

"I suppose so," she said, running a hand over dust on the bookshelf. Goosebumps popped out on her arms and a telltale tingle spider-webbed over her scalp, and she visibly shivered.

"What's with the face?" asked Tom.

She rolled her shoulders and trembled again. "I don't know. I mean, maybe a flash of something." Eyebrows knitted together, she crossed the room and searched for the rosette Ransom had turned.

The detectives exchanged a curious glance.

"Marn? What are you lookin' for?" Tom joined her at the fireplace and as he reached her, she found the right rose and the bookcase sprang open. He wheeled around and stared at the opening beyond the shelves. "What the heck?"

Danny slowly turned, not believing his eyes. "What year was this house built? Trap doors, hidden rooms? Did rumrunners own this property?"

Tom and Marnie met Danny near the opening.

"Ransom found the room when he was searching for Sam." Marnie pulled her phone from her back pocket and turned on the flashlight. She stood between the men, shining her light into the darkness.

They crept behind the bookcase and the beam revealed two sets of stairs—one going up and one traveling down; and leaning against the wall between the staircases was a school bus yellow, sixty-centimeter builder's level—the top edge bloody and clumped with nutmeg-brown hair.

"Ah, Jesus!" Tom ran a hand down his face.

"We need to bag it," said Danny, as he stepped closer to inspect the offending object.

Without a word, Marnie dashed to the kitchen to find a proper vessel for the level, returning a minute later with a large plastic garbage bag. The detectives hadn't moved, only to pull their phones from their pockets and turn on their own flashlights.

"Here. I hope this will do," she said, handing the bag to Danny.

Tom snapped pictures while Danny provided light. Then they videoed the scene.

Marnie stepped out and ran upstairs to check on the dogs because they had been unusually quiet. She found Gus snoozing on Tom's bed and Tater and Dickens curled up on their beds in her room.

"Good boys! Thank you for obeying," she praised. "C'mon! Let's go outside."

Both dogs stood and stretched, bums in the air, front paws extended. Their loud yawns brought the curious Labrador to the door, cocking his head inquisitively.

"Marnie, is everything okay?" Teddy appeared in the hallway, rubbing sleep from her eyes.

"Yeah."

"Why are you dressed?"

"I'm taking the dogs out."

"Where's Danny?"

"He and Tom are downstairs. You should go back to bed."

Teddy yawned and said, "If there's something going on, tell me."

Marnie sighed and rolled her neck. "We found the weapon that likely killed Lanie."

Teddy glanced at her toes and took a breath. "Oh."

"Yeah. I'm taking the dogs out to give the guys time to do what they have to do."

Teddy nodded.

"Listen. I hope I don't have to say this, but I'm going to, anyway. Whatever goes on while you're here, don't tattle it around town."

"I won't."

"Promise?"

"Yeah. I promise."

"Okay. The dogs and I are going downstairs."

"I'm coming with you. I don't wanna be up here by myself," said Teddy, racing back to her room.

She appeared a moment later wearing cut-offs, a Creekwood Bears T-shirt and flip-flops.

Marnie laughed. "Still supporting our high school team?"

Teddy giggled. "Once a cheerleader, always a cheerleader."

Marnie threw a fist in the air. "Go, Bears!"

"That didn't sound very enthusiastic!"

"That's why I wasn't a cheerleader," said Marnie with a shrug.

"No, that's not it. You never even tried out. You were too busy studying, playing sports and hanging around Tom."

Marnie frowned. "I didn't 'hang around' Tom. We're friends."

Teddy raised an eyebrow. "Hmm … It made it hard for him to have a girlfriend with you in the picture."

"Well, friends don't dump friends because they have a significant other. Friendship doesn't work that way."

"Yes, it does," argued Teddy.

"Nope. It really doesn't, and if that's why you dislike me and broke up with Tom when we were in high school, that's your problem. Bygones, Teddy. It's time to move on." With that, Marnie turned and walked away.

"This is nuts, Danny. How did this get into Marnie's house?"

"I don't know, Tommy, but I have my suspicions she knows something. She got quiet and then disappeared."

"Yeah. I'll get my fingerprint kit from the truck. Maybe we can lift something from the door."

"Thanks. I don't think we need to call Rick out for this. We'll take the level to him in the morning and drop off whatever prints we get. My father is already busting on me about being over budget."

"Hmm … We're only over budget 'cause people keep gettin' killed. What the heck is goin' on in our quiet little town?"

-Chapter 38-

"Did you guys get any sleep?" asked Tom, taking a gulp of black coffee.

Settled on a bench seat at the kitchen table and swaddled in a chunky cardigan with her knees pulled up to her chin, Marnie shook her head. "No. That storm early this morning kept me awake. Danny is still asleep, though. He had Tater and Dickens up on his side of the bed because he thought they were frightened. Ha! They played him. They were snoring when I came downstairs."

"I can't believe the temperature drop overnight," he said as he opened the back door. "But that rain smells so good!"

"It does." She stretched to see at the clock. "I need to get dressed. Sam will be here in an hour."

"We'll have to keep Teddy busy while we have the meeting. She'll tell everyone in town if she knows your brother is here."

"I spoke with her about that last night. She seemed to understand. See if you can drive it home. I think she gossips because she's lonely and wants to feel important. I don't think she intends harm."

Tom said, "She's been out of full-time work for a couple of years, but she's got a few part-time jobs, but nothing stable."

"Isn't she a teacher?"

"No. She worked in admin at the school. When they did those layoffs two years ago, they made her position redundant."

"Huh. I wonder if she's good with logistics?"

"No idea," he said.

"Well, let's see if we can find something for her here on the ranch. We're going to need help, and believe it or not, I kind of like her."

"Ha-ha! She doesn't like you," he replied with a cheeky smile.

"Yes, she does. She just doesn't know it yet." Marnie unfolded her legs from the bench and made her way upstairs to wake Danny and the knuckleheads and to get dressed.

"Sorry. I'm turned around. We are heading to the paddock door, not the study. If we turn left up ahead, we'll be back on track," said Sam, shining a flashlight down a labyrinth of passageways. "We will have to post directional signs for my sister."

Ransom glanced around the tunnel, noting the excellent craftsmanship of the original stonemasons. Built with granite blocks and a mortar of clay and sweetgrass, the structure had stood for over a century.

"Does the network of tunnels go far or only under the ranch and cemetery?"

"Uh … It is a complex system. I have never mapped out the entire layout, but at least one passageway goes into town. Another goes to the Hudson for offloading bootleg whiskey. People say they built the tunnels for the Underground Railroad."

"Wow!" said Ransom, his respect for the builders growing.

"It is a piece of Creekwood history I would like to study," said Sam. He pointed to the beam ahead of them and said, "Up there. My sister left the door open for us. I can see a light shining."

"Teddy, I really appreciate you doing this for me. Thanks so much," said Marnie.

"I'm happy to pitch in. Do you think you might need someone to do this full-time?"

"I think so. Are you interested?" Marnie placed four printed spread sheets on the dining room table and used a highlighter to circle several items. "These are things Carl Parkins, my business partner, has had trouble sourcing. If you could find them, it would be great!"

"Are you planning to open a cafeteria for workers?"

"Eventually. That will take time, though."

"I can help with that. It was my job at the school over in Hudson Hollow."

"Well, that's good to know."

"Let me start with this, and then we can discuss your other needs later. I'll spreadsheet the costs and suppliers first."

"Perfect! Thanks," Marnie replied. "Okay. I'll leave the knuckleheads with you. I have to get to this meeting. We'll catch up later."

As she turned to leave, Teddy said, "You know, Marnie, you can't heal yourself by helping others."

She nodded and said, "I know, but it's a nice place to start."

Danny sat in Marnie's swivel chair at her desk, writing a list of questions for Sam. Tom paced, worried about seeing his childhood friend after the traumas and turmoil of the last many years. The tapes told a story of a troubled teen abused by his psychiatrist, but the adult had committed horrible atrocities. His hand absently reached for his pistol, and he patted it to remind himself he could protect them. The study felt stuffy, so he opened the French doors to let in fresh air, but the rain bouncing off the pavers sent splashes of water into the room. He closed the doors and opted for pushing out the casement windows.

"Is that better?" he asked Danny.

"Will you sit down! You're like a cat on a hot tin roof." Danny shot him a frustrated glare, then returned to his list. The detective felt it was important to have his ducks lined up. He worried he would lose his temper and not receive the answers they all needed.

Marnie kicked open the door, carrying a tray with a coffee pot, cream, sugar, and crumb cake. She set it on a large carton and retreated to the door. "Back in a sec. I have to grab mugs." She reappeared a moment later with a second tray holding coffee mugs, napkins, and spoons.

Voices filtered up from the trapdoor, and all turned to the opening.

"I do not want her to be upset by my presence in her home. I have put her through enough."

"Chill out, Sam. She invited you," said Ransom.

"She did. But the facts are the facts. I tried to kill her and her dog. How can she trust me?"

Marnie moved to the hatch and stared down into the dimly lit tunnel. "I don't yet. But with time, who knows?"

Sam looked up at his sister, who resembled an angel, with the light from the chandelier above her forming a halo around her head. "Is it okay to come up?"

"Yeah. We're waiting for you." She stepped back, moved to the desk, and pulled herself up to sit near Danny, who had gotten to his feet—his hand resting on his sidearm.

Tom remained by the windows, standing on the middle ground. To Tom, he looked tired, battered, and thin. Sam scanned the room, making eye contact with each of them. He held his sister's gaze, then moved aside to allow Ransom to come up through the hatch.

"Good morning, people of Creekwood!" said Ransom, holding out his hand to Tom, who rolled his eyes, then accepted the greeting.

Danny stepped around the desk and offered his hand to the US Marshal. "Ransom Elliot, I presume?"

Ransom took his hand. "Nice Sherlock reference, Detective. Glad to meet you."

Danny squeezed tighter than needed before stepping back and assessing Sam, who gave him a curt nod.

"Why don't we all take a seat," said Marnie, trying to ease the tension. "We have coffee and cake for anyone who is hungry."

Danny arched his brow. "Sam, don't you shake hands with people you've just met?"

"We have met, Detective. Albeit, under unsavory circumstances."

"Yes. Let's put the first few meetings aside," he said, extending his hand to Marnie's brother. "I'm Danny Gregg, your sister's boyfriend. Good to meet you."

A lopsided smile appeared on Sam's lips, and he shook the detective's hand. "Yes, and thank you for agreeing to meet with me."

Danny waved a hand toward Tom, who stood stoically by the windows. "And you know Tom Keller."

Sam turned to his sister's best friend, but didn't know what to say.

Tom bent his head and hesitated before taking a step forward and putting out his hand, which Sam did not take.

"Please accept my apology, Tom, for all the rotten things I did to you. There is no excuse..."

"I saw the tapes," Tom said, his face stony.

Sam averted his eyes—his face reddening. "The tapes do not excuse..."

"They kinda do," said Tom, clapping him on the shoulder. "C'mon. Let's sit down and have cake. I'm starving."

Sam and Ransom sat on a brown suede sofa positioned near the hatch, which the latter closed before sitting back. Tom opted for a club chair opposite them, near the open windows. Danny returned to the swivel chair and Marnie hopped up on the desk.

Sam cleared his throat. "Before we start, I would ask that no one say my sister's name. It is an unusual request, but it is necessary."

"We watched the tapes. We understand," said Danny, getting up again to pour a cup of coffee.

"Hey, kid, have you seen the tapes?" Ransom asked Marnie.

She shook her head. "No. Not yet, but my business partner is reviewing them and Sam's journals. He'll share his findings. I read his writings. That told me more than I needed to know. Lawrence Parish manipulated my brother."

"This cake is amazing! Is this our mother's recipe?" asked Sam, taking another bite.

Marnie smiled. "It is. I add more cinnamon, but other than that, yes."

"Tastes and smells are the good things I remember. As soon as I tasted this, I was at the kitchen table with a tall glass of milk." He closed his eyes, gathering his memories.

"I'm glad you recall the good things," she said.

He opened his eyes, still filled with fond memories. "I do, like raspberry pie."

Tom jumped in. "That's my favorite! Ma ... Your sister's is every bit as good as your mother's."

Danny and Ransom sat quietly, observing the relationship between the three and listening to them reminisce.

Sam rested his forehead in his palm, before rejoining the conversation. "Sorry. My mind is overloaded, and I need to ask. Can you still access the attic at the house?"

"Yes, of course," said Marnie. "Why?"

"I stored files under the eaves and I want to hand them over to Tom and Danny."

"Tell them what you told me," said Ransom.

Head in his hands, Sam muttered, "Could I please have a glass of water?"

"Have you got another headache?" his sister asked.

"Yes. It never really goes away."

She left the room and returned minutes later with water and a bottle of naproxen.

He looked up at her, grateful for the painkillers. "Thanks, Squirt."

"You're welcome," she said, taking a seat on the hassock at his feet, which concerned the detectives. She was too close.

Danny rolled the chair sideways, then placed himself in the doorway so that he had a clear shot and watched his partner do the same.

Sam noticed the men getting into position. "Detectives, you can stand down. I will not hurt her."

Both eased back a step as Ransom sat forward. "He isn't a danger to any of us. I have spent the last several days in the same motel room with him, and I haven't needed to sleep with one eye open. He is not under Parish's influence and he is not taking medication prescribed by him."

Danny's jaw tightened, and his eyes took on a steely glint. "How do you know he isn't under Parish's influence? I'll be happier once our psychiatrist comes back to us with his prognosis. Sam, would you be willing to speak with Carl Parkins?"

"Yes. I will do anything to have my sister back in my life. Anything. Just ask."

Glancing at his partner, who was unusually quiet, Danny said, "Tommy, what's on your mind?"

"I'm thinkin' that we, meaning you and I, are going to have our asses handed to us when your father finds out we haven't taken Sam into custody."

"Yeah. That was runnin' through my mind, too," said Danny, running a hand through his thick hair, leaving it mussed and spiky.

Ransom jumped to his feet abruptly. "He is in my custody. I'm a federal agent and I take full responsibility."

Danny shot across the study and hovered over the marshal. Ransom tipped back his head, realizing he had underestimated the detective's height and body mass.

"Are you sure about that?" asked Danny. "We're not gonna find out that you're on suspension or administrative leave? Maybe we make a call and find out, huh, Tommy?"

Ransom slapped the biceps of Danny's left arm. "Settle down, Gigantor. I've got everything under control."

Danny's huge hands curled into fists, and he pulled his shoulders back.

Sam jumped up and got between the detective and the marshal.

"That is enough. There is no place for egos in this conversation. But just to be clear, if either of you attacks the other, I *will* step in. I may not be as big as you, but I am fast, strong, and was a paid assassin. So please, let's sit and behave as grown-ups."

Exchanging an amused glance, Marnie and Tom stared at the floor, covering smirks. Once everyone had returned to their "corners," Marnie said, "I'll call the tenant at the house and pick up your folders. Have you hidden anything else there?"

Sam nodded. "Yeah. The hunting rifles Dad got me are in the same cubby. If you could please get those and lock them up, I would appreciate it." He turned to Tom. "Could you clean the rifles for me? I know you know how. I taught you."

"Sure. I'd be happy to clean them." Tom sat on the corner of the hassock next to Marnie. "What's in the files, Sam?"

"Research, undeveloped film in their canisters, pictures, and evidence against two dirty agents. I hid the files in case something happened to me. I planned to write my father a letter, telling where I hid the files, and the joint task force, but I never got the chance."

"Tell them what happened?" said Marnie, placing an encouraging hand on his knee.

"Billy Williams and Ransom got themselves into a tight spot. I followed them and got blown up."

Sam explained that two federal agents had participated in a drug cover up, making it easier for cartels to transport drugs into the United States and beyond via a network of juvenile thugs. Billy and Ransom were young DEA agents who had infiltrated the group and handed information and film from surveillance cameras over to Sam, who developed the film and recognized the men as two FBI agents from his field office.

He continued, "Long story short, the two agents picked up the scent of a setup and turned the tables. They sent Billy and Ransom on a special mission to pick up a supply of crack cocaine. I heard whispers through one of my confidential informants and hightailed it to the pickup point to foul the plan. When I arrived, the guys were already in the warehouse, and it was ready to blow as soon as they picked up the package. I ran into the building, pushed Ransom and Billy out the back door, but someone was watching. They detonated the bomb before I could get out."

Ransom said, "Billy and I never saw the bosses of the operation because we hadn't worked our way far enough up the chain."

Marnie turned to Sam. "Surely your informant said something when they thought you were dead?"

With a distasteful sneer, Sam said, "No. She would have compromised herself and been dead in a matter of hours."

Marnie raised an eyebrow. "She?"

"Yes. I believe you've met her," said Sam, looking between the detectives and his sister.

"No!" shouted Marnie—eyes wide with realization. "Are you telling me your informant was Erin Matthews?"

"The one and only!"

Ransom cringed. "Gawd! I wish I could forget that psycho bitch."

The detectives' mouths hung open, and only their eyes moved as they looked at one another.

"So, who were the agents?" asked Danny.

Sam turned, his expression somber. "Remember the other night at your place? Agents Harding and Dobbs?"

"Yeah."

"They are your men."

"I knew there was something dodgy with those two!" yelled Danny, snapping his fingers.

Marnie smacked her forehead and turned to Ransom. "Hence your need for cash."

"Exactly!" Ransom nodded.

"Do you want more?"

"Always, but we don't need it right now."

A rap at the study door made them leap. When the door swung open, the dogs ran into the room and the Border Collies made a beeline for Sam, who bent and welcomed their adoration. Gus stood back and observed before joining the cuddle session.

Danny raced to the door to block Teddy's view of the room.

"Sorry!" she said. "Tater opened the door before I could stop him, but I wanted to let you know Mike Crump is here about the surveillance cameras."

"I'll be there in a minute," said Danny before closing the door and turning around. "It looks like Tater has dealt with his trust issues."

A lopsided grin lit up Sam's face. "The bacon I gave him the other morning might have something to do with it."

"Bacon will do it every time," said Tom, checking his watch. "Look, we gotta get over to Pine Ridge to check up on Kate. Do you think we could finish this up tomorrow or later tonight?"

"Yeah," said Ransom. He reached into his wallet and removed a business card, handing it to Danny, who stood closest. "You can call me here anytime. Sam, do you have anything else to share with the detectives? How about those other tapes you mentioned?"

Sam pushed himself up off the couch. "Check the wine cellar. There are four bottles of Chateau Lafite-Rothschild 2018 along the back wall. The floor beneath has a loose stone. Check under that. Then check the Champagne cooler. He has an impressive collection of 1990 Cristal Brut that retail for around twenty grand a pop. There are five thumb drives hidden in the false bottom of a dummy bottle that should make for interesting viewing."

Marnie shivered and ran her fingers over her head as a gust of wind blasted open the French doors. They jerked around as rain and wind pushed through the doors. Lawrence Parish appeared in the doorway, pointing an accusing finger at Sam. Danny's eyes darted to Marnie's and she mouthed *not real*. The detectives rushed to the doors and pushed them closed against a gust of wind. A crack of lightning sent a jolting crash through the air as the gale fought back and blew open the doors again—but the spirit was gone.

"Here comes the storm," said Marnie, wrapping herself in a hug.

-*Chapter 39-*

"Did you have to give away all the cake?" Tom asked, a childlike frown tugging at his mouth.

"I'll make another one," said Marnie, giving his shoulder a motherly pat.

"Never mind that. We've gotta get to Pine Ridge and then it's back to the Parish's to search for fancy wine," said Danny. He glanced at Teddy, who wasn't paying attention, but was adding items to a shopping list.

Marnie picked up her keys. "We'll run a couple of errands and meet you back here. Carl will be out around 10:00 with the inspector. I want to stay out of the way and let him manage it."

Teddy glanced at the clock, which read 7:30. "We should go see the caterer to discuss the party, too. You told me you had to give him the menu items as soon as possible."

"Yes! Thank you for reminding me. I've got the selections in my handbag, but I think the usual barbecue fare will be fine. Who doesn't love a pig roast?"

Danny asked, "A caterer? How many people are you thinking?"

She shrugged. "A caterer makes it easy. I'm thinking thirty or so. We'll invite the usual suspects. All of us, Carl, Andrea, Hannah, Gram, Ellie, Tom's parents, if they're in town, Alice and Allen. And of course, Rick, Jalnack and whoever else you want to invite. Put it this way, I will cater for thirty. That way, we can add others."

"What about kids? Are they invited too?" asked Tom.

"What kind of celebration would it be without kids?"

"We'll count heads while we're driving into town. You don't want to over cater," said Teddy—a comment that sent the others into fits of laughter.

"Yes, we do," said the detectives in unison.

"Ha-ha! Over catering is what we do," said Marnie. "We all love leftovers."

Dalton Hooley met the detectives at the reception desk, a smug expression on his battered face. "Miss Kate isn't interested in seeing you gentlemen," he said, straightening his frame to his full height of six-feet-eight inches.

The comment got Danny's back up; he plastered on a faux smile. "Is that right?" he said in a condescending tone. "I'm Detective Gregg, and I know you've met my partner, Detective Keller." He pulled a piece of paper from his pocket. "Now, that's too bad about Kate. We have a search warrant for her room, the grounds, and any other area we deem fit." He held out the warrant and waved it under Dalton's nose. "Lookie here! It's signed by a judge and everything, so please come with us and unlock the door."

"Marnie, do you think Tom is still interested in Danny's sister? I know they dated for a while, but feel they've broken up. Is that right?" asked Teddy, a singsong lilt in her voice.

Marnie shifted the Jeep into fourth gear, then wagged a finger. "Oh, no! Don't drag me into it. If you're interested in Tom, you can speak to him. I am not a relationship counselor for a very good reason."

"What's that?" asked Teddy, her perfect eyebrows pulled together.

"I am crap at relationships and don't think I should offer anyone advice in that area. Besides, too much drama."

"What about you and Danny?"

"That's different. He's a patient man," said Marnie with a wink. "He and I have things to work out, but we're doing okay. I have trust issues to overcome, and he needs to stop worrying about me so much."

"Trust issues are understandable after Kate and Ken. And I guess your brother too, but I didn't hear any shouting from the study this morning, so I guess you and Sam are working through things."

Marnie caught Teddy's smirk and said, "Remember what we talked about."

Teddy nodded. "I repeat nothing that happens at your house." She put her thumb and index finger to her lips, twisted her fingers, and then opened her window, tossing the imaginary key to the curb.

"That's right," said Marnie. "Where are we going? You have the list."

"Umm ... Mrs. Backus' bookstore to pick up your order. The farmer's market for Dutch carrots and, yuck, turnips. I need to go to Drake's to pick up a prescription and moisturizer. And you said something about going to your old house and a lock, but that's all I wrote because I didn't know what you wanted."

"Dang it! I forgot to ask Danny what kind of lock to buy. Oh! We need to stop at my old house to pick up some stuff." Marnie took her eyes off the road and glanced at Teddy. "Keeping secrets is important right now. If that key finds a way back into your hand, I'll..."

"No need to threaten me. I said I wouldn't say anything, and I won't."

"Promise?"

Teddy held up her hand, taking a vow of silence. "Cross my heart and hope to die."

Kate screeched and lunged at Dalton when the detectives walked into her room. "How dare you let them into my suite?! You are a worthless, horrible excuse of a man. I told you I do not want to be disturbed!"

Dalton put up an arm to fend off her attack. Before she could reach the ward, Danny scooped an arm around her waist, and she cried out in pain. But he didn't care about her broken ribs. He'd had enough. "There won't be any of your shit today! Go sit. Now!"

She slunk to her bed and sat with a coquettish pout, batting her eyelashes at the detectives.

"Why do you have to be so mean?"

Danny turned to Dalton. "You got a place you can take her? The administrator said she wouldn't be here."

"I am not leaving my room!" she shouted, her hands punching the duvet.

Tom pulled his handcuffs from his back pocket. "I'll cuff her," he said to Dalton. "We don't want your face gettin' banged up again."

The big man shook his head. "No, thanks. I can manage this."

"I am not leaving! They will go through my personal things!"

"Miss Kate, we're going to the cafeteria for a coffee and a pastry. C'mon, now." Dalton stood at the door, holding it open for her.

She stood and waltzed across the room, stopping to hiss at Tom. "I'll take care of you!"

He laughed and shook his head, but leaped back when she took a threatening step toward him.

"Miss Kate! Now! Or I'll get the guards!" said Dalton.

Indigo eyes ablaze, she sauntered out of the door with a parting hiss. Before following her, the ward reached out and opened the top drawer of her desk, pulling out the cigar box. He made eye contact with Danny and tossed it on top of the desk.

"Start there," he said, then pulled the door shut behind him.

Their search of Pine Ridge exhausted, Danny and Tom drove through the gates with more questions than when they arrived.

Tom said, "There is no way she's gettin' out of her room unless someone is helping her, but their security footage doesn't support that."

Danny rolled down his window and watched the sanitarium growing smaller in the driver's side mirror. "No. We'll have Rick's team check the video to see if it's been tampered with, but it doesn't look like it has. The security team is on top of things. And they've taken extra precautions since she escaped. Can you believe Kate did that much damage to Dalton Hooley? He's a big man. Imagine what she'd do to one of us."

"No, thank you. Those pictures they showed us are brutal."

"Thoughts on the contents of the cigar box?"

"Kate hates Marnie, me, and a lot of other people, but what it boils down to is, she's batshit crazy."

"Yeah. That's what I thought."

"Okay. On to the Parish abode. How involved do you think Kitty was in her husband's mad scientist experiments?"

"I'd hate to think. Hang on. I got a text from Garcia. Dorie got a shock when she tried to change a fuse. It threw her ten feet into a wall. She suffered a concussion, and a broken clavicle."

Danny sighed and pressed his foot down on the gas pedal. "Let's get this solved before somebody else gets fried."

"Speaking of fried … I'm starving. Can we stop at the bakery for a bear claw?"

"Throw in a couple of jelly doughnuts, and you're on!" said Danny, slowing down to exit the highway.

Marnie parked in the Town Center parking garage. "Okay. Let's tick a few things off the list. We've picked up the stuff at the house. Turnips and carrots are in the cooler. The caterer has our order. Let's hit the bookstore and drugstore, then go get a bite to eat. I'm feeling peckish."

"Ha-ha! You've been watching British shows, haven't you?"

Marnie laughed. "Yes. A good British whodunnit is one of my guilty pleasures."

"Peckish gave it away. I love them too but haven't had time to watch lately with the strange hours I've been working. I grab as many hours as I can, and I've even done a few shifts at the abattoir—I don't like it, but it's food on the table."

"Carl and my assistant Andrea are running themselves ragged. I'll introduce you to them and if it's a good fit, we can talk seriously about you working full-time with us."

"Thank you, Marnie. Living day to day is stressful."

"Where are you living?" Marnie knew Teddy's parents sold their house and were retired and traveling the country in their luxury RV.

"I've got a little pop-up camper over at the campgrounds. Six bucks a day is a bargain."

"Do your folks know?"

"God, no! It would mortify them! They are coming back to Creekwood for July fourth. I don't know…"

"What about the old gamekeeper's cottage behind my house? It needs a lot of work, but it's sort of cute. There are no broken windows, the wiring is new and so is the plumbing."

"No, Marnie, I've imposed enough."

"Okay. It's there if you need it."

Marnie tapped her steering wheel to accept an incoming call from Carl Parkins. "Hey! How did the inspection go?"

Carl's voice came through the speaker. "We got our certification! The proviso is that we need two first-aid kits for the barn, eight eyewash kits, and three more fire extinguishers. Can you check pricing while you're in town? I'll text you the list."

"No need. Teddy is with me, and she jotted down everything and is already looking up pricing and suppliers. We need to go to the liquor store for a big bottle of bubbly, too! Woo-hoo! We're certified!"

"Andrea and I will stick around if you'll be back soon."

"Sure. We'll pick up lunch on the way."

"We'll go for a walk around the property and bask in the glory of this beautiful day."

"Isn't it raining there?"

"Nope. The sun is peaking through the clouds and it's getting steamy!"

"See you soon!" Marnie hung up, turned on the radio and smiled as Billy Currington's melodious voice drifted down the airwaves, and she turned to Teddy. "We better get some beer, too."

A shiny black Humvee with polished chrome sat in the Parish's driveway when Danny and Tom pulled to the curb. The license plate read TIMBRWLF. The plate and vehicle gave away the owner. There were only two Humvees in town. Preston Belmont owned one and Marnie Reilly owned the other, not that she drove it. It had been willed to her by her deceased ex Ken Wilder, and she had been trying to get rid of it for months, but there were no takers.

"Huh. Kitty's brother must be here." Danny squinted up the driveway, turned off the engine, and stepped onto the road. "You ever met him?"

"Not formally."

Kitty's brother walked out the front door as the detectives approached the house. Dressed in a pair of khakis, a white cotton polo, and tan loafers, Belmont was a diminutive man, and his forehead furrowed as he sized them up.

"What can I do for you, gentlemen?" he asked, his deep honeyed baritone belying his stature.

Tom offered his hand. "Mr. Belmont, I am Detective Keller, and this is Detective Gregg. We're from Creekwood PD. We have a warrant to search the house."

Belmont shook hands with the detectives, his grip firm and his hands dry and rough. He held up a suitcase and grinned. "Just running errands for my sister. She's not happy wearing hospital green. You guys looking for anything in particular?"

Tom rocked on his toes. "We have a few items on our list."

"Uh-huh. I see you found Lawrence's hiding place in the study."

"Yes, sir," replied Danny.

"Would you like to know where the others are?"

"Others?" asked Tom.

"Oh, yes. My brother-in-law thought he was so clever, but he's a boob. He would have been nothing without Kitty, you know. Her money. Her brains and her license."

Danny's eyebrows shot up. "License, sir?"

"Hmm ... You didn't know about that?" Preston's face wrinkled with amusement. He chuckled, unlocked the door, and pushed it open. "Dig deeper, fellas. It's amazing what you'll find in the false bottoms of dressers, china cabinets, and credenzas."

"Thank you, Mr. Belmont," said Tom with a wide grin.

Preston stopped on the steps, and without turning around, he said, "I love my sister, but I'll be damned if she's going to walk away from this mess scot-free. Happy hunting, Detectives!" He waved, climbed up into his vehicle, and gave the horn a blast before driving away.

"I really like that guy," said Danny with a laugh.

"Marnie, what's the matter?" Teddy leaned forward, appraising her with a silent stare.

"Not sure. Something is niggling at me."

"What's that mean?"

"I have a feeling something is about to happen."

"Something good or something bad?"

Marnie giggled nervously and glanced in her rearview mirror. "A niggling feeling is never good."

"Well, we're back at the ranch now, so maybe the feeling will pass."

"Hmm … Lights are off in the house. Let's drive down to the barn to see if we can find Carl and Andrea. It looks like it's going to rain again." Marnie veered onto the lawn and bounced them over hills, stopping outside the big red barn.

"That's strange. The big door is open. I wonder if Carl and Andrea are in there." A spiderweb of energy stretched across her scalp, and she shivered. "Right back," she said, opening her door.

"I'll come with." Teddy hopped out and they both when into the barn.

"Isn't it gorgeous?" Marnie twirled to the center of the old building. "I love the way it smells in here."

"Um … It's fine as far as barns go," Teddy said with a giggle. "Where are the animals?"

"In the pasture. They come in at night or if the weather is terrible. To be honest, I don't know much about the ranch yet. That's what those books are for that we picked up today. I've got a crash course coming my way when Jonas feels up to it. Anyway, let's go. I've got unpacking to do."

Marnie stopped along the way and pulled down the light switch, then froze when the surrounding air prickled and a crackle of electricity and sparks traveled up the wall and burst into flames. "Teddy! Run!"

They raced to the door, but it swung shut as they reached it. Marnie helped Teddy push, but it would not yield.

"Oh! I feel sick!" said Teddy.

"Don't throw up!" shouted Marnie, remembering how Teddy, when they were children, would vomit when she was nervous or scared.

"I'm trying not to," she said, tears in her eyes and covering her mouth to hide a heave.

Marnie glowered and hurled her hands in the air. "What idiot would put the bar across without checking if someone was in here? Shit! If the fire reaches the hay, we're in trouble."

Teddy grabbed her arm. "Carl mentioned fire extinguishers. Are there any in here?"

"I don't know, but let's try the rear door." Marnie jogged down the center aisle and pushed on the back doors. "Gawd! These are locked from the outside too! I'll bust out a window."

"Here are the extinguishers," Teddy yelled, dragging one down from a rack on the wall. "Oh, God! Look!"

Marnie whirled around and watched in horror as the fire traveled up the wall to the haymow.

"Dammit!" Marnie grabbed a shovel and broke through a small window. She tossed a saddle blanket over the opening and told Teddy to crawl through.

"Go! Get the bar off the door and call the fire department!"

"Come with me!" Teddy shouted, her words muffled by the hand covering her mouth.

"No," said Marnie with a firm shake of her head. "I've got the extinguisher. I'm going to see if I can quell the fire."

"Marnie! C'mon!"

"Teddy! Go! Stop wasting time!"

Teddy scrambled up and through the window and called nine-one-one.

"Hello! I am at the old Billingsly Ranch on Hallowed Hills Road. We've got a fire in the barn!"

"You better pray for rain, love. Our trucks are at Pine Ridge Sanitarium. It was a false alarm, but I doubt they'll make it to you."

"Oh! Shit!" Teddy raced to the doors. She pushed up on the boom, but it wouldn't budge. "Marnie! Get out of there!"

Not knowing what to do, she called Tom.

"Hey, Teddy, we're in the middle of something..."

"Tom! The barn's on fire and Marnie's locked inside! I can't get her out!"

"We'll be there as fast as we can!"

Teddy tried thrusting up the bar again, but it was wet from the rain and wouldn't slide.

"Dammit, Marnie! Talk to me!"

"Hey! Is Marnie in there?" Carl raced to Teddy's side, with Andrea lagging a step behind.

"Yes! Get. Her. Out!" cried Teddy.

Flames licked out the door, forcing them back. The bang of the haymow doors flying open drew their attention above, where Marnie appeared at the edge, angry tears running down her face and flames dancing behind.

"I can't put it out," she yelled, then coughed into the collar of her T-shirt.

Carl shouted, "Marnie, you're going to have to jump!"

She fired back, "No shit!"

Elk and Arnie came around the side of the barn and glanced at Carl, Andrea, and Teddy, and then cast their eyes upward.

Jonas appeared and shouted, "What the hell? Hang on! I'll get a rope!"

He raced off as the others tried to lift the bar, and it finally gave way. The doors swung open and a blaze of fire and heat burst toward them.

"Shut the doors! Don't let the air in!" yelled Jonas.

He backed away from the group, gave the rope a toss and lassoed the decorative eagle sitting regally aloft the ridgepole.

"Grab the rope!" he shouted.

"Will that hold me?" she asked, coughing and pulling a doubtful expression.

"I reckon, so! That eagle carved into the ridgepole is your grandfather's handiwork."

She mumbled to herself, "So it's what? A hundred years old and has survived 400 seasons. Yeah. Sure. It'll hold me. Oh, hell, suck it up, Reilly!" She glanced to the heavens, hoping for divine guidance, but none came. With both hands gripping the rope, she gave it a firm test tug, and with a quick prayer, she swung out the door and shimmied down. Carl stood ready to make a diving catch should she fall.

Three feet from terra firma, Marnie let go of the rope and dropped, landing with a grunt.

Teddy wrapped her arms around her. "I knew you could do it!" Then she pushed her away. "Why didn't you leave with me? Jesus! You could have burned alive!" Teddy's face contorted with anger and she suddenly reeled away, throwing up in the grass.

"Ah! Teddy, I'm sorry!" she said, rubbing her back.

"Everybody move back! We gotta get this fire out!" Jonas marshaled them toward the pond as Arnie and Elk drove up in a chugging and spitting vintage pump and ladder.

Marnie's mouth dropped open. "We have a fire truck?"

"Of course!" said Jonas, a dismissive expression pinching his features.

"But there aren't any hydrants," said Andrea, scanning the pasture.

"We don't need one. We've got a pond," said Elk, rolling up his sleeves to reveal his farmer's tan. "Arnie, drop the hose!"

Arnie scooped up one end of the hose, unrolling it as he walked. He dragged it to the pond, then heaved the nozzle with all his might into the deep water in the middle.

Jonas turned on the pump as Elk positioned the firehose toward the upper level of the barn, then twisted the nozzle, producing a propulsion of pond water.

Marnie stuck her pinkies in her mouth and whistled her appreciation.

"Hey!" yelled Teddy. "Did you see that lightning over there? And listen! It's thundering."

A moment later, the sky dropped a deluge of rain, drenching them.

Marnie yelled, "C'mon! Let's get to the house before one of us gets hit by lightning!"

Carl and Andrea didn't argue. They raced to the Jeep and dove into the backseat.

Jonas said, "We'll stay here and take care of the barn. You go! Besides, we gotta get the other barn ready for livestock. Go!"

The sky crackled as a chain of lightning blazed across the sky, nipping the tail of the old windmill standing twenty feet away in the pasture.

"Oh, no!" Marnie backed away from the Jeep and stared, wide-eyed, at the spiraling blade crashing to the ground with a raucous clatter.

"Don't worry about it. We'll fix it tomorrow. It's not the first time," replied Jonas with the ease of a seasoned rancher.

"But lightning isn't supposed to strike the same spot twice," said Teddy.

Elk laughed. "Ha! That's a bullshit wives' tale. Lightning strikes wherever the hell it wants!"

-*Chapter 40-*

"That was a close call, Marn. You and Teddy ... Geez! I can't even think about it." Tom draped a protective arm around her and squeezed.

"We're okay. The barn isn't, but Jonas says it won't take much to fix it. I'll call Stu."

Danny paced from the kitchen to the dining room and back again, doing his best to calm down. "Why didn't you crawl through the window with Teddy?"

Whirling around, her green eyes flashing, she said, "Because, Detective, I'm stupid!" With an eye roll, she crossed the kitchen and filled a glass with water. "The hay was on fire. I tried to put it out with an extinguisher."

"You could've died!" he roared. "What would you have done if the doors to the haymow wouldn't open? You shouldn't have gone upstairs!"

"Coulda, woulda, shoulda. Didn't! I'm right here. Breathing and everything!" She slammed down the glass, water sloshing onto the table, and stormed out of the room. They heard her clomp up the stairs a moment later.

Danny turned to go after her, but Teddy reached out and caught his arm. "Give her a minute. She's scared. Marnie knows she should have followed me out and that she could have died. Don't tell her that again. Tell her you love her; that you're not mad at her. Get that cranky expression off your face and go upstairs in about ten minutes."

"Ten minutes?" he asked.

Teddy held up a finger, pointing to the ceiling as the sound of an upstairs shower turned on. "Because that's when the full force of what happened is going to hit. You need to go upstairs, step into the shower, clothes and all, tell her you love her, and pick her up off the cold tiles because she's going to be sitting there under the showerhead, bawling her eyes out."

Danny screwed up his face, held out his hands, and asked, "What? Why do I have to wear my clothes into the shower?"

"Chivalry," said Tom, before taking a big bite out of a bear claw.

Danny stood outside the bedroom door, willing himself to follow Teddy's instructions. Truth be told, he wasn't mad. Fear had gotten the better of him. The thought of losing Marnie made him ill. There were clues all around them, but nothing concrete stood out. The most likely suspect, Sam Reilly, wasn't a suspect at all. Or was he?

He rested his head against the door and counted. "Tom's electrical incident is three. Dorie's incident takes us back to one. The barn is two. Or is it Marnie plus Teddy, which would make three?" He thought about it, drumming his fingers on the door. "One more," he said before opening the door.

Marnie was exactly where Teddy said she would be, sitting on the cold tiles with water showering over her. But she wasn't crying; she was inspecting a blister on her big toe. She glanced up when the detective stepped in.

"What are you doing?" she asked, pulling a face.

"Trying to be chivalrous," he said, crossing his ankles and sinking to the tiles. "I'm sorry for being an ass."

"That's okay. It wasn't one of my finer moments, either." She stretched out one long leg and plonked her foot on his knee. "I burned my toes."

"I guess I'm gonna have to arrest whoever did that to you," he said, picking up her foot, tenderly kissing each digit.

She giggled. "You do that, Detective, but you better dry off first."

He brushed a tendril of hair out of her eyes and sighed. The last thing he wanted to do was leave her, but he had a killer to catch.

"Not to spoil the party…"

She nodded. "I know. You guys have to go."

"Yup. But we'll be back before you know it."

"Are you threatening me with a good time?" she teased.

He leaned forward and kissed her nose before standing and holding out his hands to help her up.

"Yes, ma'am! See you later, huh?"

"Be safe," she said, standing on tiptoes to kiss him goodbye.

When Marnie returned to the kitchen, the detectives were gone, and Teddy was making a pot of coffee.

"I hope you don't mind?" Teddy held up the pot.

"Not at all. Make yourself at home." She slumped onto a bench and leaned down to see two fluffy Border Collies and one sleek Labrador asleep under the table. "I feel horrible that Carl and Andrea took off so quickly. We didn't even open the champagne."

"Well, when Danny and Tom arrived, I think they knew the big guy was gonna explode. That man has a temper."

"That man doesn't want to lose the people he loves. He acts all gruff and roars like a bear, but it's only because he wants nothing bad to happen."

Marnie straightened her shoulders and glanced around the room.

"Gawd! Is that niggly feeling back?" Teddy asked.

"Yeah," said Marnie, scanning the room.

The dogs bolted out from under the table and barked at the back door.

The women turned to see Jonas Billingsly through the glass. He knocked once, then tried the door, which Teddy had locked. Marnie got up and calmed the dogs.

"Shh. Come on, guys," she soothed before opening the door.

"What's all that fuss about? They never bark at me." He stood at the entrance with a befuddled expression.

It was when Tater planted himself in front of his mistress that the telltale tingle returned, and Marnie knew her suspicions of Jonas were true.

"What's the verdict on the barn?" she asked.

"Stu says he can have his guys come out tomorrow or the next day to get started on repairs. I talked to Danny and Tom, though, and they want to wait for the fire chief and his investigator to have a look."

"I agree. We'll need it for our insurance, anyway. Want a coffee?" she asked, crossing to the pot.

"No. I'm gonna get back to it. I wanted to make sure you and Teddy are okay." He reached out to pat Tater, but the dog growled and bounced backward.

Jonas scowled. "What's with him?"

Marnie raised an eyebrow. "Tater and I have been chatting with Lanie."

"I don't get it. You told me she wasn't here."

"Oh, she wasn't, but she is now."

Jonas snickered. "You almost had me going for a minute! Shit, Marnie." He stepped back and opened the screen door. "C'mon, Dickens, wanna go outside?"

Dickens let out an excited yip and raced out the door, with Gus lunging after him. Tater sat and glanced back at his mistress, who shook her head sadly.

"Getting rid of the dogs won't change anything, Jonas. You killed Lanie and I can prove it."

Teddy let out a gasp, then clapped a hand over her mouth.

"Ha! What happened to client patient confidentiality? Besides, I didn't kill her. I swear on her grave."

Marnie shrugged. "Lanie says you lost your temper and whacked her with a spirit level."

Face reddening and nostrils flaring, he slammed his hands onto the table. "Stop saying that! I did not kill my wife."

"Stop taunting him," said Teddy between gritted teeth.

"Then why did we find the level in the hidden room? Who else could have put it there?"

His face darkened, and he leaped across the table, scattering paper napkins and the salt and pepper shakers.

Tater vaulted on top of the table, snapping and snarling.

"Teddy! Run!"

Marnie ordered Tater to the floor, snatched up the coffeepot and tossed the hot liquid into Jonas' face. To his pained shrieks, she strained to pick up a bench, dropping it on top of him—delivering a grunt and a groan of agony.

Teddy stood motionless, mouth open and dazed. Marnie grabbed her hand and dragged her to the study, plucking her phone off the table along the way.

Tater scurried after them, slipping on the polished floors, then sat in the doorway while Marnie pulled up the trapdoor to the tunnel.

"Down there! Go! And turn on your phone's light!"

The bench being heaved across the kitchen was the next sound the women and dog heard, then the echo of work boots tramping through the house. Teddy shrieked as she clambered down the steps, fumbling with her phone as she went.

"Tater! Come! C'mon, boy!"

The Border Collie back-walked to his mistress and waited for her to start down the stairs, then followed. Marnie pulled down the hatch, turned on her flashlight and ran, dragging Teddy with her.

"What about Dickens and Gus?" Teddy cried.

Marnie nudged her forward. "They'll be fine. Don't worry about them! Run!"

"I feel sick!"

"For God's sake, don't puke! We don't have time!"

Marnie pulled Teddy by the hand down the dark passageway, glancing back every few seconds to see if Jonas was gaining on them. When the tunnel came to a four-way, she turned left, but Teddy stopped. Tater barked, nipped her ankle, and pushed her with his nose, herding her left.

"I don't think he's following us," whispered Teddy.

"He is. You just can't see him. He grew up here and knows these tunnels better than anyone."

At another fork, Marnie stopped and assessed their position, shining the light down the paths lying ahead. She checked her internet and phone's service, but neither were available in the tunnel, giving them no option to reach out for help. On the off chance she could reach her brother telepathically, because siblings often can, she closed her eyes and sent him a message. Anything was worth a try at this point.

The crunch of boots alerted them to Jonas' location, and they spun around. He was dead ahead of them. Holding a gun.

"They'll never find you down here," he said, shining his light in their faces. "I doubt anybody but me knows about this place."

Marnie scowled and turned off her light. "Don't be stupid! The detectives and my brother know."

To Teddy, she whispered, "Turn off your light and don't throw up."

"I'm more worried about peeing my pants now," Teddy said with a whimper, and extinguished her light.

The dog growled, backed up, and sat at Marnie's feet.

Jonas laughed and took two steps forward. "They're not here, though, are they? Besides, your brother wouldn't help you."

"No, but my clairvoyance will. I have so many spirits to choose from. My parents, Lanie, Paige, my grandfather ... Any minute now, one of them *will* intervene and we'll make a run for it."

Jonas roared with laughter. "You know. I never believed that nonsense. Sure, I've humored you over the years, but let's be serious, there's no such thing as ghosts." His words barely spoken, the light of his phone turned off and darkness settled around them.

"Dammit!" he yelled.

"How did you do that?" whispered Teddy.

"I didn't do anything, but I smell the faintest hint of jasmine and musk. Can you smell it?"

"That's the horrible scent Lanie wore! She showered in it!"

"Shh!" hissed Marnie.

"What did you do to my phone?" Jonas huffed.

"Spirits drain batteries. Look behind you," said Marnie, crouching down.

His boots scrabbled the earthen floor as he jerked around, searching for a ghost. A loud sigh followed by a derisive spit came next. "There's no one there!"

"Can't you smell your wife's perfume?"

"Knock it off! You know Lanie isn't here."

Marnie grabbed Teddy's hand and pulled her down.

The women inched themselves sideways in the opposite direction, their backs to the cold stone wall. Tater slunk backward, keeping his eyes trained on Jonas.

"Marnie? Teddy? Where'd you go?"

Eyes closed with an ice pack on his forehead, Sam tried desperately to doze, but sleep would not come. He could hear Ransom tapping away on his laptop when he got the sudden urge to call his sister. He bolted upright, the ice pack clunking to the floor.

"What's wrong?" asked Ransom, closing his laptop.

"I don't know. Can you call my sister?"

Ransom unlocked his phone and tossed it to Sam. "Here you go."

Sam caught the phone and placed the call, but she didn't answer. "It went straight to voicemail," he said.

Ransom frowned. "You look worried."

"I am."

"You wanna drive over?"

Sam nodded. "Please. I would feel better knowing she is okay."

The fifteen-by-fifteen room smelled of earth, sweetgrass, and a mild whiff of creosote; its stone walls constructed with the same clay mortar as the passages.

"Shh! Close the door," said Marnie, switching on her light.

"Where are we?" asked Teddy, inspecting a row of shelves along the back wall.

"I'm not sure." Marnie reached down and gave Tater an ear scratch, then joined Teddy.

Canning jars of clear liquid lined the shelves, each with a handwritten note, crudely hole-punched, and tied to the jars with sweetgrass.

Teddy flipped over several tags and furrowed her brow. "Huh! The labels have only years on them."

Marnie poked through a rolltop desk, pulling out drawers and peeking in pigeonholes.

"What are the years?" she asked over her shoulder.

"Ah, 1919, 1921, 1930 ... Strange, right?"

"Nope. Prohibition began in 1919 in New York State, and it became federal law in 1920. Those dates aren't at all strange."

Teddy shrieked, "Is this moonshine?"

"I think so. Open one."

Teddy selected a bottle and tried to twist the lid, with no luck, so she smacked the bottom of the jar and the top loosened on the next turn. She winced and held the bottle away, afraid the odor would assault her nostrils.

Teddy held it out. "You smell it."

Which she did and nodded. "Hmm ... Corn."

"It doesn't stink?"

"Not really, but I'd bet it burns going down."

"Did you hear that?" Teddy's eyes swept to the door.

Danny turned down the car's radio and clicked his tongue on the roof of his mouth as he thought of Lanie's murder. "The only prints on that level belong to Jonas Billingsly. You think he could kill his wife?"

Tom said, "I've been thinkin' about that since Rick told us, and yeah, I do. I've known him most of my life. He's that guy who used brute force in sports just for kicks. He got me good with his cleats durin' a friendly baseball game when he slid into home and kicked my ankle. Jonas was out, and he got pissed. Marnie took me to the emergency room for stitches."

"It wasn't an accident?"

"Nah."

"Is that it?"

"Uh-uh. Before he and Lanie got together, he dated Kimberly Hamilton. Nice girl. She was two years ahead of us. Anyway, I remember one night at Oscars, you know that tavern on Ford Street, the two of them were obviously arguing. One minute she's standing there, the next she's on her butt, blood pouring out of her nose. She said he elbowed her in the face. Gave the excuse she got in the way while he was showing his buddies his golf swing. The guys backed him up, but they worked at the ranch, so they would."

"He plays golf?"

"Nope."

"We better get back to Marnie's. She knows."

Tom nodded. "Yeah. She won't be able to stop herself from sayin' something if the opportunity presents itself."

"My thoughts exactly."

The door flew open and Jonas sneered, gun drawn. Marnie grasped a bottle of moonshine and chucked it at him as hard as she could. He ducked, but Teddy sent a second missile his way, striking him in the chest before crashing to the ground and shattering. Tater clamped his jaw around Jonas' ankle and pulled him off balance.

"Jesus! Stop!"

"Tater, come!" shouted his mistress, fearing for his safety. The dog obediently fell in behind her.

Marnie hurled another, hitting Jonas' temple, followed by a blow from Teddy that knocked his weapon to the floor. Marnie dove for the pistol, dust flying up around her, a shard of glass puncturing her thigh. Jonas clamped his hands around her arms, struggling to pull her off the gun, but she kicked out and connected with his shin, causing him to lose his grip. Teddy bobbed and weaved around the two, then jumped on Jonas's back, wrapping her arms tightly around his throat. Twice her size, the farmhand easily pulled her arms free and flung onto the desk.

"Teddy!" Marnie scrambled to her feet and swung a left-hook into Jonas' face, slugging him on the chin.

"I'm going to kill you!" he growled, lurching forward.

"The fuck you are!" was the last thing Jonas heard before hitting the dirt.

Ransom bound Jonas' hands behind his back with a zip-tie before checking his vitals. "He's fine. That's quite the left-hook you've got there, kid." He glanced up and winked as he rolled the farmhand to his back. "We'll let the detectives take care of his sorry ass. Sam, you better scram before he wakes up and starts singin'."

Marnie helped Teddy sit up and checked her eyes, which focused on Sam. "She's fine, too. We'll go upstairs and call the guys."

"You better take care of that leg," said Ransom, looking down at the shard of glass poking out from her skin and the blood seeping from her thigh.

All eyes drifted to the wound, and Teddy gagged before clapping her hand over her mouth.

"Don't puke!" cried Marnie.

With an arm wrapped around his sister's waist, Sam led the women through the tunnel.

"You doing okay? I can carry you," he said.

"No thanks. We'll get there quicker if I walk. Besides, it doesn't hurt."

"Yet," said Teddy.

Ransom caught up to them. "I left Jonas behind so the detectives can say they found him."

"Ah! Creative thinking, Deputy." Sam laughed, then stopped short. "Shh!" He dragged Marnie down a passageway on their left and the others followed.

Tater poked his nose out and sniffed. His tail wagged with recognition, and a low "ow-row-row" escaped his muzzle.

"It must be Danny and Tom," said Marnie, peeking out. "It is. Come on."

"What the hell happened?" asked Danny, shining his phone's light on her leg.

"Jonas happened," she said. "Sam and Ransom got him, though. He's out cold and zip-tied."

Ransom laughed. "Ha! These two gals got him pretty good, too."

Tom bent to inspect Marnie's leg and let out a whistle. "You better get that cleaned up. Is that the bottom of a canning jar?"

"Mm-hmm. There's a stash of moonshine. Teddy and I threw it at Jonas."

"Moonshine?" asked Danny.

"Uh-huh. Can we finish this upstairs before I bleed to death?"

Tom nudged his partner. "I'll take care of Jonas. You go ahead." He turned to Ransom. "C'mon. Give me a hand."

Danny turned to Marnie and held out his arms. "Can I give you a lift, Miss Reilly?" Not waiting for an answer, he scooped her up.

-Chapter 41-

"I can't sleep. The security lights are too bright," Marnie whined, flipping her pillow for the fifth time.

Danny pulled her tenderly into the crook of his arm and she dropped her head onto his chest with a sigh.

"How's your leg feeling?"

"Like I got thirty stitches."

"That's on me. When I called your uncle, he recommended a plastic surgeon to minimize scarring."

"Hmm … I don't care about scars. Besides, Uncle Giles deals with dead people. What does he know?"

Danny chuckled. "You want a cup of hot chocolate?"

"What good is hot chocolate if I can't put schnapps in it? Antibiotics suck," she huffed.

"Okay, Miss Crankypants, wanna go downstairs?"

Both shot upright at the sound of tires in the driveway and the slamming of two doors.

Tom and Ransom walked through the back door as Danny and Marnie entered the kitchen, and a moment later, Sam came in from the downstairs bedroom. Groggy with sleep, he yawned.

"Is everything settled?" he asked.

Ransom nodded. "Yeah. We kept your name out of it. Anyone asks, *I* whacked Jonas." He turned to Marnie. "Will your friend corroborate that?"

"I saw nothing. Marnie was in the way," said Teddy, padding into the kitchen.

"Good answer," said Tom.

"No. Seriously. I didn't see who hit Jonas."

"Even better," said Sam.

"Did you get your brother's stuff out of the attic?" Ransom turned to Marnie.

"Shit! It's in the back of my car."

Tom snatched up her keys. "I'll get it."

The humidity had risen and hung oppressively over the valley. Heavy clouds rolled over the mountains and flashes of lightning strobed in the distance. Tom surveyed the front lawn, searching for lurkers in the darkness, but knew the security system would reveal any unwelcome guests. He unlocked the Jeep, slung a rifle bag over each shoulder, stacked four fireproof boxes, closed the cargo with his foot, and returned to the house. Danny met him at the back door and pushed it open.

Tom set the boxes on the table and rested the rifle bags in a corner. "Where do we start?" he asked.

The shuffle of papers, slurps of coffee, scratches of pens on notepads, and the soft snores of canines were the noises that filled the kitchen for the next three hours. The odd bleep of the app connected to motion sensors on the grounds revealed a skunk family crossing a path, a raccoon peering into a camera lens and a doe chomping clover in the pasture. Everyone inside remained focused on the task at hand, until Marnie, distracted by an incessant tapping on the window, limped to the light switch and plunged the outside into darkness.

"I cannot take those dang June bugs pinging off the glass any longer! It drives me to distraction!" She shuffled back to a bench and painfully slid into her seat.

The clock on the microwave read 3:00 AM when Tom mumbled something indiscernible.

"What?" Danny asked, rubbing the bridge of his nose, his eyes squinting with fatigue.

Tom raised his head and yelled, "I'm starving!" To prove the point, his stomach let out a roaring growl.

Marnie slid from the bench again, limped to the freezer, pulled out a cheese Danish, and stuck it in the microwave to defrost.

"This is the best I can do at this hour, but I will make you dinner tonight," she said.

"Marnie, do you want another pot of coffee?" Teddy nudged Ransom to slide off the bench so she could get out.

Head popping up, and his brow furrowed, Sam asked, "What did you just say?"

Teddy looked at him and shrugged. "I asked Marnie if she wanted coffee. Why?"

A slow smile eased across his lips, and he tipped his head. "I didn't react. You said my sister's name, and I didn't..." He yawned and his shoulders relaxed. "Say it again!"

Teddy giggled, then said it again. "Marnie."

He turned to Danny. "Now you."

"Marnie."

"Tom, you say it!"

Which he did.

"You say it," said Ransom.

Sam took a breath and said, "Marnie."

They all waited, but nothing bad happened. With a lopsided grin, he scooted out of his seat and wrapped his arms around his sister.

"Careful! Your shoulder," she said, tears dribbling down her cheeks.

"My shoulder is fine." He swung her around, then remembered her leg and set her down.

She hugged him, then leaned against the counter. "I've been reading about hypnosis and coercive mind control. You've been in a somewhat relaxed and nurturing environment for nearly a week. That, plus reading your notes, chatting with me, spending time here and saving me today ... All those things might work to remove Lawrence's influence. I knew it could happen, but I didn't think it would be so soon."

A low grumble from Tater snapped their attention to the back door, where he stood with his scruff up. Dickens and Gus joined him, muttering warnings in reply to his growls. Marnie raced to the wall switch and filled the yard with blinding light, as the detectives called up the security system on their phones.

"What the hell?" Tom glanced at Danny, who ran his fingers through his hair and stared blankly at the screen.

"What's wrong?" asked Ransom, instinctively reaching for his sidearm.

"All the security cameras are black," replied Danny.

Tater's head jerked left—his eyes focused on the cellar door. A moment later, the house plunged into darkness, except for the light from the detectives' phones, which eerily outlined their features.

They leaped to their feet, knocking over the bench. Ransom slid from his seat and followed the detectives to the cellar door.

"Marn, where's the breaker box?" asked Tom.

"There's a mechanical room at the bottom of the cellar stairs," she said, joining them near the door.

"Where's the outside entrance into the cellar?" asked Ransom.

"Under the service porch, but it's locked. I checked it earlier," she said.

The power flickered once, then the room filled with light, the microwave beeped and the clock flashed to life.

"We're being played," said Marnie, peering out the back door.

The detectives checked their phones, and every camera showed the property in real-time.

Tom rolled his shoulders and sighed. "We gotta share everything we've got. Chasin' our tails isn't gonna solve this. We've got Lanie's killer behind bars, but there are inconsistencies. Jonas swears he did not put her in that bathtub. So, who did?"

"The same person who killed Paige?" asked Teddy.

"That's what I'm thinkin'."

"Let's get together tomorrow at 3:00. That gives everyone time to put their notes together," said Danny.

Marnie asked, "Will you include Hannah and Carl?"

"Yeah. Gram, too."

"It makes sense since she knows where Creekwood's skeletons are," added Tom.

Ransom wandered to the cellar door. "I'm checking the basement before catching some Zs."

Danny agreed, "Yeah. We'll take the knuckleheads out and check the exterior door. C'mon, Tom."

Marnie and Teddy trudged upstairs ahead of the men.

"See you in the morning," said Teddy.

"I hope you get some sleep," Marnie replied, opening her bedroom door and flopping onto the bed.

A warm breeze billowed the curtains and scattered her tarot cards to the floor before slamming shut the door. With a frustrated groan, she got up to pick up the cards. Seven cards lay face up, and she fell to her knees as fear overtook her senses.

"How do I stop this?" she said, picking up the objectionable spread. The Man, Lilies, Scythe, House, Coffin, Mice, and Cross told her a story too horrid to accept. It confirmed the foreboding energy that shadowed her return to Creekwood.

Marnie's memories traveled back to Shelta Joyce, an old Irish Traveler woman who taught her to read the cards. Her tidy, quaint cottage stood at the edge of a trailer park on the outskirts of Hudson Hollow. The price to study the tarot was two hundred and fifty dollars, which included twenty one-hour lessons and one deck of cards. She had several to choose from, including Rider-Waite-Smith, the Tarot of Marseilles, and Aleister Crowley's Toth deck. But Marnie chose The Lenormand Oracle Cards named for the famed and mysterious fortune teller, Marie Anne Adelaide Lenormand. The petite deck depicted water-color images, not likely to scare a querent. Mostly.

At the scurry of dog nails on the stairs and the footfalls of the men, she scooped up the cards and dropped them in a drawer.

-Chapter 42-

"This was a great idea," said Teddy, swinging a shopping basket as they strolled through the farmer's market.

Marnie agreed, "Isn't it a beautiful morning?"

The detectives walked a few steps behind, trained eyes watching the throng of shoppers meander through the stands. There was a nip in the breeze, but the brilliant sunshine chased away the white mountain mist hanging over the valley.

"It's gonna be a hot one!" said Tom, looking up at the cloudless sky. "Is your pool warm, Marn?"

"No idea. I haven't checked it."

"You can't go swimming with those stitches," said Danny.

With a wrinkle of her nose, she pouted. "Nope." She spun around and bobbed her head toward a man leaving a strawberry stand. "Isn't that Dalton Hooley?"

"It sure is," said Tom.

"Who?" asked Teddy.

"Kate's handler," said Marnie.

The big man ambled toward them, a smile gathering when he recognized the group.

"Good morning," he said.

A chorus of 'good morning' followed, and Danny extended his hand, which Dalton heartily shook.

"Is Kate behaving herself?" asked Tom.

Dalton pursed his lips. "Not so you would notice. She's a handful."

"Did she do that to your nose?" Marnie asked.

He stood silently, then finally nodded. "Yeah. It's embarrassing that a little thing like Miss Kate could have done this to a big guy like me."

Tom clapped his shoulder. "Marnie and I grew up with her. We know how she can be. Just glad you're okay."

"Thanks. I better get going. I have to be at work soon," he said, holding up a green punnet. "Had to get strawberries for Miss Kate. She has been carrying on about how horrible the food is at Pine Ridge. I think it's fine, but I guess you can see that." The big man laughed and patted his stomach. "Have a good day!"

"You, too," said Tom, while the others offered a wave.

Marnie's green eyes scanned the crowd warily as she pulled her strawberry blonde locks into a ponytail, securing it with an elastic she wore around her wrist. "Let's grab what we need and go home. It's getting hot and I'm feeling antsy."

Tom caught her gaze and lifted a questioning eyebrow. "Antsy? In the spooky sense? As in ants crawling all over your scalp?"

"Mm-hmm ... something like that," she replied with a quiver.

Two raspberry pies cooled on the kitchen table when Carl Parkins arrived at 2:00.

"Oo! You've been baking!"

Marnie looked up from the bowl of whipped cream she was making and nodded.

"You okay?" he asked.

She turned off the mixer and shrugged. "The spirits are restless today. I can't stop the chatter."

"Have you tried meditating?"

"That made it worse. I've asked them to back off, but they won't."

"Is it your parents?"

"It's everybody," she said as she folded vanilla and sugar into the cream.

"What about a swim?"

"I can't." She pulled off her apron, revealing the stitches.

"Ow! What did you do?"

"I'll explain later."

"Okay. How about a glass of wine? I have a nice white."

"I can't. Antibiotics!" she whined.

"Yikes! Anyway, I've been through the tapes and the journals."

"What's the prognosis, Dr. Parkins?"

"Your brother needs an ethical psychotherapist, not a prison sentence."

"What do we do?"

Carl offered a sympathetic smile. "We do nothing. You let Ransom handle it."

"Should I get Sam a lawyer?"

"The best money can buy."

The savory scent of pot roast filled the house, and when the detectives came in from their swim, Tom stopped at the doorway and took a deep breath.

Tom said, "Oh, man! That smells so good!"

Danny dropped a kiss on Marnie's head. "Any chance you can keep dinner warm? We have to go to Pine Ridge. The head of security found love notes and other incriminating stuff in one of the guard's lockers."

"Yeah, of course. It's only three o'clock. We won't be ready for a few hours, anyway. I haven't even started the veggies," she said, setting a colander of red potatoes into the sink. "Is Carl in the pool?"

"Yeah. He and Teddy are floating on noodles and havin' an in-depth conversation about her parents and their unreasonable expectations," said Tom.

"Nothin' better than free therapy," she said with a giggle.

"Hmm … She needs all the therapy she can get."

Marnie wagged a finger. "Stop it!"

Gram and Hannah arrived, bringing a basket of yeasty rolls and a bottle of wine.

"Are we early?" asked Gram.

"No. Carl and Teddy are in the pool, and the guys had to run out. They've had a break in the case." Marnie crossed her fingers, then gave her visitors a hug. "Has Danny filled you in on everything?"

"Yes," said Hannah, glancing around the room, assessing the absence of people. "Are you expecting anyone else?"

"Ransom Elliot and my brother. They'll come through the tunnel."

Gram clapped her hands. "It's nice to know we're connected, isn't it?"

Marnie screwed up her face. "Connected?"

"Yes! That tunnel goes all over Creekwood, though I know it originated here. It's bricked up in some places, but I believe passages between here and the diner are still open."

"Really? So, do you know about the moonshine?"

"Many wonderful secrets … and mysteries are there to explore," she said with a titter. "I'll tell you all about it once the shenanigans have passed."

"Great," said Marnie, curious about the history of the tunnels.

The detectives returned a little after 5:00.

Danny kissed Marnie's cheek and apologized. "Sorry we took so long. We booked Hank Weston for the murder of Paige Reynolds and the attempted murder of Lanie Howard-Billingsly. He's cooling off in a holding cell until tomorrow morning."

"Wow! That's great news. You're sure it's him?"

Tom picked up a stalk of celery from the table. "Yeah. The guy had a stun gun, a fuse puller, insulated gloves, incandescent lightbulbs, and other incriminating shit in his locker."

"Did he confess?"

"Pfft! No! He lawyered up. Harry Carlisle's with him now."

"Really? Kate's lawyer?"

Tom shrugged. "Why not? He's the best defense attorney in town."

"Hmm..."

Danny draped an arm around her shoulders. "C'mon, Madame Séance. Out with it. What's bugging you?"

"Umm ... Nothing I suppose."

Her sideways glance caused her friend to bristle.

Tom pointed the celery at her accusingly. "Don't go messin' things up. We got a break!"

She lifted her shoulder in resignation. "Okay. The others are in the study. I'll be there shortly."

Danny gave her arm a loving squeeze as they left the room. But Tom issued her an "I'm watching you" warning—pointing to his eyes, then hers with his index and middle fingers before stalking off.

Marnie dragged her palms up her cheeks. "Listen up, spirits! If you want to speak with me, could you please do it one at a time? I told them I have clarity, but you're confusing me with all the chatter. You're coming through like grown-ups in a Peanuts' special. *Mwah wah wah wah mwah.* Besides, your constant nattering is giving me a headache!" she said.

Ransom was erasing a whiteboard when Marnie entered the study.

"I called Patrick, and he's on his way. I thought he could help with Sam's situation," she said, sitting in her swivel chair behind her desk. She pulled a bag of soft caramels from a drawer and scattered them across the desktop. "Help yourselves."

"Who's Patrick?" Ransom asked.

Marnie unwrapped a caramel, popped it into her mouth, and stuck it in her cheek with her tongue. "He's the DEA agent who saved my life twice last year."

Sam got out of his chair, went to the desk, and scooped up two caramels. As he unwrapped one, he frowned and studied his sister. "What did you tell him?"

"Everything."

Jaw tensed, the chords in his neck bulging, Ransom asked, "Why would you do that?"

"Because we can trust him and he's got our backs." Marnie tossed him a candy, which he caught mid-air.

The marshal turned to the detectives, who sat in chairs near the open French doors. "You both trust him?"

They nodded, and Danny replied, "More than you."

Carl stood by the back wall of bookcases, his pipe clenched between his teeth. He agreed with Marnie's actions. He casually stepped forward and removed his pipe from his mouth. "Don't worry about Patrick. He always does the righteous thing. From everything I've read, seen and heard, he'll be an ally."

Ransom shook his head. "I don't like it."

"Tough," said Marnie, flipping a caramel to Hannah, who had been silently watching her.

She caught the candy and passed it to Gram, who graciously accepted. "Any chocolate?" she asked.

Marnie opened the drawer again, withdrew a small bag of M&M's and threw it to Hannah, then she flung one to each of the detectives.

The Special Agent cleared her throat as she ripped the tiny package, dumping the colorful chocolate into her hand. "Patrick is better connected than most of you might think. He has his eyes on two suspects in the drug operation out on Hudson Pass."

"Let's pause until he gets here, then. I have to mash the potatoes and get the roasted veggies out of the oven. Besides, my spooky senses tell me Patrick has arrived and is at the kitchen door," said Marnie, pushing back her chair.

"Now, hang on a minute!" shouted Ransom.

"Her house. Her rules." Teddy leaped to her feet, following the hostess. "I'll give you a hand."

Gram sat with her thoughts as the group filed out, then retrieved from her tote a blue velvet bag closed tight with a gold cord. She untied the cord and removed an intricately carved, rose gold, elemental cross. "Air" appeared at the head of the cross and depicted a tree reaching to the sky. The foot read "Earth" with carved tree roots reaching out to the point. "Water" was engraved into the left arm with a flowing stream reaching to the center, and the word "Fire" inscribed the right arm with flames pointing east. The cross was bejeweled at the center where the four points merged with a smooth, round, smoky quartz, a gemstone Druids consider holy and one that emanates the power of Earth gods.

Gram held the cross above her head and prayed.

Grant, O Great Spirit, Thy Protection;
And in protection, strength;
And in strength, understanding;
And in understanding, knowledge;
And in knowledge, the knowledge of justice;
And in the knowledge of justice, the love of it;
And in that love, the love of all existences;
And in the love of all existences, the love of Great Spirit and the Earth our mother, and all goodness.

Bless and protect my family and those we love tonight and forevermore.

As she put away the cross, she muttered, "May my forefathers and mothers kick the ever-lovin' shite out of the bastards who dare mess with my family."

With a titter and a skip in her step, Gram joined the others in the dining room.

With the potatoes mashed and the veggies roasted, they sat around the huge oak table in the dining room, waiting for Marnie to bring in the last dish.

"Here we go!" she said, carrying an enormous, covered casserole and handing it to Tom. "Can you please put it in the middle? Your arms are longer than mine."

Tom set it down and removed the lid. "Oo! That smells good!" he said, setting the cover on the sideboard behind him.

"Gram, would you say grace?" asked Marnie.

Never sure what to expect from the older woman, Danny, Hannah, Tom, and Marnie bowed their heads with the others, but kept one eye open and on Gram.

"Father, Son, and the Holy Ghost, whoever eats the fastest, gets the most. Amen."

"Amen!" said Tom, grabbing up a spoon and filling his plate with meat and gravy.

Danny chuckled. "I don't think I've heard that one before."

"I just pulled it of my hat," said Gram, helping herself to a yeasty roll and passing the basket to Hannah.

"Are we allowed to talk shop while we eat?"

"I'm fine with that," replied Marnie.

When no one argued, Hannah turned to Patrick, who sat opposite her, next to Ransom, with Sam beside him. "Great! Danny, Tom, and Carl have filled me in on Lawrence Parish's unethical practices, and we know what led to Sam's presence in the building when it exploded.

I think Agents Harding and Dobbs were trying to extinguish a problem when they came to the cabin. I believe this, because I filed a complaint against them. They were not the agents originally put on the case. They swapped using the lame excuse of proximity to their homes. Anyway, Patrick, why don't you tell everyone what you told me yesterday?"

"F-F-First of-f-f all, anyone who isn't law enforcement, d-d-do n-n-not repeat a w-w-word of what I am about to t-t-tell you."

Marnie, Teddy, Carl, and Gram nodded their agreement.

He sipped his wine and continued. "I've been surveilling the p-pass for the l-l-last few months. The kids up there th-think I'm a crazy homeless guy who lives in a p-pup tent, so they leave me alone. I come and go, w-wander around mumbling to myself, buy the drug du jour, and crawl b-b-back into my tent. Nobody asks questions. Dobbs and Harding t-t-turn up every couple of days. They keep to the trees, dress like vagrants and pass p-packages along to their mules. There's a new guy who shows up now and again, but he keeps his face in the shadows."

"Are you sure they aren't working an op?" asked Ransom.

Sam agreed. "I was thinking the same thing."

Patrick said, "N-n-no. When I shared my f-f-findings with m-my -b-b-boss, he set things in m-motion. We've checked their financials and searched their properties. Both men live above their means. Neither has won the lottery or inherited sizeable sums of money, and they had caches of cash hidden in their holiday homes. We took everything. They are gonna be p-p-pissed when they see it's gone."

"Have you got pictures or videos?" asked Ransom.

Patrick pulled his phone from his back pocket. "You betcha!"

Heads together, Ransom and Sam watched the films and flipped through the images. Dobbs and Harding were easy to recognize. As they moved through the images, Marnie could see the gears turning in her brother's head. She knew what he was thinking: why would two career agents be so careless?

"You had search warrants?" asked Sam.

Patrick helped himself to the pot roast and confirmed, "Everything has been by the b-book."

"It's strange they wouldn't know you are on to them. They must have security cameras in their homes."

"They do, but we know how to get around those things."

"Yes, of course."

Ransom asked, "Anything else?"

Patrick's wide grin told them there was. "Dobbs and Harding d-d-don't t-trust each other. B-b-both have, or I should say h-had, video of the warehouse explosion from different angles. They were there and their voices were in the footage. I figure they kept the evidence in case the other tried to lay blame."

"You got those videos on your phone?" Ransom handed the device to Patrick, who scrolled, then passed it back.

"There you go. The next three are pertinent."

Ransom and Sam watched again; the latter visibly flinching when an explosion boomed through the tiny speaker, and Marnie and Carl glanced at each other.

When it ended, Ransom whistled and handed the phone to Danny, who sat next to him at the head of the table. Tom and Hannah hopped up from their seats and stood behind Danny to watch the chaos.

Once they finished, Marnie asked, "Patrick, is it enough to clear my brother?"

"Oh, yeah. Harding and Dobbs will be in a cell by the end of the week if Sam's files contain equally incriminating information."

Gram and Hannah said their goodbyes just after midnight, but Carl remained to speak with Sam. The two disappeared into the study while the others finished cleaning up the kitchen.

Patrick agreed to share the videos and pictures with the Creekwood Police Department. As Tom and Danny reviewed the footage and images again, the former thought the man on the pass who kept to the shadows was familiar. He replayed it several times, before giving up, and set a reminder on his phone to review the files again tomorrow with a clear head.

After running a dishcloth over the kitchen table, Marnie sat with a loud sigh. "Ransom, do you agree with Patrick? Is Sam in the clear?"

"Yeah, and for the record, I never believed he killed those cops here in Creekwood. It's not how he's wired."

Danny rested a hand protectively on Marnie's shoulder. "If you had seen him ... heard him, you wouldn't doubt it."

Ransom gave Danny a long, irritated look. "And now? What do you think?"

Danny lifted a shoulder. "Now? I don't want to believe it. Look, my father has the videos and thumb drives in his office we'll go through over the next couple of days. Once that's done and I have Carl's full report, I'll have an answer. But right now, I'm on the fence. The guy sitting at the table tonight seemed harmless. The guy who tried to break into my cabin and kill Marnie last year was not."

"Ha-ha! Harmless is not a word to describe Sam," said Tom, tapping Marnie's shoulder. "Remember how he whacked that guy with the crowbar over on the island?"

"Mm-hmm." She wasn't really listening. She was thinking of what came next, and turned to the marshal and asked, "What's next? How will you handle it from here?"

Ransom rolled his head to ease a kink out of his neck and leaned his head against the wall, before focusing his clear gray eyes on Marnie. "You tell me. What's your gut telling you?"

"That you will use the information Patrick, Danny, Tom, and Sam have gathered to write a comprehensive report. Then, you will add Carl's analysis to underpin Sam's innocence."

"That sums it up. I've started the report, and I have been communicating with my boss throughout the process. I haven't gone rogue. There are other people who believe Sam was set up."

Marnie glared at him. "Why didn't they listen or speak to me back then? You wouldn't take my calls or Tom's! The agency came down hard on both of us. They even threatened us! Why didn't you help?" Marnie's eyes filled with angry tears. "All of this time..." Her voice cracked, and she slammed her hand on the table. "All of this time wasted!"

"I'm sorry, kid. Believe it or not, I did what I could, but I didn't want to talk to you until I had answers. Now I do, so I'm here, helping."

Face red, she flew to her feet and spat, "Oh, bite me!" She stormed off, stamped up the stairs and slammed her bedroom door.

-Chapter 43-

Cloudy skies brought four days of drizzles and downpours, bringing a welcome calm to the ranch. As the raindrops washed over Creekwood, Marnie, Teddy, and Sam unpacked the remaining boxes at the farmhouse and completed plans for the July fourth bash. Elk and Arnie made repairs to the windmill and the barn, hired two more farmhands, and the former took over management of the ranch. He would move into the cottage previously occupied by Jonas and Lanie.

When asked if he would mind living in a place where someone died, Elk laughed and said, "People die where they die. There ain't an old house in Creekwood where someone hasn't croaked."

Paige Reynold's doctor finally called Giles Markson after returning from an overseas family vacation. The doctor confirmed Paige was awaiting approval from her insurance company to schedule surgery. While her pacemaker was only three years old, there were signs it was faulty which included labored breathing and chest pain. A shock to her chest with a stun gun would have been fatal.

Marnie and Teddy finally made a trip to Hackett's Hardware to buy a lock for the tunnel's trap door. Unable to help, they referred them to Larry, a local locksmith, who installed a locking mechanism guaranteed to keep out the bad guys.

The detectives, with help from the federal marshal and DEA agents, continued their investigations, reviewing tapes from the Parish's home, consulting with Carl, and preparing reports of their findings.

They cut Hank Weston loose. None of the items found in his locker had his fingerprints on them. In fact, there were no fingerprints at all, and the guy had alibis that checked out for the times of Paige's and Lanie's murders. The love notes found in his locker were from Kate. It was a game she played with all new security guards—even the women. Hank held on to them because he planned to put them in Kate's files.

Kitty Parish, still in hospital, was charged with conspiracy to commit murder and illegal manufacture of drugs. With two more boxes of videos to get through, additional charges were pending, as well as ethics charges related to her criminal activity regarding clients. The drug manufacture charge was a reach, but Rick Price and his team were testing pills found in a tiny laboratory in the Parish's cellar. One bottle of the tablets proved to be an anabolic steroid, known to cause rage in large doses. Also found were a pill press, an invoice for the online purchase of the press, foil-packed bags of pharmaceutical-grade pill binding excipient, and other powders with non-descriptive packaging, except for a number on the sachets, handwritten in black Sharpie. Kitty feigned ignorance, but her brother confirmed his sister held doctorates in pharmacology *and* psychiatry.

The news wasn't much better for Kate Parish, whose charges included murder in the first degree for the killings of Officers Webb and Weaver, another count of first-degree murder in the fatal shooting of Judge Sophia Reilly, two counts of assault with a deadly weapon with the intent to kill Detective Tom Keller and Officer Sam Jalnack.

While watching videoed sessions the Parishes had with Kate, and reading supporting notes, the police learned that Lawrence and Kitty recognized their daughter's unstable behavior when, at three years old, she killed her hamster. Her vicious treatment of small creatures was the beginning of their struggles. Their child's violence toward her mother escalated their fears, and they tried hypnotherapy and drugs, which had minimal effect.

When Sophia and Colin Reilly brought Sam to his first session with Lawrence, the Parishes seized the opportunity to cover their daughter's indiscretions. Sam, troubled by nightmares and low self-esteem following the traumatic events on the island, was an easy target. Jethro Barnes had created the Parish's first victim.

The Parishes spent years brainwashing the young man, and through unethical mind control methods, they programmed him to believe he was violent and that he hated his family, especially his sister. Over time, he blamed his trauma on his family.

Every time Kate committed a horrendous act, the psychiatrists manipulated Sam into believing he was at fault. To control him further, the Parishes "installed" trigger words into his young brain. After a few months, his sister's name conjured violent episodes, causing him to strike out at anything or anyone in his path.

The detectives combed through every document in the Parish's home, digging up the paperwork involving Sophia's case against Lawrence Parish and the letter from the medical board revoking his license. A personal journal revealed the man's hatred for the judge. There were also side notes in Kate's handwriting swearing she would avenge her father's mistreatment.

The murder of Sophia Reilly and Kate's celebration of the brutal act confirmed the Parish's earlier diagnosis. Their daughter was a psychopath, but they had a bigger problem. Sam Reilly no longer lived in Creekwood, so when he came home to grieve with his father and sister, Kate invited him to have lunch, then delivered him to her parents for manipulation. Because of her friendship with Marnie, Kate knew her friend and her father suspected Sam. After all, he and his mother had recently argued, he was driving from Creekwood to Washington, DC when the murder occurred, and Kate made sure he didn't have an alibi. While Sam was with her parents, she rifled through his truck and pilfered fuel and food receipts from his wallet, which he kept locked in the console with his gun.

Sophia's murder was an open cold case until two days ago when Ransom Elliott noticed a long gun was missing from the cabinet in the Parish's library. He searched the house and found a shotgun hidden under a squeaky wide oak floorboard in Kate Parish's bedroom. Fingerprints on the gun belonged to Lawrence and Kate Parish, and they discovered an old box of double-aught buckshot shells, the same caliber used in the murder, in the cabinet. Rick's team's tests confirmed the casing found at the scene matched the shotgun found under the floorboards. But the shotgun and shells weren't the only proof. A video of the psychiatrists manipulating Sam into believing he killed his mother showed Kate in the background, dancing gracefully behind their victim before placing the shotgun in his lap, but Sam never touched the gun. His hands remained glued to the arms of the chair in which he sat. Even under hypnosis, he knew enough to not touch the weapon.

Over a beer, Danny, Tom, Ransom, and Sam discussed the stupidity of keeping a murder weapon. In the end, Tom offered hubris as the reason.

Agents Dobbs and Harding found themselves in a pickle. Suspended without pay and under investigation, the agents scrambled to piece together a cohesive story to keep themselves out of jail, but Dobbs couldn't handle the mounting evidence and pressure and sang like a bird. His confession paved the way for Sam Reilly being cleared of suspicion of the explosion and the events leading to it. They didn't cop to the murders of the two drug dealers out on Hudson Pass, though. That case is still open.

Marnie and Carl met with Dr. Miller at Bayview Correctional to discuss his findings on the shrapnel in Sam's brain. It wasn't as bad as they thought. The fragments lay between the dura mater and the arachnoid layer of the meninges, the membrane that protects the brain. The doctor referred them to a respected neurosurgeon who had performed similar surgeries with minimal collateral damage. Sam and the surgeon have an appointment in early September.

Ransom, his boss, and Chief Gregg worked together to keep Sam out of prison and with his sister in Creekwood, where he was required to wear an ankle bracelet, and attend five ninety-minute weekly sessions with Carl Parkins. While still fighting inner demons, Sam was finding clarity.

Jed Rawlins was "in the wind" and sightings pour into a hotline set up by Ransom. They believe he is hiding out somewhere in the dense forests of the Adirondack Mountains.

The rigged lamp at Tom's house, Dorie's accident, and the fire in the barn were in the hands of the fire investigator. But two other burning questions still puzzled them. Who killed Paige Reynolds, and who put Lanie Howard-Billingsly into the bathtub?

-Chapter 44-

Ablazing fourth of July sun beat down on the pool, the water catching its reflection in the ripples created by the swimmers. With a waterproof bandage covering her wound, Marnie swam two laps, but Tom grabbed her foot on her third pass and removed all seriousness from the exercise. She swam to the side and pulled two pool noodles into the water, throwing a blue one at her best friend, and keeping the green one for herself.

"That pig roast smells so good!" she said, relaxing for the first time in weeks.

The caterers had arrived and politely thrown her out of her kitchen so they could prepare food. Green and white striped tents were being set up on the lawn to save the guests from the scorching late afternoon heat. Elk, Arnie, and their team stored away equipment and got the pump and ladder ready in case fireworks landed where they shouldn't.

The screen door of the summer kitchen squeaked open and Sam appeared, carrying a cooler. His hair and face had caught some sun, giving him reddish highlights and a healthy tan. He reached into the cooler, pulled out a can of lager, tossed it to Tom, then handed one to Danny and one to his sister. "Did you put on sunscreen?"

"No. It makes me itch," she said, poking out her tongue.

"You've been sayin' that since we were kids," said Tom, as he cannon-balled into the cool water.

Teddy shot him a dirty look from her lounge chair before wiping water from her book with a towel.

Danny said, "Hey, Sam, I'm wondering where the stuff is you and Pigeon borrowed from my garage. Do you have it at your hotel?"

Blinking and wrinkling his forehead, he said, "Pigeon took your ax, but we took nothing from your garage."

"Really? I'm missing camping equipment. If it wasn't you, who?"

Sam puffed out his cheeks and released the air. "I promise it was not us."

Marnie growled, "Great! Now we have to worry about someone else prowling the woods."

Danny dismissed it with a shrug. "Maybe not. I might have put the gear in the attic. I'll check later." Although he knew he had not.

Tom slapped the surface of the water and shouted, "Marn! We forgot about the treasure!"

She slapped the water, mimicking his astounded expression. "No, we didn't! I locked it in the safe so we can open it after all the drama passes."

"Ha! You're being optimistic!"

"Ah-ah! Cautiously optimistic!"

"Ha-ha! You two have waited how many years to open that thing?" Danny laughed. "A few more days won't kill you." He sat on the edge of the pool, dangling his feet in the water. "What time does the pyrotechnics guy get here?"

Marnie swam to his side and rested her chin on his knee. "They did their set up yesterday, so they won't be here until 8:00. Guests arrive at 5:30, which means we have another few hours to lounge."

"Good stuff. Dad said he and Cap might be on time. They offered to watch what's left of the videos so we could enjoy the sunshine. Either way, they'll be here. The captain sounds like he's looking forward to it."

Marnie pulled a face. "Really? Never thought Pete Sterling would look forward to seeing me. Ha! You coming for a swim?"

"Yeah. I'm thinkin' about the case."

"Stop! We've got a day off," said Tom, skipping a tennis ball across the pool, which created a commotion of the furry kind. Tater,

Dickens, and Gus romped across the patio and dove into the water before they could be stopped.

Mac Gregg and Pete Sterling were down to their last four tapes, and from the label dates, they were the last sessions ever recorded by Lawrence. They considered wading through them tomorrow, but it was only 1:00 PM. There was plenty of time to finish and get to the party on time.

Ellie Nikol and her wife Julie arrived early for a swim. They brought with them five-year-old Holly and seven-year-old Ben, who were Julie's children from her first marriage. Also in tow were their six rescue dogs, Magic, Eli, Barley, Levi, Dewey and Chicken, who Tater, Dickens, and Gus greeted with gusto.

"I hope you don't mind," asked Ellie.

Marnie gave the kids and dogs a hug. "They are always welcome, but we'll put them inside when the fireworks start."

"You're having fireworks?" asked Holly.

"We sure are. How about a swim first, though?"

"Yeah! Where's Tom? I want to cannonball him!" yelled Ben, racing to the pool.

"Ha-ha! Have fun!" Marnie said. "Make yourselves at home."

"We'll see you at the pool," said Ellie.

Pete Sterling pushed the last tape into the VCR while Mac called out to Officer Garcia, who cringed. She didn't want overtime on the Fourth of July.

"Garcia, can you get me everything you can find on this guy?" he asked, snapping an index card onto her desk.

"Sure, Chief. Are you looking for anything specific?"

"Yeah. Everything you can find."

Danny and Gram found Marnie sitting alone in the study—with her index fingers to her temples and her eyes closed. The detective cleared his throat to let her know they were there.

"Guests are arriving. You okay?" he asked.

"I don't know," she said. "Something feels off, and it has since I drove into town. Then my cards fell on the floor and the ones that landed upright created a dreadful spread."

Gram asked, "What did the cards say, love?"

Marnie's bottom lip trembled, and tears filled her eyes. "Someone is going to die!"

"Are you sure you read them, right?" Danny asked, moving to her side and kneeling next to her.

"Of course, I did!" she wailed, before burying her face in his shoulder and bawling.

Gram got up from her chair, went to Marnie, and rubbed her back. "There's nothin' we can do about death, love. It comes to us all."

"But I can't lose anyone else. It's too much!"

Danny understood, having lost his wife and mother. "You think something will happen to Sam, don't you?"

She choked up again and flung herself into his arms, hugging him tight.

Tom poked his head in the door. "Hey! Are you coming outside? Everyone's here."

Marnie lifted her head; her face red, blotchy, and wet with tears.

"What's goin' on?" Tom walked into the office, worry lining his handsome face.

Danny said, "She saw something bad in her cards."

"What'd you see, Marn?" asked Tom.

"Death!"

He coaxed a smile to his lips. "Nobody's gonna die today. It's Independence Day. It would be rude to ruin our holiday. C'mon," he said, offering his hand. "Wash your face and then let's get some cotton candy. We'll spoil our dinner with sugar."

She jerked out a nod, went into the bathroom and ran a cold cloth across her face.

With a cloud of pink spun sugar in hand, Marnie made the rounds to chat with her guests. Rick Price and his wife Tracy perched on a boulder overlooking the creek.

"This is a handsome property," said Rick, turning to look across the green pasture.

"Are you settling in?" asked Tracy.

"We're getting there. I'm unpacked, so that's a great start," said Marnie.

"Is this Wild Creek?" asked Rick.

"Yup. I had a look at the deed the other day, and before the Billingslys owned the land, it was called Wild Creek Ranch. The thought of changing it back is appealing. What do you think?"

"I love it!" said Tracy.

"Wild sounds right, considering the last few weeks," said Rick.

Marnie twisted her mouth to the side. "Perhaps I should consider something else."

Rick patted her shoulder. "I was teasing. Research the history of the property and give it a name that suits its past."

She giggled. "Well, we found Depression era moonshine in the tunnels."

"There you go. That brings many names to mind."

Alice Wells tapped Marnie's shoulder, and she turned.

"Alice! I'm happy you could make it."

"Allan sends his regrets. He had to make a trip to Albany to see his mother. She's unwell."

"I hope she'll be okay."

Alice rolled her eyes. "She will. She does this whenever he has plans."

Abigael and Declan Keller strolled to the group, each carrying a glass of wine.

Abigael offered Marnie a one-armed hug, and Declan brushed her cheek with a kiss.

"This place is perfect! Tom has been going on and on about it," said Abigael.

"I told him we should build him a nice little house here by the creek."

"Well, that sounds perfect. You grew up together. You may as well grow old together, too."

"That's what I think."

Declan nodded his chin toward the pack of dogs running their way. "What's with them?"

Marnie laughed. "They're chasing ghost cats. Tater and Dickens have been doing that since we moved in. There are so many of them on this property. I hope they can still catch mice. Anyway. I better get them inside before the fireworks get underway. I'll be back soon."

Pete and Mac stared at the screen, both too shocked to speak. The latter snatched up his phone and called his son.

"C'mon, Daniel! Answer!" he growled, but the call went to voicemail. "Daniel, call me when you get this message. It's urgent!"

Pete pulled his phone from his pocket. "I'll try Keller."

"Yeah. I'll try Hannah."

Officer Garcia tapped on the door, and Pete yanked it open. "Yeah!"

She held out a file. "That's everything I could find."

Pete took the file, scanned the top page, and sucked in a breath.

The chief glanced up. "What have we got, Pete?"

"Seven years in the Marines. Medical discharge. Here's what I was looking for. Says he was an electrical engineer and an explosives expert. Currently employed at Pine Ridge and Phantasmagoria Fireworks. And we know from the tapes, he's been the Parish's patient since February."

"Jesus, Mary, and Joseph!" Mac dragged a hand over his face. "Garcia, we need any officer in the vicinity of Marnie Reilly's property out on Hallowed Hills Road to get there and stop the fireworks. Can you take care of that? Call the Sheriff too. Tell them Chief Gregg and Captain Sterling of Creekwood PD are on the way, but they need to stop it now!"

"Yes, sir!" she said, scurrying back to her desk.

Mac slammed a hand down on his desk. "Dammit! No one is answering!"

Pete scooped up Mac's keys and tossed them to him. "C'mon. Let's get out there. You drive and I'll keep calling. We'll get through to one of them."

The Star-Spangled Banner echoed from the sound system as everyone gathered near the windmill and pond for the fireworks to start. Danny, Gram, Hannah, and Teddy sat on a picnic rug waiting for Tom and Marnie to return from another cotton candy run.

Patrick went to higher ground. He rested comfortably on his stomach in the open door of the haymow, his sniper rifle aimed nowhere in particular. Ransom and Sam chose lower ground, having made their way through the tunnel to a vine-covered wrought iron door on the side of a hill that looked out over the pasture.

As the partygoers settled onto their blankets, the music segued to James Brown's Living in America and a series of whistlers, horsetails, and waterfalls filled the sky with color, followed by a chorus of *Oos!* and *Ahhs!* from the crowd.

Their attention was drawn to a light show that included Niagara Falls, a spinning Catherine's wheel and a perfectly timed American flag came to life in streaks of red, white, and blue as a recording of God Bless America changed the tempo.

Danny felt his phone buzz in his pocket but ignored it to look for Marnie and his partner, who he spotted, skipping arm and arm over a knoll, singing at the top of their lungs.

Gram nudged him and laughed. "How much sugar have the two of them had?"

"Daniel!" Hannah shouted and shoved her phone at him. "Daniel! It's Pete Sterling!"

He turned to his sister, grinning widely. "What?"

"It's the captain! He says we have to stop the fireworks!"

He grabbed the phone and plugged one ear to listen.

"Cap? What's up?"

"Stop … Marnie and… Danger… Stop… Now!"

Danny got up and moved away from the noise. "Cap, I'm getting every second word."

"Stop the fireworks!"

Glancing glanced toward the highway, he saw flashing blue and white lights on the horizon. "On it!" he shouted, before tossing his sister her phone. He broke into a sprint; his destination was one hundred feet ahead: the fireworks platform near the barn. Patrick watched the detective race toward the staging area and trained his scope on the pyrotechnician below.

Sam and Ransom spotted Danny running at the stage like a linebacker. They pushed the door, but it only rattled on its hinge.

"Dammit! Put your shoulder into it!" yelled Ransom, which they both did, to no avail. "It's locked! Stand back!" The marshal pulled out his gun, shot the latch, and the door yielded.

At a dead run, the two set off toward to the stage to help Danny, as Marnie and Tom came down the hill and noticed the commotion and the open door. They whirled around to see Officers Tartetto and Connor racing toward them.

Over the blare of the music and explosion of the fireworks, Tartetto shouted, "Stop the fireworks!"

Marnie turned toward the barn and spotted Patrick in the haymow, then she saw Danny running to the platform. A second later, she watched in horror as the big man from Pine Ridge loaded something into a tube and mortar and took aim, releasing an aerial shell as Danny tackled him to the ground. But it was too late.

"Tom!" she screamed, grabbing his hand and pulling him to the opening in the hill. As they ducked through the door, the missile exploded in a blinding flash of color, blasting them into the tunnel.

-*Chapter 45-*

July 5ᵗʰ

"How's she doing, Doc?" Danny asked Giles Markson. "She's been in and out for over the last hour. I'm glad you could bring Tater and Dickens to her. It might help."

"That's not what I asked." The detective brushed her forehead with a kiss. A deep laceration lined her cheek at the hairline, purple rings outlined her eyes, and her swollen bottom lip had three tiny stitches.

"It's going to take time, Danny. Marnie has months of recovery ahead of her," said the doctor, looking at the damage Dalton Hooley had done to his goddaughter.

The detective read the doctor's mind. "Hooley confessed to everything. He told us he felt compelled to put Lanie in the bathtub when he found her dead. Compelled. Jesus! The Parishes are monsters." Danny paused for a breath, then continued, "We figured him for the barn fire, Tom's lamp, and Dorie's accident, and we were right. But we haven't found the modified stun gun he used to kill Paige Reynolds. He says it's in his apartment, but it's not. I'm worried it's in the wrong hands. Anyway, he's going away for a long time."

"Yes, your father and Pete Sterling told me about the videos. Can you believe such evil exists?"

Danny nodded grimly. "I can, unfortunately."

Sam stirred in his chair, then joined them at his sister's bedside. "Is she awake?"

The detective and the doctor shook their heads.

Tater and Dickens sat at the side of the bed, their ears flat to their heads and their mouths shut tight. Danny gently tugged Tater's ear, then bent to pick him up. He placed the Border Collie with great care onto Marnie's bed, being mindful of the IV and her broken ribs. The dog stared into her face before giving the tip of her a nose a lick. Sam called Dickens, who loped to him. He hefted up the dog and placed him opposite Tater, careful not to bump his sister's broken shoulder and injured knee. Dickens grumbled something incoherent, then lay down beside his mistress, his head resting on her thigh.

Marnie's eyelids fluttered, and she made a sucking sound, which Danny assumed was thirst. He took a cup of water from the table and held the straw to her lips, but she pushed it away.

"Tom," she mumbled.

The men eyed one another. Danny raked his fingers through his hair, thinking about his numbers game and how he had been wrong. The barn fire was one for Marnie and one for Teddy. The tunnel was one for each of them, too. Dalton Hooley finished one cycle with Marnie and started a new cycle with his partner. Two more.

Tater whimpered and bumped Marnie's hand with his nose.

She opened one eye and said, "Tater." Then she turned and Dickens smiled at her.

Sam leaned on the bedrail. "Hey, Squirt. How's your head?"

She rubbed her forehead, and tried to focus on the doorway, where her best friend stood, leaning against the doorjamb, ankles crossed—a cheeky grin on his handsome face. She stared at him, her weary eyes brimming with tears.

Turning to Danny, she whispered, "Real or not real?"

-The End-

Spoils of the Dead

By Robert Frost

Two fairies it was
On a still summer day
Came forth in the woods
With the flowers to play.

The flowers they plucked
They cast on the ground
For others, and those
For still others they found.

Flower-guided it was
That they came as they ran
On something that lay
In the shape of a man.

The snow must have made
The feathery bed
When this one fell
On the sleep of the dead.

But the snow was gone
A long time ago,
And the body he wore
Nigh gone with the snow.

The fairies drew near
And keenly espied
A ring on his hand
And a chain at his side.

They knelt in the leaves
And eerily played
With the glittering things,
And were not afraid.

And when they went home
To hide in their burrow,
They took them along
To play with to-morrow.

When you came on death,
Did you not come flower-guided
Like the elves in the wood?
I remember that I did.

But I recognized death
With sorrow and dread,
And I hated and hate
The spoils of the dead.

Resources

Sources used in the writing of this fiction book include:

A Boy's Will by Robert Frost

Medscape website, https://emedicine.medscape.com/article/913575-overview

The Mayo Clinic, https://www.mayoclinic.org/diseases-conditions/antisocial-personality-disorder/symptoms-causes/syc-20353928

Priory, https://www.priorygroup.com/mental-health/drug-induced-psychosis
Adirondack Park Agency of New York State
New York Flora Atlas
New York State Department of Environmental Conservation
American Fireworks Display

Acknowledgements

Harper, thank you for *trying* to be quiet while I write and for being my guinea pig. Thank goodness you get my weird and dark sense of humor. I couldn't have done this without your expert advice on mental health, veterans, and dog noises. I still love you more than pizza.

Big cuddles and ear scratches to Dougal, Callee, Midget, and Mags. You fill up my heart and provide lovely breaks in my day. If it not for you, I wouldn't know when to quit for the day.

Nicole Ballingal, I love your talent! The cover is striking! Pun intended. Always remember, Fatal Vow wouldn't be here if you hadn't broken your leg.

Frances, my writing and my life are richer for having met you. I can't thank you enough for your coaching, kindness, and silliness.

Jane Hackett Backus, Nicole Ballingal, Tracy Brown, Wendy Flood, Laurie Lashomb, and Karen Harper-Peck, a huge thanks to you all for reading the Beta of Fatal Vow. Apologies for causing you trauma. I'm really not evil. Read the last chapter.

Karen Harper-Peck, thank you for helping me keep your brother on his toes. Our calls about murder methods concern him.

Jane Hackett Backus, you are forever my teacher. Mrs. Backus' bookstore in Chapter 39 and Hackett's Hardware in Chapter 43 are for you.

Tracy Brown, thanks so much for pulling me into your IG writing challenges and for welcoming my crew into the fold. Oh! Danny sends his love.

Wendy, because of you, Fatal Vow is set in summer. Thank you for being a wonderful support, and for the impromptu brainstorming of book four. I look forward to a glass of champagne to celebrate with my favorite oldest sister.

Laurie Lashomb, thanks, soul sister, for your precious support, feedback, and for picking up on my hometown references. Are you still drinking lolly water?

For my fellow dog rescuers, Janet Adams and Mary and Roy Wolfwalker, Chapter 44 has something for you.

Thanks to Kevin at American Fireworks Display for the wealth of knowledge shared with me regarding pyrotechnics.

Mom and Dad, thanks for the divine guidance. I know you're there.

A huge THANKS to the Instagram Writing Community. It's comforting to have found a village where my weirdness is welcome—and encouraged.

To all the dogs I've loved before, Tater and Dickens are for you.

About the Author

Shari T. Mitchell is the author of the Marnie Reilly Mysteries thriller series, which includes Divine Guidance, Torn Veil, and Fatal Vow (coming July 2023).

Raised in Northern New York State, Shari's hometown and surrounds are the inspiration for her series' fictional town of Creekwood, New York—which is located somewhere in the Adirondack Mountains.

While Shari loves developing multidimensional characters with whom her readers can relate, her passion is plotting the twists and turns of a mystery. It feeds her analytical and creative mind.

She lives in North Carolina and shares her home with her partner in crime, Harper, and their crazy rescue dogs, Dougal, Callee, Midget, and Mags.

A thirty-plus year marketer, Shari loves spending time with her family, cooking, hiking, traveling, gardening, and reading. She is often heard chatting with her characters because they natter at her constantly!

Mystery is her favorite genre, having cut her teeth on Nancy Drew, The Hardy Boys, and Trixie Belden. Her favorite authors include Robert Frost, Agatha Christie, Mary Higgins Clark, Ruth Rendell, Michael Connelly, Jonathan Kellerman, David Baldacci, Louise Penny, Kathy Reichs, Patricia Cornwell, and Michael Koryta.

For Readers

Thank you for reading *Fatal Vow*. I hope you enjoyed the story. Please consider leaving a review on Goodreads, Amazon or wherever you purchased the book.

The Marnie Reilly Mysteries continues with Book 4. It's in the works!

Website

Visit ShariTMitchell.com for short stories, recipes, and to learn more about her books. Sign-up for her newsletter for updates from Creekwood.

Social Media

Instagram: @sharitmitchell
Goodreads: www.goodreads.com/sharitmitchell
Facebook: www.facebook.com/ShariTMitchellAuthor

THE ISLAND

A Marnie Reilly Mysteries Novella

SHARI T. MITCHELL

"C'mon, Sam! We want to go swimming!" Dressed in white shorts, a navy-blue bikini top, and red sandals, five-year-old Marnie Reilly stood impatiently on the dock waiting for her brother. Carrying her T-shirt, she bounced up and down like a bunny.

"You're being bossy again," Tom scolded, squinting his eyes against the mid-morning sun.

She scrunched up her face. "No, I'm not. I'm being a pest. There's a difference." Nose pointed to the sun, she crossed her arms and gazed up the hill at her brother.

Twelve-year-old Sam Reilly loped toward them in light blue swimming trunks, a baseball shirt, a ball cap, and flip-flops. He carried a backpack and a navy and white striped beach bag.

He called out, "Mom said you have to put on sunscreen. She said you can't go swimming until you do."

Marnie danced impatiently from one foot to the other. "Argh! I hate sunscreen! It makes me itch all over!" She performed a heebie-jeebies dance for effect, flailing her limbs and scratching her body all over like monkeys do.

Sam stopped and hooked his thumb back toward the house. "Well, argue with Mom about that. I'm not letting you go in the water without it."

His little sister threw up her arms. "Fine! I'll wear the dang stuff."

"Good! Now come get your bag. You forgot your towel, and your lunch." He held the beach bag out for her to retrieve.

"Can't you bring it to me? You're comin' down here anyway!" she huffed.

"Nope! Mom and Dad told me to stop babying you. Come on! It's yours. I'm not carrying it," he said, standing his ground.

She rolled her eyes and stomped up the hill with a dramatic pump of arms and legs.

When she reached her brother, she took her bag, set it on the ground, and pulled on his arm so that he would bend to meet her.

"Thank you for taking us swimming with you and your friends." She kissed his cheek, followed by the buzz of spit-riddled raspberries, which sent her into fits of giggles.

Sam dropped his backpack, scooped her up in his arms, and blew on her tummy. She giggled and squirmed with delight.

"Stop it!" she said between titters.

He set her down on the grass and messed up her strawberry blonde hair that hung all the way to the middle of her back.

"C'mon! I'll race you to the dock!" Sam took off running.

"Oh! I'll never catch you! You're too fast!" She charged after him, arms and legs pumping, and only caught him when he slowed down enough to let her.

"C'mon, Squirt! Get in the boat. We'll row over to the island and have lunch. Sound good?" He picked her up and swung her into the rowboat.

Marnie nodded emphatically. "Sounds good! C'mon, Tom!"

Tom stared down at his toes for a moment. He lifted his chin, and a flush of embarrassment rose in his tanned face. "Um ... I don't swim too good. My mother told me I gotta wear armbands."

Marnie giggled. "Aw, Tom! Don't be silly. I'll wear mine too. Mom packed them so that I could swim out real far—that way, if I get tired, I can float. I like to wear them sometimes."

Ruffling Tom's hair, Sam said, "How about I teach you to swim? I taught Marnie, and she's pretty good. Would you like that?"

The youngster tipped back his noggin and looked up at Marnie's big brother. "Really? You'd teach me?"

"Yeah. Sure. You're not afraid of the water, are you?"

Tom held his head up high, pulled back his shoulders, and puffed out his chest. "Nah! I'm not afraid!" he said, holding the older boy's gaze.

Sam smiled and nodded again. "Good! Let's get you into a life jacket. Then we'll head over to the island. Marnie, put yours on, please. I don't want Mom yelling at me."

Reaching into the shed, he passed the safety vests to the youngsters. Next, he grabbed a nearly deflated inner tube and an air pump. He set them down on the deck of the rowboat, untied the skiff from its cleats, dropped the stern line into the back, threw the bowline to Marnie, who placed it neatly on the bottom, before taking a seat next to Tom. Sam stepped in and settled into the middle seat. It wobbled gently and Tom sucked in a breath, grabbing for his friend's arm.

She patted his back. "Don't worry. Even if we tip, the water is really shallow here. You could stand up."

He took another deep breath, then finished putting on his life jacket.

"Ready to go?" Sam asked.

"Hang on!" Marnie scrambled around Sam to the stern, kneeled, and turned, flashing a smile at her brother. Tom, sitting warily in the back, nodded.

Calm water lapped the rowboat, and the clear sky above them promised a perfect day. A soft summer breeze cooled the heat of the sun as the tree toads called for more. Marnie leaned over and watched fish scurry beneath the boat, and marveled how she could see clear to the bottom of the pond.

She turned around and pointed. "Tom, look at the fish swimming under us!"

He hesitantly leaned, and asked, "What kind are they?"

"The big ones are probably bass, sunfish, or bullhead. If they're small, then minnow which are great bait," Sam replied.

"Do you guys go fishin'?" asked the young boy, turning in his seat to watch Sam row.

"Yeah. Sure. We go with Dad and sometimes Marnie and I go— just the two of us."

"Marn, do you like to fish?" Tom asked.

She didn't answer—her eyes locked on land.

Tom tried again. "Hey, Marn!" he shouted.

Dipping an oar into the pond, Sam splashed water onto his sister, and she spun around, wiping it off her face with her arm.

"Hey! What'd you do that for?" she roared—her brow crinkled with anger.

"Tom was speaking to you. What are you looking at?" Sam replied, squinting to see what had his sister's attention.

She nodded her chin at the island. "There's an old guy up there. I'm trying to figure if he's real or not."

Sam focused on the spot, then shrugged. "I can't see anyone. Tom, do you see anyone?"

The boy peeked around Sam, staring fiercely in the direction Marnie had nodded. He shrugged and shook his head. "Nah! I don't see an old man."

Marnie gingerly stood up in the bow and continued to concentrate on the island.

Despite the warm summer sun, Tom shivered and hugged himself against the chill trickling up his back to his neck.

The closer they got to the shore, the more certain Sam was of his sister was seeing a ghost.

"Marnie, there's nobody on the beach."

"Okay," she said, resting her elbows on the bow. She was used to people not seeing what she could, and under her breath, she muttered, "Well, I can see him, and he looks angry."

Boredom set in and she turned around. "Want me to help you row? Are you getting tired?"

"Can get back here without tipping us over?" he teased.

She made her way to the middle, causing only gentle rocking. "How was that?" she asked.

"Pretty good, Squirt!" he replied.

She sat on the seat in between her brother's legs, leaning her back against his chest, feet planted firmly on the deck and grabbed hold of the oars. A soft breeze blew her hair up into Sam's face, tickling his nose and chin.

"Geez, Marnie! Your hair is in my face! Where's your cap?" he asked.

"It's in my bag. I think."

Sam sighed. "Well, we're almost there. We'll get there faster with two rowers."

She held tight to the paddles, even though her fingers weren't long enough to wrap all the way around. Sam, of course, did most of the work, but she liked helping.

"Look! We're nearly there!" she screeched. "The guy is standing on the shore! Can you see him?"

Sam rolled his eyes. His frustration with his sister's gift was often hard to control. He knew she could see ghosts—but it was irksome sometimes.

"You know I can't. Tom, what about you?" he asked with a hint of annoyance.

He didn't. He sat behind Marnie and Sam—eyes now tightly closed. "Nah! I don't see anything."

"Well, he still looks angry about something. He's got a cranky face, and his clothes are dirty, and he looks ... famil... famil..." She furrowed her brow, searching her words.

"Familiar?" Sam asked.

She snapped her fingers, nodding emphatically. "Yeah! Like I know him!"

Sam nodded, then frowned. Who was he? No one had lived on this island in years. The bridge collapsed three years ago, but Marnie couldn't remember that because he barely did. With one last pull, the boat propelled to the pier. He set down the oars, grabbed the dock, and loosely tied off the back.

"Marnie, hop off and tie the front! Tom, give her that line that's by your feet?"

Tom scooped up the rope and held it out, waiting for Marnie to take it from him.

She scrambled onto the wooden deck, rocking the little boat as she went. Tom sucked in a breath, grabbed hold of his seat with one hand, and dangled the line above his head with the other. Marnie reached out and took it, then skipped to the cleat positioned at the bow. She planted one foot against a pylon, tugged, and with an exaggerated grunt, brought them closer to the dock. Her strong, little hands crisscrossed the rope around the cleat. She stood back and beamed.

She'd come a long way since last summer. Last year, she could barely get out of the vessel without help, and now she was pulling them to the pier.

"Well done, Squirt!" he lauded. "Soon, you'll be able to row me across."

Her eyebrows shot up and her face lit up. "Do you really think so?"

He smirked. "Well, not all the way, but some."

Deflated, her shoulders dropped—but only for a moment.

"Hey, Tom! Come on! Hop up on the dock!" She danced, encouraging her friend to join her.

"Is that cranky man still there?" Tom asked warily as he removed his life jacket.

She glanced around, then shook her head. "Nope. He's not here right now. He could be swimming with Sam's friends."

She dropped her life jacket into the bow, then lay on her tummy and reached for her bag, but she couldn't quite get it. Sam leaned forward, grabbed it, and held it out to her.

"You better put on sunscreen before you forget. Mom will kick my butt if you get burned"

She threw her head back and rolled her eyes.

Sam helped Tom up onto the dock, then followed. Fists on his hips, he stared down at his sister, who glanced up at his stern face, sat down, and took a bottle of sunscreen out of her bag. She held it out.

"Can you get my back, please?" she asked, her bottom lip out.

Tom giggled. "You're gonna trip over that lip and fall in the water."

She glared at him and wrinkled her nose.

Her brother laughed. "Or your face will freeze that way." He did as she asked, adding, "Don't forget to smear it on your face too."

"I won't forget."

Sam dug into Marnie's bag and found her baseball cap. "Here. Put on your cap so your head doesn't burn."

She snatched her hat, jammed it atop her head, and jumped to her feet. "Can we go swimming now?"

"Yeah. Help me grab the stuff," Sam said. He stepped into the rowboat and gave Marnie the inner tube, the armbands, and the air pump. "Let me pump these up so that I can leave the pump here. It'll just take a minute."

Marnie turned around with a loud huff, then skipped to the shoreline. Tom stayed to help Sam, and they looked up when they heard her talking to someone neither could see nor hear. Then her conversation escalated quickly.

With a frustrated stomp, she hollered, "No! You can't tell us we can't come here! We can swim here any time we want! You're a ghost!" She stopped and listened.

The boys watched as she nodded. Turning back, she ran to them.

"Hey, Sam! That man ... umm... he says his name is Mr. Barnes, said we can't swim here! He told me to tell you that there's a man living in his old house and that he murdered him, and he will kill us too if we find him!" She halted, took a deep breath, and hopped onto the dock.

"Marnie, are you making up stories to scare us? Is that make believe or is it true?" her brother asked.

"Swear to God, Sammy, I'm not kidding! It's true! I swear on my life!" she replied—her eyes wide, not with fear, but with determination. "You've got to believe me! Cross my heart!" She tugged on his shirt. "He's gonna hurt somebody. We gotta stop him!"

Tom slunk closer and sat down near Marnie. He pulled up his knees to his chin, hugging his legs tight to his chest. He turned to her. She hopped up and down. Her face flushed red, her aquamarine eyes wide, and her little fists wound tightly—she looked like a fighter getting ready to take a swing.

"Don't ya think we should tell our parents and call the cops?" Tom asked.

"No! We gotta warn Sam's friends! They're swimming on the other side of the island where that man is! We have to tell them to go home!" Marnie continued to bob back and forth. "Something bad's gonna happen," she said, patting her head as she surveyed the shore. When she turned back, the look in her eyes sent a chill up her brother's spine. "The top of my head is all tingly and prickly."

Sam set down the pump and rubbed his chin. His friends were on the opposite shore, waiting for them. Should he warn them? Would they believe him if he told them his sister, who sees spirits, spoke to a ghost who told her to leave? Or should he and the little ones leave? He glanced toward home, wondering if he should go get his father. He would know what to do. Yes. They would go back. He dropped the pump and inner tube into the boat and as he turned to share his plan with the others, a bloodcurdling scream ripped through the woods.

"What the heck!" Sam startled and turned.

"We gotta go get our parents!" cried Tom.

"It'll take too long. Your friends need us. Come on!" Marnie cried, pulling her brother in the scream's direction.

"No! You two need to stay here! You could get hurt. I'll go!" Sam said firmly.

"Nuh uh! I'm coming with you!" she said.

Sam scanned the dock, looking for a place where they would be safe. He saw the old generator shed. It had a hasp lock with a metal pin on the outside. If I can get her into that shed, she'll be safe, he thought.

"Well, we're going to have to find weapons. We can't fight a bad guy without a club or something to throw at him. Let's check that shed over there," he suggested.

Marnie ran ahead of him, as he had hoped she would do.

"Tom, can you help her? See if you can find something to hit him with?" Sam nudged him so would run to the shed.

The boy hopped up from his seat on the dock and raced forward. "I'll help her!" he called over his shoulder.

Reaching the door, she pulled on it, but it wouldn't open. She studied the lock, grasped the pin and pulled up, but she was too small to get it high enough. Slapping the door out of frustration, she barked, "Dang door! Dang lock!"

When Tom reached her, he stood on his tiptoes and tried, too, but nothing budged.

"You can't reach it; you're shorter than me. We need my big brother," she said with a roll of her eyes. "Sam, we can't open the door!"

"Hang on! I'll get it," he replied.

He grasped the pin, but it remained firmly fixed.

"It's rusted," he told them. He pulled harder, to no avail.

He thought for a second, searching for an alternative—but he knew they would be safer with him.

"C'mon! We'll all go but stay behind me. You understand, Marnie? You don't run ahead! If you do, I'll tell Mom and Dad that you didn't listen to me."

She ignored his threat and instead growled, "Let's get big sticks and rocks! We can hit him if he tries to get us," she said, stomping off. "Oh! Look, Sam! You could hit somebody really hard with this stick!" She struggled to pick up a large piece of driftwood.

"Marnie! What did I say?! Stay behind me!" Sam scolded, his face red with anger. "Don't run ahead!"

She skidded to a stop, dropped the wood, and turned back—bewilderment showing on her freckled face. She wasn't used to Sam getting angry with her. Annoyed, yes, but never nothing like this.

"Sorry," she said, dropping her eyes to the ground.

"Make sure you do!" he replied with a frown.

She nodded—not daring to lift her gaze to meet his. Sam bent over, picked up the piece of driftwood, and nodded with approval.

"Thanks, Squirt. This will make a decent club. I hope I don't need to use it."

She lifted her head and eyes to meet Sam's. He winked at her and tugged on the brim of her cap. He turned around to check on Tom, who stood directly behind him—his face white as a sheet, as he uneasily twisted and pulled on the hem of his T-shirt.

"C'mon, Tom. We're gonna be fine. We'll get the bad guy, huh?" he said, unsure exactly who was prey—the man or them. His friends could be in peril. He believed Marnie's gift would lead them in the right direction. She would tell him if they were running into danger. He looked down at her, holding tight to his index finger. Sensing that he was looking at her, she looked up.

"It's okay, Sam. We're alright," she assured.

"Which way should we go, Squirt?" he asked.

Marnie closed her eyes and whispered. Tom cocked his head, straining to hear her. Sam knew she was speaking with her grandfather. He also knew Papa Jack always answered when she called him.

"The water is the best way," she said.

"Thanks. Hold the back of my shirt with one hand, and Tom's hand with the other," he said.

She grasped his shirt. Tom retreated a step and stared into her green eyes.

"C'mon," she coaxed, wiggling her fingers. "We're safe. My Papa Jack is watching over us, and I'll bet if you ask her, Annie will too."

Tom closed his eyes, as Marnie had. He thought about his sister Annie, who had died recently after being hit by a car. She appeared to him and smiled. Tom's mouth lifted into a grin. He opened his eyes and grabbed hold of his friend's hand.

They set off to catch Mr. Barnes' killer. Sam led the way, gripping he driftwood.

They hurried along the reedy, pebbled shoreline. Mosquitos buzzed around their ears, and dragonfly wings glinted iridescent blue and green in the bright sunlight.

Marnie stumbled over a tree root, lost her grip, and toppled into the water with a splash. Tom, still holding onto her, stumbled sideways, clumsily reached for a sapling, saving himself from Marnie's wet fate.

"Stupid tree!" griped Marnie.

"Ow!" screeched Tom, as he scrambled to his feet.

"Shh!" Sam held a finger to his lips and offered his hand to his sister.

As the little ones collected themselves, another scream jolted them. Sam turned toward the shriek, then back to the youngsters.

"Stay put! I'm going to help. Crouch down. Don't move! I'll come back to get you. If anyone comes near, throw rocks at them really hard!" Sam darted off, leaving them alone at the edge of the pond.

Frowning, Marnie rang out the water from her hair.

"I want to help, too," she said with determination.

Tom wrinkled his nose. "He'll get mad if we follow him."

Marnie shook her head, stooped and started picking up stones. "Nah! He'll be happy to see us. We're gonna take these stones and chuck them real hard at the bad guy," she replied, shoving them into the pockets of her shorts. "Come on! Fill your pockets!"

Tom kicked the dirt, frustrated with his friend.

Marnie side-eyed him. "Alright. You stay. Mr. Barnes will keep you company. I need to help my brother!"

Tom's violet eyes grew as large as saucers. "He's here? Right now?" he asked, pointing at the ground.

"Can't you see him?"

His eyes darted left, then right. He spun in a circle, then back to Marnie. "Nah! I don't see anybody! You're just tryin' to scare me!"

She quirked up the corner of her mouth and shrugged. "Okay. I'm leaving."

Marnie waited as Tom gnawed at his bottom lip and thought about his options. Stay with Mr. Barnes—the dead guy, or go with Marnie, get yelled at by Sam, and run into a bad guy. He glanced from left to right. His furrowed brow relaxed slightly when he spied a rusty crowbar leaning against a tree, and as he bent to pick it up, another scream echoed. His face clouded with anger. He swung the crowbar onto his shoulder, clutched her arm and tugged her up the path.

"C'mon, Marn! We're gonna get that man! Making girls scream—that's … that's… Well, I'm gonna whack him!"

She grinned. "Yeah! Let's beat him up!"

They marched around pond's shoreline, clinging to each other. As they drew closer to the sounds of splashing and murmured conversations, they slowed their pace and crouched down. Peeking through the long grass, they could see Sam speaking with a group of kids about his age. He turned in their direction but didn't see them hiding.

"I'll be back. I've gotta get my sister and her friend. If I had known about that tree swing over the pond, I wouldn't have worried. Why do girls always have to scream?" Sam laughed and headed back to the the little ones, who exchanged glances.

"We better go back to where Sam said to stay," Tom whispered.

They raced to the spot where her brother had left them, but they stopped dead in their tracks. A man loomed before them—he was huge — bigger than anyone Marnie had ever seen in her life. Mr. Barnes appeared beside the fellow—shooing them away, but both the children froze, mouths agape.

He towered over them, and Marnie frowned while she studied his features; taller than her dad, with sooty black hair, a broad, flat forehead, bushy eyebrows, black eyes, and an enormous mouth. She decided he had fat lips. His earlobes were fat, too, but he was thin—wiry was what her mom would say. As she analyzed him, Marnie became agitated—sad—angry. She saw something evil in him, but she also felt sorry for him. She sensed a terrible pain in her right knee, then her head ached, and left ear buzzed. When her vision grew fuzzy, and her stomach lurched, she knew that these were his symptoms—not her own.

Being an empath is often confusing, especially for a child. But Marnie's mother told her that if she was ever to experience what she was now experiencing, she needed to focus on something positive—something nice—focus on anything but the person causing her to feel bad. So, she looked at Tom. When their eyes met, she felt panicked—terrified. She focused on the pond—calm washed over her, and her courage returned. She took a step forward, puffed out her chest, and scowled.

"Hey! What are you doing on Mr. Barnes' island? Did you hurt him?" she asked, head high and shoulders straight. Planting her feet firmly, she raised an eyebrow.

He stared down at her—eyes empty.

"Can you talk?" she asked, as she studied him, her frown slowly disappearing. "Hey! Why are you so grumpy? You know, you should get some aspirin for your knee and your head. It must hurt an awful lot. You might not be grumpy. Maybe Mr. Barnes has some at his house. You should go check."

Tom nudged her. "I don't think he wants to talk to us. We oughta get Sam."

She agreed, "Yeah. Let's go."

Grabbing her hair, he pulled her back, and she screeched.

"Ow! Let go of me! Tom! Run! Find Sam!" she screamed, flailing. "Let go of me, you stupid head!"

Her friend faltered, stared wide-eyed at her, and raced off.

The man clutched Marnie's arms and tightly clasped a mitt over her mouth. She twisted to free herself and stomped down hard on his foot. He held tighter, squeezing her middle as he lifted her. Kicking back, she connected with his knee, and he screeched in pain.

"Argh! You little bitch! You're dead!" he roared, his grip on her tightening.

She turned away, freeing her mouth from his rough and grimy paw. Sucking in a breath, she threw back her head into his nose, and sunk her teeth into his thumb. He hurled her to the ground, and as she scrambled to get to her feet, he slapped her across the face. Marnie saw stars—her ears buzzed, and she fell backward into the reeds.

Sam stopped on a cedar-covered path. The humidity had crept up. He tugged his shirt away from his damp skin, lifted the hem and wiped sweat from his face. The soft breeze from earlier in the day had faded, and the buzz of mosquitos and flies filled the sticky air. He wished he hadn't taken a shortcut through the trees but had rather walked along the shore. Swatting away a mosquito from his ear, he narrowed his eyes, searching in every direction. He was certain he had heard his sister screech. Cupping his hands like a megaphone, he called out.

"Marnie! Are you okay? I'll be right there!"

When she didn't answer, he hollered again.

Tom stopped running, turning toward Sam's voice.

"Over here!" he called, his voice filled with desperation.

"Is Marnie with you?" Sam asked, panic rising in his voice.

"That bad man has her! He grabbed her hair! She sent me to get you!" The fear-filled shout sent chills up Sam's spine.

He raced toward Tom's shouts, and running as fast as his legs would carry him, Tom ran toward the sound of Sam's voice.

"Where are you?" shrieked Tom.

"Here, buddy!" Sam called in reply. He could see the boy's head bobbing and weaving through the thickets and brambles of the overgrown woods. Then he didn't.

Tom took a sharp turn around a boulder, heard Marnie screech again, and pivoted, colliding with her brother.

Marnie kicked and shoved her captor away and scrambled back through the reeds and into the pond. She held her breath, dunked herself, and swam in awkward circles. When she came up for air, he grabbed her hair and yanked her out of the water, then swung her around like a rag-doll, before huddling her onto his hip and under his arm. She thrashed violently and shrieked, flailing her arms and legs—anything to regain her freedom.

"My brother's gonna beat you up! My dad's gonna murder you!" she cried.

Swinging her around, he grasped her under her armpits until they were nose to nose. He glared into her face and she scrunched up her nose.

"You stink! You smell like you haven't brushed your teeth!" she shrieked.

Marnie looked into eyes as dead as Mr. Barnes', but she was certain he wasn't a ghost. A spirit wouldn't be able to pick her up or slap her. She was sure of it. Eyes as big as saucers, she saw something in this man—and it wasn't good—it was evil. Pure evil! A cold chill inched up her spine, and goosebumps puckered her skin. The top of her head tingled, a sure sign something bad was about to happen. She squirmed and kicked wildly so that he would drop her, but his grip tightened, and a menacing sneer appeared on his unshaven face. His fingers dug into her little arms, and she winced with pain.

"I'll have fun killing you, little one. I'll bite off your fingers one by one, then your toes, your ears, and last, your nose." Licking his lips, he pulled her closer. Their noses nearly touching. Marnie could see the wickedness growing within him, knowing he would do exactly what he was threatening.

She summoned as much courage as her fear would allow and screamed, "You better put me down!" Kicking out, she jammed her little feet into his stomach.

Unfazed, he shook her, bobbing her head back violently. Marnie snapped forward, smashing the bridge of his beak with her skull, and she cringed at the audible crunch of bones. Blinded by pain, he dropped her and brought his palms to his face. She pulled herself up, and kneeling on a carpet of pine needles, she watched with morbid fascination as he growled with pain. Then he put two fingers along either side of his nose and pushed it back into place, blood oozing to the ground. Eyes wide and mouth agape, Marnie read his thoughts. She scrambled to her feet, and as she turned to flee, he lunged forward.

"I'll kill you!" he wailed.

"No, you are not!" roared Sam, swinging Tom's rusty crowbar at the man's head.

He hit the ground with a dull thud—a loud groan escaping from his throat but not before Tom had pulled Marnie from harm's way.

Sam stood over the monster, the weapon raised over his head. "I swear I will kill you if you get up! Don't you move or I'll hit you again!" He glanced up. "Tom, I want you to run and get my friends as fast as you can!"

Without a word, Tom darted off.

"Marnie, open your bag. Let's see what we have to tie him up."

Groaning, the guy rolled over, and reached the boy's leg. Sam crashed the crowbar onto the outstretched digits and kicked dirt into the ogre's face.

Hearing the crack of bar on bone, Marnie's head popped up from inspecting the contents of her bag. Her eyes welled with tears—partly from fear—partly from frustration. She couldn't find anything to tie up her tormentor.

"Nothing!" she whined. She stood and tipped everything out, sitting down to sift through the contents. "I don't have anything..."

Reaching for Sam's ankle again, the big dude grunted and lurched forward.

"Look out!" Marnie shrieked.

Sam swung his weapon down, smashing his forearm. A sickening crack followed, and he fell back with pain. His head lolled to one side and his glare fixed on Marnie.

She rolled her nose and put up her fists. "I'll take a swing at you next! You're a demon! My brother'll whack your other arm if you keep moving around and trying to grab him!"

The sound of thundering feet, breaking branches, and rustling leaves turned their attention to the woods. A moment later, Sam's friends skidded to a halt in the clearing. Tom, red-faced and winded, trailed behind them. Marcus, a teenager about thirteen, stepped into the clearing first. His dark brown hair was flat to his head—either from sweat or from swimming. His hazel eyes widened when he saw the guy slumped on the ground, groaning under the threat of the raised crowbar.

"What the hell happened?" Marcus asked, disbelief and confusion clouding his features.

Marnie hopped up, pointing at the sprawled figure. "He tried to kill me!"

The teen glanced at her—then at Sam.

The other children, including three tween boys, one boy who was about Marnie's age, a tall willowy girl; and three petite girls stepped into the clearing and stared down at the groaning beast. Their ages ranged from six to thirteen. The disgust on their faces ranged from "Holy crap! Sam really messed this guy up!" to "Oh my god! This man is grotesque!"

The villain's right arm had a huge goose egg and a nasty bruise rising on the forearm, and his left hand seeped blood, and looked to be broken. His nose was slightly askew and bulbous, and dribbles of dried blood splotched his lips and chin. His graying white T-shirt and jeans were grubby, with specks of red dotting the fabrics.

Sam relaxed his stance—but kept the crow bar raised.

"Marcus, can you please go to my house, get some rope, and ask my parents to call the cops?" asked Sam—no emotion in his voice. "They are going to take forever getting out to the island. My dad can help. We'll tie this guy up, then wait for the police. Oh, tell them to send paramedics, too."

Still staring down at the injured man, Marcus nodded. "Yeah. I can go. I have my father's boat." He turned to run back to his boat, snapped his fingers, and pivoted. "You know! I've got tow rope to tie up this dude."

Glancing up, Sam clenched his jaw, and nodded. "Thanks, Marcus." Turning to the tall, willowy girl, he said, "Stephanie, can you please go with Marcus and bring back the rope? I want to get him tied up sooner rather than later. I don't trust him."

"Sure. I'll do that for you." Stephanie blushed, then she and Marcus raced through the woods to get the rope.

Distracted by his crush's coy smile, Sam relaxed and lowered the metal bar to his side. He really liked Stephanie. He planned to ask her to go with him to the Creekwood Summer Festival Dance coming up next weekend.

"Sam! Look out!" Marnie screeched.

Her assailant kicked the boy's legs from beneath him. Then he weakly grabbed the crowbar with his mangled mitt. Marnie scrambled to get to her brother, but she stumbled on another tree root. The man scooted across the ground on his butt, and wrapped his right arm around Marnie's throat, while still gripping the bar tightly.

"Don't move! Any of you! I'll break her neck! I will squeeze the life out of her!" rasped out her foe.

"Argh! Stop!" Marnie screeched and thrashed.

"Don't fight me! I will kill you! I'll squeeze the life out of you, and I'll do it quicker if you struggle!" he threatened.

He scooted on his backside across the mossy ground until his back was against a large cedar tree. He planted the edge of his boots into the ground, and using the tree as leverage, he pushed himself up onto his feet. Marnie's neck still firmly trapped in the crook of his right arm, he stood and weakly took two backward steps away from Sam and his group of friends.

Eyes closed, Tom sank down to the dirt, covering his face with his forearm. He whispered, "Annie, please help my friend!"

Sam took a threatening step.

The kidnapper grinned and squeezed.

"You're hurting me!" she squeaked out, tears running down her frightened face.

Sam took another step forward.

"Not one more!" growled the enemy. "I will snap her neck like a twig!"

The roar of a boat engine echoed as it rounded the island. Sam hoped it was Marcus speeding toward the Reilly's dock. He scanned the faces of his friends, looking for options. David and Stuart, the Reilly children's close friends, looked between Sam and Marnie. Stuart was Sam's age, and David was a year older than Marnie. Sam knew if he could count on anyone, it was them, so he looked to Stuart for guidance, who put his hands out flat in front of himself, a sign for him to stand down. Sam nodded and retreated a step.

"Good boy!" said the brute with a wicked sneer. He walked backward through the brush, dragging Marnie into the forest with him. Tears streamed down her face and while her mouth was moving, she was too frightened to make a sound.

Sam turned around, searching for Tom, who was creeping through the trees.

"Get back here!"

The boy stopped for a moment, made eye contact with the teen, shook his head firmly, and darted off—trailing behind the monster who was carrying away his friend.

"You better let me go!" Marnie cried. "The cops are coming!"

"Will you shut up!" he growled.

Tears of pain pooled in his eyes as he half-carried and half-dragged Marnie to a shabby Gothic Carpenter house on the eastern side of the island. Made of timber, the house featured a large, dilapidated veranda, chipped paint and a crumbling brick chimney.

Cobwebs and trumpet creeper clung to the veranda's columns, and a picture window had a crack running through it.

The man lugged her up the front steps onto the porch and pushed open the door with his backside. Once inside, he dragged Marnie across the room and down a short hallway to the cellar stairs and clumsily hauled her to the earthen floor below.

"This is your home for the next coupla hours," he barked. Still holding her in the crook of his arm, he scanned the dark and dank room for a place to lock her away for an hour or two. An old leather sea chest sat in the far corner. His mouth curled up in a sneer. He knew lugging the child across the room and into that chest wouldn't be easy, but he would do it to shut her up.

"My dad'll be here soon. He's gonna be really mad at you for hurting me," she said meekly.

Taunting her, he laughed. "Your father and the cops ain't gonna do shit! You're goin' in this trunk; I'll go kill your friends, come back, kill you, and be gone by the time the cops come!"

Marnie stomped down on his foot, but her flip-flops had fallen off while he dragged her through the woods, and her small, bare feet did nothing to faze him.

"Haha! Didn't hurt!" he said, adding a wicked laugh.

Stooping to open the lid, his swollen fingers struggled to grasp the hasp.

"Open it!" he ordered, leaning her closer.

"No!" she squealed.

He squeezed her neck. "Open it! Damn you! Now!"

"Ow! Stop it, stupid-head!"

He squeezed harder, and she reached out and pulled up, but it wouldn't open. He bent and grabbed the hasp. With a pained grunt, he pulled up the lid. There was nothing in the chest but old rope and fishing nets. He grabbed Marnie by the scruff and shoved her inside, dropping the lid quickly, locking it.

Kicking and screaming, she cried, "Let me out! Let me out!"

He booted the side, hollering, "Shut up! If you don't, I'm going upstairs to get my gun. I will shoot you! I'll kill you right now!"

She lay still, hearing his footsteps on the stairs. The slam of the cellar door jiggled the windows, and the echo of his steps grew faint. Marnie strained to hear the distant footfalls—maybe in the kitchen or perhaps on the veranda. She closed her eyes and whispered, hoping Papa Jack would hear her and tell her what to do.

Tom snuck behind the house, peered through a kitchen window, and ducked down when his friend's captor walked into the room. He squatted behind a scrubby shrub, feeling the thud of his heart beating against his chest, and heard it drumming in his ears. He tried breathing through his nose, but it didn't work. No matter how hard he tried not to be frightened—he was terrified. Closing his eyes, he counted to ten, and thought of Annie, only this time she didn't appear.

Slam! Jerking, the boy stiffened when the front door banged shut. He ducked down further, tucking himself against the foundation.

Uh-oh! He winced, as the crunch of dirt and old leaves under boots grew louder. The baddie appeared at the side of the house where the little guy crouched.

Tom held his breath, counted to fifteen, and just as a breath nearly burst from his lungs, the monster walked back to the front of the dwelling. He exhaled loudly, sucked in air, and breathed a sigh of relief when he saw the monster walk off to the far side of the island where Sam's friends had been swimming and laughing moments before. He stood and wiped dirt and gravel from his palms onto his shorts.

"Where are you, Marnie? Where'd he take you?" he muttered to himself.

"Papa Jack, are you sure?" Marnie asked. She shuddered in a breath. Clumsily rolling to her side, she sighed, opened her eyes and listened. Silence. The creep was gone.

A door closed quietly. Light footsteps above—someone was moving around upstairs. Marnie thumped her fists on the walls. She moved awkwardly to her back and kicked the lid and banged on the sides. Then she lay silent. A door opened, and she heard feet on the cellar stairs. She froze.

"What if it's the bad guy and he got his gun? He's gonna shoot me!" she said to herself.

She cocked her head, hearing a whisper. Then she heard someone utter her name.

"Marn, are you down here?" Tom whispered loudly.

She pushed herself up onto an elbow. "Get me out of here!" she shouted.

He gripped the hasp and yanked it upward.

"Dang it! It's stuck!" he yelled. "I'm gonna find somethin' to open it!"

Dust floated in the air and the grimy windows rippled with age, but enough light shone through that he wasn't in pitch blackness. A workbench sat against the side wall, and he spotted a set of screwdrivers hanging above it.

"That'll work," he said.

"Tom!" Marnie cried.

He ran back, screwdriver at the ready. "I'm right here! I'll get you out!"

Pushing the tip between the trunk and the hasp, he finagled the lock free, then dropped the tool and threw open the lid. Marnie popped up to her feet, scrambled over the side, and gave the boy a big bear hug.

He pushed her away. "Stop it! We gotta get outta here before he comes back!"

She put a finger to her lips. "Shh! I've got to tell you something," she whispered.

He leaned close—his eyebrows knitting together. "What?"

She pressed her lips to his ear and whispered, "Mr. Barnes has a secret. My Papa Jack said so."

He stepped back and stared at her. "What did he say?"

She glanced around to see if anyone was listening to their conversation. When she saw no one—living or dead—hiding in the shadows of the cellar, she whispered, "Mr. Barnes killed his wife, and she's buried under the bridge near an old ice shack."

The boy crinkled his nose. "An ice shack? What the heck is that?"

Marnie stuck out her bottom lip and shrugged. "Not sure. That's what Papa Jack told me. He said there's a treasure hidden in the coal chute, too."

Tom quirked up one side of his mouth. "What's that?"

She shrugged again. "I dunno, but I bet it's down here."

They wandered through the cellar looking for a coal chute. Neither knew what one was, but Marnie knew they would know it if they saw it. Tom stumbled over a cardboard box and fell against her, and she lurched headlong into a wooden bin.

She spit and sputtered. "Blah! Blah! What ... I'm all dirty! You pushed me into dirt!" she bellowed, looking at the black dust covering her.

Tom's eyes widened. "Sorry! I tripped!"

She turned in a half circle. "Hey! I think this is coal dust. I know what it looks like. Dad told me and Sam that if we didn't help with chores, Santa was going to leave it in our stockings. He even brought some home to show us." Marnie bent and picked up a chunk of coal from the bin. "See! This is coal!"

"I've seen that stuff before. My grandpa puts it in his barbecue!" Tom said with pride.

Marnie cocked her head and examined the wall on which the coal bin sat. She took three steps closer to the wall, and her upper body disappeared into a hole. "Look! That must be the coal chute! Look! It goes outside! I can see light up there!" Her muffled words echoed up the chute, but Tom understood everything she said.

He climbed into the box and joined his friend. Both stood looking up at the daylight shining down.

"Where's the treasure?" he asked.

She pointed up. "There it is! It's right there!" She reached up and pulled a piece of twine, and an oilcloth sack fell into her arms. "Wow! It's heavy! I bet it's a genie lantern!"

"Nah! Genies aren't real! That's only in movies! It's probably a pirate's treasure! Gold and silver!"

"Well, lots of people say ghosts aren't either—and they're wrong! So, genies could be, too!" she argued.

"C'mon, Marn! Open it!" Tom said as he climbed out of the coal bin.

She gave him the sack and scrambled over the side onto the dusty cellar floor.

Shaking her head, she said, "No, let's wait until we get outside. We've got to leave now! That man's gonna come back!"

He agreed, "Let's get outta here!"

They raced up the stairs, and as they reached the top, the door flew open, and Mr. Barnes loomed over them—his face scary and dark.

Marnie was one step ahead of Tom. She pointed her finger at the specter. "You need to go now! We're not afraid of you! We know what you did!"

Bumping her with his shoulder, he whispered, "Please don't make him mad."

"He can't hurt us. He's a ghost."

"I can do more than you think!" bellowed the spirit, his words echoing through the house. "Put my treasure back where you found it!"

"No!" Marnie growled. "Out of our way! We're going to get the cops!" She took a step up and a frigid blast of wind pushed her backward into Tom, and they tumbled down the stairs to the cold cement floor beneath.

Tom hit his head on the stone foundation at the bottom. Marnie's landing was softer as she fell on top of Tom, her top teeth biting through her bottom lip. Stunned and scared, they looked up. Mr. Barnes slammed shut the door, and they heard the latch turn.

"Geez! Why'd you make him mad?" Tom struggled to sit up.

Marnie rolled off him and stood up. "He was already mad! He told us to leave when we got here, remember?"

"Yeah," he said, reaching to feel the bump growing. Bending over, he asked, "Marn, am I bleeding?"

She inspected his skull, but there wasn't any blood—only a huge goose egg.

"Nah! What about me?" She pushed out her bottom lip for him to inspect.

"Yeah! That doesn't look too good!" he said, scrunching up his face.

"It's just another scar. I'll bet when I'm a grown-up I'll have better ones. It's a little cut, right?" she asked.

He shrugged his shoulder. "I guess so. Hey! How are we gonna get out of here?"

Marnie glanced around the cellar. The windows were too high for them to reach, but she had an idea. Tongue poking out the side of her mouth in concentration, she snapped her fingers awkwardly.

"The coal chute!" she said. "We're gonna put the treasure back up there so that Mr. Barnes doesn't chase us. Then we'll crawl up the walls like Santa Claus does when he goes up the chimney. We'll come back to get it."

Sam paced frantically up and down the forest floor. He ran his fingers through his hair and gave an inward groan. Staring up at the tree branches overhead, he sighed. "Hey, guys, I've gotta go find my sister—and her buddy. My dad will be here soon. If they aren't with me, he's gonna kick my butt."

Strolling to his side, Stephanie tucked her arm through his. "This isn't your fault. You didn't know there was a madman here. How could you have known?"

He stared straight ahead, focused on the path where Tom had darted away. He clenched his jaw. "My sister warned me. If she tells my father, well, I'll get grounded for the rest of the summer."

"Marnie isn't a tattletale," David Bennett assured.

Shaking his head, Sam said, "Not on purpose, no. She tattles accidentally, but she doesn't get me into trouble on purpose. She blurts things out without even realizing what she's saying."

Wrinkling her forehead, Stephanie shot a glance sideways. "What do you mean, your sister warned you? How could she warn you if you came to the island together?"

Sam sighed and turned to Stephanie. "My sister sees stuff, hears things the rest of us don't. Ghosts." Realizing he had outed his sister's gift to his friends, he turned his back on the group.

Stephanie burst out laughing. Two of the girls shot each other glances and giggled, and the other two stared down at their toes. The Bennett boys nodded knowingly, while the others gawked blankly—not sure what to make of his strange admission.

The teen's face reddened with anger, and he spun around, glaring at them. "It's not funny! A psycho kidnapped Marnie! What's funny about that?!"

Her shoulders stiffened. "Geez, Sam! We're only teasing, but seriously! Your sister sees ghosts? It obviously embarrasses you! You turned your back on us!" She giggled, and the other girls joined her.

Furrowing his brow, Sam cocked his head to one side. "I am not embarrassed that Marnie can see ghosts. I'm angry with myself because I broke my promise to her to not tell anyone about her gift." His frown deepened. "Wow, Stephanie! I didn't realize that you were one of the mean girls. I thought you were different. Ha! I was going to ask you to the dance next weekend. I guess I'll take a girl who doesn't make fun of my sister—especially when her life is in danger."

Stuart, David, and the other boys side-eyed one another, as Stephanie's friends rallied around her.

"Sam Reilly, don't be mean. How dare you say I am! I think it's ridiculous that you believe your sister can see ghosts! Of course, she can't! Ghosts aren't real!" Stephanie stomped away from the group. Two of her girlfriends chased after her, but the other two remained with Sam and the boys.

Pushing a spiny pinecone around with his toe, Sam announced, "I gotta search for Marnie. Everybody stick together. If that big guy comes back, you don't want to be wandering alone."

"We'll come with you," replied Stuart, hooking a thumb at his brother David. "Joe and Alex can stay here with the girls. You shouldn't go alone."

With a reluctant nod, Sam agreed, "Yeah. That's a good idea. He has the crowbar. We'll have to find some big sticks and rocks along the way. He's injured, but he's strong."

The boys agreed with nods of their heads.

"We were going to catch some fish for lunch, so I've got my filet knife in my bag. I'll bring that," Stuart suggested.

Sucking on his bottom lip, Sam considered the consequences. "Hmm. We sure don't want him to get hold of that! He's got Marnie! If he gets it away from you ... It's a risk, Stuart. Until we find her... He's already taken the crowbar. What if he got hold of your knife?"

Stuart gasped then whistled. "Geez! I hadn't thought of that! I guess it was kind of stupid." He dropped his head and his shoulders.

"It wasn't stupid, Stu. It's just ... well... I need to make sure the kids are safe, that's all. Let's find big sticks or rocks and leave the knife behind."

"Okay. Let's go get them."

Turning to Joe and Alex, Sam said, "If my dad gets here before we get back, tell him where we went."

"If that dude returns, we'll holler," Joe said.

"Same for us," said Sam, glancing at Stephanie and the girls. He thought he should apologize for getting angry, then quickly changed his mind. She *had* been mean and shouldn't have said that. *Dang it! I'm not apologizing. She should apologize to me.*

"Let's go get my sister!" He took a confident step forward and disappeared into the woods, with the Bennett boys trailing him.

"Hey, Marn, we should take the screwdriver with us—you know, to stab him if he comes after us!" Tom ran back and picked it up, wielding it as a pirate would a sword. "What do you reckon?"

"That's a good idea," she agreed. With a glance about the cellar, she twisted her mouth in thought. "Umm ... What else is down here that we can hit him with?"

"Is that a matchstick? That looks like the one my dad used to whack down weeds in our yard," said Tom.

Marnie's eyes followed his to a machete. It hung on a peg over Mr. Barnes' workbench.

"If you boost me up, I can get it! That looks scary. I'll bet that icky man would be afraid of that! He has stinky breath. I don't think he has a toothbrush." She skipped across the dusty floor and stood next to the workbench.

"What? Everybody has one," said Tom, getting on his hands and knees; Marnie stepped onto his back and crawled onto the workbench. She reached up, grabbed the handle of the machete, and pulled it out and off the peg. Giving it carefully to Tom, she hopped down.

"It's pretty rusty," he said.

With a shrug, Marnie said, "We can still whack him with it."

They went back to the coal bin, dropped the screwdriver and machete into the bin, and scuttled over the side.

"How the heck are we gonna get up there?" Tom asked, staring up the chute.

"How should I know?" she said, shoving the treasure back where they had found it. "Oh! What's that?"

Eyes wide, they shared frightened glances. Footsteps crunching on the leaves and the gravel road echoed down the chute from outside, and Marnie held a finger to her lips.

Sam, Stuart, and David approached the house. They kept low so no one would see them should they be looking out the window.

"You think he's got Marnie in there?" Stuart whispered.

"He could. She has to be here somewhere. We've looked everywhere else," said Sam. "If he's in there, and she is too, we'll never get her out without my father or the cops."

"Maybe he stashed her and came for us?" suggested David.

"Wait here." Sam crept to the back windows, stood on his toes, and peeked into the kitchen. He couldn't see anyone, and so went around to a side window, but again, no one appeared to be home. He turned back to David and Stuart, motioning for them to join him.

Hearing voices from outside the house, Marnie and Tom could see feet through a rippled window.

"Look! Flip-flops!" She grabbed Tom's arm. "It's my brother and his friends!"

Tom wrapped his arms around her in a huge bear hug and twirled her around.

"Yell really loud!" she said.

They screamed at the top of their lungs. "Down here! We're in the cellar! Sam!"

He turned to face the house. "You guys hear that?" A smile spread across his face. "That's my sister! They're here! Listen!"

Colin Reilly tied his boat up to the dock—wrinkles of worry lining his forehead. He stooped and took the rifle that his wife, Sophia, was passing up to him. He wore khaki cargo shorts, a gray New York Giants shirt, and tan boat shoes. His strawberry blonde hair, freckled nose, and green eyes told anyone who cared to notice that Marnie took after her father. Colin's broad shoulders, long, lean build, and strong, rough hands gave away his career as a tradesman. He was a carpenter—probably the best in Creekwood. Well-known about town, he was the guy who could get anything done, and done right. He coached the town's Little League program; sat on the school board; volunteered at the Boys and Girls Club, and was an avid hunter, angler, and the pitcher on his softball team.

Sophia held out her hand to her husband. He helped her navigate her way off the boat and onto the rickety dock. Sophia wore cutoff denim shorts, a white tank top, and white Keds; and around her waist, she wore a black canvas fanny pack. Her honey blonde ponytail poked neatly out the back of her navy blue Creekwood PD baseball cap. Sophia was a force of nature. She ran 5 miles every day; belonged to the PTA; coached the girls' high school volleyball team; and she volunteered at the local animal shelter every weekend. Marnie's and Sam's mother had a reputation for speaking her mind—honestly and fairly. She also had a reputation for not suffering fools easily, which was a good thing because she was Creekwood's town judge.

Marcus arrived moments after the Reillys.

"Can you anchor and swim in? There won't be room for the police boat if you dock here?" called Colin.

He waved his understanding. Colin helped him aboard and Sophia passed him a towel.

"What can I do to help?" asked Marcus.

"How about you stay here so that you can wave in the police?" Colin suggested.

"Happy to help any way I can." He sat back into a seat, warily assessing the shore.

Sophia noticed the concern on Marcus's face. She nudged her husband and directed her gaze in the boy's direction.

"There's a flare gun under the captain's chair. If you have any trouble, send up a flare, then reload," recommended Colin.

He grinned. "Thanks. I was just thinking that man might come this way. He might want to get off the island, and I doubt he would worry about stealing a boat."

"You're probably right. We'll be back once we gather everyone. You said the Bennett boys are here, two other boys and five girls. Is that right?" asked Colin.

"Yes, sir. They were all together in a clearing in the heart of the woods."

"Don't worry. We'll find everyone," Sophia assured him.

Marcus's eyes grew wide, and a frown spread across his face. "He's a really big dude! Be careful!"

Colin laughed. "Hmm. He took Marnie. He had better be careful. That little girl is a force of nature, like her mother. Our own little tempest, and if Sam is as angry as you say he is, he'll tail that big dude, and he'll be sorry he wrangled with the Reilly family."

Sam picked up a large rock and shattered the cellar window. He cleared away the glass and stuck his head through the opening.

"Man, am I happy to see you!" he said.

"Sammy Bear!" Marnie hopped from foot to foot, arms waving.

Tom inspected the broken window, face tight with worry. "Mr. Barnes is gonna be mad!"

"I don't care if he's mad. Are you locked down there? Can you come up through the house?" Sam asked.

Marnie said, "Mr. Barnes knocked us downstairs and locked the door! He's an ass!"

"Don't cuss!" Sam scolded.

She dropped her eyes to the floor, then up to Sam. "Well, he is an ass. He's mean!"

Turning his head to hide a grin, he said, "Okay, Marnie. He's an ass. Now, c'mon over here. Stu and David will hold my feet. I'll stretch my arms down, you're going to grab me so I can pull you up."

"Tom, you go first. I'll matchstick that guy if he comes down here to get me," Marnie said, holding up the machete like a sword.

"You sure, Marn? I can matchstick him!" Tom offered.

"One of you, get over here! We don't have a lot of time!" scolded Sam.

Tom jumped, surprised by Sam's tone. He ran to the window, held onto Sam, and he pulled him up and through the window.

"C'mon, Marnie! Let's go!" Sam scooted back through the window and held out his arms.

She raced to the window and gave her brother the machete. "Here, take the matchstick! We can whack the bad guy with it!"

"It's called a machete," Sam corrected her, and took the blade carefully. He gave it to Stuart, then he reached down for his sibling, who held tight as he rescued her from the cellar. He got to his feet and brushed gravel and dirt from his clothes before giving his sister a tight embrace.

"Thank you for getting us out of there!" She hugged him back and asked, "Is that meanie coming back?"

"Don't know. C'mon!"

They rounded the corner of the porch and stopped dead. The big dude stood in front of them with a gun—aimed directly at Marnie.

"You're not going anywhere!" he growled.

Stuart, who was in the lead, quickly hid the machete behind his back. Sam saw it and moved a step closer to him. Marnie darted away, snatching up a fistful of gravel. With all her might, she heaved it, peppering the monster. As he turned to re-aim his weapon, Tom grabbed a handful of stones and let it fly. David did the same.

Sam took the weapon from Stuart's and charged forward. Dazed by the commotion, the villain pivoted left, then right, then he aimed at Sam.

Marnie scooped up two fistfuls of gravel and flung it at his face. The others all bombarded their enemy with flying stones and dirt as Sam charged forward, wildly waving the machete. Confused, the enemy retreated, and pointed the weapon at Sam again.

A fist-sized chunk of granite tore through the trees, hitting its target on the shoulder. He wavered and spun around, now aiming his pistol to his right—into the woods.

Shush-shick!

Birds scattered and Sam eased back, knowing his father had arrived, and he had brought along his hunting rifle.

Without revealing his position, Colin yelled, "Drop your weapon! Now!"

He refused, turning it on Marnie.

Chick-chick!

The distinct click a round being chambered drew his attention left.

Sophia, pistol drawn, aimed at her enemy's chest, and emerged from the brush on the opposite side of the house. She quickly scanned the children's faces, then planted her Keds.

"Freeze, asshole!"

He met Sophia's gaze—a slight grin appearing on his face—daring her to shoot.

Colin moved from his position in the woods, directly opposite his wife—his rifle aimed at the man's leg. "Put the gun down. We don't want to shoot you. Put it down and kick it over here." He worked hard to hide his fear with his cool, steady tone.

Glancing warily between Sophia and Colin, he considered his options. Marnie scrunched up her nose and poked out her tongue. His decision was simple. He took aim at the little girl.

Birds scattered in the woods behind, and the big dude craned his neck, as Sam lunged forward with the machete. He whacked his adversary's right arm, and a pained shriek echoed across the island. Their foe dropped his weapon.

David zig-zagged around the big guy and kneeled behind him. Stuart rushed forward, driving his shoulder into his stomach—forcing him to trip backward over his brother. Landing hard on a bed of pine needles—his bloody left mitt clung to his wounded right arm. Another shriek of pain escaped him as Colin placed his foot on his arm and pointed the rifle at his head.

"Don't move!" he growled.

"Careful, Dad! He's fast! He got away from us today!" Sam raced to his father's side and glowered down.

"Don't worry, son. I heard the police arrive."

Sophia put her gun into her fanny pack and ran to Marnie. She checked her from head to toe, making sure she had no broken bones; she hugged her quickly, then examined the others. Rejoining her husband, she retrieved her gun from her pack, training it on the bad guy's chest.

She glanced up at her son, then back down at the figure wincing beneath her husband's foot. "Sam, are you hurt?"

"I'm fine, Mom," he responded with a shrug.

She studied her son. "Look at me."

His gray eyes met his mother's soft blue gaze. He looked older to her than when they had left for the island this morning. She knew he wasn't okay, and that this had been a terrible ordeal for everyone. "Thank you for taking such good care of your sister," Sophia said—a warm smile spread across her face, and her eyes teared up.

Frowning, Sam replied, "Yeah! I did a great job. I let him kidnap her."

"Did you get her back? Did you do everything you could to protect her?" Colin asked, taking his eyes off his prisoner so he could see his son's face.

Sam nodded.

"Well, then you did the best you could, and it's better than a lot of boys your age could have done. You did well, son." Colin looked around at the group of children. "You've all done well."

Struggling to hide tears, Sam stared into the woods and Marnie skipped to his side and wound her arms around him.

Two police officers in uniform and a man wearing jeans, a T-shirt, suit jacket, and boots raced into the clearing.

"Mr. and Mrs. Reilly, please put down your weapons. We'll take it from here."

"Whew! Are we glad to see you!" Colin sighed, lowering his rifle.

"Yeah. The cavalry's here," Officer Pete Sterling replied.

"How are the kids doin'?" asked Officer Lou Beaumont, nodding toward the children.

"They're as well as you'd expect. Marnie and Sam have minor bumps, cuts, and bruises..." Sophia began—only to be interrupted by her daughter.

"Tom has a big, bumpy goose egg on his head!"

"Well, if none of them need care urgently, we'd appreciate it if you could take the kids to the hospital after we've spoken with them. We don't want them to forget anything," said Officer Sterling.

Sophia wrapped an arm around her son's shoulders. "Could take this to our house? It's been a strenuous day, and we'd like the children to be comfortable when they speak with you."

She glanced at Tom. Looking at Sterling, she said, "I've tried to reach Tom's parents but haven't been able to get through to them. They've been in Saratoga Springs most of the day and plan to pick him up at 7:00. I think it's best we get the kids home."

Marnie poked her head around her mother and looked up at Officer Sterling. "Yeah! And I'm hungry! We didn't get to eat our lunch 'cause that man kidnapped me!" Bringing her fists to her hips, she glared bravely at the prisoner.

The policeman, wearing jeans, stepped forward. "That's fine. We'll finish up here, then meet you at your house. Pete, you know where the Reilly's live, right?"

"Yeah. I know."

The jeans-cladded man said, "I'm Lieutenant Mac Gregg. I'm here in Creekwood helping for a few days while their boss is on vacation. We'll come over as soon as we've finished."

Sophia smiled warmly. "Thanks so much. It's just that the children..."

With dismissive wave, he said, "No need to explain. I'd want to get them home, too. I have two myself—about Marnie's age." The lieutenant ruffled her hair.

She glowered at him. "Hey! How did you know my name?"

"Ha-ha! She's a pistol, isn't she?" Lieutenant Gregg kneeled and smiled. "Well, Marnie, your mom mentioned your name when we first arrived. Why don't you go home with your mom and dad, have something to eat, and we'll see you soon."

She gave him a sideways glance—one strawberry blonde eyebrow raised. Sophia recognized the look on her daughter's face, and before the child could blurt out something inappropriate, she agreed wholeheartedly with the lieutenant.

"Yes, I think that is for the best. We'll get the kids home and fed. After that, they'll be ready to have a nice long chat with you."

Colin playfully messed up Marnie's hair and agreed, "Yeah, and she won't be so grumpy once she's been fed."

"Don't bet on it!" she growled.

Colin laughed, glancing at the prisoner. "Any idea who this guy is?"

Lieutenant Gregg raked his fingers through his thick brown mop. Pulling a notepad from his pocket, he said, "Yeah. His name is Jethro Barnes. He's Cy Barnes' adopted son, and he's bad news. He's been in and out of trouble since he was 15. His mother, Ida, married Cy when Jethro was five. From what I can tell, it wasn't a happy family. Jethro got out of Bayview a couple years ago. His parole officer lost him, and we've been looking for him in connection with a few armed robberies. Ida Barnes has no known whereabouts. It has to be six years since Cy Barnes put in a missing person on Ida. We've always figured she got fed up and took off."

"When did Cy pass away? I don't remember anything in the newspaper," asked Colin.

"A couple of officers came over two years ago to do a welfare check because people in town hadn't seen him in a while. Anyway, they found him dead in his vegetable garden. They thought it was a stroke, but I'm wondering now," replied Lieutenant Gregg, glancing over his shoulder at Jethro.

Officers Beaumont and Sterling had helped Barnes sit up, securing his hands behind his back with cuffs.

Marnie eased toward Jethro Barnes, stopped a foot away, and narrowed her eyes. She leaned forward and whispered, "I know you killed Mr. Barnes, and that he killed Mrs. Barnes. I'm gonna tell the cops when they come to my house tonight. You're a bad man!"

"If you tell them anything, you are dead," Barnes growled.

"You're gonna get locked up. You can't hurt me," she whispered.

"Get away from him!" said Colin.

"Hang on a sec, Dad! I want to see if his nose still hurts!" she called back. She turned back to Barnes. "Does it?"

"A little girl like you isn't gonna hurt someone like me," replied Barnes—a malicious grin spreading across his ugly face.

Marnie took one step back, rolled her little fingers into a tight fist...

"No!" shouted Colin.

She peeked at her father for a split-second before punching the monster square in the nose.

"Does it hurt now?" she said, glowering at him.

"Oh, Marnie!" Sophia covered her eyes, shaking her head.

Nudging one another, the children giggled and quietly celebrated her pugilistic effort. The police officers hid their amusement by turning their backs.

Barnes blinked back tears of pain as blood oozed down his anger-reddened face. "I will kill you!"

"You're going to jail!" She screwed up her face and poked out her tongue, before running to her father's side. Arms wrapped around one of his legs, she tipped her head up and grinned.

"Marnie, you don't punch people!" he scolded. He kneeled next to her. "We've talked about this!"

"He hurt me! He locked me in that dang trunk, and he hit Sam, and he shook me real hard, and he killed Mr. Barnes, and ... and..." she gasped for a breath, fell into the safety of her father's arms and wailed.

Colin hugged her close, picked her up, and turned to his wife. "It's time to get these kids home. She's exhausted. They all must be."

The aroma of grilled hamburgers and hot dogs, and the sounds of barking dogs, children laughing, silverware clattering and Johnny Cash on the stereo greeted the policemen when they arrived at the Reilly home at a little past 6:30.

Marnie and her two dogs met them at the door. "Hi! My parents are in the kitchen. This is Murphy and this is Jack." She pushed open the screen door, and the dogs sniffed at the men as they entered the house.

Lieutenant Gregg scratched Murphy's ears and bent to pat the top of Jack's head. Officer Sterling walked around the dogs with wary eyes, and Officer Beaumont patted Marnie's head.

"C'mon! I'll take you to my parents!" She grabbed Lieutenant Gregg's index finger and pulled him through her home to the big country kitchen, the others following.

An old oak trestle table with long bench seats sat in a nook by a bay window that looked over the backyard. The table held a stack of paper plates, silverware, plastic cups, and napkins with mustards, ketchup, salad dressings, and relish bottles in the middle with bowls of potato, macaroni, and green salad. Two pitchers of lemonade and two of ice water sat on a sideboard on the back wall near the backdoor.

"The cops are here!" Marnie announced. She pulled out a bench and sat at the table. Murphy and Jack curled up at her feet. "Can I have a hot dog with sauerkraut and mustard, please?"

Sophia appeared from the pantry with hamburger and hot dog rolls. "Yes, bossy boots. I'll check on dinner with your father. Officers, would you like to join us? We have hamburgers, hot dogs, and three types of salad."

Beaumont rubbed his palms together. "That would be great! I'll take a hot dog with everything!"

"We're not here for dinner, Lou." Sterling sighed deeply. "We're here to question the children."

"I think something to eat would be fine. We can sit with the kids—get to know them a bit better. It may make them more comfortable," suggested Lieutenant Gregg. "Uh … where are the others?"

"They're outside—except for Tom. He's in the den watching TV. He has a headache from that bump on his head. I keep checking on him to make sure he's awake. Poor thing. I don't think he has a concussion, but that bump will hurt for a few days," said Sophia.

Colin came in the back door, carrying a tray of hamburgers. Sam followed with a plate of hot dogs. The rest of the children trooped in behind, and hovered over the table, waiting their turn. Tom wandered into the kitchen moments later and slid onto the bench next to Marnie. David sat on the other bench opposite them.

"Dad, can we go out and sit at the picnic table?" asked Sam.

"Sure. Does everybody have a drink?"

"And a napkin? Don't wipe food on your clothes," Sophia said. "Put your plates in the garbage when you're finished. And bring the silverware into the house—do not throw it out!"

"Alright, Mom!" said Sam, rolling his eyes.

The screen door slammed, and the teenagers were gone.

Sterling took a seat next to David, and Officer Beaumont took one beside Tom.

Sitting at the breakfast counter, Sophia and Colin positioned themselves where they could easily hear the conversation without intruding.

"Can I sit with you?" asked the lieutenant, standing beside Marnie—who was swinging her legs under the table.

"Sure." She shrugged and tried to take a bite of her hot dog, winced, and set it down. "Ow!" she said, scrunching up her nose, she put her fingers to her swollen lip.

"Your lip looks mighty sore. Did Jethro Barnes do that?" asked the lieutenant.

"Nah! Mr. Barnes did. He pushed us down the stairs. That's how Tom got the goose egg!"

"Mr. Barnes?" asked the lieutenant. "But he wasn't there."

"Yes, he was! Ask Tom! He'll tell ya!"

Tom took a big bite out of his hamburger and nodded. "Yup!"

"That's impossible. He died two years ago," said Officer Sterling from across the table.

Lieutenant Gregg narrowed his eyes and shook his head at Sterling, who purposely did not look in the commanding officer's direction.

"Pfft! I know that! He killed his wife, you know! My Papa Jack told me he murdered her. She's buried under the bridge near the ice shack. He said he got killed by Jethro!"

"Who is Papa Jack?"

"My grandfather. He talks to me sometimes. He's a ghost, like Mr. Barnes—but he is a friendly ghost. Mr. Barnes is nasty," she said matter-of-factly, looking at Tom, who nodded in agreement.

Sterling smirked. "A ghost? My goodness, you two have active imaginations!"

"I don't get it." Marnie frowned and threw up her arms. "Why are you laughing at us?"

Colin and Sophia shared a look, knowing this was going to be a hard conversation.

Sterling smugly replied, "Well, Marnie, I'm a grown-up. I don't believe in ghosts."

"That's okay. They don't believe in you either," she replied with a shrug. "That lady behind you called you a nincompoop. She says you were born grumpy and grew up to be ... umm..." Marnie squinted her eyes and cocked her head to one side. Her aquamarine eyes focused directly over Sterling's head. "Bombastic! That's what she said! Bombastic!" Marnie shrugged. "I don't know that word. What does it mean?"

Sterling gasped. "Who told you that?"

"She says she's your mom and that you've been a pain in the ass your whole life and that she told you so!" She grinned, picked up her hot dog, and turned to her parents. "Dad, can you cut this up for me? It's ouching my lip."

The adults contained their laughter to save Officer Sterling's dignity, but David and Tom giggled.

"Ha-ha! Marnie, you said a swear word." Tom roared with laughter.

She pointed at the officer. "No! His mom said the swear word. She told me to say it."

"Hey, Pete, how about you go out back and get statements from the other kids? Beau, go with him. You can divide the kids up, and we can finish this quicker so that the Reillys can get on with their night." Lieutenant Gregg stood and walked out the back door with the officers.

"Bombastic! It's fun to say! Bombastic! What does it mean?" Marnie's wide-eyed innocence of naively insulting Officer Sterling made her father smile.

"How about we talk about that later? We'll get out the dictionary and look it up once everyone has gone home. How does that sound?"

"Is it a naughty word?"

Colin stood over his daughter, cutting up the hot dog. "No, it's not a naughty word, but you shouldn't use it to describe people. It could hurt their feelings."

Glancing sideways in thought, Marnie asked, "Is Officer Sterling bombastic?"

Her father burst out laughing, turned his back and stepped outside. He knew Marnie would continue her line of questioning if she had an audience.

"Perhaps a bit." Sophia nodded curtly.

"Ah! It means he's annoying." Marnie picked up a bit of the hot dog and popped it into her mouth.

Sophia turned away to hide a grin as the lieutenant returned.

"Marnie, can we have a chat?" he asked.

"Sure!" she said.

Marnie told the lieutenant about everything that had happened on the island, with Tom and David adding to the story. He left twice—once when she told him about Mrs. Barnes's body being near the ice shack under the bridge; and again, to hide his amusement when she asked him if he thought Officer Sterling was bombastic.

Lieutenant Gregg pushed back his chair and stood. "Thank you, everyone, for your help. You did very well. I'm heading to the station to write my reports, and I'll let you know if I have any more questions. Do you have questions for me?"

Tom sat forward, leaning his arms on the tabletop. "Do you always carry your gun?"

"I carry it everywhere, but at home. I lock it in a cupboard," said the lieutenant.

"Have ya ever shot anyone?" asked David.

"Yes, but not in a very long time." He glanced away, picked up his notebook and pen, and tucked them in his pocket.

Marnie put up a hand—her eyes filling with tears. "Stop asking him about that! It makes him sad!" She wiped away tears.

A knock at the front door, and the squeak of the screen door opening, interrupted the children's questions.

Tom's mother called out from the foyer. "Hello! We're back! It's Abigeal and Declan! Sorry we're a little late. We had a flat tire on the way home!"

Their son hopped up from his seat and ran to the door. "Mom! Dad! We went to the island today, and I got a bump on my head, and Marnie got locked in a trunk, and..."

"Whoa! What did you say? You bumped your head?" Abigeal Keller pulled her son to her and checked his head for the bump. "Oh, my goodness, that is quite a goose egg. Tom, look at me."

"I'm okay! C'mon in the kitchen. We're talkin' to the cops!" He turned and raced back.

His parents exchanged bemused glances.

Abigeal nudged her husband. "We better go find out what mischief Tom and Marnie have gotten into this time."

A call came through for Lieutenant Gregg while the Reillys were giving the Kellers a rundown of the day's events. He excused himself and stepped outside.

When he returned, he studied Marnie for a moment. How could this little girl know where to find Ida Barnes' body? Is it possible she really sees ghosts and speaks with them too? His own son talked about ghosts often, but he thought it was simply the overactive imagination of a child. His wife Carol had disagreed. She told him it was common for children to see spirits. She also told him that her mother, Margaret, was quite "gifted" in speaking to the dead. He had considered it was nonsense—until now.

Colin offered a cup of coffee to Lieutenant Gregg. "Coffee? Hey, everything alright?"

The lieutenant accepted the cup. "Ah, thanks. Mr. Reilly, does your daughter really see ghosts? I'm asking because Ida Barnes was exactly where Marnie said she was. She couldn't have known that. The officers found nothing in the house supplying a location of Ida Barnes's corpse."

"She tells us things all the time." Colin laughed. "Things she would have no way of knowing, unless she was 'conferring with spirits', as her mother calls it. She's been doing that since she could talk—and before, she would smile or frown or cry or laugh at things we couldn't see. I guess I believe she speaks to them because she is never wrong."

The lieutenant furrowed his brow. "Huh. My son tells me he sees ghosts. I may have to take it seriously. Thanks."

"No worries. Are you all set? Do you need any more information from the kids?"

"All good. I'm heading back up North in a few days, but I'll be back for the trial—if it gets that far. Pete and Lou will take it from here," replied the lieutenant.

"Hey, mister! Are you leaving?" Marnie tugged his pant leg—a chocolate fudgesicle smile smeared on her face.

"Yes, I have work to do. It was very nice meeting you."

She grasped his index finger and pulled him toward her. Lieutenant Gregg stooped so that his eyes met the child's. Marnie kissed him on the cheek, leaving an imprint of chocolate lips.

"Thanks for locking up Jethro Barnes, sir," she said with an impish grin.

"You're very welcome. Thank you for helping us get him."

Marnie giggled. "No sweat! See ya!"

She raced off to join Tom and David in the backyard. It was a perfect night to catch fireflies.

Sam appeared in Marnie's bedroom doorway with his sleeping bag and a pillow in his arms.

"Hey, Squirt, do you mind if I crash in here with you tonight?"

She sat up and patted the side of her bed, inviting him into her room. "Are you scared, Sam?"

"Nope. Is it okay if I sleep on your floor?" he asked.

"Sure! We can have a slumber party!"

"Are *you* scared?" he asked.

"Nah! You won't let anything get me, will you?"

"I'll always protect you," he said.

"Cross your heart?" she asked.

"And hope to die."

-The End-